Presents

Andrea Taylor's
Baby Mother

Published by
THE X PRESS, 55 BROADWAY MARKET, LONDON E8 4PH.
TEL: 0171 729 1199   FAX: 0171 729 1771
E-MAIL: Xpress @ maxis.co.uk

© Andrea Taylor 1996.

All the characters, company names and events in this book are totally fictitious and any resemblance to real life persons, or companies with the same or similar names, is purely coincidental.

All rights reserved. No part of this book may be reproduced in any form without written permission from the Publisher.

Distributed by Turnaround, 27 Horsell Road, London N5 1XL
Tel: 0171 609 7836

Printed by BPC Paperbacks Ltd, Aylesbury, Bucks.

ISBN   1-874509-16-6

Baby Mother

(When a Man Leaves his Woman)

THIS BOOK IS FOR:

*My mum Miss P,
who made the phrase 'baby mother'
nothing to be ashamed about.
Love you loads.*

*To my little big sis Jennifer (1974-1993),
who was never a mother in the real sense,
but a surrogate mother to all the children
she minded including my own.
I miss you.*

*My babies Kaisha and Letitia.
Mummy thanks you for being the bestest children
a mother could wish to have.*

*To my sistas and spars everywhere.
TURN THOSE DREAMS INTO REALITY!*

*To CW,
If it wasn't for you I would never have got this far.
Live good.*

ONE

Puddin cyaan bake widout fire

Jennifer Edwards sighed deeply. "Sod's law," she muttered before dashing the laddered pair of tights aside and searching her drawer in vain for another pair. She had only been home half an hour — straight from the courtroom and into the shower — yet had succeeded in doing her hair and make-up with minutes to spare. Everything had gone smoothly, except for the tights.

Panicking, she rushed out of the bedroom in her lacy bra and panties and called to her sister. "Donna!"

From across the landing the other bedroom door opened and Donna appeared, dressed in the rude gal's uniform of tight, coloured jeans and a top that just skimmed her belly button. "Yeah, Sis?"

Jennifer often wondered what her sister would look like in a classic cut suit. Getting her into one voluntarily would be nothing short of a miracle. For once Donna wasn't modelling a hat or that bandanna she'd taken to wearing. Her hair, tied back at the nape of her neck with a shiny cotton band, was relaxed and easily came to her shoulders.

"Tights D, tights. I've just laddered my last pair."

"I've got a couple of yours, hold on."

Donna disappeared into her room leaving the door open for Jennifer to face the life-size poster of a bare-chested Tupac Shakur — tattoos and all — on the opposite wall. Written large in gold ink across Tupac's torso was the legend, 'MINE.' Jennifer shook her head disbelievingly before returning to her pine-mirrored wardrobe to find something suitable and ready to wear. Nothing except her work suits. It had been so long since she'd been out raving that she no longer possessed any party dresses. One of the suits would have to do. She pulled out the least formal two-piece then went to her other wardrobe for a blouse.

This reunion had better be worth it. Jennifer had had to break sweat to get home from court in time. It was an open and shut case, but for the over-enthusiastic foreman, the jury were only expected to retire for an hour or two. In the event, they were out for four hours. Then on her way home in the taxi, she ended up in a roadblock. Well, the main thing was that she'd won the case. Sometimes that was all that mattered.

"Here," Donna handed her two pairs of black tights.

"Why do you never replace my things? Come to that why don't you ask if you can borrow them first?" Jennifer snapped, snatching her tights from her sister.

Donna flicked a few wisps of hair over her shoulder and waved away her sister's complaint. "Don't stress me, man." She sloped back to her bedroom, shutting the door behind her.

Kids! Donna was lucky she was her sister and not her daughter.

Jennifer sat on the edge of the bed and eased the tights onto her smooth legs, before slipping into the lilac suit. She stood briefly in front of the mirror to straighten her clothes and admire herself. She looked good and felt good. Her hair, clipped to perfection by Splinters of Mayfair, was cut mid-length into a chic bob and caressed the back of her neck sensuously. Her linen suit, obviously expensive, was worn over a silk blouse; its skirt, nearly touching her ankles, was cut to fit her waist and curve naturally and smoothly over her hips. Below the skirt, her black stockinged legs peeked out briefly before ending in shoes with two inch heels and just a shade darker than her suit. *Yes!* Tonight, she was going to show her class that she had class. Snatching a handbag from the shelf in her wardrobe, she pressed the 'off' button on her cassette player before skipping out of the room.

"D, I'm gone. Okay?"

The reply came back to her through the closed door, "Right Sis, enjoy yourself."

Downstairs she went through her day-to-day handbag, taking only the essentials: keys, money, credit cards, pen and address book. She'd left her lipstick upstairs. Clattering back up the wrought-iron spiral staircase, she grabbed her lipstick from the dressing-table in her room and headed again for the stairs.

Her white Volkswagen Cabriolet stood in the driveway. *Damn!* She had forgotten to lock the door and set the car alarm last night.

She scolded herself as she eased into the comfortable front seat. That wasn't the kind of mistake you could afford to make in south London, or north London for that matter. She glanced at her watch. She was late. At least the drive from Honor Oak to Crofton Park wouldn't take long. As she slipped the car into gear, her mind drifted to the evening at hand. She couldn't wait to see her old school friends again. Apart from the odd chance meeting she hadn't seen most of them since leaving to college almost ten years ago. She backed the Volkswagen into the road, wondering what her old friends had been up to all these years.

"...This is how we do it,
It's Friday night and I feel all right,
the party's here on the west side..."

"Go Montell!"

Dressed in an off-the-shoulder blue lycra dress, that showed every movement of her well-toned muscles, Elaine Johnson waved her long, sinewy arms in the air, trying to get the party moving — preferably onto the dance floor. She was fit, energetic and disliked spending her evenings sitting down.

A young man in a silk suit stood watching the ladies from the nearby bar, propping up the counter with his fine self. Karen was the first to notice him and she was sure he was staring in her direction. She was one of Elaine's closest friends and had a lusty sensual look which men rarely failed to notice. He had the biggest, brightest eyes she had ever seen. Discreetly, Karen coaxed up the front of her short black velvet dress to make her tiny bosom look larger.

"Get back in your chair, girl, before you shame the lot of us," she told Elaine. "Anybody'd think Montell Jordan was singing live and direct right here beside us." Then she turned her attention back to the handsome stranger and gave him the full come-on through her grey-green contact lenses. He smiled back. Karen wet her lips.

Beverly, who had spent two days trying to find something in her wardrobe to fit before admitting defeat and buying a cheap, size sixteen rose-printed dress, was gazing expectantly towards the entrance door. "Look who Cynthia's with!"

Her friends' heads swiveled in Cynthia's direction. Elaine's mouth fell open. "Isn't that...?"

"Jason Adams!" Beverly finished.

"The year below us at school." Elaine reached for their bottle of complimentary wine, her eyes following the couple as they made their way to a table near the centre of the hall.

Karen screwed up her pretty mouth, and shook a cigarette from the Benson & Hedges packet. "Oh yeah. Wasn't he...y'know...gay?"

Beverly slapped one chubby hand to her ample chest. "Get outta here!"

Elaine patted her beehived hair with slim fingers, the nails carefully manicured and crimsoned. "He most certainly was not gay. I can personally vouch for him."

Karen leaned back in her chair, lighting the cigarette that hung between her lips. "Eh-eh! You can personally vouch for him!"

A knowing glance passed between Beverly and Karen, followed by a burst of laughter around the table.

"He was simply obsessed with his looks back then. The relaxed hair, precision pressed clothes, he was immaculate from head to toe. Apart from his hair, the man don't look like he's changed a bit."

The most mingling was going on inside the huge hall. The guests walked tentatively from person to person, unsure of identities or reactions. Smiling, chatting, sipping alcohol, swapping phone numbers, business cards even, from those who looked like they had made it big time.

Elaine scanned the crowd, pausing only to flirtatiously eyeball the nattily-dressed Jason Adams.

"I suppose you wanna say hello?" Karen asked her.

"We-ell..."

"Come nuh. We can pass his table on the way to the buffet." Karen got up without waiting for an answer, stubbed out her cigarette and pushed back her chair. She smoothed her short velvet dress over her hips and made her way across the hall, followed by her friends.

The hall was rapidly filling up with Crofton School's students of yesteryear. Some were already at the bar where the food and drink was, while others were checking out the dance floor. Most had already secured seats and tables for their old crews. Tonight was going to be a good reunion rave.

"Don't get Cynthia jealous now, it looks like she's put on a bit of weight!" Karen had to shout to be heard above the music as they neared the dance floor and the speakers.

Elaine heard, but chose to ignore the advice of her homegirl. When the threesome sauntered over to Jason's table, she immediately leaned over between him and Cynthia. "Hi Jason, remember me?"

Cynthia caught Elaine's eyes and the two women stared at each other impassively.

"Blast from the past!" Jason was quick to jump up and give her a hug. "How are you girl?"

She looked him over and memories of the cold brick wall she had let him thrust her up against all those years ago came rushing back to her. He had smelt good then too.

"Can't you tell?" She did a slow twirl, showing off her aerobic instructor's taut body. Cynthia, a sour look on her face, ignored her completely.

Jason could hardly believe the female body builder physique before him. He whistled despite himself, then remembered who he was there with. "You know my wife?"

Elaine raised an eyebrow. "Do I?"

"Cynthia."

Behind Elaine, Karen laughed hoarsely.

"One wedding I didn't get an invite to," Elaine said.

"Sorry about that." Jason took her hand. "Before you go let me have your number, maybe we can get together."

Cynthia shot her husband a disapproving glare. If looks could kill...

"I might just do that," Elaine said, loud enough for Cynthia to hear.

"Later, yeah?"

Elaine pouted her lips provocatively and let her hand slip out of his. Married men were the worst flirts. She hoped Allan would never turn into one once they were married.

The women set off again through the crowd and took their place in the queue for the buffet. Elaine bopped her head to the music. Karen greeted several people she knew and went over briefly to talk to a man who had waved her over. An assortment of cold meats, curried chicken, savouries and salads, with several variations on coleslaw, awaited them when they got to the front of the queue, not to talk of the free drinks already sliding down their throats. The crew were getting into the party spirit.

"Is that all you're eating?" Karen stared at Beverly's plate of a single leaf of lettuce, a spoonful of coleslaw and half a tomato.

"It's healthy, isn't it?"

"It's only healthy when you eat enough to stay alive."

"I'm dieting. I mean look at the size of me. Since I had Jerome I've put on two stone. Remember at school, I was the one who could eat anything without gaining a pound. Now I only have to look at a cake and I put on half a stone."

"You know what works for me?" Elaine waited until she had both their attentions. "Ginseng, lemon tea and aerobic exercise at least once a day."

"Really. Ginseng? Isn't that the root that makes men stay hard longer?" Karen asked.

"I heard that," Beverly grinned.

"You'd have to ask Allan about that, I don't know about men, but it sure keeps me going," Elaine said with a mischievous glint in her eye.

"Bwoy, you look good girl. Whether it's the ginseng or the man, you're a walking advert for it," Beverly complimented. "I can't afford no expensive herbs or aerobic classes. I haven't even got time for exercise."

"Listen Bev, even if you lose weight you've still gotta tone up."

"But you don't wanna end up like Elaine, pumping too much iron and not enough men," Karen laughed.

Elaine thumped her friend's arm but laughed anyway.

Karen speared a piece of chicken with her fork. "When was the last time you had a man, Bev?"

Beverly pushed the half tomato around on her plate with her fork.

Elaine glared at Karen. "Nuh mind her, me dear," she said, touching Beverly's hand. "Karen thinks that having a man is the be all and end all. Believe me, you don't need them."

"Give over Elaine. You're only saying that because you've got Allan."

"I'm just saying Beverly is a good woman, she doesn't have to search for a man. Lose a bit of weight and start fixing herself up and the decent men are bound to flock to her. But in the meantime she needs to put the whole ah dem outta her mind and concentrate on her baby."

"Jennifer was good at banishing men from her thoughts. Remember?"

"Yeah...Jennifer Edwards, now she was a sister with sense," Elaine agreed. "Anyone know if she's coming tonight?"

"She is," Beverly said. "First letter I got from her in years was to say, 'Looking forward to seeing you again at the reunion'. I was going to write back but never got round to it."

"How come I didn't get one?" Karen whined.

Elaine consoled her. "You've moved around so much since we left school she probably hasn't got your address."

"Oh look, there's our old drama teacher. What was her name?"

"Barry. Mrs. Barry. Remember that time Maureen squirted invisible ink over her blouse?" Beverly giggled.

"Yeah, the whole class burst out laughing and she burst into tears. We got a real ticking off at registration."

"God, I remember now. It was April Fools Day and her husband had just told her he wanted a divorce. She broke down and confessed the whole thing to us," Elaine joined in.

"Bwoy, we felt so guilty afterwards we chipped in to buy her flowers."

"She was all right, Mrs. Barry. Gone a bit grey now though, she must be at least fifty odd," Beverly said watching their former teacher laugh at a joke.

"So Elaine, why didn't you bring Allan with you?" Karen asked.

"Allan wouldn't come to one of these things. He doesn't know anybody and he hates people asking personal questions. He's a very private person."

"Shy is he?" Beverly asked.

Karen smirked. "Not in the bedroom though, I'll bet."

"That's why I didn't bring him. D'you think we could talk about men like this with him sitting here?"

"Did Jennifer ever get married?" Karen asked Beverly.

"There was no mention of a husband in her letter."

Elaine crossed her supple legs, waxed smooth just yesterday. "The few times I've seen her she's always been Miss Single Black Female."

"After all these years?" said Beverly.

"Don't look so shocked," Karen said. "It doesn't mean she ain't getting any. I haven't got a husband either, but I've got a man who services me regularly and my kids have got me."

Elaine looked concerned. "Your kids, yes. Do they ever get to see their father?"

"Once a fortnight, once a month. When he feels like it. Sometimes he even sends some money," she said ironically.

"I know Allan would never do that to me. When we decide to have kids we'll be married and the kids will be planned."

"Y'know that's exactly what Charles said to me when I met him," Karen said.

"Well he was obviously just saying that to keep you interested," Elaine replied tactlessly.

"He stayed with me for five years! Natasha had a father for the first four years of her life," Karen snapped back.

"All right, girl, calm down. I'm not blaming you. It was Charles who decided fatherhood and domesticity was not for him."

"Men! I wonder how many of the women here are in mine and Karen's position. Baby mothers."

"How can you call yourself that?" Elaine said. "That's just a phrase invented by today's black man to claim you as his property."

"It's true, Bev. Once a man starts calling you his baby mother it's like he's putting you in a stable. Part of his harem," Karen chuckled.

Elaine laughed at the idea, but it was true. The first woman to have a man's child was his baby mother and, as long as she was the only one, she was special. But once the man has more children with other women, everything changes. Then, the one with the most children earns the most respect.

"Besides...no disrespect intended, but you can't call yourself a baby mother when the man did dig and lef' you before the baby was even born, in fact as soon as he found out. He can't lay no claim on you or your child."

"What goes through those guys' heads? I mean one minute they love you, can't get enough of your sweetness. Then you tell them you're pregnant and WHAM! It's like everything they saw in you was never there," Elaine said.

"Nah, that's not how it goes. It's not you they run from, it's the fact that money haffe start coming outta dem wallet to pay fe de chile. That's why nowadays I'm just out for what I can get. Why d'you think I haven't got a regular boyfriend? Because I'm not setting myself up to take that shit again."

"But what about mental stimulation, you telling me you prefer sex to that?" Beverly asked unbelievably. Her bed had been empty for almost a year and she would take either without question if it was offered.

"Yeah man, every time. That deep emotional stuff only leads to trouble. I don't want a guy getting to know me inside out, because before you know it he thinks he owns you and starts taking liberties. I play them at their own game. If I was a man I'd be the Don, my spars all bigging me up. My lifestyle's ideal. First sign of any of that 'You're my girl shit,' and he's out the door. Treat 'em like dirt."

"Karen, how can you say that? I know Allan and he knows me, we've been going out for two years and neither of us is taking liberties."

"Okay that's you, right, but look at Beverly. The man was around even through her putting on weight, health problems, and her parents dissing him, right?"

Beverly nodded. Behind them the atmosphere was buzzing as old school friends reminisced and caught up on lost years and exchanged telephone numbers to the sound of *Return of the Mack*.

"Okay, then she tells him she's pregnant," Karen continued, "and the man couldn't be seen for dust. There are millions of women out there with the same story."

Karen had only just finished speaking when she noticed someone waving at them from across the hall. She waved back, embarrassed, and Elaine and Beverly looked round.

"Who the hell is that?" Elaine wondered.

"Jackie Palmer," Beverly whispered back.

Jackie was coming over, red high-heels clicking and a red leather mini-dress tight around her waist. Her brunette-coloured weave hung down to the middle of her back and she wore make-up so thick it clung to her face for dear life.

"Karen love, how are you? Lovely to see you again," she screeched, planting imaginary kisses on either side of Karen's cheeks.

"Jacks, long time no see," she faked a pleasant surprise. "You remember Elaine and Beverly."

"Elaine, yes you were in Mrs. White's class too, weren't you?" She reached for Elaine's hand with a handful of red-painted false nails.

Elaine rubbed her chin thoughtfully. "It's coming back to me now," she said, shaking her hand. "You were in Mr. Dixon's class, used to move with us when your best friend wasn't at school."

Flustered, Jackie giggled nervously and moved on to Beverly. "So how are you Beverly? You look...well..."

Beverly pursed her lips sulkily. It didn't take a genius to figure out that Jackie was referring to the extra weight she was carrying. "I've just had a baby," she said by way of an excuse.

"How lovely," Jackie clapped her hands together. "How long have you been married?"

"I'm not."

"Oh..." Jackie hastily turned back to Karen. "So what about you? You have to be married. One of the most popular girls in school you were."

"Married no, kids two, boyfriend no, lover yes, job part-time. Did I miss anything?"

Elaine and Beverly stifled laughs as they rose and, leaving Karen with Jackie, headed towards the ladies.

The toilets were surprisingly clean and empty.

"Can you believe that Jackie?" Elaine said, heading for the mirror.

"I'm surprised Karen even bothered to give her the time of day."

"That's the trouble with reunions, everybody pretends they were friends from time. It ain't until afterwards that you remember you either couldn't stand the person or never really knew them in the first place."

"Mmm," Beverly said from inside the cubicle, "I didn't see many of the black boys from school out there."

"Saw a few of the white guys from the sixth form. You know how black man don't reach until after midnight."

"It finishes at one."

"Well they don't know what they're missing," Elaine said flatly. She opened her purse and took out a lip pencil and looking in the mirror, she outlined her well-shaped mouth carefully and re-applied her dark brown lipstick. "I could've brought Allan, you know, someone to dance with later..."

Her last words were drowned out by the sound of the lavatory flushing. Beverly emerged and washed her hands. "What did you say?"

"We're gonna be short of men to dance with." She moved away from the small mirror and watched Beverly re-adjusting her bra.

"I'm not bothered about that. Shit, I knew I should have worn the white one, damn thing keeps digging into me. I don't know what bra size I am since I've been breast feeding. I've been three different sizes already. I usually feed Jerome at this time of the evening, that's why I'm so full." She lifted her heavy breasts with both hands.

"Perks of the job,"Elaine laughed. "Geddit? Big breasts...Perks?"

"Oh yeah," Beverly laughed with her. Elaine's chest was high and firm, along with her bottom and could hardly be described as big.

"Karen hasn't changed though, has she?"

"What d'you mean?" Beverly squirted her neck and chest with *Soft Musk* perfume.

Elaine wet her fingers under the tap and slicked down one of her sideburns. "Well, you know, still blatant. I bet she still flirts like mad."

Beverly seemed to remember it was Elaine who was the flirt, always jealous of Karen's popularity. "She isn't a flirt, she doesn't have to. Especially since she started going out with Charles in the sixth form. That was love, she didn't even look at another man."

"Still dressed like a tart though."

"Elaine!" Beverly thumped her gently on the arm.

"I'm only saying..." Elaine shrugged innocently. "I love Karen too."

They opened the door that led back into the hallway and re-entered the party atmosphere.

"I wonder if Charles will turn up," Beverly said above the music.

"No, not if he thinks *she's* going to be here."

When Beverly and Elaine arrived back at their table Karen had already dispatched with Jackie, been to the bar and refilled their glasses. Next to her was a man neither of them recognized. Elaine took in his silk suit and the heavy gold around his neck and wrist.

"Girls, this is Roger. Apparently he was in the sixth form and he recognizes me."

"Hi Roger."

"Hello Roger."

He smiled at both of them, his eyes mesmerized by Elaine's chest. Elaine's chest always had that effect on people, even women. She had that 'perfect' chest from the dirty magazines that schoolboys drool over behind the bike shed.

"Roger just happens to be single and on the lookout for a wife," Karen announced rapturously, her eyelashes fluttering in his direction. Could he see the colour of her eyes in this light, she wondered?

"Good luck, Roger," Elaine said coolly taking her seat again. "I'm engaged, Beverly here has just had a baby, and I guess you already know about Karen."

Karen's mouth dropped open as Roger announced that he had just remembered something that needed attending to urgently on the other side of the hall and hastily said his goodbyes before sloping off.

"What d'you do that for?"

"Karen, he's a no-hoper. Any man who has to go around telling women he's looking for a wife is looking for a meal ticket."

"And how d'you work that out?"

"Experience." Elaine sipped her Malibu and pineapple. "Anyway Karen, you've got a man."

Karen kissed her teeth. "How many times do I have to tell you, he's not my man, he's my bed companion. They're easier to replace." She turned to catch Roger's behind disappearing across the dance-floor.

"What happened to your friend Jackie?" Beverly asked.

"Gone back to her husband." Karen mimicked Jackie's squeaky voice, " 'Better get back to Johnny, he'll be missing me...' Jeeze, I can't believe we used to let her hang around with us."

"She always had gossip and spare change, remember?" Beverly said.

"She's married! Where's the poor victim?" Elaine asked.

Karen swiveled around and pointed to a table against the back wall. "There they are, Mr and Mrs Price."

Elaine squinted her eyes to peer across through the dimly-lit hall. "The white guy?"

Beverly shook her head. "You're having us on. He must be nearly fifty!"

"As sure as I'm sitting here, that old white man is her husband. Big diamond and gold wedding ring on her finger. Dat ain't all either."

Elaine and Beverly turned back to face her.

"She's pregnant."

Elaine nearly choked on her drink. "Bwoy, you'd think ten years would change a person. But she's still a bimbo."

"At least she's married," Beverly said wistfully.

"To a white man!" Karen added.

"At least she won't end up being called 'baby mother'. You can't call a white man 'baby faada' can you?"

Karen and Elaine laughed at the image of Jackie's husband as a polygamous yardie in string vest and baggy jeans.

All of a sudden the music changed and Elaine felt herself being transported back to their school days. "Rufus and Chaka Khan...!" She stood up, dancing on the spot. "You guys gotta get up now. Come on, they're playing our music."

Karen raised a disapproving eyebrow. "How many drinks you had?"

"Don't tell me you've come here to sit down all night. Let's party."

Happened so naturally didn't I know it was love
Next thing I felt was you, holding me close
What was I gonna do I let myself go
Now we're flying through the stars
Hope this night will last forever...

"Come on they're playing tunes." Elaine hollered as her fit body bounced.

Ain't nobody, love me better
Makes me happy, makes me feel this way

Ain't nobody...

Elaine's enthusiasm was becoming too much for her friends. Karen took a swig of her Bacardi and coke and got up. "Okay, let's show 'em we ain't no old timers yet."

"Go girl!"

Beverly's breast milk had started to flow and she felt too uncomfortable to dance. As her mind drifted to thoughts of ducking out early her eyes wandered to the exit. "Hold on, isn't that Jennifer?"

All eyes turned towards the door as the silhouette of a tall woman stood just inside the doorway, underneath the bright red, 'EASTER REUNION — CLASS OF '86' sign.

Karen waved Jennifer over. As the newly-arrived woman crossed the dancefloor, the eyes and heads of the gathered guests turned and followed her to her seat. Certain men didn't even realize that their tongues hung from their mouths as they ogled, while more than one pair of women's eyes burned with envy.

"Jen, you look wicked," Karen said, hugging Jennifer with true affection.

"Karen," Jennifer's voice was deep, sophisticated, cultured. She noticed Karen's green eyes, but wasn't sure if she was supposed to. "You haven't changed a bit."

"Don't lie to me now," Karen laughed.

"Jen, remember me?"

Jennifer turned to greet Elaine who was standing behind her. "How could I forget the one person who was always rational when the rest of us were seeing red. Hi Eileen."

The look on Elaine's face told her she had got it wrong.

"It's Elaine. How you doing?"

"Good, thanks. I don't even have to ask you, you look terrific." Jennifer's gaze swept over Elaine's trim figure.

"Believe me, I wasn't even this healthy as a teenager," Elaine boasted.

"And Bev..." Jennifer walked around the table, arms outstretched.

Beverly stood to greet her. There were real tears in her eyes as Jennifer's arms embraced her.

"Let me look at you all," Jennifer said, stepping back to admire her old friends. "If it wasn't for the fancy clothes I could imagine we were all sixteen again."

They all laughed.

"Bwoy, have we got some catching up to do," Karen said, rubbing her hands together. "First, what do you want to drink?"

"Oh...ah, Southern Comfort and lemonade, please."

Karen disappeared towards the bar. From there she watched Jennifer gesticulating in animated conversation with the other two. Back in their schooldays Karen had always been the centre of attention, not least because she always wore the latest fashions which her friends could not afford and regularly had her hair relaxed at the salon. It was Karen to whom most of the boys flocked when they all started dating seriously because she was allowed to stay out as late as she wanted and had always been good for a laugh. *Looks like being serious paid off for Jennifer Edwards*, she mused with self-regret.

Back at the table, Jennifer was definitely the centre of attraction.

"Yeah," Beverly was saying when Karen returned with the drinks, "by the looks of you, you're making a good living as a lawyer."

Karen sat herself down sideways on her chair and crossed her legs. "Either that or you're making a good living on the game," she joked.

"Has she been like this all evening?" Jennifer smiled, an appealing dimple appearing in her left cheek.

"Does a fish live in water?" Elaine said, her head still bobbing to *Joy and Pain*, bubbling through the speakers.

"So what's it like being a solicitor?" Elaine asked, curious as to what you had to do to look as good as Jennifer. It was one thing to be able to stop traffic with your figure, but Jennifer could do it with her aura alone. That was something special.

"Actually, I'm a barrister."

"Eh-eh," Karen said, obviously impressed. "You mean one of those that wear a gown and the wig? Like on the telly?"

"Something like that," she smiled. "I'm aiming to be a QC — a Queen's Counsel — only another ten years or so to go."

"Go girl!" Elaine said, playfully punching her arm. "More power to the sistas."

"Had any juicy murder cases?" Karen asked, green eyes almost catlike.

"I've assisted on one or two, but I mostly get domestics." Jennifer felt real warmth from Elaine whereas Karen seemed to be cold towards her. "Enough about me, so what are you all doing now?"

"I'm an aerobics dash afrobics instructor, not that you needed telling," Elaine jokingly boasted, throwing her muscular arms open dramatically to show off her trim waist.

"Shut up about your body already. Bwoy, Allan must be half dead having you work on him every night," Karen teased.

"Allan? Are you married then?" Jennifer asked.

"Strike one," Elaine chuckled.

"Neither am I," Jennifer admitted. "Sometimes a woman's got to stay single to survive. Sometimes that's the only way to achieve your goals."

"But I am engaged though," Elaine stretched out her hand showing Jennifer the ring, "to Allan of course. No date yet though."

"So what about you two?"

"I came close, but it turned out he didn't deserve me," Karen replied flippantly.

Everyone waited for Beverly's answer.

She looked up meeting their eyes, shrugged her shoulders. "I just haven't met the right man yet."

"Aaah the old cliché," Jennifer empathized. "Not one of us?"

Karen placed a comforting hand on Beverly's shoulder. "Children are what we have. Children with no fathers." Her voice was deep and slurred.

Jennifer waited for an explanation.

"Beverly here has a beautiful baby boy of six months — Jerome."

Beverly reached into her handbag for the photo album she always carried around with her. She handed it to Jennifer while Karen continued.

"You heard of Amway?"

Jennifer nodded. They were a firm with agents all over the world selling their everyday household products at tupperware parties for commission. Some did it part-time, for others it was their full-time job.

"Well, I work for them, and I have two children Natasha and Kyle. Five and nine."

"We're planning to have children after we're married," Elaine added.

"That's the only way, girl. Especially in this day and age," Jennifer said, then qualified herself when she caught a glint of fire in Karen's eyes. "Only a man can make a child fatherless, so tying him down seems like a good idea to me."

"Whatever happened to your younger sister, what was her name again?"

"Donna. She's living with me now. Pure worries, believe me."

"Worries? But she must be, what, how old now?"

"Seventeen."

They each nodded sympathetically, remembering the age well. The killer years.

"It's like Donna's always got something to prove. She's got to prove she's independent, that she's a *woman* now. Behind it all she's still a child of course. She doesn't realize that I've been through all that before."

"You talking housework or men?"

"Men. Every time she stays out all night it worries the hell out of me."

Beverly empathised, she was the eldest of five children. "You don't need to have a child when you've got a little sister living with you."

"Don't I know it."

"But your sister was so quiet at school. Used to get the mickey taken out of her because she had to go church every Saturday, Seventh Day Adventist wasn't it?"

"Mmm-hmm. Those were the days. She raves every night now and wears little more than her underwear to clubs. Skirts barely skimming her bottom, fishnet stockings..."

"Me dear!" Karen exclaimed.

"...Thigh high boots, a studded bra with sequins and see-through blouses and jackets. The amount of times I've told her that the way you dress is the way you're treated."

"Especially by men," Elaine added.

"The other day I saw her with that Fitzroy Lucas. You remember, the one who got a girl pregnant before we even left school."

Karen exhaled deeply, shaking her head slowly. "Fitzroy, bwoy he was sweet."

Beverly was taken aback. "Karen, you didn't!"

"Well...he was offering," she replied deadpan.

"But the guy was a slag," Elaine grimaced.

"Maybe, but he always made a girl feel like the one and only."

That had to be the attraction, Jennifer thought. Sweet talk and sex was all guys like that knew about treating a woman. "I don't want him around my sister. He's too experienced and Lord knows how many children he's fathered."

Elaine took her compact from her purse and dabbed the shine from her nose. "I'm sure somebody told me he'd settled down about a year ago."

"You know, I saw him with a woman in Lewisham only a couple of months ago," Karen clicked her fingers in the air. "Yeah, yeah he was pushing a pram."

"Looks like you've got nothing to worry about then," Beverly consoled.

"You don't understand," Jennifer was becoming more and more anxious by what she was hearing, "they're more than just friends. She's even stayed over at his house."

"Oh boy. Looks like Fitzroy's hooked another one," Karen whistled, looking around the hall for any stray unattached men. "I don't think he can afford to get another girl pregnant though. From what I heard, the CSA are looking for him to pay maintenance on at least five kids already."

"All right girl, don't give our Jen a heart attack," Elaine said, clocking Jennifer's expression.

"I know how she feels though," Karen said, returning her attention to the table. "Look how many young girls you see pushing prams with no man beside them and no ring 'pon dem finger. Simply because guys like Fitzroy have had their fun and done a runner. Jennifer wants to spare her sister the kind of prejudice we single mothers have to put up with."

Jennifer nodded.

"Both of my children were planned," Karen continued, "Charles wanted me to have the first baby when I was only seventeen," she kissed her teeth. "You see what love do to yuh?" She looked up in time to see a familiar face from the past swerving towards them.

"Yaow sis!"

A can of Tennants came crashing down on the table between them. Jennifer caught her breath sharply and looked up at Lloyd Campbell's leering grin. He was six foot three and hairy, a fact he was proud to display by wearing his shirt open down to his belly button. He sported an unfashionable mini afro and what looked like the same jacket he'd worn back in school, the sleeves now grown back to the elbows.

"Hell fire!" Karen blurted, sitting up straight in her chair.

"Yuh nuh 'member me, Miss Sweetness?" He leaned closer breathing lager and cigarette fumes over everyone.

Jennifer leaned back, a look of distaste on her face. "I remember." Lloyd had plagued her last year at Crofton sixth form. He was the type of admirer that every woman dreaded. He was rude, brainless, untidy, and when he had the hots for a woman, he never gave up. In her final year, Jennifer just happened to be that woman.

His grin widened, groggy eyes ran down her body. "I was hoping

I would see you, y'know..."

"Well it's good to see that some things don't change, eh Lloyd?" Elaine looked at him mockingly with one delicately raised eyebrow.

He ignored her and resumed his flattery of Jennifer. "You look good, yuh know...still fit...yuh know how me mean?"

Jennifer felt like gagging and was about to get up and move when someone tapped Lloyd on his back and he stood up straight to challenge the intruder.

The ladies sat with their mouths open. It was Jonathan. Only five foot nine to Lloyd's six three, but somehow he managed to seem more imposing. He was dressed in an up-to-the-minute style suit, a khaki green cut to fit a man of class — a man who had the body to carry it off. He wore a very low fade haircut and a ring on his little finger was his only jewellery. His friend, a taller dark-skinned man, stood just behind him. Jonathan's natural hazel eyes met Lloyd's mean ones.

"This man bothering you ladies?"

"You could say that," Jennifer breathed a sigh of relief. How long had she gone out with Jonathan, she wondered to herself. A mere two months before finishing it because of other women throwing themselves at him. He had too much temptation in his way for her liking. *Looks like he's doing well.* She always knew he would.

"What's it got to do wid you?"

"Look Lloyd, we don't want any trouble. The ladies are here to..."

"Fuck you!"

Jonathan's friend stepped forward so that the two men flanked Lloyd on either side. Karen licked her lips in anticipation of a ruckus.

"Come on, man." Jonathan picked up the can of Tennants and handed it to Lloyd. "Go drink yuh drink somewhere else."

Lloyd looked up at the tall friend and then back at Jonathan. There was a loaded pause. He reckoned he could take this little squirt, when he was sober, but the two of them? Lloyd backed up shakily. "Later Sweetness...I comin' back fe me dance."

Jonathan and his tall friend touched fists before turning back to the table.

"Jennifer, long time no see."

"Were you looking?"

"I'm looking now."

He leaned closer to Jennifer and a waft of fruit and masculine spice aftershave tickled her nose. Jonathan looked good, smelled good and still had that same penetrating look that used to go through her like a blow torch.

"Didn't your mother ever tell you not to stare?" Jennifer couldn't resist flirting. She leaned back casually so that her wrapover skirt flapped back revealing tight long calves.

"It's more polite than doing what I'm thinking..."

"Oooh, gimme some ah dat," Karen oozed.

Natural hazel eyes met contact lense green. "Hi..." Jonathan said, a quizzical look on his face.

"Karen," she filled in, giving him what she thought was her most appealing smile. Why was he pretending he couldn't remember her name?

He smiled around the table, shaking the other's hands, "Jonathan."

"We know," Elaine purred holding onto his hand a little longer than necessary.

His eyes met Jennifer's again. A profound silence followed...a cool silence.

"I would join you but a group of us have come down from Luton...where I'm living now," his voice was wistful.

"That's a shame," Jennifer meant it. "What are you doing now...?"

"I'm an accountant...freelance. You?"

Jennifer's eyes were filled with admiration. "A barrister," she said with airy modesty. He raised an eyebrow, equally impressed.

Karen's green eyes watched the intimacy between her friend and the man she knew would never be interested in her no matter what. *Let her have him, he's probably a stuck-up snob anyway.*

Jonathan kissed Jennifer on her cheek like a cautious man would if he thought a lady might be offended by it. "I'll see you later maybe...?"

"Maybe." Jennifer watched the two men walk away and wondered how she had let Jonathan get away. All the ambition in the world couldn't change the fact that she was a red-blooded woman and still had an eye for a charming man. Was there a whole life out there she had missed while she'd had her head stuck in books and spent all her spare time in libraries? She shook her head, no, if she had ended up with him she wouldn't be where she was today. *Sometimes a woman's gotta stay single to survive*, she reminded herself.

On their route to the bar for more drinks Elaine and Karen engaged in a game of 'spot the face' as they eased their way past the growing crowd of ex-pupils and teachers from yesteryear wanting to know what they were now doing. By the time they weaved their way back to the table, a group of guys had noticed that sistas were thin on the ground and wanted to join up. But they looked too desperate to even contemplate.

Jennifer leant her elbows on the table. "Is it my imagination or is it getting weirder out there...I mean, being single?"

"We're just getting older."

"It's a new era," Elaine offered, "romance is a thing of the past."

"Bullshit...It's just that men are fucked-up! There aren't any good men anymore," Karen said. When she thought about how seldom she got to go out because she was now strapped with bringing up two young children on her own, and in a job that didn't offer her the luxuries of life, she became bitter. Her life was fucked-up because Charles had decided he wanted to be a single man again. He couldn't even keep his promise to contribute regular money for the kids. *Arsehole!*

"Let's change the subject," Beverly intervened. "We were both going to go to college together, remember Jen? Instead you went while I had to go to work to support my family."

"I know," Jennifer frowned. "Did you ever think of going back to school? You could still do it, you know that don't you?"

"Not with Jerome and no money to pay for child care."

"Study at home if you have to. There's nothing stopping you except yourself."

Beverly knew that Jennifer was right. Years of menial cleaning jobs and temporary clerical were all she thought she was good for. So many years wasted at the service of others, while her goals lay abandoned by the roadside. She could have been Jennifer Edwards. Elegant, confident, rich...unburdened. She could still be Jennifer Edwards. Easier said than done.

"*...Going to a show tonight, after working hard nine to five.
Not talking bout a movie no, on a Broadway stage, show with lights...*"

"Oh my God! *Encore!*" Elaine jumped up, "No way am I sitting here through this. Cheryl Lynn! Remember going to Nations when this came out...?" She was already dancing her way onto the dance floor.

"I guess we bes' follow her for her own safety," Karen said and they all got up together and made their way after Elaine's gyrating figure.

It was as though the entire party had chosen to get up and dance at the same time. The dancehall filled quickly.

Encore was followed by *All This Love That I'm Giving,* by Gwen McCrae and Jocelyn Brown's, *Somebody Else's Guy.*

Elaine was singing along and strutting her stuff. For Jennifer this brought back memories of her youth. She had to learn all over again how to 'shock out'. Jennifer mopped the light perspiration from her forehead. The memories were bittersweet. What had happened to these women, she wondered? In the sixth form they all had ambition. They all wanted careers. Elaine had been an athlete and they had all thought that one day she would run for England. Karen was going to run her own restaurant, and Beverly was going to study for a degree. All they had to show for the passing of the years was that two of them were now single parents and, as far as Jennifer could see, Elaine might be next, despite her engagement ring. So much talent gone to waste. The more she thought about the old days and what could have been for her sisters in spirit, the more Jennifer felt depressed.

And what they had told her about Fitzroy didn't help either. The question mark hanging over his head was how many baby mothers he had out there. A sudden panic flared in Jennifer's chest. Like her old school mates, Donna had dreams. She wanted to be a graphic designer, but Jennifer couldn't see how Fitzroy Lucas could possibly assist her in that ambition.

She made a mental note to fill Donna in on 'Mister Loverman' just as soon as she saw her next.

The reunion was over. Endless choruses of *Auld Lang Syne* had been sung and those who could remember the words had even added a verse or two of the old school song. Karen ran to catch up with her friends as they waited by the exit.

"Got his number did you?" Elaine asked.

"Might come in handy," Karen waved the slip of paper at them. The cold air hit them as they walked out of the school building in a huddle and the women pulled their coats around their bodies as they walked up the pathway towards Manwood Road and Jennifer's car.

"Jerome must be missing me," Beverly said throwing her scarf over her shoulder. "This is the first night I've been away from him."

"I'll bet he hasn't even noticed," Karen yawned.

Jennifer removed her car keys from her bag and began to cross the street. "He's her baby, course he will."

"Babies need a break as well, you know. It's good for you to do your own thing every once in a while," Elaine wrapped an arm around Bev's huge shoulders.

"Karen!"

"If one more person calls my name I'm gonna slap 'em silly."

They all turned to see a man running up the road towards them, his jacket flapping behind him.

"Looks like you've got another admirer," Elaine giggled.

Karen frowned, "Mmm."

Just a bit taller than Karen with a dark complexion and friendly smile, the man came up to them. Karen was clearly embarrassed.

"Karen, I'm glad I caught you."

Karen's green contacts smouldered. "Philip, what are you doing here?"

"I came to give you a lift home." He looked over at the huddled group of bemused females. They were wondering who the fit-looking stranger was.

"Evening ladies."

"Evening," they chorused.

"Philip!" Karen called back his attention. She didn't bother introducing him. "I told you I'd call you tomorrow."

"I know, but I don't see why you should have to wait on a cab and pay a stranger when I've got a car," he caressed her shoulder softly. "I've been waiting out here for two hours."

Elaine giggled. Beverly poked her in the ribs.

Karen's cheeks felt hot despite the bitter wind that had blown up. "Why?" she said simply.

Philip shrugged. "They wouldn't let me in, 'cause I didn't have an invitation."

"Look Karen, it's okay," Jennifer moved forward, "We'll meet again soon. I'll call you."

Karen threw Philip a dirty look. "I'm sorry girls. Looks like certain man can't wait to get their daily 'slam'."

They all laughed.

"I'll call you tomorrow," Elaine kissed Karen's cheek. "Don't wear him out," she whispered. "Looks like you've got a real loverbwoy there."

"Bev, kiss Jerome for me." They embraced.

"Will do."

"Any of you going our way, I could drop you?" Philip offered. Karen threw him another dirty look. What the hell was he was playing at? *First he offers to babysit the kids for the night, now this.* He had better not be getting serious on her. It would be a shame to say goodbye so soon, besides she was enjoying being waited on hand and foot.

"No, no we're fine," they agreed. The girls said their goodbyes and watched Karen and Philip walk away arm in arm.

They held their tongues until they were in the car and then let rip.

"Whoy, looks like we've just met Mr Karen."

"Naaa," Elaine shook her head. "She jus' told us, she only want a man for one t'ing. She'll use him an' dump him. She's probably putting him under manners as we speak, for not doing as he was told."

Elaine was right. She knew Karen well. But love, true love, has a habit of finding a way.

It was almost two o'clock Saturday morning when Jennifer returned to her maisonette on the top two floors of the large Victorian four-storey house overlooking Honor Oak Park. As late as it was, the first thing she did when she stepped through the door was call out for her sister.

"Donna!"

Still no answer. She shed her outdoor clothes, hanging her coat on the classic wooden stand by the front door, and climbed up the wrought-iron spiral staircase in the middle of the lower floor living room up to the bedrooms above. She went straight for her sister's room.

"Donna!" she called again, this time louder. "Donna! Are you in there?" Still no answer. She let herself into her younger sister's domain. The bedroom was filled with the normal hoardings of a seventeen year old. Records and CDs sat atop the stereo — a Christmas present from Jennifer. Her jackets, ranging from denim to padded puffa, hung on the wall-mounted coat rack. Her college books, folders and papers littered her desk, the parquet floor, bookcase and the bed. Tupac steered down at her from the life-size poster, a leery look on his face. A poster of ragga queen Patra caught Jennifer's eye. *Another one of Donna's role models!* Jennifer sighed. Donna's dressing-table showed signs of a hurried make-over. A hair magazine propped up against the mirror, her tongs, brushes and comb were left where they fell. An open tub of gel sat on the floor by her chair over which hung discarded garments.

The bed in the middle of the room had clearly not been slept in. Donna's teddy bears were lined up against the pillows exactly as they were every morning. Where was she? She hadn't mentioned going out. But then again, a phone call from one of her ragamuffin friends was usually all it took to tease Donna out of the front door.

Jennifer went down to the living room to call Donna on her mobile. Cordless phone in hand she sat in her favourite armchair. Favourite because her fax, two telephones, desk and filing cabinets were all within easy reach. On either side of her stood bookshelves stacked with law books. This corner of the room was designed for work and study.

She dialled quickly and held the phone to her ear. *Engaged!* She pressed redial. *Still engaged.* She was beginning to feel anxious about her sister and king rat, Fitzroy. What did Donna see in him? As she paced the floor of her newly fitted kitchen she wondered how mothers of teenagers managed.

Only this week they had received a letter from their parents in Jamaica. Mummy wanted to know when they were coming to visit next. She missed them and always worried about them not eating properly. But most of all she worried about her daughters going out with 'wokless men'. The only thing that eased her fears, she said, was knowing that they were together and watching out for each other, especially where men were concerned. She wanted to be kept informed, of everything, and told them off for not writing enough. At the bottom of the letter she had again written their Jamaican phone number in large bold print.

Jennifer grimaced. There was no way she could tell her mother about Donna's new man. She'd probably have a heart attack! No, she'd have to make Donna see sense. The streets at night were no place for a girl her age. That, however, was not her main concern. The thought of her sister ensconced in Fitzroy's flat...in his bedroom...him, barechested and horny...ragga music playing on his stereo and God knows what happening on his bed...

With that nightmare vision in her head, Jennifer took her drink back to the living room and dialled again. This time she got the voice box answering service and had to endure the intro to *Undercover Lover* before her sister's bubbly voice announced, "You have reached the voice box of Donna Edwards...You know what to do and when to do it."

"D, it's me...your sister. It's after two in the morning, where are you? Call me as soon as you get this message...I'm at home."

Sighing, Jennifer walked over to the stereo system and flicked it on. The tuner was pre-programmed to her favourite Choice FM. The sweet and sultry vocals of Jenni Francis oozed out of the speakers giving a shout to, "...All those women out there who are on their own tonight...this one's going out to you all, sistas."

Jennifer flopped onto the huge five-seater sofa as the sounds of Barry White's *Practice What You Preach* filled the room. She was so tired that before she knew it she had slipped into a deep slumber.

Donna Edwards had spent the night having a wicked time! Fitzroy had a car and had insisted on visiting five parties for the night. By the time they came home, Donna's feet were killing her, she couldn't wait to pull off her new knee-length leather boots. On the way back she'd complained to Fitzroy how much her toes were killing her.

"Wha' me tell yuh? Ya doan wear new boot out ah dance."

They were exhausted, drunk, high on each other's company. They giggled all the way up the communal stairwell. Fitzroy was feeling good and could barely keep his hands off his woman. If he wasn't tickling her, he was whispering into her ears teasingly. Donna did try to hush him, but it did no good. He was in a playful mood and couldn't bring himself to consider anyone else in the building who might be trying to get to sleep when he was having so much fun with his girl. Outside the flat Donna struggled to line the key up while Fitzroy tickled her. It slipped in eventually and Fitzroy made a joke about fitting a key in her lock. Giggling, they fell into the darkened living room.

"Quiet Fitz," Donna hissed, "you'll wake Jen up."

"Ah wha' dis, you nevah worry 'bout making noise before," he whispered back, nibbling the back of her neck.

"Yeah, well, we weren't on our feet then, an' we weren't in my sister's flat neither," Donna hissed, running a hand over his short twisted locks.

"Cho', dat sister ah yours, she's going on too stush if you ask me. Just 'cause she's a lawyer. Ah nuh she one live yah, y'know. Jus' tell her dat Fitzroy seh she haffe settle an' cool, seen?"

"Why don't you tell me yourself?" The voice came from the other side of the room and made both Donna and Fitzroy jump into each others arms.

"Ah wha' de blood...?!" Fitzroy exclaimed, his head spinning in the direction of the voice.

Donna hit the light switch by the door and illuminated the room.

Jennifer was standing over by the bay windows, her arms folded and a pissed-off look on her face.

"Oh Sis. Didn't know you were still up. Did you fall asleep on the sofa again?"

Jennifer took in the short lycra dress her sister was wrapped in and the way Fitzroy's hand slipped to her backside. "I must have done. Which is just as well, otherwise I wouldn't have heard what your friend thought of me."

"Heh...heh...hey!" he stuttered not liking the way she put him down with that single word 'Friend'.

"Didn't you get my message on your mobile?" Jennifer asked.

"Oh yeah...the message. Yeah I got it. What about it?" her sister replied.

"Well why didn't you call me back?"

" 'Cause we were almost home by the time I got it. I figured it could wait until morning. What was so urgent anyway? Has somebody died? Don't tell me that something's happened to mum and dad."

Jennifer exhaled. Her lips twisted into an angry pout. Wasn't it obvious what was wrong? *The child comes in here six o'clock in the morning. The sun is up, the milkman has done his rounds. Did she even think to leave a note to say where she was going? No! That would have been too easy. Then she doesn't come home alone, but with this...this degenerate, who looks as though he's wanted by the police.*

"Well...what is it?"

"It can wait for now." Jennifer's stern attention was now focused on Fitzroy Lucas who had unzipped the heavy leather coat he was wearing to reveal a limp string vest over a well-toned, slim torso and unbuckled baggy jeans. He threw himself on the sofa, his legs splayed out in front of him. "We'll talk about it in the morning," Jennifer said bitterly, making her way to the spiral staircase.

"I thought it was urgent," Donna said.

"It was," Jennifer replied. "And it still will be tomorrow morning. But it'll have to wait. I'm tired, I'm going to turn in. I'd appreciate if you told your guest to keep the noise down. It is after all nearly dawn." With that Jennifer climbed up the staircase to her bedroom, leaving Fitzroy stuttering, "Eh...eh...eh," after her.

Jennifer awoke later that Saturday morning, her head feeling as though she had spent the night in a cement mixer. She had only had two glasses of wine and was well within her limit. But wine and worries don't mix and right now she had a trailerload of worries in the shape of an unruly little sister and the company she kept.

Jennifer glanced across the landing. Donna's bedroom, its door wide open, was empty. She heard noises coming from the kitchen downstairs. She secured her silk dressing gown at the waist and went downstairs for some juice before her morning jog.

She sensed Fitzroy's presence even before she entered the kitchen. He was dressed in baggy jeans which hung at the hips, revealing the red and white striped boxer shorts beneath. He stood over the stove barechested, cooking himself a fry up. The kitchen was awash with the smell of oils and fatty food. After all, what did someone like him know about a luxury such as an extractor fan.

Jennifer cleared her throat to alert him to her presence.

"Yuh awright, Jen?" Fitzroy turned with the frying pan in his hand, and a grin that showed off his two gold teeth.

Jennifer ignored him and crossed to the fridge, pulling out a carton of grapefruit juice.

Fitzroy kissed his teeth. "Cho', some people need to learn manners more than adders."

Irritation gathered within her. "If you're referring to me, just remember whose house you're in."

He turned to her and leant against the counter. "What 'appen to yuh, eh? One time me did t'ink seh you was criss. Now you so stush I man cyant even 'ave a decent conversation."

"Tell that to one of your baby mothers."

"Ah wha' you ah seh?'

"Don't act ignorant," she said. "I know all about you and I'm going to make sure Donna knows too."

"Know wha'?"

It was all a game to Fitzroy. Even though he hadn't been back to the Caribbean since he was thirteen, he spoke as though he'd just stepped off the plane from back-a-yard.

Jennifer walked towards the spiral staircase. "Just make sure you clean up the kitchen when you finish doing whatever you're doing."

She heard him kiss his teeth again as she climbed up the steps. Fitzroy needed babysitting. Where the hell was Donna? Jennifer had things to do and didn't want Mr Loverman in her home when she got back.

Jennifer sat patiently in her Volkswagen with the roof down. The Lewisham Centre's three car parks were rammed to capacity. Usually she would have waited until Sunday to do her shopping, but she couldn't bare to stay indoors a moment longer with HIM around. He was still there when she got back from her morning jog, going through her record collection, a spliff in hand. She had to talk to Donna and soon. She didn't want Fitzroy in her home no way, no more.

The streets of Lewisham were going through reconstruction. Lewisham 2000 they called it. The old clock tower had come down the previous year, and was now replaced by a new one. The old Army and Navy store had vanished. Knocked down to the ground, along with the glass overhead walkway that had joined the department store to the shopping centre. The actual shopping centre hadn't changed much over the years. A lot of the shops had been around since Jennifer was at school. Boots the chemist, Argos, Our Price, Etams, where she used to buy her school uniform (come to think of it didn't she get her first bra from there too?) The commonly known 'Black market' was just that, a market that sold goods for black people. There was a black hairdresser, a black hair care shop, a greeting card shop, that also sold posters, black dolls, incense and books. Finch's sold patties, hard dough bread and bun, and competed with the hair care shops with it's own stock of beauty products. There was a black man who sold kids and baby wear, mostly socks, vests and pants, he always had a smile and a joke for everybody. Jennifer remembered that someone had told her Errol used to be a famous boxer, and now here he was years later selling baby's knickers.

Jennifer bought herself a pattie and browsed around. She checked out a pair of leather boots in River Island and eased her earlier tension by purchasing a stack of books from the Black Writers section at Wordsworth Books on the High Street. Then she went back in the Centre, deciding to treat herself to some new clothes. She was so engrossed with comparing outfits in Marks and Spencer, that when a hand tapped her on the shoulder it took her by surprise.

"Jen! Bit jumpy aren't you? Did I catch you doing something you weren't supposed to?" Elaine, her hair pulled back into a bun, dressed in jogging bottoms and leotard with a jumper casually draped over her shoulders, stood grinning beside her.

Jennifer laughed and hung the tartan skirt she had been considering back on the rack. "Elaine, I don't see you in years and then bump into you a day after the reunion."

"Funny how life works out, isn't it?" Elaine admired Jennifer's casual weekend style. Lemon lambswool jumper tucked into black denims, ending in a pair of polished black ankle boots. Her short leather jacket looked and felt as soft as rose petals. Quality. Even her hair looked as though she had just stepped out of a salon. Elaine, in contrast, had dressed minimalist and her fit body was barely concealed by the tight-fitting leotard.

"What are you doing out dressed like that, it's only spring."

"I'm taking an Afrobics class down at the Riverdale. You should come along one day, they're fun plus you get a body like mine thrown in for free."

Jennifer smiled. Elaine did look good, but Jennifer preferred her body to look a little more feminine. In her book, rock hard muscles were for men. "I will when I get a chance. I don't have a lot of spare time. And when I do I find myself having to watch out for Donna. Who'd have thought that at the age of twenty seven I'd be playing mother to a seventeen year old?"

"What?"

"It doesn't matter."

Elaine remembered last night's conversation. "You mean your sister?"

"Who else?"

They walked together, pausing outside Ravel's to browse at shoes.

"You'll never guess who I've just seen."

Jennifer seemed less than interested. There was a pair of pink and cream platforms in the shop window that reminded her of shoes her mum was wearing in one of the photographs they had at home of their parents taken in the seventies.

"One of Fitzroy's baby mothers!"

Elaine immediately had Jennifer's attention. "Where?"

"In Sainsbury's. She's got their kid with her. I only know her because she don't live that far from me."

Jennifer was immediately gripped with an overwhelming urge to meet this woman. "Show me," she demanded urgently.

"You're joking aren't you?" Elaine regarded her with jovial concern. "What are you going to do, go up to her and ask how she's living?"

Jennifer shook her head. "Elaine, I just need some questions answered. This woman...What's her name?"

"Celia."

Jennifer grabbed Elaine's arm, leading her back towards

Sainsbury's. "She might have some answers for me."

"All right woman, you don't need to kidnap me," Elaine protested as she was whisked away.

They entered Sainsbury's through the main entrance and weaved through crowds of shoppers with shopping trolleys and baskets and children. The pair kept their heads high and searched up and down each aisle. Jennifer pointed to a woman with a young boy by her side. Elaine shook her head. They were just about to give up when Elaine spotted the woman in question and directed Jennifer towards the tills at the far end of the supermarket. They barged towards the front of the queue.

"Celia!" Elaine called. The young woman looked up, her brow furrowed at having her name shouted out in a public.

Celia was a big woman. Not big in the fat sense but she looked like she could have held her own in a wrestling match. Her large black leather jacket covered most of her bulk, but still she was an imposing figure. Her hair gelled to her head in Marcell waves, she wore gold sandals on her feet. Jennifer was only too aware that this was a woman from the streets.

"Elaine, whatcha running me down for, man? Didn't I jus' see you?"

"Celia this is a friend of mine, Jennifer. You have something in common."

Celia looked Jennifer up and down as though she couldn't possibly have. "Yeah?"

"I'm a..." Jennifer struggled to find a word to describe her relationship with the man they knew in common, "...an acquaintance of Fitzroy's."

Celia's son grinned cheekily up at Jennifer. A familiar grin. Celia turned to Elaine then back to Jennifer and screwed up her mouth, pushed up her chest and set her feet in a fighting stance. "You want trouble?" she challenged.

"No, you don't understand," Jennifer turned to the little boy, two years old at the most. "Is this his baby?"

Celia still wasn't convinced Jennifer was a friend and not foe. "What's that got to do with you?"

Elaine stepped in. She could see a situation developing here that could leave Jennifer lying flat on her back. "Easy nuh, C. Jen's just trying to get some information for her sister."

"I'm not no advice bureau, y'know."

"Fitzroy's seeing my sister, okay? I just want to make sure she knows what she's getting into."

"What Fitzroy does is his own business."

"I don't want to interfere with whatever you and Fitzroy have. I'm just trying to make my sister see that he's no good."

"You know where he is?"

"Yeah at the moment I do."

"Well you can tell him from me he is a no good dirty bastard who owes me three months money. His son needs new shoes and a coat that fits an' if he don't find his raas down my yard by weekend gone, I'm sending my bruddas for him..."

"Well Celia, nice seeing you again, we'll make sure he gets the message," Elaine said, dragging Jennifer away. "Them kinda people you don't mess with," she advised.

" 'Them kinda people', as you put it, is who my sister's already messing with. But I'm not going to let Fitzroy turn my sister into that woman," Jennifer replied forcefully. Her blood was boiling. As she walked Elaine back to her class at the Riverdale, Jennifer resolved that she would have to make Donna see sense one way or another.

Four shopping bags later Jennifer arrived back home and found that her sister still wasn't there. Fitzroy had made himself at home on her sofa and was eating lunch.

"Jen, remember these programmes?" he said through a mouthful of bun and cheese.

Jennifer looked over at the TV screen. He was watching Batman. The original action series. "Don't you have anything better to do?"

"No, but if yuh 'ave sup'm in mind..." Fitzroy had one hand down the front of his jeans.

Jennifer shook her head with disgust. "Why don't you go home?" She moved around the living room clearing up his mess. Newspaper pages scattered on the floor. "Don't start taking my place as a doss house."

"Me ah wait fe Donna. Yuh 'ave one serious problem, y'know," he said sitting up straight, crumbs fell from his chest into his lap.

"Yes. You."

"See how I mean?" he gestured. "Frustration, man. Pure frustration. It nuh good fe yuh," he stood up and came up behind her as she plumped up the cushions.

"What d'you think you're doing?"

"Jus' easing yuh mind," he touched her shoulders and was immediately pushed aside.

"Don't play those games with me Fitzroy, I'm not my sister."

With that she left him and climbed the stairs to her room for some peace and quiet. When Donna eventually showed up, Jennifer still didn't get a chance to talk to her because Fitzroy stayed for tea and even supper and emptied the fridge of every can of Red Stripe. By nightfall he was too drunk to leave and Donna said he might as well stay, much to Jennifer's chagrin.

The clock radio woke her up at exactly 9.15 when the voice of Alaister Cooke with his *Letter From America* filled the bedroom. Jennifer opened her eyes to the bright and beautiful Sunday morning. It looked like it was going to be one of those lazy ones. For a busy barrister who didn't have time to listen to the radio as much as she would like, Radio 4 on a Sunday morning was the perfect review of the week. Listening to Alaister Cooke, the Morning Service and the Pick Of The Week put her in the right mood to enjoy her day of rest. But this morning, her attention was only partly on the broadcast, because her mind kept wondering back to the current problem in her life. Donna was next door in the bedroom with Fitzroy and while they were there together, Jennifer couldn't help being tense and uptight.

She got up hurriedly, and went next door. She stood outside Donna's bedroom for a moment, with her head against the door, listening. She couldn't hear anything. She wanted to wake them up and get Fitzroy out of the house so that she could get a chance to finally talk to her sister woman to woman about the man in her life. She knocked loudly on the door.

"Donna! Donna, are you awake?" There was no response. She put her head to the door again. This time she could just about make out a deep, guttural snore — the kind that could only have come from a man. Jennifer grimaced and went back into her bedroom where she climbed out of her pyjamas and changed quickly into her track suit. She slipped on her new Nikes and headband, the one with just the logo on it, before skipping down the stairs, out of the flat and out the main entrance of the house.

The route wasn't always the same, depending on the weather. Dry weather would see her tracking the slopes of Honor Oak Park. Wet mornings would take her down Devonshire Road, its hills were just as steep as the park's. Distance was always the same, two miles every day. Then after her circuit, she would jog over to the newsagents down the road and pick up a copy of each of the broadsheets.

She walked back leisurely to her place. The sun was shining bright and there wasn't a cloud in the sky. She filled her lungs with a deep breath of air which made her feel charged enough to face the rest of the day.

Back at the flat, Fitzroy and Donna were still not up. Jennifer slipped out of her running gear and into the bathroom for a leisurely shower, after which she dressed in a simple cotton dress and went downstairs to read the papers over a bowl of muesli. She turned first to the business pages as usual. Even though she was making a steady climb in her career as a barrister, she had ambitions for bigger things. Criminal and civil law was not where she wanted to be in five years time. She saw herself more as a company lawyer. That was where the real money was and in the hierarchy of things, that was where all the cudos was. So now she made a point of keeping abreast of all the business news and kept herself aware of all the little changes in company law, so that she would be prepared to make the move when she was given the opportunity.

After browsing the business pages, she turned to the Home News sections. There was an article on how the CSA were getting tough on absent fathers. Apparently, they were now offering rewards for information leading to the successful apprehension of any of the 100 absent fathers on their 'Britain's Most Wanted' hit list. They had also hit upon the novel idea of putting up the 'Wanted' posters of these fugitives in pubs, bookies and football grounds up and down the country. Jennifer couldn't help thinking of Fitzroy and whether or not his name was on that hit list. She mentally calculated how much she would get for turning him in.

The horrible thought entered her head that it might already be too late. Donna could after all already be pregnant. If so, she couldn't see Fitzroy making any contribution to a child. Not ever. He didn't work and seemed to have no inclination to get up off his backside to find a job. Even though she had previously presented him with the Evening Standard's classified jobs pages, Fitzroy had failed to get the message, saying only that there wasn't no job out there which could pay him what he was really worth so therefore that it was better that he just took time to set up something for himself. He was working on it, he said. Working on it just like he had over the years since leaving school with no qualifications. What did her sister see in this guy? She just couldn't understand. It had to be the sex.

Almost on cue, she heard the quiet giggling from the bedroom above, followed by the rhythmic squeaking of the bed springs. Her heart began to beat fast and furiously. She got up, her face contorted in anger and her nostrils flaring. She climbed up the stairs fast, taking them two at a time. Almost before she realized it, she was outside Donna's room. She paused for a moment to catch her breath. The heavy breathing was more audible now. Jennifer winced and started knocking loudly on the door. She heard herself call, "Donna! Are you awake yet?!"

A faint "Bumboclaat!" came from within. It was Fitzroy's voice.

Undeterred, she knocked loudly again. "D, wake up, I need to speak to you. Urgently!"

After a moment she heard her sister's breathless voice. "Yes...? What is it? What d'you want Sis?"

What did she want? So much was her haste in running upstairs to do what she could to break up any tenderness between her sister and Fitzroy that she hadn't even prepared an excuse. And now when she had to conjure one up, she couldn't come up with anything. She scanned her imagination for a good one, but the best she could do was say, "I just wanted to ask if you fancied going for a little picnic in the park a little later? It's such a beautiful warm day, there isn't a cloud in the sky."

Again she heard Fitzroy's exasperated voice from within: "Picnic?!?! Wha' de bumboclaat! She ah mek noise 'bout picnic?!"

She heard Donna's whispered giggle, "Shush!" Then her voice rose to reply, "Are you serious?"

"Well, what d'you think?" she couldn't believe she was doing this. "Shame to waste the day away in bed."

There was a silence before Donna shouted back, "I'll be down later."

"You want to go out then?"

"Leave it out, Jen. I'll be down soon."

Jennifer heard the whispering of their voices behind the door and then laughter. They were laughing at her! She felt like a fool. What could she do to save her sister from this dangerous liaison? She stomped down the stairs making as much noise as possible.

Five minutes later she heard the two of them come out of the bedroom having a conversation about some ragga DJ they were on different sides of the fence about. Then their voices faded into the bathroom. Half an hour later they emerged downstairs smelling fresh and dressed casually. By the look of things Fitzroy had every intention of enjoying the hospitality further. He acted like Jennifer wasn't even in the room. With both remote controls in his hand, he spread his body out on the sofa. The telly went on in one corner, the stereo in the other.

"Don't you have a home to go to, Fitzroy?"

"Yeah, an' if Donna want me fe go, me will go."

"We could always go back upstairs if you want your peace," Donna suggested. A look passed between her and Fitzroy which meant exactly what Jennifer thought it did.

"No, that won't be necessary. I want us to spend some time alone D. How often are we both at home on a Sunday?"

Fitzroy pulled his girlfriend closer. "You want to spend time wid yuh sister?"

Donna giggled. "I want to spend time with you."

"Me know dat a'ready."

One of those looks again.

"I'll make us some breakfast." As Donna stood up to go to the kitchen Fitzroy smacked her bottom playfully.

Jennifer had had enough. As soon as Donna was out of the room she got up and switched the stereo off, leaving the church choir singing on the television.

She stood in front of it with her arms crossed, "Don't you have a church service to attend Fitzroy?"

"Wha' you mean?"

"It is Sunday. Didn't your mother always tell you to repent your sins in church every Sunday, I'm sure you've got a lot to catch up on."

"You don't know me, y'know. Talk to yuh sister, man, she will tell you she don't want anyt'ing else from me, but me," he threw his legs over the arm of the sofa and reached for one of the Sunday supplements on the coffee table.

"I'm sure there are others out there who don't want anything else but your money. N'est ce pas?"

"Why yuh always haffe talk in riddles fa?"

"I bumped into a woman yesterday whose name was..." Jennifer paused, a finger on her chin for effect, "...Celia..."

She watched Fitzroy's expression, but he was still nonchalant, "Yeah, and...?"

"It was funny really, because she got very excited when I mentioned your name. She said something about you not bringing her any money for three months. When I told her I knew where you were she got even more excited, said something about her brothers wanting a word with you. Does any of this mean anything?"

Fitzroy's eyes suddenly came alive. "De 'ooman, she did 'ave a pickney wid her?"

"A boy, yes."

"Yuh nevah tell her weh me deh?" He shot up now, studying Jennifer anxiously.

Jennifer shrugged. "I did as a matter of fact, told her that this afternoon would be a good time to call around." She had to turn her back to avoid him seeing the smirk bubbling up from her belly.

"A lie yuh ah tell!" He jumped up from the sofa and rushed to look out of the window in case the woman's arrival was imminent.

"I would have told you earlier but you were in bed so late that it slipped my mind..."

"I...I jus' remember, me 'ave sup'm fe her, y'know. Maybe me will...uhm...jus' drop by, y'know. Save her de trouble..." Fitzroy was already at the doorway before he finished the sentence. "Yaow D," he called, "me gawn, seen?"

Donna came to meet him in the passageway wiping her hands on a tea towel.

"I jus' remember me 'ave some bizness to tek care ah. Is a'right. Me will call you, seen?"

Fitzroy hit the road, his shirt tail full of wind.

Alone at last the sisters sat at the kitchen table while Donna ate her breakfast.

"How about the picnic? The sun is still out." Jennifer asked tentatively.

Donna gave her sister a look that told her what she thought of that idea. She swept her hair off her face with one hand. She had what people back home called 'good hair', Jennifer thought, not for the first time.

"Get real, Jen. I can think of better things to do on a hot Sunday."

Jennifer stared into her cup of warm coffee. "We should do more things together. Then you wouldn't have to spend so much time with Fitzroy."

"Sorry Sis, but you can't do for me what Fitzroy does," Donna bit into her buttered toast and smiled cheekily.

Jennifer winced. She hated the way Donna made a joke of everything. They'd had the argument about having sex under her sister's roof a year ago. Donna had asked her if she'd rather she did it on the streets. Jennifer couldn't argue with that and had little choice but to accept that her baby sister was going to bring boys home and that they were going to be using her bedroom for their carnal knowledge.

"I know that, but I'm not going to get you in trouble the way Fitzroy will."

"What makes you so sure that Fitzroy is going to get me in trouble? You don't know him."

"You wanna bet? Donna, he's ten years older than you. He's got three women pregnant that I know about and God knows how many more."

"I suppose you've got proof that the kids are his, right?" Donna tilted her head in question. "Fitzroy told me that ever since school women told lies about him because he didn't want them. They'd get pregnant and blame it on him because he was an easy target."

"And you believed that?"

Donna shrugged. "I can't see what the problem is. Even if it was true, do you think I'm stupid enough to let myself get pregnant?"

"No. I'm saying he's devious enough to make you pregnant."

Donna got up from her seat and paced the kitchen. "You're never gonna let me make my own decisions are you? You're never gonna trust my instincts, my judgments. You know what, Jen, why don't you just live my life for me?"

"If you would only listen to me..."

"What, like you listen to me?"

"Don't raise your voice to me young lady. Sit down."

Slowly, Donna sat down at the dining table and faced her sister sulkily.

"I know women who, years ago when they were your age, thought they were grown up enough to make their own mistakes. No matter what people told them they never listened, as far as they were concerned they knew what they were doing."

Donna sighed, expressing her boredom. "Mum and dad had you at my age."

"That was in those days..."

"That wasn't all that long ago, y'know. Or what, are you saying you're an old woman already?"

"This isn't about Mum and Dad. These days you're on your own. And if you can't deal with it your kids end up in crime or in care...And then when the father reappears fifteen years later he can have rights to the kid and can upset any kind of relationship the mother has managed to establish with the child. I've bumped into old school friends who ended up as single mothers and they all regret it and wish they had their time again. They would rather be out clubbing than at home every weekend because they've got no one to help them. These are women who wanted to travel the world as teenagers, yet hardly travel further than the corner shop now and who have to juggle benefits to make ends meet."

Jennifer rested her arms on the kitchen table and made Donna meet her eyes. "You've got to realize that there's no future in a relationship with Fitzroy. All someone like him can offer you is a life in menial jobs with no career prospects, or a future raising children on your own. He might turn up at Christmas with a twenty pound note for you and the kid, but nothing more."

Donna picked at her fingernail, seemingly unconcerned.

"Mum and Dad cared about us enough to make sure we got a good education," Jennifer continued. "The least you can do is carry on the way they brought you up. Whatever happened to the baby sister who used to follow me around everywhere and want to be like me?"

"You really want to know? I grew up. Look, I'm not Jamaican, I'm British. So there was no point in Mum and Dad bringing me up like they would have in Jamaica."

Jennifer sat back in her chair ready, listening. She could hear the kitchen clock ticking away behind her.

Donna continued. "When you moved out, I was left at home with them. You know how old-fashioned they are, I always had to wear your hand-me-downs. And they still cooked food for four after you left and made me eat extra because they couldn't understand why there was food left over."

Jennifer chuckled at that.

"It's true. So not only was I wearing hand-me-downs and my Dad's old glasses, but I was also getting fat just so that mum wouldn't have to waste any food."

"I'm sorry, D," Jennifer laughed, "but that is funny."

Donna laughed too. "You don't understand why I enjoy how Fitzroy makes me feel because you didn't lead my life. When I wanted to go out with my friends after school, Mum and Dad made me come straight home and do my homework. I wanted to relax my hair and style it myself, but Mum plaited it in them cornrows every week from primary until they went back to Jamaica."

Jennifer's expression was thoughtful. "So what you're saying is that you're rebelling against what they taught you."

"I don't see it that way. The way I see it, I've finally got the chance to express myself and that's exactly what I'm doing."

"Don't you think I've heard that before from women who are now single with babies coming out of their ears?"

Donna stood up abruptly. "Jennifer, I love you, but you've got to trust me. I know what I'm doing. I can handle Fitzroy."

Jennifer mumbled. "Let's hope so."

"Pardon?"

"Beware of young men that give so little and take so much."

"Yeah, right Sis," Donna shook her head in mirth.

Jennifer decided to give Donna a couple more days to come to her senses about Fitzroy. After that she would start laying down the law. That was her prerogative because she paid the bills and her sister's expenses which enabled her to go to college. Maybe the only way to force Donna to get rid of Fitzroy would be to cut her weekly allowance. It had worked for their parents when they were kids.

TWO
If yuh cyan do bettah, yuh mus' do bettah

By ten o'clock Monday morning Jennifer had already taken four paracetamols for a headache that just wouldn't go away. The senior clerk Julian Holland, a small grey-haired man with a Greek nose, was the first to greet her when she arrived at chambers.

"Good morning, Miss Edwards," he handed her fax messages and mail.

"Morning, Julian."

"Miss Edwards, I've placed a brief in your tray, an industrial injury case we're considering. Let me know as soon as you've read it and I'll arrange a conference."

She smiled a thank you at the clerk and walked on to her room to be met by a pile of early morning phone messages placed in the centre of her desk. There were two messages from a Mr. Harvey who was claiming to be a lawyer from some society. He wanted to meet with her. She threw it into her pending tray. The others were from lawyers and clients who wanted follow-ups, or updates on their cases. As she was due in court in fifteen minutes she delegated the calls to the clerk.

The woman took the stand in disguise. No one would have guessed that she was recently nominated Businesswoman of the Year by a black newspaper.

The first time she had met Mrs. Matthews, Jennifer had asked where she had purchased the beautifully made beige three-piece suit she was wearing. Now the woman who took the stand looked as though she was on benefit and had to borrow her mother's clothes for her day in court. She wore a long, flowery, oversized dress with a grey cardigan and an old coat that might have been fashionable twenty years ago. She wore no make-up and her hair was simply brushed back off her face.

Mrs Matthews coughed timidly into a white hanky, before speaking. "He walked out on me an the children eighteen months ago," she sniffed.

Jennifer's 'learned friend' Patrick Wilson, representing the plaintiff, was a tall thin man with a beard, who wore his gown like a tent. He faced the witness on the stand. "And have you seen Mr. Matthews in those eighteen months?"

"He came by last year to ask me for his share of our house."

"The house that you no longer own?"

"That's right."

"What happened to your home, Mrs. Matthews?"

Mrs Matthew clutched her handbag tightly. "Had to sell it, couldn't afford to stay in that big house no more on only one salary."

"And the proceeds from the house, Mrs. Matthews, what happened to that?"

"It's all gone...I had debts to pay and the kids needed stuff and when the council put us in that flat we had to buy furniture and stuff."

"But the house was worth half a million. Do you expect the court to believe that you simply spent the money on furniture?"

"Yes sir...I mean no, I put some into my business...and...I donated money to a gipsy settlement...but they've moved on without trace." She paused and looked straight at the barrister. "...Money don't last forever, y'know."

"Does your husband have any rights to that money, Mrs Matthews?"

"No sir, the house was in my name."

"But wasn't the mortgage being paid out of his salary until he left you?"

"That's right, but then when he ran off with his slut he stopped paying...nearly had us thrown out on the street." Mrs Matthews crossed her fingers behind her back, "I even turned to prostitution to pay the mortgage before the house was sold."

"He is still the father of your children, of which he now has custody, do you not feel that he has a right to his share from the sale of your home?"

"No!" she said adamantly. "I slaved for that man for years. Years of washing, cleaning, sexing him..."

"Thank you Mrs. Matthews," the judge interrupted. "Any further questions?"

"Yes your honour," Jennifer stood while Patrick Wilson took his seat.

Mrs Matthews looked increasingly uncomfortable, her fingers were clenching and unclenching her handbag, controlling her anger.

"Mrs Matthews, would you please tell the court why the family home was in your name only."

Mrs Matthews visibly relaxed. "It was because Victor...Mr Matthews, always said that if we ever divorced then the house would belong to me and the children, that we wouldn't have to go through this..." she indicated the courtroom.

"And why do you believe Mr. Matthews changed his mind about this arrangement?"

"Because without my money he had NOTHING!" Mrs Matthews threw a look of scorn across the court at her ex-husband.

Jennifer smiled at her reassuringly, though deep down she was beginning to regret having this case assigned to her. "No further questions," she said and sat down.

"Any further questions, Mr. Wilson?" the judge asked.

The senior barrister stood. "No further questions, m'lud."

The judge turned to the witness box. "You may step down Mrs Matthews."

The next witness for the prosecution was a detective whom Mr. Matthews had hired to prove that Mrs Matthews still had the money and was living wealthy from it.

The detective took the stand. *A black man!* And a Denzel lookalike! Jennifer did her best to hide her amazement as she listened to this cool operator's testimony. Then she began her questioning.

"Mr..." she referred to her papers, "...Carnegie, my client is a small business woman, with a struggling business I might add. She now lives in a council-owned maisonette on the Peckham North estate. Does this strike you as the lifestyle of a woman who has half a million pounds at her disposal?"

"That's simple, Miss Edwards, Mrs Matthews has chosen to live this way ever since she realized that her husband was going to claim half of the house's worth." His voice was youthful and almost musical.

"How would you go about proving such a claim, Mr. Carnegie?"

"I've followed her, watched how she spends her money, where she spends her money. I've observed the way she dresses, what transportation she uses to get around..."

Jennifer looked up from her notes and was sure she detected a smirk on his face. She began to take a dislike to this ruggedly handsome witness. He was too smooth by half and she had a sudden urge to cut him down to size.

"Mr. Carnegie, you say you saw my client, Mrs. Matthews, shopping in town recently. What exactly did you see?"

The private investigator, Tony Carnegie, unbuttoned his jacket slowly, like a male stripper about to go into a routine, and pulled out a leather bound notebook from his inside pocket. He flicked through it until he came to the relevant page. "On the morning of April 12th, Mrs. Matthews walked into the Croydon branch of Dorothy Perkins and browsed for approximately fifteen minutes. During this time she picked up five items of clothing, a skirt, a pair of trousers, two dresses and a blouse."

"Did she purchase any of these items?"

"Yes," he turned to the next page. "Mrs. Matthews purchased the two dresses, the skirt and the blouse on her credit card. A total of one hundred and fifty pounds altogether."

Mr Matthews let out a loud whistle of astonishment. "Coulda fed the pickney fe a month on dat."

"Are you sure," Jennifer continued, "that the purchases were for herself?"

"Yes. Definitely," he said with another smirk. "They were in her size, she paid for them with her credit card."

"Are you in the habit, Mr. Carnegie, of purchasing women's clothing?"

Tony Carnegie jumped back defensively. "No!"

"Then I put it to you that the items of clothing Mrs. Matthews purchased could possibly have been for someone else. A present? A purchase for a friend with the same size in clothes? It's not unusual."

"Miss Edwards," Carnegie said suavely, his head tilted a little to the side, "I assure you that I know women, sometimes better than they know themselves. I could look at a woman and tell which shops she buys her clothes from, how much she spends on clothes, whether she does her hair herself or pays an expensive hairdresser. That's what I do for a living — study people. Especially women." His eyes looked her up and down. "I've been trailing Mrs. Matthews for two months and in that time I've learnt her clothes size, shoe size, her tastes in food and men, and her desires and aspirations."

Jennifer hated the man's arrogance. Next he'd be telling her he knew what she fantasized about while she lay in bed at night.

"Also..." he referred again to his notebook, "Mrs Matthews wore one of the dresses purchased on the date of April 12th to a luncheon at a restaurant called 'Chez Noir' where she again paid by credit card."

"M'lud, as self-employed, Mrs Matthews does have a business expense account. I'm sure you will find that her restaurant bill is noted in her company's books."

The judge referred to the account book he had in front of him and waved the proceedings on. Jennifer walked back to the desk and picked out a sheet of paper from her file.

"Mr Matthews left his wife a year and a half ago, leaving her to raise their two children Donna and Jason alone. A year ago Mr. Matthews came back into their lives and threatened to file for custody on the grounds of neglect. Mrs Matthews let him take the children because she accepted they needed to spend more time with their father and because she wanted to pursue a life-long dream of setting up her own business. In the time that the children were living with their mother Mr. Matthews made no contribution to their parenting, financially or otherwise. Or do you have any evidence to the contrary Mr. Carnegie?"

"Urr..." Tony Carnegie swallows. "No." He wasn't sure he knew where the questioning was heading.

The judge raised his mallet. "Miss Edwards I must remind you of the reason Mr. Carnegie is on the stand. He is here to give us evidence of his investigation into Mrs. Matthews' expenses and finances. Not to give evidence as to why Mr. Matthews did not pay maintenance. Are we clear on that?"

"Yes, Your Honour. I was coming to that." Jennifer sucked her cheeks in and her lips pouted. "It is my belief that Mr. Matthews only sought custody of the children because he felt it was the only way he could get his hands on the proceeds of the house. That is the only reason he employed you to tail his wife, isn't it Mr. Carnegie?"

"That is quite possible Miss Edwards, but then, who would you say had the greatest need for that money, a struggling unemployed single father, or a successful businesswoman?"

Jennifer's chest heaved, she sighed internally. "Do you have any more evidence as to Mrs. Matthews' financial status, Mr. Carnegie?"

"As a matter of fact I do." He proceeded to reel off a series of spending sprees that included parties, presents for a boyfriend and redecoration of her flat, plus modernization of her work premises. Holidays abroad.

In the middle of it Mrs Matthews, who had restrained herself as best as she could throughout, jumped up out of her seat and ran over to her estranged husband and grabbed him by the throat. "I gave you everything a man could ask for: a beautiful home, two beautiful children. You bastard, what did you do in return? Dump me for an eighteen year old slag and now you're trying to take my money too..."

Her outburst was too much for the judge and as Mrs. Matthews was dragged away yelling by a court guard, he ruled against her and ordered Mrs Matthews to pay Mr. Matthews his share of the house — two hundred and fifty thousand pounds — and his court fees.

Jennifer shook her head and sighed as she put her things in the leather briefcase her parents had bought her on graduation. Monogrammed with her initials it was one of her most treasured possessions.

She hurried out of the court room, the sound of her high-heeled stilettos echoing as she went along. She had a case at another court in the afternoon and would only have time for a quick snack.

"Excuse me...Miss Edwards...?"

Jennifer turned in the direction of the voice. It was the private investigator.

She looked him up and down as he swaggered down the corridor towards her. There was something about him...she couldn't put her finger on it. *Something...?* She didn't have time to sum it up however, before he stood right in front of her smiling warmly, the kind of smile that expected to be reciprocated. He had a small scar in one eyebrow and the cutest smile she had ever seen on a grown man.

"I just wanted to tell you how much I enjoyed your performance in court," he said, the smile broadening.

"I'm sure you did," she replied brusquely, walking on towards the exit. "After all, you won the day."

"Yes, but no matter what the judge says, I think that your arguments were really a lot better. What does the judge know," he said, following her.

Jennifer felt his presence behind her. He was patronizing her, winding her up. She was sure of it. She just kept walking, her stilettos sounding a little tap dance with every two-step combination.

"Hey!" Tony Carnegie called after. "No hard feelings. Just because you lost the case. That's how it goes in life, there are winners and losers. I thought you would know all about that, being a barrister and all. Today for me, tomorrow for you."

Jennifer stopped momentarily and turned to look Tony dead in the eyes, trying to see if he was laughing at her, but all she could find was a charming twinkle in his eye. She thought that he must have been a real rascal as a youngster. However, she had better things to do right now than stare into his eyes. She carried on towards the exit. Tony stepped ahead enough to reach the exit before her. He smiled holding the door open, catching the scent of her perfume as she stepped out of the building. *Class*. The single word was like a price tag in his mind.

"Well," Jennifer addressed Tony when they were both outside, "I'm sure we won't be meeting again, so I'll say goodbye..." She turned to go.

"No wait," Tony called after her. "If we won't be meeting again that's all the more reason to give me the pleasure of joining me for lunch."

"Thanks, but no thanks," she told him politely but firmly.

"No...don't tell me you're turning me down..."

"It was nice of you to offer, but I'm otherwise engaged. I need to get back to chambers. Thanks anyway."

"I should have known," said Carnegie almost dejectedly, "you put one over on a woman and she won't forgive you," his voice held a distinct edge of sarcasm.

" 'Put one over'? Excuse me, you gave a testimony in a court case, that's all. If you want to kid yourself into thinking that you put one over on me go ahead, but I think that's taking it too far."

Tony looked pleased with himself. "But you have to admit that if you had won that court case or if I was testifying on your behalf, you wouldn't be so averse to lunching with me."

"Look, I've got better things to do with my time than to shed tears over a case. I really am busy and I need to get back. Anyway I'm surprised that you have time for lunches, I thought you'd be too busy stalking some poor woman somewhere, on behalf of her ex-husband."

Tony seemed unfazed by Jennifer's wit. He looked as if he had heard comments like that about his profession many times before and, indeed, he had. "I don't only snoop after women, I also investigate men...on a professional basis that is," Tony reminded her. "My services are open to any members of the general public." He smiled charmingly. "Anyway, I see you're not interested in any of that and as you would rather die than have lunch with me, I'll say goodbye."

With that Tony Carnegie made his way slowly down the steps at the front of the court house and looked up and down the road for a taxi. Jennifer remained standing on the top step, staring at him. She was thinking...Something he said was sticking in her mind.

Tony had flagged down a black taxi and was just about to climb in when Jennifer called out: "Wait...!"

Tony turned around, looking Jennifer hard in the eyes.

"I've changed my mind...I see that I have got a few minutes to spare for lunch...maybe just a snack."

"As you wish," he replied with that inviting smile.

"But I insist, *I'm* taking *you* to lunch," she said.

"I wouldn't dream of it," he smiled. "The only women I allow to buy me dinner are clients."

"Then I'll have to become a client," Jennifer said with an equally inviting smile. Tony held the cab door open as she stepped in, then he climbed in behind her.

El Montenegro's was crowded as usual. It was one of the favourite City haunts for people in the law. Situated on Fleet Street, it used to be popular amongst journalists on the national daily newspapers before they all moved to Wapping. Now it was a popular watering hole amongst the barristers and solicitors and clerks of the law who congregated around the Old Bailey and the Central Criminal Court. Jennifer returned from the bar with a dry white wine for herself and a Mexican bottled beer for Tony.

Taking a sip of his beer, Tony raised the glass in a toast. "To adversaries and all who sail in them," he said smiling.

"Quite," said Jennifer stiffly. "Now, what I want to see you about..."

"Whoa! Do we have to rush into this business thing straight away?"

Jennifer looked at her watch hurriedly. "Yes, if you don't mind. I don't have much time."

"How do you know if you can afford my fee?"

"Because, I suspect that you probably couldn't afford mine," she replied quick time.

"Touché!" Tony knew when he was beaten. "Nuff said."

"Back to the matter at hand. I want you to do some investigating for me. Do you think you can handle it?"

"That's my business...you have a problem and I take care of it."

"Well, it's not me exactly who needs the help. It's someone I know...she's in trouble. She's got a man who she doesn't know if she can trust. She wants to know if her man's got any children by any other woman. Or other women, as the case may be. And if so, how many?"

Tony studied her critically, "Who is this friend of yours exactly?"

"I'd rather not say," Jennifer sipped her drink.

Tony leant forward on the table. "Sorry. No can do. I need to know the facts."

"Okay, if you must know, it's my baby sister," she said frankly.

"Let me get this straight...your sister's got a man who you don't trust...?"

"I didn't say that, I said she suspects..."

"Yes, but what people say and what they mean aren't necessarily the same thing are they, counsel? You're a lawyer, you know that...So you're the big sister and you want to stop this man being with your kid sister by any means necessary. *You* don't trust him."

"Okay, I admit it. I want you to check this man out. My sister's young and naive. He's taking advantage of her."

"He is from your point of view."

"He is from anybody's point of view. It's quite obvious to everybody but my sister. You know how it is when you think you're in love."

"How is it?" Tony said with a glint in his eyes.

Jennifer felt self-conscious, his eyes were almost undressing her. "Well, you know...you fall in love and suddenly you become blind to what's really going on around you. You believe that the sun shines out of your lover's backside."

Tony sighed. "Yeah, I've been there...but it's been a while. It's only a fading memory now...So he's taking advantage of her and it's obvious from everybody's point of view except baby sister's. Am I right?"

Jennifer nodded. That's exactly how it was. "Look, I wouldn't be asking you to check this out if I didn't already have some proof. I've personally spoken to a woman who has had a baby for him, but from the gossip that's reaching me he's got a whole army of kids out there that he's not admitting to."

"And you think that your sister will drop him the moment she finds out exactly how many children he has?"

"Well, I hope so..."

"Let me ask you one thing, you're a barrister, an attractive sista. I'd say you were between twenty six and twenty eight years old, about five feet nine inches tall and around ten stone in weight, you speak well, you've got an air of success about you plus the kind of looks that many men would describe as 'criss'..."

"Please!" said Jennifer, embarrassed. "Go easy on the sugary stuff."

"No, but seriously...why are you so concerned about your sister's man? Why not let your sister make her own mistakes?"

"She's seventeen for goodness sake. I'm not going to let her throw her life away before she even knows the meaning of it."

"But maybe she's really in love...maybe it won't make any difference what I find out about her boyfriend. Maybe your sister's just crazy about this guy."

"I'll cross that bridge when I come to it."

Tony sat pondering as he took a long slow swig from his glass of beer. He pondered too long for Jennifer's liking.

"Look," she said getting up to go, "maybe this was all a mistake...you're obviously not the right person for this job."

"Woah...hold on. I didn't say that I wouldn't take the case. Sit down. Please relax. I just have a couple more questions to ask you. I need to know the facts."

Jennifer considered it a moment before easing herself back down on the seat.

"Are you sure that this isn't all about jealousy on your part?"

Jennifer was about to explode inside, but she restrained herself. "I consider that question to be out of order," she said simply.

"I could say that about some of the questions you were asking me in court. But I didn't. In fact, standing in the witness box and testifying, I ended up enjoying them and looked forward to your next question."

Jennifer looked at him hard. What was his game? Was she wasting her time even bothering to discuss her problems with this man? "Look," she said, "I've told you the situation as best I can. I want you to find out some information about Fitzroy that I may be able to use in preventing him from turning my sister into yet another single mother statistic in a world full of baby fathers. It's as simple as that. If you can find me any useful information on him you could be saving a young black teenager from ruining her life by one careless night of passion with 'Johnny-too-bad'."

The private investigator smiled admiringly. "Fair enough. That sounds reasonable to me."

"Jen, could you do my hair for me please," Donna called out.

Jennifer put down the legal papers she was reading. The sound of swing music floated out of her sister's bedroom and down the staircase. "Fitzroy coming round is he?" she called back.

Donna came down the spiral staircase, her blow-dried hair sticking up all over her head. "Fitzroy's not the only person I try to look good for, y'know. I'm going out with Shanika."

Jennifer sighed. Shanika was just as bad as Fitzroy. Either of them could get Donna pregnant. One directly, the other by leading her to it. "But it's a week night. Haven't you got homework from college to do?"

"Nothing that can't wait until tomorrow. Look, if you don't want to do my hair just say so. I don't need a lecture."

"It's all right I'll do it," Jennifer followed her back upstairs.

Donna sat on the swivel chair in front of her dresser mirror. "By the way, what's all this?" Donna held up a small blue and white cellophane wrapped packet.

Embarrassed, Jennifer avoided her sister's gaze. "Condoms," she replied.

"I know that," Donna rolled her eyes. "But how did they get under my pillow?"

"Look D, I put them there because I wanted to make sure you would always have some. I was in the chemist anyway, so I thought... When they run out I've got more."

"Jen, they give them out free at the family planning clinic." Donna pulled open her bottom drawer and opened an old chocolate box stuffed with an array of different coloured condom packets. "I have plenty, thank you very much. And I use 'em."

Jennifer now felt like the naive schoolgirl she was taking her sister for. "Sorry. I just thought..."

"All right, jus' don't do it again," Donna grinned.

"Did you still want me to do your hair, or did you just want to embarrass me?"

"I want you to help with my hair," Donna said turning back to her dresser. Containers of hair gel, combs, brushes and make-up were laid out in front of her. Her curling tongs were already heating up on a flannel she'd placed on the table.

"So what style do you want?"

"See that magazine on the bed..."

Jennifer picked up the magazine. It was open on a page full of glamorous women wearing various extensions. "You want one of these?"

"Don't say it like that. It's what's in now. You see that one with the ponytails and the sideburns?" Jennifer stood by her side and Donna pointed out the style she wanted. "That one."

"I can't do extensions."

"I'll direct you, Sis. I just can't do it myself without it looking naff. It'll be quicker with four hands."

Jennifer looked at the picture again. "If you're sure."

Teenage girls certainly were more daring these days. They dressed in baggy jeans half the time and shaved off their hair like the boys with all sorts of patterns cut into it. Otherwise they were adding extensions and colouring their hair several different colours. Donna had even toyed with the idea of having an earring in her nose!

Half an hour later, Donna's hair could have featured in Black Beauty and Hair Magazine. With a zig zag parting, multi-coloured spiral extensions creating two high ponytails either side of her head and slicked down waved sideburns, she couldn't help but get noticed. Jennifer had to admit she was proud of her effort. Then she noticed Donna's outfit hanging from the wardrobe door and decided that her sister had either bought the hair to match the outfit or vice versa.

"Good job, Sis. Betcha didn't know you had the talent in ya."

Jennifer chuckled. "If I ever need a sideline to pay the bills I'll open up a salon."

The doorbell rang. Jennifer went down the stairs knowing it had to be for her sister.

Shanika was eighteen and had gone to the same school as Donna. Of course she hadn't even noticed Donna until she'd started to change her image. Since then, Shanika had been a bad influence, in Jennifer's opinion. Shanika had had a well-developed body since early in her teens when she was often mistaken for a more mature woman. Her mother had brought her and her sisters up alone. Three sisters, three different fathers. None of these facts endeared her to Jennifer.

Tonight Shanika was dressed in a yellow puffa coat that reached her knees. She wore lace tights and knee-high boots identical to the ones Donna had recently purchased. Her hair was cut short, the front lengthened with the help of a row of weave-on hair. Stripes of red and gold went through it.

Jennifer turned from the front door and called up the stairs. "Donna your friend is here. She's just getting dressed," she told the girl. She wished she could pick and choose Donna's friends.

Shanika followed her into the living room. "All right, Jen?" she asked.

"Yes. You?" She sat down on the sofa and picked up one of Donna's beauty magazines absentmindedly.

"Yeah man. We're going to rave tonight."

"Where are you going?"

"What! Donna didn't tell you?"

"Does she tell me anything these days?"

"Granaries, man. They have this male stripper every Friday. You musta heard of Friday Night Raw." Shanika threw herself down in the armchair opposite Jennifer and shrugged off her puffa jacket, revealing a very short black leather skirt and see-through lace body suit.

"Friday Night Raw! Male strippers? You must be desperate."

"Chill, Jen man. We ain't gonna rape him or not'n," her mouth worked on her chewing gum. "It's a laugh."

"Isn't there an age limit in that club?"

She popped her gum making Jennifer wince before replying. "Yeah so?"

Shanika had grown accustomed to pushing up her chest in bouncers' faces to prove her age.

"And how's your baby? Naomi, isn't it?"

"Naomi's safe. My mum's got her."

"Her father not around anymore?"

"Him? He comes round. He's all right though, y'know, 'cause anything she wants she can have."

"What about you, do you get what you want from him?"

"I'm getting enough. I'm not his woman anymore, but I'm still his baby mother."

That phrase again. So many black women were beginning to use that to describe themselves. But Shanika wasn't fooling her. Jennifer had heard Donna's conversations with Shanika, and knew that anything Shanika got from Delroy, her baby father, she had to beg for.

Donna came down and rescued her friend. "Shan why didn't you come up, man, I was waiting for you?"

"I was keeping Jen company. Weren't I, Jen?"

"Something like that." Jennifer turned to see what her sister was wearing. The black lycra catsuit wasn't too bad until she turned to the sides, made out of yellow lace, and you could tell she wore nothing underneath. Jennifer bit her tongue to stop herself nagging. "D, have you got enough money?"

"Well actually, Jen, I am a bit short. Don't want the others to think I'm scrounging off 'em."

Jennifer got her handbag from the desk and gave Donna a tenner. "If you need a lift home, make sure you call me."

"Sure Sis, but we'll be all right, Val's driving."

The girls left and the house was suddenly quiet. Jennifer felt an emptiness, like she was an old maid, alone, her children grown up and gone and all she was left with was the television and her thoughts for company.

She tidied and cleaned the kitchen, half-listening to the radio in the background, dipping in and out of the angst of the soap characters as the programme drifted on, but too worried about Donna to give it her full attention.

Was it always going to be like this now that Donna was old enough to stay out all night. The two of them used to enjoy sitting together in front of the telly, watching videos. They would eat ice cream, their legs covered with a duvet, watching horror films. Some evenings they would get the old photo albums out and look and laugh at themselves as children. Plaited hair and missing teeth. Flared trousers, tank tops and frilled collars. Platform shoes and plimsoles.

She missed those simple evenings with a vengeance now. She gazed at the phone, it remained silent. She hadn't needed a social life of her own before, Donna had always been there when she needed a chat, a hug, a laugh, someone to go out with. She needed to get out more, meet new people. Most of all she needed to take her mind off family matters. She found a half-empty bottle of wine. That would be her company for the rest of the evening, she decided, curling up on the sofa with the latest issue of Essence at her side.

As Friday night turned to Saturday morning, Jennifer found comfort in a tub of Haagen Dazs at the bottom of the freezer. The ice cream went down smoothly. She hit the television remote control. An old black and white film on Channel Four was the best option, and for a while she watched James Stewart in *Vertigo*.

Soon her mind drifted to thoughts of her parents in Jamaica. She hadn't written to them in weeks and hadn't made a phone call for months. The sudden urge to speak to Daddy made her reach for the phone without bothering to work out the time difference. The phone rang unanswered. They were probably on the beach, swimming in the beautiful Caribbean sea together, she figured. Jamaica at this time of year was made for romance.

Jennifer had been in love only once in her life. Kenny had been her knight in shining armour. It had been so good. She was twenty one and he was ten years her senior. She found she had little in common with men her own age. Her independence always seemed to challenge them. Kenny was a banker, the kind of success story she had had fantasies about marrying throughout her teenage years. They had met in a wine bar in the city. He told her about his climb to the top and she told him about her dreams to get to that same status. After two wonderful years together she had fallen so deeply in love with the fairy tale that even when his ex-wife, whom she knew about, turned up at her front door with the son she didn't know about, she refused to drop him. She hadn't realized the kind of man he really was until she told Kenny that she wanted them to get married and have children and the very next day he turned up with a pre-nuptial agreement for her signature. She blew her top. The agreement required her to give up all rights to anything and everything. It was stalemate. She wasn't going to sign the agreement and he didn't intend on marrying without it being signed.

The relationship had gone steadily downhill from there. He had eventually given her an ultimatum that left her no choice but to let him go. Whenever she thought of how worthless he had made her seem, it still hurt. Since then she had had nothing but what she called brief encounters. She kept men as acquaintances and stayed at ease with herself and reminded herself often that, 'Sometimes a woman's got to stay single to survive'.

Jennifer knew what she was worth on the market. The more success she had in her career the more men, of all shades and colours, wanted her. The City was full of fortysomethings searching for Miss Right. And she still had an interest in men, she just didn't trust them with her feelings. It was going to take a lot for a man to sweep her off her feet again. She fell asleep in front of the flickering television with dreams of a wedding that never happened.

Monday morning at chambers. There was another message from Paul Harvey: *I don't know if you've received my last two messages. Please call me. We could be an asset to one another.*

'We could be assets to one another'. What was that, a chat up line?

Jennifer picked up the phone and called a colleague, another female barrister, and asked her if she knew of Paul Harvey. Angela knew a lot about Paul Harvey and filled Jennifer in on his reputation. He was an up and coming black barrister who fancied himself as every sista's dream in a profession where the black women outnumbered the men. He knew people in power and ran the Worshipful Company of Black Barristers, a networking group. The rumour was, Angela added, that Paul Harvey had an extremely large penis. "Hung like a horse, apparently," she giggled.

Hung like a horse or not, Jennifer was always interested in meeting powerful professional contacts. She dialled his number. It was answered by a husky voiced black woman.

"Oh Miss Edwards. Yes, Mr. Harvey has been trying to get hold of you for days. I'll put you through."

There was a click on the line.

"Hello Ms Edwards," a male voice came on the line.

"Mr Harvey?"

"Yes. Thanks for returning my call."

"I was curious Mr Harvey."

"Please call me Paul."

"Okay, Paul. What can I do for you?"

"I've seen you in action. In court. But when I checked we didn't appear to have you listed on our network. The Worshipful Company of Black Barristers I mean."

"Right. I'm already a member of the Society of Black Lawyers and the Association of Women Barristers."

"Ah. But why limit yourself? You'll find that the Worshipful Company of Black Barristers is altogether different from those organisations. And that's why I'm calling you, I've heard some good things about you and your work. Can we meet, say over lunch?"

"Sure."

"Tomorrow, if you're free."

"I'll just check my diary," Jennifer flipped over two pages of her diary knowing full well that she was free. "Tomorrow afternoon? That's fine."

"Great. I'll pick you up at one."

"Fine."

Jennifer hung up, feeling intrigued. He didn't seem too bad. A lunch date with an intelligent black man would make a refreshing change.

At a corner table in an upmarket restaurant Jennifer found herself in deep conversation with a man she'd met for the first time two hours ago. She had dressed formally to imply that this was strictly a business lunch. She wore a navy trouser suit with Chinese collar buttoned to the neck.

Paul Harvey towered five inches above her, with a body that already showed it was succumbing to the excesses allowed by a generous expense account. Nevertheless, he was a striking figure of a man. His skin complexion was dark chocolate and though his recently trimmed short hair was thinning on top, overall his look was manicured. His expensive suit set off the look and complimented his immaculate moustache.

They'd started off with drinks and then moved onto the restaurant for their meal. Paul was leaning towards her, his chin resting on a bridge he'd made with his hands. His engaging brown eyes contained a powerful mixture of impudence and assurance. Right now they were fastened on her face as she spoke.

"It's not even the fact that I'm a woman that isolates me," she was saying, waving her wine glass back and forth, "it's the fact that I'm a black woman. They look at me and I know that they're thinking this woman obviously got where she is today because of positive discrimination, positive action and every other employment act under the sun. And you know why? It's because of this old boy network that still exists in the legal system."

Paul shook his head as she held out her glass for a refill.

"You trying to tell me I've had too much?"

"Let's put it this way, the tablecloth is starting to see a lot more of your wine than you are."

"Point taken." She placed her glass back on the table and leaned back in her chair. She must have made such a bad first impression. Going on about discrimination in the legal system and about her baby sister. He must be bored silly. She'd told him all about her climb up the career ladder and he had sat there charmingly taking it all in. She didn't meet many black men who she felt equalled her, status wise. Paul was an exception. If she was looking for a male companion she could do a lot worse.

"I'm sorry Paul. I've been a little uptight recently. I really do need to unwind."

"No, it's okay," he flashed a killer smile. "I've had a delightful time and I happen to know what you're feeling."

Jennifer seriously doubted that he did but she let it go.

"We've all been there," Paul continued. He reached for her hand and laid his own over it on the table. "I do a good line in massages."

She raised her eyebrows at him, "Excuse me?"

Paul smirked, "Did that sound too forward? I apologize. All I meant was it's a good way to relieve tension...but then you probably have someone to do that for you," he said, meeting her eyes over the burning candle.

He was fishing and Jennifer knew it. It might have been the fact that she'd had too much to drink for a lunch time, or the fact that she actually felt a strong attraction to this man, but she wanted him to know that she was available.

"No," she ran a finger around the rim of her glass, "there is no one to relieve my tension."

Paul squeezed her hand meaningfully. For a while his eyes locked with hers in a disconcerted gaze. It was as though the rest of the room had vanished. There was just the dining table and the two of them. Jennifer broke the look and as an excuse she took her hand back to beckon the waiter with.

"We shouldn't have to wait this long for coffee," she said to Paul whose gaze had not wavered.

The waiter came over, took their order and left again. Jennifer started feeling that the sooner this lunch was over the better. She had felt things she had no right to feel at this stage. But it had been so long since she had had anyone special in her life.

"Jennifer."

"Mmm," she replied picking up the menu from the table, she scanned the pages without reading them.

"Can I have your attention for a moment."

"Of course Paul," she smiled her 'Buddy' smile and tried to forget the way she had tingled at the touch from his hand.

"Today has been very special to me. I feel so foolish saying this but I have this feeling that the two of us were brought together by fate."

Jennifer's menu closed and she laid it flat on the table. Her brow creased into a frown. "Yes?"

"Yes. You told me before how few black men there are in our profession..."

"Black women too," she interrupted. She had an idea where this was leading and was trying to avoid it.

"Yes, granted. But my point is that very rarely would you find two people so clearly made for each other within our profession."

"And which two people might that be?" Jennifer was completely serious.

"Why, us of course," his smile widened.

Jennifer did not believe in the saying, 'Flattery gets you everywhere.' She was worth more than flattery. Paul would have to work harder.

"Paul did I say or do something to lead you to that conclusion? Because if you feel that I did then there's been a misunderstanding, and I apologize."

Unfazed Paul continued his quest. "This isn't about actions or words Jennifer," he said her name like no one else. It flowed off his tongue like treacle. "Can't you feel it? I want you in my life. I'm even willing to let you choose the terms."

Jennifer couldn't believe what she was hearing. She wanted to laugh, she wanted to curse. She wanted to get up and pour her wine over his head and leave him sitting there embarrassed like in the movies. She had to admit that she was enjoying the idea of a simple business lunch turning into a flirtatious rendezvous? Paul Harvey was having an effect on her, whatever it was, they had it going on.

"Paul, we barely know each other," she told him placing her napkin on the table. She chuckled, "I mean, for a minute there I thought you were going to propose."

He smiled. "You're right Jennifer. We're two professional people. In our early thirties, years ahead of us. What's the rush."

Just then the waiter came back with the coffee. Then he whisked away the menus and left them alone.

Paul stirred cream into his cup as he talked. "Okay, forget the relationship. But why sleep miles apart. Why sleep with a cold empty space on the other side of our double beds? Aren't we allowed to fill that space with someone who we feel is special? Someone we want to touch..." his voice dropped to a seductive whisper.

"Mr. Harvey, I think...no...I know you are being far too personal. I thought we were having a business lunch, then you turn up with flowers, bring me to an exclusive restaurant. Your touch is too familiar and you're talking to me as though I've known you for months instead of hours."

"Well, that's the way I feel."

"I can't help your feelings, Mr. Harvey. Let me tell you one thing about me that you haven't noticed. I know what I want in my life. I'll know when I'm ready to settle down. Meanwhile I can control my lustful cravings. I suggest you start learning." With that she stood up and grabbed her bag and coat and strode towards the door.

"Jennifer, please."

"I believe our meeting is over Mr. Harvey," she said over her shoulder.

They were all the same. Give a man the time of day and he'd think it was his cue to try to get you into bed. Paul Harvey was no different. If she had a pound for every man who had try to get into her knickers she'd be a rich woman.

Jennifer waved down a taxi outside the restaurant and sat in the back full of disappointment.

She'd hoped Paul would be different. It had been a long time since anyone had stirred up her orgasmic juices. Stirred! He could have had them boiling, but he'd blown it. Talking dirty didn't work on her anymore. What Jennifer craved was sweetness. Paul could have told her over the phone that he wanted to get her into bed and saved them both a whole lot of trouble.

Three quarters of an hour later the cab pulled up outside her home and was greeted by the heavy bass of jungle music coming from the direction of Jennifer's flat.

The noise, because that's exactly what it was, was coming from the living room. Jennifer ran up the steps and flung open the door to her flat. "Donna!" she screamed.

Two faces peeped up to meet hers from the sofa.

"Oh God, Jen!" Donna leapt up from the sofa clinging to her unbuttoned blouse. Fitzroy got up fumbling with his jeans and pulling up his flies nonchalantly. "Awright Jen?"

"What you doing home?" Donna asked.

Jennifer glared at Fitzroy. "It doesn't matter what I'm doing, I live here, but it looks as though I was just in time."

"We weren't doing nothing. Jus' mucking around."

"Don't," Jennifer held up her hand to stop the excuses. Her head was thumping and she could feel heat rising from her neck up to her eyes. She turned to Fitzroy. "Get out of my house."

"Jennifer! What d'you think you're doing?"

Fitzroy was already getting up and pulling on his jacket, "Me nah budda wid dis, seen? Donna, call me when yuh ready."

"Hang on, jus' stay there," Donna stood between her sister and her man. "We both live here and when I moved in you told me that this was our home. How can you walk in here and diss my friends like that?"

"Exactly, this is our home, but every time I come home lately, this layabout is here eating my food, messing up my front room..."

"Ours Jennifer, ours. You can't treat me like no baby no more. I'm seventeen for God's sake. You know what, I get the feeling you're jealous," Donna said snidely. "Jealous because I've got a man who makes me feel like a woman, what have you got? You're still a woman y'know, feelings and flesh. You can't do nothing about me having a man, so you may as well go and get one of your own."

Jennifer stepped forward raising her hand to her sister. Fitzroy stepped forward. "Hey..."

Donna flinched and held out a hand to stop Fitzroy, but stood her ground. "Slap me nuh."

Jennifer hadn't realized her hand was in the air until her sister pointed it out. Had things between them got so bad that she was willing to beat sense into her? Her hand came down slowly.

"Me gone, seen," Fitzroy, a man of few words moved around Jennifer to the door.

" 'Ole up Fitz, I'm coming with you."

"Donna, you're not leaving this house with him. Not until you hear what I have to say," Jennifer followed her into the hallway.

"No? How you gonna stop me?"

Fitzroy handed Donna her jacket and stood with hands in pockets sizing up Jennifer. He was enjoying her loss of control.

"Donna you don't know what you're doing. Are you expecting him to look after you? He can't even look after his own flesh and blood."

"I can look after myself, Jen. An' you know what, I'm gonna prove it to ya." Donna grabbed Fitzroy's arm and the two of them left, the door slamming behind them.

The jungle music still hollered in Jennifer's ears as she ran a hand through her hair and slid slowly down the passage wall. "Shit, shit, shit."

Paul Harvey's clerk called the very next day to make apologizes for their misunderstanding. He was having a social gathering on behalf of the Worshipful Company of Black Barristers this evening, would she be interested in coming along? Mr. Harvey expressed himself so well through his clerk that Jennifer was tempted to say yes straight away, but she told the clerk she would have to check with her secretary and get back to her. Socializing was the last thing on her mind. Donna hadn't called. She had no idea where she was or even where Fitzroy lived. She'd waited up until after midnight. By then it was too late to start calling round all her friends.

That evening Jennifer found herself parking her car in the underground car park at Lauderdale Tower, one of The Barbican's skyscraping residential tower blocks. She wore a long black satin figure-hugging dress, with a lime green shawl draped across her bare shoulders. Other upwardly mobile black men and women were making their way to the same entrance, and Jennifer felt conspicuous going in on her own. They made their way up to the second floor where they had to sign a guest book before entering.

Inside, Billie Holiday was playing just loud enough to be heard but not to hinder conversation. Jennifer marveled at the perfection of the flat's interior design. Pine contrasted with stark black. To her right was a fake log fireplace with a black chimney piece bordered by a real pine wall. The floor was polished parquet and the double sofas were a midnight blue. Two sculptured lamps and Art Deco statuettes stood on a heavy marble and glass coffee table. Uniformed waiters circulated, carrying trays of champagne. Jennifer spotted Paul almost immediately. He was looking casually fine in a navy blue wool suit with a black polo neck shirt. Jennifer made her way over to his side of the room without being too obvious. Her plan worked. Paul spotted her and paused to pick up a glass of champagne before approaching.

"Good evening," he greeted. His eyes took in her well-groomed hair and the way her dress fitted her curves like a second skin.

"Hello again," she said.

"I'm sorry..." he began.

"I apologize..." they said in unison then smiled at one another.

"Paul, there's no need for you to apologize. I was having a bad day. It didn't end too well either."

"Be that as it may. I did come on too strong," he handed her the glass of bubbly.

"So did I. With the ticking off I meant."

"Well enjoy the evening. Let me introduce you to a few people." They crossed the room together and Paul presented her to a woman around her own age who had just passed her law degree. "Jennifer could make a great mentor for you," he said leaving them to talk.

Paul Harvey's sixty or so well-heeled guests sipped champagne and manoeuvred to get their share of the vast buffet. Jennifer was not interested in either. She was conscious of only one person in the noisy throng. Although she made a deliberate effort to avoid looking at him, they still made eye contact from time to time. Paul Harvey wore the confidence of a man who was definitely making it. He was great at mingling, moving smoothly from one person to another without leaving anyone standing alone. He would introduce someone to someone else, then leave them to get acquainted. Or he would join a conversation and compliment it, adding his own point of view whilst flirting with the many intelligent and attractive women there.

Jennifer had been cornered by a man she had no interest in whatsoever. He was boring and told stale law jokes. "What haven't you got if you've got three lawyers buried up to their necks in sand?"

"Not enough sand," Jennifer answered drily. She spotted the legal representative from the Daily Mail and took the opportunity to excuse herself from the bore. The only thing she could remember about him was that he was a law student.

Every time Paul came near her Jennifer felt hot and was sure he had to be feeling it too. She wasn't surprised when even before all the guests had left he asked her to stay behind until after the waiters had packed up and gone, for a chance to talk quietly.

Jennifer sat on the firm sofa and relaxed. Paul said he hadn't had a bite to eat all evening and went off to put a plate of food together. Jennifer had been in bachelor pads before but nothing like this. It was hard to know just what type of man lived here, apart from the fact that he had to have money. A mix of bachelor with a hint of the soul of a woman.

"More champagne?" he offered coming back in.

"Thank you."

He disappeared again. She heard the low pop of a cork before he came back carrying two glasses, the bottle and his plate of food. He placed them on the coffee table and sat in the adjacent armchair. They had a table between them but there was body heat in the air. He poured for both of them and passed her a glass.

"To us and a bountiful relationship," Paul toasted.

Jennifer raised her glass.

He tucked into his food, commenting occasionally about how well the night had gone. Every now and again he offered her various morsels from his plate saying, "Do try this. It's wonderful the way it slides down your throat." It was too tempting to refuse, even though she wasn't hungry.

They debated on everything from politics to why black women wore weaves. She found his conversation refreshing. He didn't think it unusual that she agreed with those women who were against the principle of marriage. After all, he said, it wasn't the piece of paper that mattered but the bond between the two people. He was curious about her and she had to think hard about her responses to his questions. It had been a long time since she had conversed with a man about what she was feeling deep down in her soul.

Paul was well-read and quoted lines from poetry effortlessly. He sympathized with her lack of free time but warned of the dangers of only mixing in like-minded professional circles. "You end up losing touch with the rest of the world," he said.

To emphasize a point Paul would touch Jennifer's hand or arm, leaving his fingers a second longer than was necessary. Jennifer was bewildered by the mix of apprehension and excitement running around in her mind. She was actually longing for each touch of his hand.

She discovered that he had lived on his own for ten years now, though he had not exactly been celibate. He had bedded many women, this much was obvious without him saying so. After all he was an unmarried, attractive, eligible bachelor.

Paul told her that when he met a woman he was attracted to she had to pass certain criteria before he would take it seriously. He was very quick to point out that the criteria had nothing to do with what shape body the woman had. It was more to do with the meeting of minds. His heart always told him when something was right. Like now.

They were onto coffee when the music from the stereo stopped and Paul got up to change the CD.

"What's that?" Jennifer asked cocking her head to one side. She could hear a musical tinkling coming from one side of the room.

"You mean the chimes."

"Windchimes?"

"Yes I collect them on my travels. Would you like to see my collection?"

She smiled delightedly. There was so much to this man that she had yet to find out. "Yes please."

He took her hand as the music started again and led her to the back of the room where he drew back a ceiling to floor curtain to reveal a huge balcony which had remained concealed throughout the party. The door slid across and he lead her outside. The night was warm. The chimes hung about a foot apart around the perimeter of the overhanging roof of the balcony.

Miniature African masks, delicate oriental petals, silver crafted planetary shapes, tiny sea shells, multi coloured discs and crystals were amongst the feast of windchimes before her. While she marveled at their beauty Paul ducked back inside to bring out their coffees.

"Impressed?"

"You have an eye for beauty."

"Handcrafted or made by nature," he stated his eyes meeting hers.

Jennifer felt she'd walked straight into that head-on, but she didn't mind, she had already made up her mind that she was going to allow Mr Paul Harvey to seduce her.

"I've had a terrific evening," he said.

"Me too."

Keith Washington's *Make Time For Love* was playing in the living room. Jennifer breathed in the scent of spring from the flowers in the hanging baskets on the balcony.

"Look at that sky," Paul said, pointing up at the star-studded velvet above their heads. Jennifer followed his gaze. "Superman's a lucky guy," he said.

Jennifer laughed, "What?"

"To be able to carry his woman up into the stars," he explained. "Couldn't you just imagine riding on a cloud through a night like this?"

Jennifer was enthralled. Speechless. Her heart was racing and when he put his hand on her shoulder and turned her to him a warmth tingled its way through her body. She wanted him to kiss her so badly that she nearly made the first move. Paul kissed her gently on the cheek and said. "It's late," he glanced at his watch. "Four in the morning already. I apologize for keeping you so late."

"No apologies needed. I've enjoyed your company," she moved closer so that their chests touched.

But Paul was already leading her back into the flat, straight to the coat rack where he retrieved her shawl. "Will you be all right driving home this late?"

Jennifer was confused. Was it so long since she'd had a man that she was mixing up the signs? Hadn't the whole evening been constructed to seduce her? "I'll, be fine. Thanks for a wonderful evening."

"We'll do it again very soon. Maybe we could go out sometime?"

"I'd like that." They kissed cheeks again and Paul waited by the door as she got into the lift. Downstairs and feeling as horny as she ever had, she climbed into her car and drove away quickly.

For six weeks Jennifer and Paul dated. He was always the perfect gentleman and Jennifer began to wonder if this was the real Paul Harvey. He never laid a hand on her unless it was to kiss her good night or to show friendly affection. He seemed a very different man from the guy who had laid it on thick the first time they'd gone out. It probably normally worked too, but not with this lady. They dined out, dined in, went to the cinema and theatre and spent the evening at his flat watching videos, worked out together and gave each other healthy eating tips. But they never made love. They never even got near making love, much to Jennifer's disappointment.

She had even gone so far as to pretend to fall asleep in his flat one night. Paul had given her his bed and slept on the sofa in the living room. All night she had lain awake waiting to hear him creep into the bedroom, but her fantasies remained unfulfilled. Despite the setbacks she was determined to get her man. There was no way she was going to give up on him. He was the perfect type of black man, someone who always paid when they went out. Jennifer would always make sure she offered, but Paul insisted it was his pleasure. There was no mistaking what she was feeling. A mixture of hot, passionate lust and the beginnings of love, she was sure this was it.

There had to be a way of making Mr Cool hot, and it was about time Jennifer found out what it was. She called his office early on Wednesday and invited him round to dinner for Friday evening.

"...Come into my bedroom, baby don't you know you belong to me, ah yes you do.
Come in, close the door baby, your body belongs to me, tonight..."

Jennifer smoothed cocoa butter over her waxed legs and then reached for her new bottle of perfume. Tonight would be the night. She began to feel like a mistress waiting for the married man to turn up so that she could seduce him into thinking she was the one he should be with and not his wife. The whole house smelt of her expensive perfume, she'd sprinkled a little on the furniture, curtains and carpet. What the heck it was only money! She hoped she hadn't forgotten anything. Wine, flowers, music, a drop-dead outfit, plus she had the place to herself with Donna still too stubborn to come home. When the doorbell rang she took her time walking to the door. Didn't want him to think that she had been waiting for him impatiently. Although Paul was dead on time, Jennifer had been ready and nervously waiting a good half an hour earlier.

Jennifer opened the door wearing the nearly see-through chiffon blouse and loose flowing trousers, that had set her back more, much more, than a bob or two. Paul stood there, a bunch of flowers and a bottle of her favourite wine in his arms. His hair had been waved with some kind of texturised perm. It looked good.

"Good evening," he planted a friendly kiss on her cheek and handed her the wine and flowers.

"It will be." Jennifer placed the wine and flowers on the narrow table by the front door and helped him off with his jacket. She stood on tiptoe to kiss the back of his neck.

He shivered and turned to her with a surprised look in his eye. "What did I do to deserve that?"

"You're here aren't you?" She gave him her sexiest smile and they embraced.

"New perfume?"

"Mmmm, Champagne, I treated myself."

Paul took a seat on the sofa. On the centre table was a flower display to rival a professional florists. Roses and orchids, just as Paul had on his balcony. She knew he liked them but he didn't comment.

"Dinner is nearly ready, can I get you a drink?"

"Mineral water please, I'll save the hot stuff for dinner."

Jennifer skipped back to the kitchen singing along to the Keith Sweat CD. He was still acting cool, hadn't commented on her outfit but she was determined to warm it up. It may have been a long time between relationships but not so long that she had forgotten how to turn a man on.

She returned with his water and a glass of wine for herself and sat next to him on the sofa. "So here we are again," she clinked her glass to his.

"Cheers."

She admired the charming, attractive man beside her. For some reason she found herself wondering whether there was any truth to the gossip about the size of his penis. To have that kind of gossip hanging over him he had to be a ladies man. But why was he not making a move on her? She hoped that the gossip had been started by women and not men.

"It's been a long day," he said catching her eye.

Jennifer sipped her drink. "Has it?"

"You know when you think you're just about to reach a goal and something jumps in and halts your progress..."

"Ye-es."

"My career in law is becoming that barrier," Paul sighed and took a sip of water.

Jennifer waited for an explanation.

"I've got bigger ambitions than the legal profession can offer. I want to be where the real power is. I want to be part of the decision making process in this country. And that's politics."

Jennifer listened intently.

"But it's just not happening at the moment. All I need is a break, a foot in the door and I'm there."

"Nothing happens that quickly. Not without hard work."

"Ah but it can," he raised a finger in the air. "Look how many of our colleagues and acquaintances have made it to QC or MP on the old boys network." He fingered his tie. "You attend the right public school and all it takes are a few words to the right people."

Jennifer nodded, she knew all about it. That was what kept most women back in the professions. "But where's the satisfaction in that? Wouldn't you rather know that you got to where you are because of merit, hard work?"

"You're missing the point. Whether I got there on merit or by climbing on the backs of others the result is the same."

Jennifer disagreed but didn't say so. "I'll check on dinner, it should be about ready now."

"The food smells delicious, I hope you haven't gone to a lot of trouble. I'm not a big eater anymore, as you know."

Paul was referring to the diet he had recently embarked on after the embarrassment of being puffed out after a mere five minutes of squash.

"I've cooked all your favourites. Tonight is your night. You've given me so much." Hearing that seemed to please him. He patted her knee endearingly.

Over a candlelit dinner and soft music, Paul talked of his wish to get into politics and of becoming an MP. He saw himself becoming Britain's first black Prime Minister.

"You never mentioned this passion of yours before."

He placed his fork on the side of the plate. "Somewhere along the line it became buried." His eyes searched hers. "Occasionally we start out to do one thing and it ends up as something else, but that's okay because it's along the same lines...and then you realize it's not as fulfilling as your original plan."

"And which party would you run for?"

"Well obviously I'm a Tory by nature, but I'd consider any party that would guarantee me a safe seat. You see it's all about getting your foot in the door, then after that I can switch my allegiance like the wind. 'By any means necessary' as Malcolm the Tenth once said."

Jennifer laughed. Paul had never been quite this witty before. She was seeing a new side to him that he hadn't revealed before.

"This old boy network you mentioned before...imagine if black women got together and started their own networks."

"I don't see why not," Paul resumed eating.

"You know what my ambition is now?"

"To marry a rich man..."

She watched his face and a smile broke that told her he was joking. She wagged her finger at him, "I was about to come down hard on you, don't run those chauvinistic jokes in front of me."

"I'm sorry," he smiled, "I know you're not the type to marry for power or money."

I wouldn't go that far, she thought but kept it to herself. "My ambition is to start my own good ol' sistas network, bring in other women behind me. All I'd need to do is to learn the ol' boy's network game."

"That would take forever. It's much simpler to marry for status."

"I wouldn't do that. I might marry because that person is my equal, but not to elevate me into something I'm not."

"It's not about that. If you marry someone that gets you into the right circles, compliments your ideals, it's like taking advantage of a good thing. It's about giving, sharing, balancing. What's the problem?"

Love, Jennifer wanted to say but didn't. She wanted to avoid being seen as a romantic. Her career was more important to her than marrying for status. Paul's mind seemed to dart from one subject to the other, but she still hadn't got the drift of the evening. Since the candlelit dinner and smouldering eyes hadn't worked, Jennifer decided to be a little less tactful. She knocked back another glass of wine and unbuttoned the top two buttons on her blouse, revealing a little cleavage. But all Paul did in response was loosen his tie a little and undo the top button of his shirt.

They talked some more about law and their futures, the future for black professionals in this country, everything except their relationship. Every time Jennifer brought up couples and relationships, Paul managed to steer the conversation back to work. But as she emptied another bottle of wine and the subdued lighting lulled her into a relaxed warmth, Jennifer found herself confiding in Paul about her fears for her sister, and her worry that there would never be time for love in her own life. Paul nodded and empathised. He moved over to the sofa and took her hand. "I understand. Some of us make sacrifices for our careers, others make sacrifices for our families. It's a matter of priorities."

He was the closest he'd been all evening and Jennifer decided this was it. She moved up closer so that their lips were almost touching, then suddenly Paul looked at his watch. "It's quarter to one," he announced, "I've done it again, haven't I? Kept you up late..."

"No, it's quite all right."

"No," he pushed her gently aside. "I wouldn't want you getting a bad reputation with your neighbours...you know, seeing me leave late at night." He stood up straightening his clothes.

Screw the neighbours, she wanted to say. "I wish we had more time together. The night just seems to go so fast," Jennifer said, standing facing him. The look on her face should have told him what she was thinking, but Paul either didn't see it or chose to ignore it.

He kissed her cheek as he would his mother's. "We are so alike aren't we?"

"You noticed it too."

"Like minds..."

Jennifer touched a finger to his lips. "I thought it was opposites attract."

"I don't want to ruin our friendship."

"How could it?"

"How could what, Jennifer?"

"It doesn't matter." By this time they had reached the front door.

"Pity," he said.

Jennifer felt desperately tired as the adrenaline ebbed away. Perhaps he was only teasing her, but then why? He must know what she was thinking and she was sure that he was thinking the same thing. Did she have to make all the moves? Jennifer reached for the front door. "Yes it is. Two people in our position couldn't possibly get sexually involved could we?" There, she'd said it. She turned her back to him, so she didn't see when his hand went into his inside pocket and removed the small leather box.

"But there is one way..."

Jennifer turned around to him, and before she saw the glint in his eyes she noticed the jewellery box. Her mind was thinking 'ring' but she was too confused to make sense of it.

"What's that?" was all she could utter.

Slowly, Paul opened the box and revealed the diamond cluster ring. "Jennifer, will you marry me?"

One hand flew to her throat. "It's...it's all a bit sudden...unexpected..."

Paul dropped down on one knee, taking her left hand in both of his, he asked again, "Miss Jennifer Edwards, will you be my wife?"

She looked down at him, tears of joy welling up in her eyes. "No!" she said breathlessly, "...I mean yes."

Paul kissed her hand before scrambling to his feet and easing the diamond ring onto the appropriate finger. He was delighted. "Thank you, you have no idea how happy you've made me. From the moment we met I knew we could be an asset to one another. A match made in heaven." He held her face in his hands. "What advantages our children will have."

Jennifer was grinning too much to reply. Had she just said 'yes' to marrying a man she'd known for only two months? She had. Why? Because it was right, it felt right. She fell into his arms and as they kissed passionately, she couldn't help wondering about those rumours...

She stepped back from him just long enough to savour the moment.

"Are you okay? This is what you want isn't it?"

"I think...I'm scared."

"Don't be," he filled the space between them again. "Leave everything to me."

His lips caressed her neck. She clung nervously to his shoulders. "Paul..."

"Mmm," he sucked the flesh on her neck so gently it made her weak at the knees.

"Will you still respect me in the morning?" she sighed dreamily.

He met her eyes and held her face in his hands, gently. "My darling, you're mine now. Everything I have is yours..." he kissed her lips, "...including my respect."

"Oh Paul!" a husky cry escaped her lips. At the same time she felt his strong hands holding her by the waist, pulling her towards him, belly to belly, chest to chest. They walked backwards into the seductively-lit living room and to the sofa where he flopped on top of her, surprisingly aggressive in his need. His lips were filled with hunger. This had to be love!

She felt his weight on her legs as they fumbled to remove clothes. He undid a couple of the buttons on his shirt hurriedly, loosened his tie some more and unzipped his flies before abandoning the job half done.

"Paul, slow down, I'm not going anywhere."

"I can't help myself," he mumbled as he took one firm breast in his hand and with eager long fingers, pushed aside the flimsy material of her lacy white bra. "You are so adorable." He showered her cheeks, neck and chest in tiny urgent kisses. He kneaded a nipple into hardness before devouring it like a hungry infant. Without missing a beat he turned to the other one, covering it with his hot saliva and licking it to a firm peak.

Jennifer gasped as she was carried away on a tidal wave of emotion and lust. Their clothes hung from their steaming bodies. Paul had suddenly now become hungry for everything the evening had promised. Jennifer felt as though she had fallen from a great cliff and instead of going down she was rising to dizzy ecstasy. It was a rush like nothing before. She opened her eyes and he was looking straight at her, the raw intensity of his need burning through her. This wasn't how she had imagined the first time with Paul Harvey would be. Was this the same calm, controlled gentleman she had got to know or had he transformed in the heat of lust? He was tracing a path down her hard stomach, sucking on that tender hip erogenous zone that not many men seemed to know about.

He's in love with me, was all she could think as she abandoned herself to his wild kisses. He was all over her...wanting her...needing her. And God, she wanted him right back. He rose again to take her lips passionately, finding her tongue and engaging it in a tantalising dance. He pressed two fingers into her vagina, touching her magic button with experienced precision, causing her to arch her back and groan. His erection was pressing into her thigh and, moaning with excitement, she reached down to help it out of the confines of his suit trousers.

Jennifer purred with pleasure, and clawed his back as he pressed himself inside her just a little, then pulled out again and as he entered her again everything else in the world disappeared. Donna, Fitzroy, work, the room she was in, the sofa underneath her, all her worries — none of them mattered. She sought his lips and whispered, "I want you...all of you."

In reply, his hips thrust upwards driving his penis deeper and deeper. He was giving, she was taking. They were made for each other, he'd said and he was right. Physically, mentally, two pieces of the same puzzle. Him, her fiancé. The passion started exploding inside her first and an overwhelming feeling of joy burned with a heat that swept from her genitals to every part of her body.

"Ohhhh, you feel soooo good...Aaahh...!!" she heard him groan and his orgasm seemed to collide with her own, as they thrust their groins towards each other simultaneously with a final burst of energy.

Jennifer cried out as her orgasm completely dominated her. His groan accompanied hers and he pushed deeper one last time before shuddering to stillness.

They lay exhausted, breathing heavily, holding each other close as their chests heaved in syncopation. His penis became soft and limp inside her.

"I hope you enjoyed that as much as I did," he breathed into her neck.

Her arms were under his shirt, her fingers now relaxed and spread out like starfish on his back, her head was bent at an awkward and uncomfortable angle against the sofa's arm. Her blouse tangled around her arm, one breast hanging over the top of the cup of her bra. She reassured him with a squeeze, not wanting to say it had all been over too quickly and that she would have preferred it if they had at least taken their clothes off, even taken it into the bedroom perhaps, and made love instead of just having sex. She didn't say any of those things because all in all she had enjoyed herself and it was enough to have the satisfaction of having reached orgasm on her first time with the man she was going to spend the rest of her life with.

They lay like that for a long time, Paul dozing off and his body becoming dead weight. Jennifer wanted to drift back to reality 'sloooowly', but the magic of the moment was beginning to wear off as she developed a cramp in her neck. She tried to move but she couldn't shift him. She cleared her throat, hoping to rouse him, praying that Donna didn't walk in just now. Paul groaned but didn't budge.

"Paul, could you..." She shoved and he rolled off the low sofa onto the carpet, his eyes still closed and a blissful smile on his face. She raised herself up on her hands. Her chiffon blouse hung loosely from her shoulders, one white button was stuck onto her naked skin, ripped loose in the heat of the moment. She looked down at the face of her new fiancé. Her eyes travelled down to his crushed sweaty shirt and shrivelled cock, his trousers tangled around his ankles. Jennifer stood astride him, looking down. He was so vulnerable. Holding her left hand up she looked at the ring and smiled smugly to herself. It had all happened so quickly. She was now an engaged woman. She ran a hand over her hair and felt the untidy peaks. Her hair was a ruffled mess!

Sitting up at last, Paul's eyes opened. "Jennifer...?"

She pulled her blouse closed over her chest, suddenly embarrassed. "Why don't you make some coffee, I'll be down in a minute." Quickly she gathered her clothing and headed for the hallway, climbing the stairs as though she were on a cloud. She had just broken her two year drought and as she remembered the act she shivered. It had definitely been worth it. She felt happier than she had ever felt before and decided that nothing, *nothing* was going to spoil it.

The warm water of the shower cascaded over her taut body and she again felt rejuvenated. She couldn't stop admiring the ring. Emeralds and diamonds set in a beautiful circle. Doubts had no space in her mind now. Jennifer wanted to be Mrs. Paul Harvey. *A woman's gotta stay single to survive!* Her own advice echoed back to her until she succeeded in banishing it from her memory. Lost in her own thoughts she lost track of time.

The knock on the bathroom door startled her. "Yes?" she gasped.

Paul's voice came back to her through the wooden door. "I'll take our drinks to the bedroom shall I?"

He was planning to stay! There hadn't been a man in her bed for two years, how was it going to feel? "That's fine," she called back, "it's the door opposite the bathroom." Paul wasn't just any man, he was her fiancé, the man she was going to marry and spend the rest of her life with.

"Okay."

She heard her bedroom door open. He would be lying in bed between her cotton sheets waiting for her when she entered with just a towel wrapped around her naked body. Would he be ready to go again?

She needn't have worried about Paul waiting hungrily for more because by the time Jennifer got to the bedroom he was snoring peacefully under her duvet. One thing she had learnt tonight, the rumours about his size were just that. It wasn't its size that was special, but its shape. It was a 'hit the G spot' shape and she should know. *Rumours!*

In the city a couple of weeks later, a damage lawsuit that had dragged on for months, came to an unexpected and gratifying end. The plaintiff agreed to settle out of court for an amount nothing short of stunning. Jennifer wasted no time in getting her clerk to prepare the settlement document and had it signed by the plaintiff the same day. The plaintiff's lawyer had stood by shaking his head in dismay and disbelief, while Jennifer sat behind her desk with a strong, silent look on her face. The good guy had won. Victory tasted so good! Jennifer had called Angela at her chambers and arranged to meet for lunch.

"Darling," Angela kissed Jennifer on both cheeks.

They sat in the bistro style restaurant by a tinted window overlooking the street. Jennifer glanced at the passers-by. Were any of them as happy as she was? The waiter poured Frascati for them.

"Congratulations on the case, but what I want to know is how are things going with Paul?" Angela leaned towards her and whispered conspiratorially, "Are the rumours true?"

Jennifer feigned innocence. "Angela! I don't know what you mean, I'm sure."

"I'll bet you do," Angela grinned.

Jennifer's face cracked into a smile too. She decided to lie. "The rumours are most definitely true, and I'm going to be the very last woman to testify to it."

But Angela didn't get the drift, which was just as well because Jennifer wanted to tell Donna the big news first.

"Go on," Angela squealed with delight and brought her hands together. "Tell me all."

Jennifer did.

A call from Donna awaited Jennifer when she got back to chambers that afternoon.

"Hi Sis."

"Hello Donna. How are you?"

"I'm good..."

"And Fitzroy?"

"I suppose he's fine."

Surely that sounded like disenchantment. *Rejoice!* It had been nine weeks since Donna moved out.

"So when am I going to see you? You haven't called in two weeks."

"I was planning on coming round tonight...We could go out, eat, talk. How about the pictures?"

"I suppose I'll be paying for the pleasure of your company?"

"You stopped my money remember? If you don't want me to come round then..."

"Don't be silly. We'll go to the pictures."

"It's a date then."

They confirmed that they would meet at home for seven o'clock.

"Oh and I've got some BIG news to tell you," Jennifer said.

Donna arrived back home, wearing a micro mini denim skirt with opaque black tights and a long shirt with her hair braided, short and two toned. Because the argument that led to her moving out had never really been resolved, she hovered in the hallway, words hanging in the air, feeling uncomfortable carrying her overnight bag.

Jennifer noticed the bag. "You're staying?"

"Just the night, I'm seeing Fitzroy tomorrow night." She looked away and picked at the scarlet varnish on her long fingernails.

"So everything's just fine with you two."

"Yeah," Donna insisted a little too quickly.

Jennifer drove to the cinema. On the way, Donna informed her that Fitzroy had taught her to drive and that she was going for her test. Jennifer told her that was wonderful. "How are you going to afford a car though?"

"I've got an interview for a job next week."

"Doing what?"

"A holiday job. In Tescos, Lewisham."

"Haven't you got exams to think about?"

"It won't interfere with that. I'll only be doing seventeen hours a week."

"Seventeen hours!" Jennifer shook her head. She felt a pang of guilt about her sister's allowance, but decided that Donna could have it when she finally came to her senses.

They drove past McDonalds on Peckham Rye. Donna waved to a couple of boys, both wearing yellow and navy Michigan puffa jackets and baggy jeans. The current *gangsta lick*.

"So what's it like being an independent woman?" Jennifer asked as they queued outside the huge multi-screen cinema.

"Awright, sometimes. Fitzroy's got some nasty habits..."

Jennifer could imagine.

"...He needs a mother not a lover."

"Let's not talk about him. Let's just have a good time and then when we get back tonight we'll sit up all night chatting."

Donna smiled and they went into the cinema to see a box office smash that the black community had raved about for months.

After the film the sisters bought fried chicken. Back home they changed into their night clothes and, like little girls allowed to stay up late during the holidays, settled down in front of the television to watch a romantic comedy video. In the 'intermission' Jennifer opened a bottle of wine while Donna warmed up chicken, corn on the cob, fries and coleslaw. A late night feast accompanied the rest of the film. Then they lay on their backs on the polished parquet flooring, facing the ceiling.

"Remember Aunt Iris' parties?" Donna giggled. "I was about eight years old and used to hide under the table and, when no one was looking, I would reach up and drink the drinks."

"Mmm," Jennifer said through a mouthful of chicken, "and you got sick, I remember that. Dad took you home and made you sleep in the bath in case you were sick again in the night." She laughed at the memory.

"I don't think I was myself again for a week."

Jennifer felt Donna was relaxed enough now for her to tell her about Paul. "Donna...you know that when you left...I was single..."

"You still are, aren't you? Unless you're hiding him in the wardrobe."

"A lot has happened since you left..."

Donna turned sideways on the floor, with a glint in her eye, she looked at her sister. "You got laid didn't you?"

"Donna!" Jennifer kicked her sister's leg lightly. "I wouldn't quite put it like that. I started seeing another barrister. His name's Paul Harvey. He's thirty five, single and he's asked me to marry him."

"No!" Donna sat up excited.

"And I said...yes..."

Donna's jaw fall open. She leapt up and with arms wide open threw herself on her sister who was still lying flat on her back. "You work faas eeh?" she teased.

Jennifer frowned, her sister was beginning to sound more and more like that ruffneck boyfriend of hers. She only just managed to push Donna off her and sit up. "Sis, it wasn't like that. I mean, we didn't do...anything for weeks nearly two months and then he asked me to marry him before we did...He's perfect, trust me."

"You fell in love and got engaged in two months?"

"It happens."

No one had yet asked Jennifer whether she loved him or not and she declined to bring it up. It didn't seem to matter to anyone. She was getting married, that was blessing enough.

"I can't believe this. So why didn't you say anything?"

"I wanted it to be special. Just us, here."

"So you're going to marry him?"

"I'm going to marry him, yes."

"Well...what's he like?" Donna was on the edge of her seat.

"He's attractive, very professional, ambitious, caring and he is very interested in me..."

Donna twisted her mouth dubiously, "So does he make you laugh?"

"We laugh together."

"Is he fun, sexy, exciting..."

"D I'm not going to marry a male stripper."

Donna reached up to the coffee table for her glass of wine.

"So what do you think?"

Donna swilled her wine in her mouth a little before turning to her sister thoughtfully. "I seem to remember someone saying to me over and over again... 'a woman's gotta stay single to survive'," she furrowed her brow. "Was that by any chance you?"

"Donna, you know why I said that?"

Donna looked at her and shrugged.

Jennifer continued. "A woman can't achieve her goals once a man becomes a part of her life. Her only goal then is children."

"So why are you getting married?"

"Because I've reached my goals. I'm what I set out to be — a barrister. Plus, my fiancé..." she liked using that word, "...shares my goals, we couldn't be more perfect for each other."

Donna seemed to be considering it. "And where will you live?"

"I don't know. I suppose we'll buy somewhere together..."

Donna sighed and when she looked up at her sister her eyes were glistening. "I get to be bridesmaid?"

Jennifer grinned back at her. "If you're good you can be chief bridesmaid."

Donna smiled broadly. "Congratulations, Sis," she hugged her.

Donna still had reservations, that much was obvious. *All those questions.* Why was it that kids were so cynical?

"I do want the best for you, y'know."

"You too D."

It was almost morning, but neither of them felt like sleeping. It had been so long since they last talked like this and, as it was a weekend, they had all day and all night. They switched on the stereo and listened to sweet soul on Choice FM and talked about everything. Almost. Donna didn't mention that she had spent the past week on her friend Val's sofa since she caught Fitzroy chatting up another girl at a dance they had gone to together. The closest she got to bringing it up was to say that she was thinking of asking the council for a place of her own.

Talking with her now, Jennifer realized how much she missed not having Donna around, missed telling her off for leaving the butter out of the fridge, not washing out the bath after her or for leaving crumbs on the living room floor after she'd had a snack. There were, she had to admit, advantages to not having Donna around. She now realized that she had been so caught up in her sister's life because nothing was happening in her own. But now spring had turned into summer and with it Jennifer floated on air. Now when she put something somewhere it stayed there. Now when she tidied up she was the only one who messed it up again. And she could work at home without having to put up with a jungle or ragga bass as accompaniment. She didn't find hairpieces in the bathroom, or false fingernails on the kitchen table. And, most importantly, she didn't have to put up with Fitzroy sprawled all over her home. Still, she wished there could be many more long nights together with Donna like tonight, but it seemed like they were slowly drifting apart.

The sun was streaming in through the living room windows when they finally decided to wearily climb the wrought-iron staircase up to their bedrooms. When they woke up several hours later Donna went back to 'Fitzroy's' and Jennifer was again left in peace, perfect peace.

A few weeks later Jennifer was unpacking Marks and Spencer bags when she opened the refrigerator and her attention was drawn to the empty space where only this morning there had been a tub of yoghurt. Donna had been home again and had helped herself to the food in the freezer. Little sister had a habit of sneaking in, like a thief in the night, to feed herself whilst big sister was at work.

Paul. Over the last few weeks Jennifer hadn't really had the time to worry about Donna because Paul had literally taken her breath away and swept her off her feet with style and charisma. He was a man who knew where he was going and he was taking her with him. He had chosen her to be his life long companion.

She focused on the coming evening. Tonight she would get the chance to show Paul off. She had invited her girlfriends around to announce her impending nuptials. She wanted to shout it out loud to her old schoolfriends. Nobody knew yet. They knew about Paul Harvey but not about the engagement. She had wanted to let it sink in first, relish the fact that this was for real.

She continued unpacking the pre-packed meals. Perfect, the vegetables only needed to be popped into a saucepan and heated. Good old M&S always came to the rescue whenever Jennifer didn't have time to spend on anything so mundane as cooking a meal.

She set the table for eight. The tablecloth was brilliant white, the glasses sparkled. Candlesticks shone and the silver gleamed. It was perfect, set to impress. Satisfied with her preparations, she poured herself a Bacardi and coke with ice and took it upstairs with her to get ready.

Eight for eight thirty she'd told them. At eight o'clock precisely, just as she was putting her earrings in, the doorbell rang. Hurriedly she fastened the gold hoops and zipped up the back of the red halter neck dress she was wearing. She hurried to answer it, hoping it was Paul. It wasn't.

"Angela, as punctual as you are in court," Jennifer took the bottle of champagne from her.

"But of course, that's how I got my reputation," the petite brunette stepped over the threshold into Jennifer's hallway, her eyes flitting around. "My husband, John," she introduced him without turning around as he followed her in.

John was the living model for Barbie's Ken doll. A fine dark-haired version. "Nice to meet you."

"Likewise," he replied. "Are we early?"

"No, perfect timing. Let me take your coats and you can go on through to the living room."

Angela unbuttoned her dark camel hair coat and handed it to Jennifer. She wore a simple black V shape swing dress and had dressed it up with gold jewellery, a choker and bracelet. Simple but effective. "You look fabulous Jennifer, bit different from the old wig and gown, eh?" Angela smiled through cigarette-stained teeth.

Jennifer caught the hint that Angela wanted a compliment back. "Just something I threw on, but you...that outfit must have cost more than..."

"Please," Angela pushed back her perfect hair, "a lady never reveals how much her clothes cost in front of her husband," she laughed and John and Jennifer laughed with her.

Jennifer hung the coats up before following them in. "What will you have to drink?"

"My usual, G & T please, Jennifer."

Jennifer turned to John. "Whisky and soda's my poison," he said with a trace of a Welsh accent?

"Mr Harvey hiding upstairs is he?"

"No," Jennifer felt a nervous twinge in her stomach. "He isn't here yet."

"He's cutting it fine isn't he? Oh I know, he wants to make an entrance."

Jennifer giggled. "Yes that must be it. Lemon?"

"Please. You have a lovely home. Maybe I can have a tour later."

"Sure, when you're too drunk to notice the cracks and rising damp," Jennifer joked.

She handed them their drinks and made small talk. John appeared to be preoccupied with the CD collection and was making no effort to join in the conversation.

The doorbell rang and they all looked towards the door. Jennifer put her drink down and excused herself. *Please let it be Paul.*

It was Elaine and Allan.

Jennifer tried to mask her disappointment and greeted Elaine with an awkward hug, both women trying not to smudge their make-up.

"This is Allan?" Elaine grinned at her fiancé.

He was a lot darker than Elaine with big eyes that looked as sensitive as a child's. He looked like a body builder and had an air of purpose and control about him. Even though he was wearing a suit, the defined outline of his well-toned pecs bulged through. Jennifer took his hand and shook it lightly. "I've heard so much about you," she said.

"You too, but Elaine's obviously not too good with descriptions," he smiled. He had lovely teeth that shone out of his dark face like beacons. "Nice to meet you."

"You too. Angela and John are inside, introduce yourselves while I check on the food."

At this rate everyone will be here before Paul. That wasn't how she wanted it. By now Paul was supposed to be mixing their guests' drinks and introducing himself, while she served canapes and looked beautiful.

Karen and Beverly arrived together at half past eight. Paul still hadn't turned up. Jennifer had dialled his office and home numbers but neither answered. Jennifer started to panic.

Everyone else seemed to be getting along fine. Angela and John saw nothing wrong with Karen and Beverly bringing up their children on their own and if they did they hid it well. Beverly told them of her plans to go back to school and study law and they encouraged her to go for it. Elaine and Allan revealed that they had now set a date for their wedding in August, two months away. It would be a small church wedding, with only one bridesmaid and a best man — Karen and Allan's brother respectively. The reception would be held at their flat. Everyone congratulated them. Elaine's news made Jennifer even more anxious about Paul showing up.

By nine Karen had started to complain about how hungry she was and Beverly was saying the babysitter was only staying until midnight.

"He's bound to turn up soon," Angela said reassuringly.

Jennifer nodded, but her heart sank. She shrugged and began to remove Paul's place setting. Then she lit the candles on the dining table.

"Need a hand?" Karen came into the kitchen behind her.

Jennifer was decanting the food from the plastic cartons into serving bowls and looked embarrassed as she saw Karen's smirk.

"Good old M & S, eh?" she said, indicating the packaging.

They laughed together. "Thanks. There's the vegetables to drain and put into the green bowls."

"Been stood up?" Karen had a way of saying what nobody else dared to.

"I don't know where he is. He's ruined my surprise..."

"Surprise?"

"Yes..." Jennifer leant against the counter. "I was going to make an announcement, about us."

Karen came closer, her lively eyes fixed on Jennifer's. "Yeah?"

"I should wait and tell you all together..."

"Naaah...you can't leave me hanging like this. What?"

"Paul asked me to marry him."

"Aarrgh!" Karen screamed, rushing forward to hug her friend.

"I take it that's congratulations."

"You lucky dog. Shit, I knew you'd be the one to get married. Gonna be a big one an' all innit?"

"Well we haven't got that far yet..."

"So why didn't you say something when Elaine was going on about her little wedding?"

"I wanted Paul to be here when I announced it."

"But you still gonna do it, ain't you?"

"Well..."

"You've got to. You've got us all here, your other friend Angela and her husband, the food and drink..."

"You're right, I will."

Together they carried in the plates and food and drink, and invited everyone to take their places in the dining room. The aroma of the food made Jennifer forget her disappointment and reminded her that she had been too nervous to eat all day.

Jennifer had to rearrange the seats so that she wouldn't be facing an empty chair at the other end of the table. She began to unscrew the cork of a wine bottle, but Angela stopped her.

"Let John do that, it's a man's job. You don't mind do you darling."

John took the bottle from her hand. "Of course not." Jennifer got the feeling that he felt slightly uncomfortable in a room full of black people, but he was coping.

"Hold on, before everyone starts eating and drinking and stuff, Jennifer's got an announcement to make," Karen said standing up, she looked at Jennifer encouragingly.

Jennifer stood up nervously, all faces were turned up towards her. Some looked concerned, others excited, the men were just hungry.

"As you've noticed Paul hasn't managed to make it tonight. We were planning...I was planning on having all my friends here so that I could announce my engagement to the man I've been waiting for all my life...and this evening..."

For a second no one moved, then mouths dropped open and eyes opened wider. Elaine, Beverly and Angela stepped forward and showered Jennifer with kisses, hugs and congratulations, while the men poured champagne into everyone's glasses.

Then the questions came. "When?" "How have you kept it so quiet?" "Let me see the ring." "Why didn't you tell me sooner?" "How and where did he ask you?" "I can't wait to meet the man who managed to conquer Jennifer Edwards." Excitement vibrated over the table.

Jennifer's heart danced around in her chest throughout, beating madly, wildly. Paul still hadn't turned up but in the euphoria of the moment she couldn't feel angry with him. He was bound to have a very good reason for his absence. He was probably tied up with a client or finishing important paperwork. She'd been there herself often enough.

As they sat down to eat, Jennifer answered all the questions and told the guests of her future plans. She had had two days to think about it and decided she wanted a spectacular wedding that would make the society pages of the national papers.

THREE
When breeze blow fowl fedder, yuh fine out seh fowl got skin

Jennifer was late for her tennis lesson. She jogged out onto the court where her coach waited. He was not pleased.

"I'm sorry Carl, had to make a stop off on the way."

Carl was a short, muscular, fair-skinned black man who wasn't quite good looking, but not exactly ugly either. "You're paying, Jen."

"I'll pay Carl, let's get going."

After a hopeless year of squash, Jennifer had decided to try another racket sport. Athletics had been her forte at school, but her arms needed exercise too. Angela and John often played tennis and had invited her over to one of their lawn parties. She didn't want to appear to be an amateur, hence the lessons.

She stood with a serving stance, her calf muscles already aching. The ball whooshed towards her racket. She made a half-hearted swipe at it but missed.

"Jennifer," Carl complained, "concentrate."

"Sorry Carl, my mind must be elsewhere."

"Well call it back will you," he walked slowly back from the net. Carl had hairy legs with rigid thigh muscles that disappeared into white shorts. Jennifer found herself wondering if his buttocks were just as hard and immediately scolded herself. She was soon to be a married woman. Thoughts like that were for single swingers.

She adopted an athletic stance and returned the next oncoming ball gracefully.

"That's good, keep it coming," he encouraged.

Grinning, she lobbed the ball back a second time and darted nimbly across the court for another volley.

An hour and a half later it was over. Sweating and aching Jennifer made her way back to the changing rooms. Carl patted her on the back. "You doing good, girl."

It was the way he said it. Now she was sure he was gay.

Jennifer climbed into her third shower of the day. She felt tired and just a little queasy. She wondered if the ginseng and multivitamins were doing her any good. They were supposed to give you energy, stop colds, improve your skin, your eyesight, oil your joints, but she felt wrecked.

She had arranged to meet Paul for dinner tonight, he was going to explain why he hadn't shown up for their engagement announcement, but now she just wanted to go home, fall into bed and sleep until tomorrow evening.

She dried herself and climbed out of the shower, then dressed in a light cotton dress and slipped her trainers back on over her ankle socks. No, she was in no condition to go out to dinner, she felt completely exhausted and needed to sleep. She would call Paul and cancel dinner, he could explain things another time. She yawned loudly and stretched her arms.

Jennifer turned over in bed and focused her bleary eyes on the alarm clock. It was five past four in the morning and still dark. She threw back the duvet and dragged herself to the bathroom. She felt terrible.

After emptying her bladder she leant against the sink basin, a wave of nausea overwhelming her. She retched and spat into the sink. Light-headed and breathless she sat on the lid of the toilet bowl and breathed deeply. She was hot and needed air, but her legs shook when she tried to stand again. It had to be that summer flu bug that was going around.

It was time she saw a doctor. A week of this was too much. Bile rose in her throat again and she quickly raised the lid of the wc and heaved into the disinfected water. It was too late or even too early to call a doctor. She would have to get a replacement to stand in for her in court in order to make a trip to the surgery as soon as they were open. Five minutes later the nausea had passed. After rinsing her mouth with Listerine she ran the shower.

She woke up early and called Julian Holland to arrange for one of the other barristers in chambers to cover for her. That sorted, she flopped back on her bed and slept until well into the afternoon. When she finally lifted herself up, a message on her answering machine awaited her from Paul. *Shit!* She forgot to cancel dinner. The message was brief. He apologised for missing her dinner party, said that he had been trying to get hold of her since yesterday because he had been invited by America's Black Attorney's Group to replace the Society of Black Lawyer's Peter Herbert at the last minute on a mini lecture tour of universities over there. He was leaving on a flight from Heathrow in a few hours. He said he would call her from Washington when he arrived. Jennifer's heart sank. He was leaving the country, already she missed him.

Jennifer went downstairs and rustled up a bowl of cornflakes for a late *late* breakfast. She decided that she probably wouldn't be able to get an appointment with the doctor at this time of day and anyway, she felt much better this morning, all the sickness of the night before had disappeared. She was going to take the rest of the day off. She felt like going out though and, impulsively, she dialled Beverly's number and asked if she fancied a shopping trip to the West End. Beverly agreed so long as she could bring Jerome.

The sun beamed down on the three of them as they crossed Regent Street. Jennifer fanned herself feverishly with the magazine she had just bought, glad she had worn the full-length summer dress. It kept the scorching heat off her legs and fanned her body with it's swaying as she walked.

"Are you okay, Jen?" Beverly asked, strapping Jerome back into his pushchair.

"Yes, why?"

"Oh nothing...your cheeks look a little flushed, that's all." Beverly's ample bosom heaved under the yellow sun dress. "People used to say that I looked flushed all the way through my pregnancy. Really pissed me off."

"Really." Jennifer's forehead and cheeks felt a little warm, but then so did the weather.

Nine month old Jerome was chewing on a teething biscuit. He was Beverly's burden, the millstone around her neck, and made every simple trip to the newsagents seem like a major expedition. Beverly complained that with Jerome, her work was never done. It always took forever to get him to sleep and when she finally succeeded she would be stuck indoors for the duration because there was no way you dared disturb a dozing child who had problems sleeping at the best of times.

They crossed over to Old Compton Street. Everywhere Jennifer looked she saw babies. Babies in push chairs and carried in pouches. There seemed to have been a baby boom while she was asleep.

"I hadn't noticed," Beverly said, "but then, when you've got your own to concentrate on you haven't got time to be looking at other babies," she gazed lovingly at Jerome. "Do you and Paul want children?"

Jennifer fumbled for the right answer. "I suppose so, but not right away, we both have some career goals to fulfil first."

"But you won't have to work when you're married to him, will you?"

"I may not have to, but I will." Jennifer played her motto over in her head again. 'A woman's got to stay single to survive.' She would have to modify that a little after she was married. 'A woman has to stay focused to survive,' or 'a woman's got to stay childless to survive.' She would work on it.

They came to a gift shop and Jennifer waited outside with the pushchair while Beverly rushed in to buy something that she knew her mum would love.

"What a lovely baby boy." Jennifer looked up at the sound of the American accent. She smiled at the white woman who came up and gazed at Jerome.

"He's so cute. Looks like his Momma."

It took a moment for Jennifer to register that the woman mistook her for Jerome's mother. "Oh...No, he's not mine."

"But you are expecting aren't you? I can tell, you got that look aboutcha."

Jennifer threw her a dirty look. *Woman, doesn't know what she's talking about.* She caught her reflection in the shop window. What was it about her today? Earlier, a pregnant woman holding the hand of a toddler had come up alongside her and started going on about how expensive babies were and had even asked her when hers was due. *Maybe it's a sign.* To warn her about Donna. Could baby sister be pregnant? Jennifer felt tears come to her eyes. How many times had she told, warned her sister to be careful? How many times had she given Donna the facts and figures of careless sex. Fitzroy Lucas had a lot to answer for. The only thing that would cure a persistent baby father such as him was a 'Bobbit' and Jennifer wished she had the bottle to do it herself. Men like him didn't deserve to have a sexual organ if he couldn't be responsible for it.

Donna sauntered in around six o'clock, wearing a new red felt hat, her hair still braided and looking good.

Jennifer cooked dinner, her sister's favourite curry goat, rice and peas.

"Sup'm smells good," Donna said.

"I'm glad you think so."

"I'm starving..."

"D, do you have something important you want to tell me?"

Donna thought about it. "No, I don't think so."

"Something about Fitzroy?"

Something flickered in her eyes. "How did you find out?"

"Instinct," Jennifer lied. "Do you want to tell me about it?"

Donna rested her head against the back of the sofa and sighed. "He didn't like the way I cussed about his kid. I told him I didn't want them living with us..."

"You didn't want Fitzroy's baby?"

"Well he didn't have to let her stay did he? I mean was I wrong to get upset?"

Jennifer frowned. "Who?"

"Fitzroy's baby mother of course. Come crying on his doorstep a few weeks ago. Her mum chucked her out telling her to find someone else to look after the baby and she comes running to him."

Jennifer stared at her. "That's all you had to tell me?"

"Well...yes. What did you think?"

"I...I..." her voice died away. Jennifer shook her head and said, "I just knew something was wrong and I needed you to tell me...that's all."

"You thought he was beating on me or something?"

"Well, maybe not that serious, but I was concerned."

"We argued...he got rid of her. I couldn't have that woman sleeping on the sofa with her toddler running around the flat with no leash."

"I understand," Jennifer touched her sister's hair affectionately. "You see what I told you, that woman should have stayed single..."

"...To survive," Donna added.

They laughed together as Jennifer dished up the hot food.

88

"And is there any chance you might be pregnant?" the white-coated doctor asked.

The question took Jennifer by surprise. She had been feeling sick again but had managed to avoid that option. "It's a possibility, but I'm usually very careful."

The doctor looked over his glasses at her. "Have you had unprotected sex within the last few months?"

"Yes," she replied, feeling like an adolescent being scolded.

The doctor huffed exasperatedly. "Okay then," he put his pen down and stood up. Behind his desk were two white, wall-mounted cabinets. One, glass-fronted, contained empty vials, tissues, medical swabs, syringes and spatulas. The other locked one was probably where the doctor kept the drugs.

He produced a small white-capped sample bottle from the glass-fronted cabinet, filled in a label and stuck it on the container before handing it to her. "Take a urine sample first thing in the morning and bring it in to reception." He didn't look up again as he filled in her notes. "We'll have the results within a couple of hours after that."

"It's not gastric flu, or something then? I've had that before you see."

"These things happen," he looked at her name on the records, "*Miss* Edwards. But why don't we just wait and see."

Patronizing old man, she thought, putting her sample bottle out of sight inside her handbag. She got up and left, stepping out of the surgery and into a heavy downpour.

Pregnant indeed! She unfolded her telescopic umbrella. It was impossible and the test tomorrow would prove that smug grey-haired fool wrong beyond a doubt, she told herself, hurrying across the road to her car.

Nevertheless the thought followed her. When had she had her last period? She had forgotten, they were so irregular these days. Then she remembered she'd had a period last month, she hadn't missed one. Jennifer breathed a sigh of relief, climbed into her Cabriolet and slipped in the Keith Sweat cassette. She smiled to herself.

Tuesday, Wednesday, Thursday passed with Jennifer working hard. She picked up one single white envelope in the mail on Friday. Inside was Elaine's wedding invitation:

Mr and Mrs Reginald Johnson
request the pleasure of your company at the marriage of their daughter
Elaine to Mr. Allan Goulden
at
St. Mark's church, Ladywell

On the back was the address of the flat they shared where the reception was being held. Jennifer felt happiness well up inside her. She went into her living room and propped the invite up on her mantelpiece.

Dressed in her favourite navy suit, the skirt just covering her calves, the jacket fashionably dropping past her hips, her jewellery was understated but elegant, she began her weekly handbag clearout when the clear sample bottle rolled off the table and onto the floor. *The pregnancy test!* She'd completely forgotten. *Girl, sort yourself out, get the test done. Today!* She ran a hand below her stomach, her bladder felt like it was about to explode.

The wedding was small, family and close friends only. The newlyweds were saving for their own house and wanted a white wedding, but not an expensive one. The reception was held in Elaine's front room and she wore a modern off-the-shoulder, knee-length, layered white lace dress with a matching hat. She had a glow that didn't falter all day.

Her father, a small bald man in his fifties, was in tears as he made his speech. Holding his daughter's hand he told of how close they were and he was proud to have played a part in producing such a beautiful successful daughter. He then turned to his wife and kissed her saying, "Thank you." Tears filled Jennifer's eyes as she watched this touching family scene, and when Allan's voice broke as he told of his love for Elaine, there was no holding back, Jennifer mopped tears of joy from her cheeks.

Monday morning. A message from Paul on the answering machine. He was back from the States but even that failed to raise a smile. The call from the doctor's surgery was totally unexpected. Jennifer had been so preoccupied with other things she had forgotten about her test result. Sitting behind her huge desk she put the phone down, threw her head back and sunk into her swivel chair. *How could this be?* She had to get out, get hold of Paul. If there was anyone she had to talk to it was him.

She dialled his work number. "Hello, it's Jennifer Edwards, is Paul Harvey available?"

"Miss Edwards...please hold."

A few seconds later Paul's faithful clerk came back on the line. "Mr. Harvey's in conference, Miss Edwards. Can I take a message?"

"Just ask him to call me as soon as possible will you."

"Certainly. Goodbye."

She replaced the receiver. If he was busy, he was busy. What the hell was she going to say to him anyway? 'Hi Paul, guess what I'm pregnant...we're going to have a baby...how do you feel about kids? I know we said we wanted to have kids one day, so how about in seven months time?' Somehow she didn't think it was going to be that easy.

She could always bawl her eyes out and blame it on the pill that she wasn't on. Would Paul feel deceived and leave her? Then she'd have to tell Donna and her parents and that was the hardest part. Maybe she was being too pessimistic. Paul might actually love the idea of a baby right now.

She rubbed a hand over her belly. *Why me and why now?* How was she going to juggle her career and a child? And after all she had said and the way she had behaved, how could she admit to her little sister that she had got pregnant?

She got her coat from the coat stand by the door and her handbag from her locker and stepped out into the adjoining office. Catrin, her pupil, stopped typing and looked up inquiringly. "Can I get you something?"

"I'm not feeling too good. I think I'll go home."

"Sure. You haven't been looking too good lately. There are no more appointments this afternoon and I can handle any calls so don't worry."

With that Jennifer departed. On her way out she checked that her mobile phone was on and entered the hubbub of the London streets, walking towards the tube.

She got off at Oxford Circus and was soon in Hennes department store. One of her favourite places to shop.

She flicked disinterestedly and automatically through a rack of clothes and wondered bitterly why buying herself a new outfit didn't have the same thrill anymore. She felt the warning sting of tears behind her eyes. She felt so alone. Fine example she turned out to be.

She was staring at nothingness when she felt someone watching her. She turned her head to find a sales assistant hovering uncertainly.

"Everything all right?" the assistant asked.

"Everything's just fine," Jennifer sniffed.

The assistant in her stiff navy blue uniform tidied the rack beside her.

"I'm pregnant."

"Are you?" The assistant looked at Jennifer's flat stomach. "You look so slim."

"Two months," she replied, wondering why she was telling a complete stranger her business. Was she looking for sympathy?

"What do you want, boy or girl?"

That was the furthest thing from Jennifer's mind. She was beginning to feel sick again.

"Girls are easier," the assistant went on. "My sister's got one of each and she says girls are easier. Hers always slept through the night, even at one month old."

Jennifer looked at her watch, hoping the woman would get the message.

"You ought to have a look at the maternity wear upstairs. They don't look like maternity these days, you can even wear them afterwards."

Obviously she couldn't take a hint.

"Most people don't get their figures back straight away, they stay baggy," she continued. "Everything just drops. My sister put on a stone with each baby."

Jennifer imagined herself being blown up slowly and unwillingly like a balloon. A tight and painful process. Then, when she could expand no more, the air being let out quickly leaving her body like an overstretched balloon, all the tightness gone.

She leant down to pick up her handbag. "Thanks," she said.

The assistant looked surprised. "You're welcome."

"You've made me decide to get rid of it."

When Karen had received the call from Jennifer on that afternoon, the first thing she'd thought was, *good*. It was a chance to get out of work for a couple of hours and have a good old chin wag. They had arranged to meet in the cafe at the Crofton Leisure Centre, a convenient meeting place for both of them.

Karen hadn't been expecting the look of a worried woman sitting on her own by a window overlooking the tennis courts.

"Bwoy Jen, you don't look too good, y'know," Karen said, taking a seat opposite her.

"Nice to see you too, Kaz."

"Wassup?"

"We should have met in a bar instead. I need a drink."

"Hold on, I'm sure we can get a glass of wine in this place." She left her friend gazing out of the window and went to get them both a drink.

"I bribed him into giving us some Bacardi," she grinned on her return.

"Thanks," Jennifer said, taking her drink.

"So, what's up, girl?"

Jennifer couldn't even bring herself to say it. Why had she picked Karen to tell anyway? Why did she need to tell anyone when she had already decided not to have this baby?

Karen watched all the confusion in Jennifer's face and became even more intrigued. "Is it yuh sister? I know how dat gal gets to you. You must be a saint to put up with her. If I was in your place I'da kicked her arse out long time...She's got no gratitude. I tell..."

"It's not Donna..."

Jennifer reached inside her handbag and produced a card which she handed to her friend.

Karen took the card from Jennifer's shaking hand. "An ante-natal appointment card," she said falteringly.

"Exactly."

"With your name 'pon it."

Jennifer gulped the Bacardi down. Their eyes met across the table. Jennifer's sad and devoid of feeling, Karen's incredulous and searching.

"This is a joke, right Jen?"

"Does it look like I'm laughing."

"Eh-eh!" Karen's hand flew to her mouth stifling a laugh. *Jennifer Edwards got knocked up!* She never thought she'd live to see the day. For all her upper class hoity toity Jennifer, the big-shot barrister, was on the same level as her.

"Karen!"

"I'm sorry, Jen. This is just so unreal."

"You're telling me!"

Karen crossed her forearms on the table and scrutinized Jennifer's face. "Bwoy, this hit you hard didn't it?"

Jennifer nodded.

"So how did you let yourself get knocked up?"

"It was the night when he proposed. I was walking on air. I guess contraception was the last thing on my mind."

"Your fiancé...Paul?"

"Yes, it's his. My first sexual encounter in two years and I mess up big time."

"Mmm-hmm. These men with money and charm are the worst. They mess you up man."

Again Jennifer wondered why she had chosen Karen, the least sympathetic of her friends to confide in.

"So does he know?"

"No, not yet."

"Are you going to tell him?"

"I'll only tell him if I decide to keep it."

"If?"

Jennifer stared down at two men on the badminton court below. "I didn't plan for this to happen. I have absolutely no idea what to do with a baby." She threw her hands up in despair. "I never wanted this."

"Who does? At least you're not going to be left on your own. You're getting married in two months, remember. It's not the end of the world."

There was a silence between the two women. A group of school kids came up the stairs, rowdily discussing a punishment they were about to incur from their teacher.

"That Mr. Baxter needs a slap, y'know."

"Needs more dan dat. I should get my Uncle down here with his shotgun, man. Sort him out quick time." The boy clapped his hands together for effect.

"Y'know whose fault dis is, it's dat Kevin. You wait 'til I ketch up wid 'im, he ain't gonna show his face around for months."

If only those kids knew that their problems would seem petty compared to the real troubles that awaited them in adulthood, Jennifer mused.

"I don't want you thinking that I'm on the side of the opposition, but I think you should tell the father."

Jennifer shrugged.

"Well you still haven't decided whether you want to go through with it or not and I think the father's attitude could sway your decision."

"What a mess...A child's life in my hands."

"You manage all right with Donna."

Jennifer half smiled. Donna was a separate problem. "All the times I warned her about getting pregnant..." she swallowed the rest of her drink.

"You got a lot of thinking to do. Go home Jen, call Paul and talk to him."

Karen was right. Sooner or later Paul would have to be told.

Jennifer leaned across the arm of the sofa and picked up the phone on the third ring. "Hello."

"Jennifer," Paul's deep tones came down the line.

"Paul, you got my message then?" she asked casually.

"Ah yes, eventually. Listen, can I see you tonight? I have some good news."

Bemused at the coincidence, Jennifer replied, "Yes of course. I have some good news for you too. Why don't you come over."

"Great. I'll see you in an hour."

"I'll be waiting." She hung up and immediately started to make herself presentable. She took the ponytail out of her hair and combed it into it's usual bob haircut, retouched her make-up and changed into a casual dress, showing off the best of her smooth athletic legs.

Paul was always punctual. An hour later he was on her doorstep, a bunch of red roses in his arms. He kissed her full on the lips. "I can't believe it's been so long."

"Good trip?"

"Perfect, I can't wait to tell you my news."

They went into Jennifer's sitting room and he unbuttoned his jacket before making himself comfortable on the sofa. Jennifer had already popped the cork on a bottle of champagne and placed it in an ice bucket.

"What a day I've had," Paul breathed deeply, spreading his arms along the back of the sofa.

"Wait until I tell you about mine." She filled two glasses with bubbly and cuddled up beside him. "But you first."

"Well it all started with a chance meeting about a month ago. I was sitting in chambers going through piles of paper work, when my secretary buzzed me to say there was an old friend in reception to see me. It was somebody I hadn't seen in months and, to tell you the truth, never expected to see again. Anyway, to cut a long story short, after several meetings and telephone calls, we've come to an agreement." Paul fidgeted excitedly.

"Well, come on tell me."

"I am now halfway up the ladder to my new career," he grabbed her arms. "Can you believe it?"

"Paul, I'm overjoyed, but what are you talking about exactly?"

"Politics, my love. That good ole boy's network really does work!" He clapped his hands together.

Jennifer was becoming irritated. "Yes, and...?"

"I've always said it's not what you know but whom." He leant forward, elbows on his knees and clasped his hands. "...Jennifer, we may have to postpone the wedding."

Jennifer shot him a cold look. "I don't think so Paul, you see there's a tiny complication to our plans...I'm going to have a baby."

Paul's face remained expressionless. Maybe it hadn't registered. She knew the feeling.

"Ah," was all he said.

"*Our* baby, Paul..."

He seemed to come out of his shock. "But of course," he removed his hand from her knee, smoothed his moustache nervously and stood up. "I'm terribly sorry Jennifer. How could I have been so careless...In this day and age you would think a man my age would be more responsible."

"Paul, I'm not accusing you..."

"I know, honey. Next you're going to tell me it takes two."

"Well...yes."

Jennifer's eyes followed her fiancé as he paced back and forth. Her heart was beating much too fast. Could you get a heart attack from giving somebody bad news? Paul finally stopped his pacing. His arms fell to his side and he smiled.

"Jennifer," he breathed deeply, "Jennifer, Jennifer, Jennifer..." His voice rose higher and his smile broadened with each mention of her name. "You know something...this really isn't a problem." Paul sat beside her on the sofa and took her hands in his.

Jennifer was surprised but glad at his reaction.

"In fact, this is an added bonus to my astounding good luck."

Now Jennifer was flabbergasted. "B...But..."

"No my love," he touched a finger to her lips, "what more could I have wished for, a wife and child, at the same time as my star ascends careerwise. You are beautiful, did you know that?"

Paul kissed her tenderly and Jennifer forgot all the angst and agony she had been through. He wanted her and he wanted their baby. Life couldn't be sweeter.

Despite morning sickness Jennifer floated on air over the next two weeks. She felt as happy as she could possibly be. She was engaged and pregnant and had a man who wanted her that way. Karen warned her to keep her feet on the ground when she told her.

"Yuh t'ink he's still gonna want you when you look like a baby elephant compared to the Naomi Campbell lookalikes out deh?"

"Paul doesn't look at other woman in that way. Paul appreciates women with brains."

Karen kissed her teeth. She had known too many men, it would take a lot to convince her that Paul Harvey was some other species. But Jennifer knew it. *He hadn't even mentioned abortion!*

The wedding was brought forward. They would still marry in a church but the reception was going to be limited to a reasonable two hundred guests. Preparations were stepped up. She enlisted the help of her friends and her sister to help organize and go shopping with her. The wedding buzz even seemed to enhance her performance in court.

"It's like this you see..."

Paul had come around to Jennifer's flat late that night after standing her up yet again. He had an apology to make. She'd waited on the other end of the phone for him to make it, but he insisted on seeing her. He hadn't even kissed her when he'd arrived. He avoided her gaze and refused any refreshment, saying he wasn't staying long. Something was wrong.

"More good news?" she asked.

"For one of us," he replied solemnly, rubbing his hands as he paced the living room.

"This new career I've been telling you about...Well, it's more than a job."

"More than a job?" Alarm bells sounded in Jennifer's mind.

"The post was given to me under false pretences," he paused, cleared his throat and smoothed his moustache nervously. "I don't quite know how to put this...I told them that I was unattached. They are totally against...attachments as it were."

"What kind of antiquated criteria system is that?"

"That's not quite it," Paul glanced at her out of the corner of his eyes before focusing on the ceiling. "You see, the person who put me forward for the post was a woman..."

Jennifer's mouth clamped shut as if she knew what was coming.

Paul continued. "When I first started out in law I was introduced to a beautiful, intelligent, well-off young woman whose father just happens to be a powerful Tory politician. At the time he was a judge, one of the most powerful in the country. I strived to get close to her father, I strived to get her, but I was never good enough," he swallowed and began pacing again, a little smile touched the corners of his mouth.

Jennifer sat rigid, feeling empty and numb, while swirling in her guts was a volcano about to erupt.

"...Then she comes back into my life, she's heard of my accomplishments and hands me a proposal on a plate, a proposal I've been waiting for all my life. She offers to practically grease my career path into parliament. I would get selected, win a safe seat..." he was ranting. Jennifer sat impassively on the sofa. "...After a few years a government post and, who knows, maybe even my own department eventually. In twenty years from now I could become Britain's first black prime minister. Now...you wouldn't want to stand in the way of all of that, would you?"

"I'm sorry, did I miss something...? " Jennifer cleared her dry throat and narrowed her eyes. "I'm sure there's a message for me somewhere in all of this but I didn't quite catch it."

Paul ran an itchy finger around the inside of his collar. "I...I," he coughed and turned his back to her, "I can't marry you Jennifer."

"What?" Jennifer suddenly felt hot and dizzy as the living room seemed to spin round fast.

"I'm sorry..."

Jennifer raised a hand to her forehead. "What you're saying is that you're pushing me aside to take up with this woman?"

"No! Not exactly. It's a career move. Being pregnant you're not in a position to understand. But if you weren't, maybe we could have still..."

"Still what?"

"Well I have to be unattached at the moment, unmarried, no dependents...but once I make it to government... It's just that I couldn't possibly leave you hanging on, never knowing when I'd be coming back, or whether we were still going to be married some day. It just wouldn't be fair to you or the baby."

Jennifer stood slowly frowning. "And this woman, she's the reason you don't want anything to do with me or my baby?!" Her voice rose without effort, she didn't even realize she was shouting.

"Jennifer! Come now, we don't need to get hostile over this. It's nobody's fault, it's just the luck of the draw. Career comes first, you know that. Anyway you'll be okay, women like yourself have so many options nowadays."

Jennifer winced, feeling like a volcano about to spew lava. "You mean abortion, kill my child?"

"If you wish. Look, this woman is my passport to the very top. One silly mistake on my part is all it would take to wreck the opportunity. I can't afford to let that happen."

Jennifer glared at him. To Paul it was nothing more than a game of musical chairs. But this was her life he was juggling, and the life of her baby. "You know what Paul, I should have followed my first instinct."

"And what was that?"

"To kick you in the balls and make a run for it!"

Paul chuckled nervously. "Jennifer, darling, one thing I always loved about you was your ability to stay in control. Don't disappoint me. Who knows, maybe when you've sorted yourself out...I could visit...stay over occasionally."

The eyes he looked into were as hard as bricks. Jennifer wanted to scream. *Become his mistress!* Did she come across as desperate? *He must think he's speaking to a child.* Jennifer's right hand took the initiative and before Paul could defend himself she had slapped him so hard in his face that her hand stung.

"Jennifer!!!" Paul's hand went to his injured cheek.

She was shaking with hurt and humiliation. "Don't even utter my name from your filthy mouth again. I trusted you, I gave you everything and this is how you repay me..." She suddenly remembered that she still wore his ring. She ripped it off her finger and threw it in his face. "... Treating me like some old garment that has lost its use!" Tears rolled down her cheeks.

Paul moved towards the door his eyes widening. "I...I think I'd better...leave. I'll call you in the morning when you've had a chance to calm down."

"Go, yes, by all means but don't call me or show your conniving, disrespectful face anywhere near me or my family again."

Paul hurried out the flat. "I thought of all people you would understand how much this meant to me, Jennifer..." he called back.

"Get out! Just get outta my house!" She slammed the door behind him and collapsed against it.

FOUR
When water t'row weh it cyant pick up back

Jennifer sat in Beverly's front room making a paper plane out of a till receipt. Beverly was babysitting for Karen, whose two children were proving difficult to contain in the modern flat in Lewisham. Toys littered the small front room — teddies, building bricks and a plastic tricycle. Jerome was walking now and was trying to reach a porcelain clown on a shelving unit. Jennifer watched as he cocked a leg up trying to get some leverage and then fell back onto his backside. Undeterred he tried again.

Nobody knew the wedding was off yet, but unprofessionally, she had taken the whole week off work to rest. The clerk for her set, Julian Holland, had not been happy. "Who am I supposed to get to cover you at such short notice?"

"I'm sure Terence can handle it, he was assisting on the Mellows case."

"Mr Childs will also need an assisting barrister," Julian pointed out.

"Do what you can please Julian, I really need this break." She burst into tears after hanging up. She had spent too many nights laying awake, just thinking about things and she now felt it was time to get it all off her chest. She waited patiently for the right opportunity to tell Beverly her story.

"Sorry about the mess, Jen. Children!" Beverly handed her a cool glass of pineapple juice.

Jennifer took the drink and looked around the room as if noticing it for the first time. "It's not that bad."

"I've just started a college course in the evenings and when I get back I just about drag myself to bed. I don't know how Karen manages to do so many things. And she's got two kids. I can't find the energy to follow Jerome around, clearing up after him."

Beverly had decided to dedicate herself to self-improvement. The college course was just the start. Maybe she would stick at it and maybe she wouldn't, but life was too short to waste sitting at home playing with her son every day. When she had her qualifications and could provide for him a lot better they would have ample time to play together, Beverly reasoned.

She stepped over a squeaky toy and flopped down on the sofa beside Jennifer. Jerome had given up trying to scale the unit and noticing the women's drinks began to bawl for one too. The only way he knew how to ask for something was to open and close his fist in a beckoning gesture. "You want drink, Jerry?"

Jerome just bawled some more. "I'll be right with you, Jen." The toddler followed his mother out of the room.

"Look Bev, if you're busy, I'll talk to you another time...!"

The large woman popped her head back in the doorway with a carton of fruit juice in her hand. "Don't be silly Jen, sit down. Jerome will probably have a nap soon." She filled the baby's feeder cup, pressed the lid on and handed it to him.

Beverly sat down again, and looked over at her friend. "Karen always tells me when she hears from you. We really should get together more often."

"I know," Jennifer said wistfully. "Time is so precious nowadays, isn't it?"

"Especially when you're about to get married."

Jennifer met Beverly's eyes. "I'm not...anymore."

"Not what?"

"Not getting married. It's over."

Beverly moved up on the sofa closer to Jennifer and took her hand.

"You're not wearing your engagement ring."

"I gave it back. I had no choice. You see he..."

"Jennifer, you don't have to tell me this if you don't want to." Those were Beverly's words but her tone said, let it all out, I want to listen, lean on me.

"I want to. Bottling things up makes me unwell."

"I hear ya," Beverly nodded. Jerome snuggled up to his mother and pushed himself up onto her lap.

"Paul and I broke up because of another woman."

"Oh Jen, poor thing. That's always the way. And pregnant too?"

Jennifer's head whiplashed in Beverly's direction and as their eyes met, Bev realized too late that it was Karen and not Jennifer who had told her about the baby. "I'm sorry..."

Jennifer related the events of the other evening to Beverly and was soon in tears. She had felt numb for days but was feeling it now. Beverly had been there herself. Devon had left her pregnant. Hadn't even been back to find out if he had a boy or a girl. And even though his family had told him he still hadn't visited.

Beverly was truly sorry for Jennifer who had always been so sensible at school, always knew where to draw the line with boys and stuck to her studies. Jennifer who had succeeded in her chosen career, bought her own home, brand new car and had everything going for her including one of London's most eligible black men, yet now... Beverly looked down at Jerome sleeping in her lap and realized that Jennifer would soon, as she herself had done, learn that the world is full of possibilities and opportunities when you don't have to bring children up on your own.

"Couldn't you call him, try and make things up?"

Jennifer dried her eyes. Beverly obviously didn't understand or else she wouldn't be suggesting that things might not be as bad as they seemed. Things were bad. Really bad. Worse than they seemed, because she had decided not to keep the baby, but she couldn't bring herself to tell anyone.

"So what are you going to do?"

Jennifer shrugged. "I'm going to have to cancel everything..."

Guests would have to be notified. The dresses had already been bought and paid for, but the caterers would have to be called and the food orders halted. It was too late to cancel the cake, so maybe she would throw it at Paul instead. At least she'd get some satisfaction out of it.

"Imagine getting this close and then this happens. I can't say I know how you feel but I know how I'd feel."

Jennifer felt humiliated.

The early October sun beamed through the window onto the chintz armchairs. The clinic was private, homely and civilized, yet Jennifer was unable to relax. The sun was giving her a headache. Was that a flutter of movement she'd felt in her abdomen? She poked her stomach spitefully. Turning on her heels she made towards the small coffee table where a kettle, cups and individual packets of coffee stood waiting. She poured herself a cup.

"Jennifer Edwards?" the female voice called from the doorway.

"Yes." She picked up her handbag and somehow her trembling legs carried her into the consulting room. This was the real thing, she thought looking around. An examination bed and a trolley laid out with a blood pressure monitor and a stethoscope, kidney-shaped bowls and plastic gloves. Jennifer sat opposite the doctor, on the other side of a huge desk, unsmiling.

"Relax Jennifer, this is just an examination. We tested your urine, it's positive," she smiled. "You're definitely pregnant."

That much was already certain. Three tests and no period for three months left little doubt. Tears of genuine self-pity welled in her eyes nonetheless.

"I thought you knew..." The doctor handed her a box of tissues.

Jennifer felt for the box and pinched out a tissue, dabbing her eyes carefully. "Yes, but every time I hear that word it hits me again."

"Bad news has a habit of doing that. When was the date of your last period?" The doctor raised her eyebrow when Jennifer told her. "Left it late, didn't you?"

"I thought I was getting married up until recently," Jennifer explained.

"All right, just take your pants and stockings off and lie on the bed for me."

Jennifer did as she was told, lying stiffly on the unyielding surface. The doctor advanced, pulling rubber gloves on and examined her inside and out. She shook her head doubtfully. "You can get dressed now."

Jennifer got off the bed, pulled her underwear on slowly. The doctor scribbled in a file. Jennifer stared at her, trying to read her face for clues. "Well?" She took her seat again.

The doctor's hazel eyes were clear, but her eyelids dropped and she shrugged. "I'm sorry Jennifer, you're too far gone. Maybe if you had come a few weeks ago..." The doctor smiled, a smile that said there was really nothing to smile about. "You knew already, didn't you?"

Jennifer was already putting her coat back on and heading for the door.

"Jennifer, any doctor will give you the same opinion, you're nearly five months pregnant..."

Thoughts, all kinds of thoughts were running through Jennifer's head. One thought especially...an option...a dangerous one...but at the moment, she was a desperate woman clutching at straws and it seemed that any option would do.

"Look, I know what's going through your mind," the doctor looked at her wistfully. "I know because I've seen hundreds of women in the same situation as yourself. And the same thoughts have gone through their minds. All I can say is, don't even think about it..."

Mind readers! Jennifer hated every one of them. She slammed the door behind her and walked the path of no return.

The candle flickered as hot wax dripped down the sides of the Chianti bottle. Jennifer looked around the small Italian restaurant. More than one male diner had his eyes on this stylishly-dressed attractive black woman sitting alone. She hardly noticed them. She had more important things on her mind.

It wasn't the kind of place she cared to be seen in, far less spend the most nerve-racking evening of her life, but Tony Carnegie, private investigator, had called to say he had some good news for her and she desperately needed some.

"Anything to drink while you're waiting, madam?"

"No," she said, dismissing the waiter with a wave of her hand. She glanced at her watch. He was late. A moment later the waiter was on his way back to her table, followed by Tony Carnegie. "Your guest has arrived, madam." He pulled out the chair opposite for Tony to sit on and handed them the menus. Tony smiled warmly at Jennifer.

"You're late."

He grinned. Tony looked confident and, dressed casually, seemed younger. He placed a box file on the table to his right and placed his menu open on top of it.

"I know," he said studying the menu. "Have you decided?"

"Just wine please, I'm not hungry."

"A bottle of dry white please," Tony said to the waiter.

"This isn't a bar, sir, you have to eat..." the waiter held his small writing pad in front of him pointedly. Tony pulled a funny face, Jennifer stifled a smile.

"What do you recommend?"

"Spaghetti?"

"Whatever..." Tony handed him back the menu and the waiter turned to Jennifer.

"Twice," she answered before the question was asked. Then turning to Tony as the waiter walked away, "Now, tell me the news."

"You mean we're not going to eat first?"

"Mr Carnegie, I really didn't come here to socialize."

Tony's smile disappeared. "Fine," he mumbled. He placed his hand on the file and pulled it in front of him. "As I've said, it's good news from your point of view," he looked up from the papers in his hand. "Fitzroy Lucas is no more a criminal than I am, but he's also not a very private dick, as I am," Tony grinned wickedly, expecting at least a smile from Jennifer, but her face remained blank.

"Okay," he continued, "he's given ten women pickney in Birmingham, Manchester and London. A few concentrated in the Lewisham borough. I went to Somerset House, had to go through the registry of all the children born since Fitzroy was fourteen. His name crops up a dozen times."

Jennifer was stunned. She had suspected at least five women, but ten, and twelve children!

Tony turned over another few pages in the file. "Young Mr Lucas is one of Britain's most wanted men. The CSA are after him, he owes them £300,000 in unpaid child maintenance!" He laughed. "The guy's a rude bwoy...a ladies man, but the only crime he's guilty of is smoking weed and I'm sure you already knew that."

Jennifer was still reeling from the revelations. "Mr Carnegie, how can a man just walk out on his children without any guilt? Answer that. Okay, I agree about safe sex, but it's both person's responsibility and thereafter also. If you think you're responsible enough to have sex, then you should be equally responsible for the consequences.""

Tony shrugged. "Don't look at me. I'm not my brothas' keeper."

Jennifer turned to his report and muttered, "I could have done better myself." She pushed the file away from her. "I should get my money back."

"You haven't paid me yet."

Good judgment on my part, she thought shrewdly. Tony Carnegie was just another arrogant cock sure man. Her first instincts were always right but why was it she never followed them?

The waiter appeared, carrying two steaming bowls of spaghetti on a tray. Jennifer felt her stomach juices rising.

"Pepper? Parmesan?" the waiter was asking.

Jennifer leaned across the table and told Tony very softly, "I'm sure you know what you're doing, you're probably very good at your job, but this time you just haven't helped."

"It wouldn't be the first time," Tony requested more parmesan over his spaghetti. Jennifer sipped her wine, watching as he chopped up his spaghetti with a knife.

"My sister is everything to me. I have to save her."

Tony looked up from the bowl he was twirling his fork around in. "We should all learn by making our own mistakes, my mum always said."

Donna had said exactly the same thing. Maybe they were right. Tony looked up from the last mouthful and raised his eyebrows at Jennifer's untouched bowl of spaghetti.

"You're not eating that?"

"I said I wasn't hungry."

"Can I have it?"

Jennifer couldn't get mad at him even if she wanted to. There was something touching about the way he asked.

"Help yourself," she slid her bowl across to him. She watched as he gave the spaghetti the sauce treatment. He wound some spaghetti onto his fork and shoved it into his mouth. There was a certain intimacy in having your food eaten by someone else, Jennifer felt. It took her back to the first time she had been in Paul's apartment. He had fed her from his own plate then. Tony was cute, almost little boy cute, unlike Paul's manly look. And Tony didn't put on airs and graces to impress. With him what you saw was what you got.

After spending a couple of depressing hours alone in a bar, Jennifer was not looking forward to spending yet another solitary weekend alone with her gloomy thoughts. When she stepped through the front door, however, she was greeted by the smell of a spicy hot Indian takeaway and a jungle track on the living room stereo. Donna was home again. Walking wearily into the hallway she half-expected to see Fitzroy sprawled on her sofa. He wasn't.

"Jen!" Donna rushed at her from the kitchen, her braids flying behind her and greeted Jennifer with a hug and a peck on her cheek, like a long lost friend.

"You're back home then?"

"For good this time. Can't get rid of me that easily." Donna headed back to the kitchen. "Did you miss me?"

Jennifer followed. "If you gave me a chance to, I might have."

The washing machine was on and a holdall on the floor contained more of Donna's dirty clothes.

Jennifer put the kettle on. "So what happened to what's his name?"

"It's finished innit," she shrugged. "Expected me to be his personal slave...tidying up, washing his briefs, dragging bags down to the laundry...I had enough. No way, no more."

Jennifer couldn't suppress the smile. "So you're completely finished?"

"Yeah man," she said as she ate her curry. "Been living on junk for months. I need some home cooking."

Jennifer had to laugh. "That's good news, D." The saying 'learn by your own mistakes' came to mind again. Tony Carnegie's investigations had been meaningless after all. All it had taken to cure Donna of her infatuation was for her to spend more time with Fitzroy, not less as Jennifer had believed.

Donna winked at her sister. "Thought you'd be pleased. An' something else..." she pulled a sheet of paper out of her back pocket and waved it above her head. She couldn't control her proud smile as she handed the certificate to her sister.

"You passed your test! Congratulations. First time as well."

"Yeah man. Fitzroy was good for summink after all... Shanika's coming round later, we're gonna celebrate."

"You're going out tonight?"

"Yeah probably only local though." Donna popped a spoonful of rice in her mouth.

Jennifer grimaced. She needed to tell Donna everything tonight before she lost her nerve. The kettle clicked off behind her and she turned to the cupboard to get a mug for her coffee. "Any chance you could stay in tonight?"

"You did miss me," Donna giggled.

If it meant she stayed in... "Yes, I missed you."

"I ain't seen much a Shan lately, y'know."

"I know, but you haven't seen much of me either," Jennifer sipped at her coffee. "It's just that there's uhmm...something I've got to tell you as well."

"You split up with that lawyer geezer, I know."

"How did you know?"

"Saw Karen in Lewisham."

Jennifer's heart leapt into her throat. "Did Karen say anything else?"

"Like what?"

"Well...uhmmm...there are going to be a few changes around

here."

"Oh yeah?"

Jennifer clasped her hands around her mug on the dining table in front of her. She mumbled, "I'm pregnant."

"What Jen?" Donna leant forward. She hadn't caught the important word.

Jennifer made her eyes meet her sister's just long enough to repeat herself. "I'm going to have a baby."

Donna jumped up. "You?! Whose baby? I know you gotta be adopting."

Admitting this to her little sister was the biggest hurdle. Shame engulfed Jennifer, unlike any shame she had ever felt.

Seeing her sister's reaction Donna sat down again, her eyes becoming serious. "You're pregnant, Sis?" she asked gently.

Jennifer nodded. There was a few seconds of silence as it sank in.

"Backside!" The laughter escaped unexpected and Donna didn't try to stop it. She slapped the table, rocking back and forth in mirth. "Wait 'til I tell Shanika bwoy, you're lucky I'm not even talking to Fitzroy, he'd never let it go."

Jennifer was shaking her head. "I'm sorry, D..."

"What you sorry for? I'm not having the pickney, you are! God, d'you realize what that means?"

Jennifer looked up at her sister. She thought she could guess what was coming. Donna was going to say, that her sister was going to be a baby mother.

"I'm going to be an auntie, 'bout time too." Donna continued eating. "Mum's going to freak, probably come flying back to England to look for her grandkid."

Don't. Jennifer didn't need to be reminded that she had yet to face her parents when she would have to admit that every lesson they'd ever taught her... *Oh, the shame of it!*

"The kid can have my room. I'll sleep in the living room."

"D how do you really feel about it?"

Donna tilted her head to the side. "Bwoy Sis," she shook her head, "what can I say, man? You messed up big time. Big career woman like you, couldn't even find a decent man to have your kids with — times are hard, guy." A cheeky grin spread across her face. "Remember how you used to say I should find a man like Paul?" Donna laughed again, slapping the table.

Jennifer lowered her head.

"Jen, man, it's tough...all right it's happened. You thought about abortion?"

"Too late. Baby's due in February."

Donna shook her head again and sucked air through her teeth. "When you mess up you mess up big!" She took her plate to the sink and ran hot water onto it.

Jennifer began to sob.

Donna dropped what she was doing and and rushed to her sister's side.

"Jen, it's not that bad. It's not like you're a kid. You're an independent woman. Okay, you ain't got a man, but you've got me." She punched Jennifer's shoulder playfully. "I'll be Daddy, yeah? Since I wear the trousers in this house anyway."

Jennifer smiled despite her feelings. Donna poked her stomach gently. "I thought that was just wind," she said.

They laughed together. Standing in the middle of the kitchen, the two women hugged each other tight.

PART TWO

FIVE

If yuh 'llow nanny goat fe tie up eena yuh field, mek up yuh mine fe yuh field get nyam dung.

I knew I was going into labour.
Knew it.
Didn't think it. Didn't wonder if this was it. I, Jennifer Edwards knew.
Four weeks early, in court, in the middle of the biggest case of my career. I felt a contraction that was nothing like the ones I had been having for the past week. It gripped me around my middle like a vice, taking my breath away for the few seconds that it lasted. Like a fool I thought it was better to conduct myself in a professional manner and I carried on summing up the evidence against my client.

It was at this point that my waters broke. I doubled over in pain. It was obvious to everyone what was happening. The court was immediately adjourned, an ambulance called and I was dispatched to a couch in the judge's chambers.

The embarrassment and humiliation of it all. Didn't these things usually happen in the middle of the night? I'd spent months building up this case. Had witnesses and a detective waiting to give evidence and I go into labour!

Strange men were asking what they could get me. Water? Tea? Whisky? All I really wanted was to go home and sleep. Oh why did I have to be a woman? Why did I have to get pregnant? And why hadn't I listened when everyone had warned me about cutting it fine?

I got someone to call Donna, who had agreed delightedly to be my birthing partner. Fortunately she was at home studying and knew the drill off by heart. She got to the hospital before I did.

I was shaking uncontrollably by the time I got into the ambulance. Suddenly I was scared. I felt so alone. Alone and in pain. The medic who accompanied me in the back of the ambulance turned around and said,

"You'll be all right love, got hours to go yet."

Thank you very much. I grinned through gritted teeth. Hours more of pain and frustration and being so damned out of control. I could feel the child aching and dancing in my belly.

Unfortunately the ambulance driver was right.

Donna was at the hospital waiting for me. I'd never been so happy to see anyone in my whole life. By the time Donna had helped me to wash and change into night wear, the midwives had wired me up to the monitor, the labour was in full swing. The baby was on its way.

I had been through this moment a hundred times in my mind. I had imagined the pains and the anxiety, but never really felt them.

I found myself thinking of the good times I'd had with past boyfriends. Those who I could, perhaps should, have had kids with. Would I be here by myself if I had got it together with one of them?

I remember saying to the midwife, "I think I've made a terrible mistake." Hours later, drowsy under the influence of pethidine, I was still repeating the same thing as an army of doctors, nurses and midwives examined between my legs. Neither they nor the drugs could stifle the wave after wave of unbearable pain. Donna simply stared at me, punctuating my every scream with, "Oh Gawd. Thanks Jen, you've put me off getting pregnant for life, guy. I'm never going t'rough dis."

I could have slapped her, but I was too busy panting, gritting my teeth and pleading, "It hurts, get this thing out of me!!!" It was unbearable. How women go through this again and again I'll never know. All those months of ante natal clinic appointments and literature should have prepared me for this, but no. Somehow they managed to miss out the words, extreme and pain. The pain was in my back, in my sides, in my abdomen, in my chest for Christ's sake. I hollered, and breathed. Breathed just like the midwife told me to.

From the time I realized I was going to have to keep this baby I had planned a natural birth. No painkillers, I wanted to be able to walk about, crouch, stand, listen to my favourite music, 'Computer Love' by Zapp. How comforting was fiction. Donna had remembered the music but I couldn't hear it. Forget the alternative childbirth, I just wanted to lie there and push. I couldn't believe that just lying there was as painful as this. At one stage I held my breath to see if it would take the pain away but that just gave me a headache.

I wondered what Paul was doing now, probably sipping iced tea on a balcony overlooking the beach with his bitch rubbing sun block into his shoulders. Bastard! Despite the pain and the way I felt about him I found myself screaming out his name.

"Who is Paul dear? Your husband? Do you have a number, I could call him for you?"

"Nooo!!!" I screamed, sounding just like the possessed girl in 'The Exorcist'.

The midwife patted my hand and turned to Donna, "This is quite normal. You should hear some of the things I get called. Remember your breathing, Jennifer, nice and easy..."

Thank you, ma'am. I've been breathing all my life and this baby isn't changing anything.

By three o'clock that afternoon, the contractions went from every ten minutes to every two minutes. I was sick until I didn't have any sick left. I pushed when I was told to. Pushed until it felt as though a team of horses was dragging my vagina inside out.

Disjointed voices floated around the room. "I can see his head," Donna screamed. *His head! How did she know what sex it was?*

"One more push and we'll have his shoulders," a doctor ordered.

"Nearly there, it's coming keep pushing."

It's coming and I'm splitting in half. It felt as though a watermelon was being forced out of me. A hole that had had trouble accepting a penis was now expected to open its doors to a baby's head. I noticed the red weals on Donna's forearms, recognized each digit of my fingers. Finally, the head was within reach and the midwife brought the child into the world...

"It's a boy!" The doctor held up a tiny, wailing creature covered in white slime.

"A boy, Jen!" Donna kissed my cheek. "My nephew. Wicked!"

I closed my eyes, I didn't want to look, I was exhausted. A moment later I felt a hot, slippery body on my bare stomach and, I swear, I screamed. My eyes flew open and for a split second I saw Paul's face on that baby's head. My nightmare became reality. I blinked and felt a sigh of relief deep down within me. He was all right...he had been born with all his little fingers and tiny toes...both his eyes and ears and legs and arms. I swear, I felt like I wanted a tall glass of whisky, straight, no chaser.

Donna was the first to hold him after they'd cut the cord and cleaned him up. When she offered him to me I pretended to be too tired. Just when I thought it was all over, I felt another contraction. "Nurse, it's starting again! Oh God, not twins."

The midwife came to my side. "It's the afterbirth dear. One final push and it'll all be over."

The worst was over but, still, I had to control the urge not to strangle the cause of all my pain when he was placed on my chest to suckle my sore nipple. He sucked so hard I was sure it would come off in his mouth. But my *milk wasn't coming and the baby began to scream, and kept screaming. I saw the rest of my life dissolve into one long high-pitched scream and I burst into tears.*

The hospital staff were all sweet and condescending over the next two days. I was patronized by midwives telling me what a good little mother I was going to be, and that child birth had its teething problems...

I was never alone. Doctors checked up on me several times a day, paediatricians checked on the baby and an endless flow of medical students studied me as though I was part of a biology lesson. And as well as the other new mothers in the adjoining beds, I had to share the ward with their families and friends who came to visit. Every time I tried to get a bit of privacy from the lovey dovey mothers and fathers and doting grandparents by pulling the curtain around my bed and putting my headphones on, a member of staff would come along and whip the curtains back. "Sorry it's not allowed unless you're actually indisposed."

Motherhood! From where I was lying, it seemed like a farce. Wasn't I supposed to be bonding with this infant because of all we had been through together? But I couldn't bring myself to love him. I had no feelings for him other than that he had come to ruin my life and the more I thought about it the more determined I was that he wasn't going to succeed.

The next day Jennifer's milk came in full force. The baby was still having trouble sucking, and the doctors advised her to stay in for a couple of days until he was settled, they even coerced her into trying him on the breast again, despite the pain. By now Jennifer's breasts were so full that between feeds she would have to go into the bathroom and squeeze them to let the milk go. Sucking, she discovered, seemed to only produce more.

Jennifer felt numb.

She shared a ward with four other women and so far she'd kept to herself, just sitting on the sidelines listening. Josey, a bleach blonde, wild haired white woman was a chain smoker and kept having to "pop out for a fag." Her baby had been born premature and spent most of its time in an incubator. Her husband was a bricklayer, who had a habit of coming to visit with his jeans hanging halfway down his backside and his belly hanging out from the bottom of his jumper.

Janine was a small cockney brunette, at fourteen years of age a mere infant herself. She was still pregnant and was to be induced any day now. Not that she could possibly understand. Janine spent most of her time walking around with her headphones on and gazing out of the windows. She never had any visitors.

Maureen was about the same age as Jennifer. A nervous looking black woman who was always gazing adoringly at her baby girl. She had plenty of visitors but not the baby's father.

Lorraine was middle-class, white, married. Her husband always wore a suit no matter what time of day he visited. She'd had a caeserian section and walked as though she had a disability. She didn't talk much to the others. She bottle-fed her son and dressed him in the same colour clothes she wore every day. Unlike the others Lorraine didn't walk around in her nightie, but went to the trouble of getting dressed every day, in clothes that still looked like maternity wear.

Jennifer got up to make herself a cup of tea from the tiny kitchen along the corridor. She carried the coffee into the day room where three of the women from her ward sat. Josey was smoking as usual, Janine was nodding to her headphones, and Maureen was knitting a baby sized cardigan.

"Hiya," Josey raised her cigarette. "Come and join us, love. Good to see ya up an' about."

Jennifer smiled uneasily and took a seat as far away from Josey as she could without being rude.

Maureen looked up from her knitting. "Your sister coming back today?"

They had obviously picked up bits of information about Jennifer by eavesdropping as she had. "Yes, I expect so."

"It's good that she comes isn't it?" Maureen leaned forward whispering. "Janine doesn't get any visitors, parents threw her out and boyfriend didn't want to know."

Jennifer nodded. She didn't want to discuss her business with these people, it was enough that she had to share a ward with them.

"You not married then?" Josey asked, placing her cigarette into the clay ashtray on the worn-out surface of the small wooden coffee table.

"No."

"Boyfriend?" Maureen leaned in.

"No."

"Poor cow," Josey puffed, pulling her mass of bleached hair back off her face.

"Are you married?" Jennifer asked Maureen out of politeness.

"Not yet, my boyfriend's overseas. Training in Germany for the T.A."

"The T.A.?"

"You know, the territorial army. We'll get married when he gets back."

Josey rolled her eyes, showing Jennifer that she didn't believe a word of it. Janine took her headphones off and studied Jennifer sceptically.

Jennifer gave her a friendly smile. "Hi. I'm Jennifer."

"Awright. You don't look the type to not be married, don't sound like it neither."

"Well," Jennifer shrugged, "nobody's infallible."

"Hey?"

"Everyone can make mistakes."

"Oh."

The day room door swung open. Jennifer turned to see the midwife who staffed their ward. She carried a cup of hot beverage and made her way to the only vacant chair in their circle. One of those ageless black women, there were few signs of the passing years on her Caribbean face. She was tall and slim and her attitude alone betrayed the fact that she was in her mid-forties. "Good afternoon ladies."

They each greeted her in their own ways.

"Just taking a well-deserved break. You lot better mek de most ah your free time," she advised.

"I know all about not 'aving free time, I got three o' the bleeders already," Josey puffed.

Jennifer winced at how crude the woman was and wondered at her bringing children up to be just like her. She shuddered.

"So yuh becoming acquainted?"

"Kind of," Maureen chirped in, "Jennifer just joined us."

"How are you Jennifer?" the nurse asked.

Jennifer got the feeling that the question was asked just for the sake of it and not because the woman really wanted to know. "Tired, if you must know."

The nurse chuckled. "What me tell yuh? You will haffe get use to it cah it ah go be a long time before you get to sleep when you feel like it."

"Wha' d'you do for a livin', Jen?" Janine asked.

"I'm a barrister," Jennifer replied proudly.

Janine's mouth hung open.

Josey stubbed her cigarette out. "A barrister! What, in all dem gowns and wigs an' stuff?" She fished another cigarette out of the packet.

"Yes."

"That's like a dressed-up lawyer innit?"

"I suppose so... Do you work?"

"Did. Used to do night shifts at the local cabbies."

Jennifer couldn't think of anything encouraging to say about that. "Right..."

The nurse sat on the edge of her chair and turned her stern face towards Jennifer. "How a woman like you manage to end up pregnant and alone?"

"The usual way — sex," Jennifer said flippantly. All the other women, except the nurse, laughed.

"Don't ask me that, I was at school see," said Janine, before waiting to find out if she was going to be asked. "Got pregnant on my first time...well, unless you count those times in the back of the car, or under the stairs..." she giggled, "...babysitting at my mum's friend's house...kissing, sucking, biting," her eyes had a far away look and for a moment Jennifer thought she saw Donna's face in Janine's.

"...Let him in just a little, just the tip, but not all the way, that's what he said. Said he was just going to come in a tiny bit, but not all the way, but before I knew it he was inside, the whole of him! Before I knew it he'd come hadn't he?"

"Where's he now?" Josey asked her.

"Who?"

"The kid's father?"

"Gone off, couldn't take it when I told him..."

"Off where?" Maureen sounded more concerned than Janine was herself.

"Fuck knows," she joined her hands together like a bird, "Evaporated into thin air."

"Wass his name? I might know him," Josey dusted ash off her cheap kimono.

"Can't remember."

"Oh come on, don't be a spoilsport, we're all in the same paddling boat, travelling down the same river..."

"He was a black guy, all right? He din't wanna know..."

Josey rolled her eyes again. "White guys are just the same as black guys when it comes to bed, love."

The black nurse kissed her teeth. "See where all your lust and feelings get you? Is not me having to hide away, too ashamed to face people," she shook her head. "Why couldn't you have waited for someone nice and respectable to come along. A real man who wasn't just looking for a bed companion."

"It weren't like that...I loved him."

"Love! If he loved you, he'd have married you...what you did was a sin. You're not'n but a baby yuhself."

"Love isn't a sin, it's the most religious act there is," Maureen put her knitting aside and decided to stand up for Janine.

"Love is not an act, it's an emotion, and sex is a sin in my church. It's a sin...what she called love was nothing but lust, no matter how ole you are. Unless of course you're married, and even then yuh only supposed to do it to start a family, it's a sin to do it fe fun."

Josey glared out of the corner of her eye at the midwife. "I take it you're a virgin then."

"I tek it yuh should mine yuh own bizness."

Maureen cleared her throat, cutting through the sudden tension in the air. "I hate this being alone, don't you?" she said to Jennifer.

"I'm not really alone. I live with my sister."

"Yes, but your sister doesn't share your bed or wrap her arms around you and make love to you when you're feeling the need."

Jennifer hid her eyes behind her cold cup of coffee as she took a sip.

"When I get outta 'ere I'm going back to school," Janine boasted.

"And who will look after your baby?" Jennifer asked.

"I'm not keeping it. Din't you know? I thought that news would 'ave got round."

The midwife took it upon herself to explain Janine's situation. "Janine was going to have an abortion, until the boyfriend's mother said she couldn't let her kill her grandchild. Told her to go ahead an have it an she would tek care ah it."

Janine interrupted. "Only they move away, don't they? No forwarding address. By then it's too late to get the abortion an' so I went for the next option, adoption. Abortion, adoption, sounds the same dun it?"

Jennifer felt a tinge of empathy with the girl. Their experiences were quite similar in a funny sort of way. They had both made mistakes, but at least she had Donna to lean on. Janine didn't have anyone.

"I've decided to have my tubes tied," Josey lay her head back in the huge worn armchair, the cloud of blond hairs falling over the back. "Jus' gotta get Steve to agree."

"Three children already and you're going home with a fourth, how can you stay so calm? I'm tearing my hair out trying to figure out how I'm going to manage with one," Jennifer marvelled.

Josey's laugh bordered on a smoker's cough. "I'm calm 'cause I have to be. What's done is done."

"I'll be all right when my Geoffrey gets home. We're going to have a big church wedding. He called yesterday, you know, couldn't talk for long but he says he's written to me, I should get it soon."

"How long has he been away?" Jennifer almost envied Maureen. Her man so many miles away and phoning to remind her how much he loves her. *Damn Paul Harvey!*

"Two months, due back any day now."

The nurse stood up, regarded Maureen with a shake of her head and a look of sympathy. "Right ladies, doan feget yuh have kids out deh." She left them to go back to work.

"She's got a problem that one. Her an' her Christianity. Needs a good seeing to more like it," Josey laughed again and this time she coughed something up from deep down in her throat.

Janine stood up and stretched.

"Can't wait to get rid o' this lump."

Jennifer smiled to herself as she stood to go back to the ward. The lump, that's just what she'd called hers.

I'd given Donna a list of things to bring for me and when she struggled in carrying my small suitcase, I almost laughed.

"Was there really that much on the list?"

"Your portable telly, your laptop computer, hairdryer, curling tongs and make-up. More baby clothes, nappies, nighties, and clothes so that you don't have to go around in your nightie all day."

"Did you remember my mail and that casebook...?"

"Yes Sis, I ticked it all off. There's even some chicken and rice and peas in there from Aunt Iris." Donna went over to the crib and looked down at our new relative. She took her coat off and hung it over the back of the chair by the bed. *"Why's he always sleeping?"*

"Because he spends the whole night making sure that I don't get any sleep."

"Really," she grinned. *"Can't wait to get him home."*

Home. I had almost forgotten that I had one. Donna lifted up the baby and peeled back the shawl he was wrapped in. Why was it that I was the only one who could resist the urge to pick him up? Why? I didn't want him to be woken up because as soon as he started to cry they would immediately hand him over to me. Donna stayed an hour before getting up and embracing me and promising to come back tomorrow. I picked up my laptop after she left and started writing. There were so many feelings I needed to get out of my system. I needed someone to complain to and my good old Powerbook was the perfect listener. And when I started 'talking' I didn't stop until I had relived the embarrassment of going into labour in the middle of a courtroom and my murderous emotions towards Paul Harvey as I screamed with pain in that delivery room.

An hour later I realized the lights were going out and our evangelical midwife was doing her rounds again checking up on our repentance. She stopped by my bed and pulled back the blanket covering my baby's head. "He'll get too hot yuh know. It's not good fe dem skin."

"He sleeps longer covered up."

She raised her eyebrows at the computer on my lap. "Working already? You can't wait 'til you get home?"

I closed the laptop. "I made a promise to myself, Mrs Thompson, that I wouldn't let a baby disrupt my life. I'm a professional."

"You may have made that promise but did your baby?"

I squared my shoulders, "Look, I didn't plan this baby, but even when I found out I never, in my wildest dreams, imagined that I would be a single mother. How do you think I felt when I told my fiancé I was going to have his baby and all he could say was, 'sorry'? Well I'm sorry too, but I can't be expected to give up everything in order to bring up a child on my own. My life is too important to me to let it come second to anyone."

There was fire in her eyes. All of a sudden I was terrified. "Women like you mek me sick," the nurse lowered her voice so that only I could hear. "You're in a position to give your baby everyt'ing he needs in dis world. So what if he doesn't have a father? You should still be strong and do it all on your own...if he doesn't want to know, then fine. Look at all these other women...they really got sup'm to moan about...they've got nothing to hang on to. Even Maureen who goes on about her man comin' back, maybe he will one day but she doesn't know where he is or when she'll see 'im again. And he's the only thing she's hanging on to." Her hands clenched into angry fists. "I want to tek your world and shake it. You don't know is better yuh lose yuh time than yuh character?" she said through clenched teeth, "Put yourself in their place — no money, no house of their own, and no man."

The other women were coming back in from the day room. "Why don't you just go ahead and sign the adoption papers?" Janine was saying to Maureen as they walked back to their beds.

"No I couldn't do that...I could never..."

"Auntie giving ya a lecture, is she, Jen?" Josey bounced in, the scent of cigarette smoke trailing her.

I smiled at her humour. Mrs Thompson shot me a look that wiped it off my face.

"Let me tell you somet'ing," she scanned all of us. "You t'ink dat you're the first people to have gone t'rough dis...you all t'ink dat your private hell is de worse...but believe me, I seen hundreds of gal like yuhself in dis situation. You t'ink t'ings so bad, because you've given birt' to a chile and your man's not around, the faada's disappeared..."

Maureen clung to the neck of her dressing gown as if protecting her chest. Josey just rolled her eyes. She had a man around even if he was a no good layabout.

Mrs Thompson continued. "Well, imagine if it had been twins, or worse, triplets? How would you have coped then?" I looked around at the other women and we all had the same expression on our faces, what the hell was she talking about?

Mrs Thompson walked away from my bed to the window that covered one whole wall from the waist upwards. "I been t'rough the same t'ing meself," the nurse continued. "Believe me..."

We must have all gasped at the same time, even Lorraine who pretended to be reading her book suddenly looked up aghast. Mrs Thompson looked and talked like a spinster who despised younger women still able to have children when opportunity had long past her.

There were many rumours about her background. One had claimed that she had once been in love herself, long ago, but had been abandoned at the altar by her betrothed and that since then she had remained a spinster. Another was that the guy she loved and was about to marry had been killed in an accident and since then her heart had refused every other possible suitor. No one knew for sure whether there was any truth in the rumours, only that they had been passed on from one group of women in the ward to the next.

"...Yes, I been t'rough the same t'ing," she continued, gazing absentmindedly out of the window, "it was many years ago. When I see all you women going t'rough the same t'ing, my mine can't help remembering. Yes, I had a man once!" she almost shouted. She looked at each of us accusingly before turning back to the window.

"He was a musician, a very good saxophonist...a jazz musician. Travel de world wid dat saxophone, I even went wid him once or twice...to Paris, to Amsterdam, Copenhagen. It was wonderful. I loved him. He could lighten up my day wid a flash of his eyes and his smile never cease to warm my heart and, when he laughed..." she smiled and we got a glimpse of what she must have looked like as a twenty year old. "...the angels blew their trumpets in praise. He could make a rainy day sunny and he could make a sunny day *warm... When I was with him, I had no worries, everyt'ing was just perfect. I was as happy as I could be and he was as gentle as de summer breeze. And when he had to go away to play wid his band, wherever it was, he would always call me at night to tell me how much he was missing me."*

We were all sitting on our beds in hushed silence like attentive primary school children at story time.

"...And before long I was pregnant," Nurse Thompson sniffed. *"...I couldn't help it, this was the man I wanted in my life and I knew that he was going to tek care of my baby. He watched my stomach get bigger and bigger, day by day and made me promise many times over that if anyt'ing happened to him I would tek care of his baby. Ah course, I didn't want him to speak like dat. Not'n was going to 'appen to him and we were going to bring up baby together, that I was sure of."* She looked over at Maureen who held her eyes for a few seconds before breaking the gaze.

"I even got ready to marry him. He had insisted that we should do things properly and I had chosen a white dress and was getting everyt'ing prepared. The day before the wedding we had arranged to meet at our favourite spot, under a large blossoming tree by de stream. But he didn't show up. I tried to call him all day, and the next day, but it was like he had vanished completely..."

By now tears were streaming down Nurse Thompson's face. I wanted to go to her, to put my arms around her, but at the same time I didn't want her to stop talking. I wanted to hear the rest of the story.

"...A week later, my son was born. Even when I lay there in the maternity ward, just like you are now, I hoped, expected that he would show up. I had left messages for him everywhere I could think of and I prayed that he would get one of dem. Even if he didn't, he knew I was due, he had no excuse. Okay, he missed the wedding, but how could he miss the birth of our child which he had often talked about being present at. Well, I didn't hear a word from him an' you know how not'n soon stretches into not'n. By the time I accepted that he wasn't going to ever show up, my son was already on the way." She produced a tissue from her pocket and mopped tears from her brown cheeks.

"I bought myself a wedding ring and went away for a few weeks to give birth to my baby. When I returned I told everyone my husband had drowned on our honeymoon. I became a widow, so dat people in the church wouldn't have to keep asking me questions as to where the child's faada was. You see, it was different back then. In those days, you could bring shame on top of the whole family by giving birth out ah wedlock. It's different nowadays. Some of you women even get praise, but not from me, be sure ah dat... Because I've paid for my hot moment of passion many times over. All that's left for me to

do now is to work hard and look after my child as best as I can. That's what you ladies should be doing." The hard opinionated side to her personality returned. *"You all fill in yuh breakfast menus yet?"*

Speechless, we simply nodded. "Good, You know where I am if you want me." She marched out of the ward taking deep breaths and straightening her starched uniform as she went.

How can life be so unfair? If men could see the devastation they left in women's lives when they betrayed them, wouldn't they become more responsible? If it were their lives that were turned upside down, inside out, never to be the same again, wouldn't they all become celibate? Maybe not. The only guaranteed way to get a baby father to understand the pain of a woman is to hang him upside down by the balls.

I lay there the next morning listening to our silence. The baby on my chest, lulled to sleep by my heartbeat, blew a saliva bubble. I rose slowly and placed him back in his crib. I still haven't felt this bond that I'm supposed to. And I'm hardly likely to, because every time I look at him I see his father and all the other men who have ruined women's lives.

The other sounds of the hospital floated in to me, breakfast being served, the shifts changing over and medication being given out.

Maureen was sitting on her bed folding a letter.

"From your boyfriend?"

She looked up. "Uh...yes," she quickly unfolded it and handed it to me.

I put a hand up to stop her. "Oh no, I didn't mean to be nosey."

"No that's okay I'd like you to read it." I took the letter from her outstretched hand. *"He'll be home in a week, says I might as well go home and wait for him."*

I scanned the letter not really reading it. "That's great." I felt pity for this woman with her delusions. She still couldn't believe that her man didn't feel the same way about their child as she did.

"I'm leaving today." She was glowing, but it seemed like a mask covering a sadness. I wanted to change the subject, I wasn't too good at acting. I looked over at the bed opposite mine. *"Where's Janine?"*

"Her labour started an hour ago. They wheeled her away to theatre. Poor kid. She's going to go through all that pain and not even get to see or hold her baby."

I wouldn't see Janine again. They put her on a ward with no babies and no pregnant women. I lay on the bed, all my dreams and hopes had burst like bubbles in front of my eyes. Where were my dreams of walking down the Champs-Elysee with a panther by my side, just as Josephine Baker had done and of flying my own private jet across the ocean? The longer I stayed in the maternity ward, the more I was reminded that I was nothing more than a baby mother. For my sanity's sake, I had to get out.

The next day, without warning, Elaine, Karen and Beverly strolled into the maternity ward, eager to give the new baby the once over. Jennifer put her laptop down when she saw them and they each showered her with hugs and congratulations.

Karen peered into the crib. "Bwoy 'im small, eeh?" She shrugged off her coat, revealing her tiny belted waist and pulled up a seat. Jennifer looked on enviously, she hadn't been able to wear a belt for months. Karen's hair had also recently been seen to by a hairdresser and she wore it short with a feathered cut. One of the first things Jennifer promised to treat herself to when she got out of the hospital was an appointment at the hairdressers to take the extensions out of her hair.

Beverly, still big, maybe bigger than ever, was already lifting him out of the crib. "How much did he weigh?" she said, smiling down at him.

Why do people always ask that? Jennifer wondered. "Seven pounds, four ounces." *How come when Beverly picks him up his head and arms don't flop the way they do when I pick him up?*

"My two both weighed nearly nine pounds," Karen quipped, "but then they were both a week late too."

"You know why that happened Karen?" Elaine asked taking off her scarf. She had a dark red love bite on her neck which she had obviously forgotten about. "Because your baby heard you cussing and decided to stay in a while longer to buil' itself up first. Nuh true?"

"Don't budda mek me start 'pon you an' dat excuse for a man you 'ave deh," Karen retorted. 'Cause if he was any kinda man he woulda had you knocked-up by now."

"Oooh," Beverly chimed, "you gonna let her get away with that?"

Elaine was about to say something when Jennifer cut in. "Ladies please, you're in a maternity ward."

Elaine held her peace. Beverly turned her attentions back to the baby. "He looks nothing like you, Jen. Do ya," she cooed, "look nothing like mummy."

Cheer me up Bev, why don't you. Jennifer sighed, "I know." She moved up on the bed to let Elaine sit down and felt her stitches strain.

She immediately straightened her legs again. Sucker had torn her flesh just coming into this world. "You never met Paul but you see that determined little mouth? It's his."

"Bastard! Never mind Jen, what goes around comes around, he'll find out the hard way."

Jennifer wished she could agree, but in her experience it was always the shits that prospered.

"My Natasha's like that, she has her damned father's eyes. She even gives me his stare when she's upset," Karen shuddered. "Spooky."

"God knows who Jerome looks like. He certainly doesn't look like either of us — his parents." Beverly rocked the baby in her arms, as he started to wriggle. "I sometimes wonder if they mixed the black babies up in the maternity ward just for a laugh."

"I hope my baby looks like Allan, he is just so handsome. The baby's got to have my teeth though 'cause Allan's leave a lot to be desired."

The other three women all stared at Elaine as if waiting for an announcement. "Well, you pregnant?" Karen snapped finally.

"No...not yet but we've decided to try...properly. Now that we're married."

"You've been married nearly six months, what's the hold up?"

Elaine ignored Karen and took the baby's little ski cap off his head instead. His hair was his best feature in Jennifer's opinion.

"You haven't said what you're gonna call him."

Jennifer didn't have a name for him yet and she was in no hurry. Names bred familiarity and she couldn't risk being too attached to him. "I haven't decided yet." Her friends looked at her like she was crazy. "But I'm open to offers."

"You 'ave nine months to mek up yuh mine an' nuh do it yet?"

"You know how it is," she protested, "you don't know if it's going to be a boy or a girl..."

Beverly nodded her head understandingly. "I didn't pick Jerome's name until he was a week old. I had a list of girl and boy names and when I knew it was a boy I just picked one that suited him."

The baby was now in Karen's arms. She sat by the window with him on her lap, his legs curled up towards his stomach and sucking on his fist noiselessly.

"Uh-uh, you know what dat means? Breastfeeding used to make me so horny, I'd have to jump on Charles as soon as I finished feeding."

Jennifer forced a smile, but felt deflated. He needed feeding *again*? Where the hell did he put it all? She preferred to wait until he was actually crying for it, but Karen was already handing him back to her.

Even as the thought of feeding came into her mind Jennifer's breasts filled up with milk. Now she was ready to do almost anything that would get rid of the feeling of carrying around two lumpy rugby balls in her bra.

Her friends stood around the bed engrossed with the process of his feeding. Jennifer ladled one rock hard breast from her white maternity bra and gingerly guided the tender nipple to his gaping mouth just as she'd been shown by the midwife. *Oh God!* It hurt, her toes curled and her buttocks clenched as he sucked his mother's flesh eagerly.

Jennifer assured herself that she was only putting up with this now because she had been told it would stop him being a sickly baby, no colds or sniffles. Apparently breastfeeding was also good for the mother because it helped to contract the womb muscles. She could definitely do with some of that.

"I breast fed Kyle for six weeks and then stopped," Karen offered. "I didn't have time to sit around for hours with my tit stuck in the kid's mouth."

"Exactly," Jennifer agreed. "Every time he wakes up he's hungry."

"That'll settle down," Beverly said. "Don't worry, motherhood has its ups and downs but you deal with it. I'm still breast feeding Jerome, y'know."

They all stared at her horrified. Her son had to be nearly eighteen months old.

Karen slapped her arm, "No!"

"The milk's still coming. It's our bonding time, while he's on the breast I read to him."

"Fuck that!" Karen said, then immediately slapped a hand to her mouth. Other visitors and mothers had turned to stare. Jennifer shared her sentiments exactly. There was absolutely no way that this child was going to have access to her nipples once he had teeth in his head.

Elaine stroked one of his tiny brown hands. "Babies. They're so precious aren't they? I mean, who'd have thought that a simple act like sex could create another human being?"

"It's been happening for millions of years, El," Beverly chuckled.

"I know that, but..." her words died away.

"Anyway," Karen interrupted, "we should have brought some

champagne...wet de baby head, plus welcome Jennifer to the club."

"What club?" Jennifer asked.

There was a mischievous glint in Karen's eyes. "The baby mother club of course."

A shiver ran down Jennifer's back.

SIX
No cuss long man til yuh sure yuh done grow

The day Jennifer was due to leave the hospital it was snowing. Donna had gone out and bought a baby seat and arrived at the hospital in her sister's car on time. Jennifer felt strange carrying her baby to the car park, Donna beside her carrying her personal effects. She felt totally alienated to the woman she had become. Since being in hospital she had put on ten pounds, rather than lost it as she assumed she would once she gave birth, she had a chest which looked like it belonged to a Swedish masseur and she was still having to wear a maternity dress, which only added to her feeling of unease.

The journey home was like a sentimental journey down the streets she used to know in her former life. Looking out the car window she noticed a young woman outside a newsagents, noticed the way she flicked her hair off her face as she chatted to her boyfriend, noticed her youthful body, noticed her taut, size ten denim-covered buttocks, a behind like she used to have before all this. Jennifer was filled with dismay, depression oozed into her mind. She knew what she had to do. She would renew her membership at the health club and start going to Elaine's Afrobics class. She would even invest in an exercise bike to snatch some extra workout time at home. Pretty soon no one would even suspect that she had been pregnant.

To Jennifer's surprise the flat was actually tidy when they got home. Donna had even cleaned the cooker which was a first, mopped and polished the floors and there wasn't a single dirty garment in the wash basket!

Jennifer handed the baby to her sister as they climbed the spiral staircase to the bedrooms. Donna had prepared her room for him. She had put sheets in his cot and hung a musical mobile up over it. Everything was perfect.

"You better put your feet up while Junior's asleep. I'll make you some tea."

It was good to be home again. Her own bed, own food, her own privacy. Jennifer had made up her mind that he could have breast milk but she had no intention of going around with a baby attached to her nipple. She would buy one of those machines to express her milk. That way Donna could feed him sometimes.

After putting the baby down and switching the intercom on, Jennifer went downstairs to the living room for the tea. She sat down on the comfortable Chesterfield sofa, picked a magazine from the stack in the wicker basket and flicked on the state of the art widescreen television. In the middle of her desk was a pile of letters already opened. She looked around the room, considering its potential. She had already set her sights on her home as an office.

"D, this mail, have I seen it all?"

"A couple came this morning, Sis," she called from the kitchen.

She picked the new ones off the top. The first envelope contained a card, the front of which showed a black woman and her husband holding their baby proudly between them. Intrigued, Jennifer opened it.

When Donna brought in the tea, Jennifer was frozen stiff, a ghostly look on her face. "What's up, Sis?"

"He sent a card...with some guilt money inside." Jennifer handed the card to Donna. It was signed by Paul and contained a cheque for two hundred pounds.

"I suppose he feels this makes up for everything..."

"I don't want it." Jennifer was already opening the other envelopes.

"Don't be silly, Sis, it's money and you and Junior deserve it."

"If I accept it he'll think everything's all right, as though I was saying the money makes up for it all."

"But he says here that he'll be sending you a cheque every month."

Jennifer was silent, reading a letter from the office. The case she had had adjourned because of her untimely labour was coming up again in three weeks. She had just three weeks to fill herself in again, contact the witnesses and read up on her briefs.

"Damn, I'm going to have to start working immediately," she said reaching for her laptop.

"Sis, you've just got out of the hospital. Don't you wanna ketch some Zees."

"I'm fine, D, couldn't wait to get back."

"What should I do with the cheque?"

"You have it...or better yet open an account for Junior with it."

Donna shrugged, "Don't stay up for too long y'know. The baby's gonna need you when he wakes up. I read up on it, you're supposed to rest when he does, so that you don't tire yourself out."

Jennifer knew this but she had things that needed doing now. Not later or tomorrow. Now. She carried a file back to her desk and picked up the phone. There were more important things in heaven and earth than her son's sleeping habits. If she and 'Junior' were to agree he would quickly have to become an asset instead of a ball and chain.

Junior, as Donna had named him, woke up an hour later and cried until I was forced to stop work. I'd been so engrossed in my work to even notice that the pizza Donna had laid out for me was now cold. In that hour I had almost begun to feel like my old self again. Not Jennifer Edwards, the single mother, but Jennifer Edwards, barrister.

Donna's fallen in love with the baby and talks to him as though he can understand. Every little noise, she's jumping up to see to him. She doesn't seem to mind carrying him around the house all day whispering to him, cuddling him. She's even taken a week off college to help me look after him. Sis is better than a husband — she's a lot more helpful and she doesn't insist that I have sex with her when I'm exhausted. Like I always say: 'A woman's gotta stay single to survive'. Without a man around I can do as I damn well please.

At bedtime I ran up the iron staircase, while Donna carried Junior. It felt so good, I ran down and then up again like a child. Donna just shook her head. She had no idea what it felt like to be free of that unwanted lump. Thank goodness! Pregnant, I was breathless walking ten feet, climbing stairs had been like climbing Everest. Now that I had been given a list of breathing, pelvic floor muscles and stomach exercises to do, I intended to start them all right away.

"I want to go for a jog," I announced.

"Are you mad? Get upstairs to bed now."

My goodness Donna was starting to sound more and more like the old me. The old me? Had motherhood changed me? I hoped not.

There was no point in Donna sleeping on the living room sofa, so that night she shared her old bedroom with Junior. But as soon as he needed feed-

ing she brought him in to me. It didn't take long for me to fall back asleep with him sucking on my breast. Roll on tomorrow.

The next day the three of us went out. Junior was now nine days old and I badly needed to get out and about. Top of my list was the breast pump, then to the town hall to register my son. The trouble is he still didn't have a name. Donna and I deliberated and decided to carry on using Junior, we could always change it by deed poll later. Of course I called him Edwards, he was definitely not having 'Bastard' as his surname like his father.

Donna had started carrying Junior in a baby pouch. I had told her that I couldn't manage that much weight putting a strain on my back. The truth was I wasn't ready to be seen in public with a baby and no husband.

On the way into Lewisham shopping centre two handsome young men nearer Donna's age than mine grinned at us. Donna ignored them and walked on, but I was stupid enough to turn and give them an inviting smile. It was the first time a man had looked at me in that way in months.

"You have a nice backside there, ya know!" one of them shouted after me and then I heard their laughter.

Yes, I told myself. I have got a nice backside. It's for sure you'll never see it though. Peasants!

The shopping centre was overflowing with women and their new babies. In Mothercare we bought Junior some proper baby boys clothes to make a change from all the yellow unisex babygrows he had. Donna was carrying on like a kid in a sweet shop.

"Jen, look at this," Donna held up a navy blue corduroy suit with matching hat. "We've just gotta get one...Sis, you see these?" It was a pair of lemon bootees with bows. "Junior needs some, can't be taking him out in socks all the time. An' we'll have to get him a christening outfit soon. Innit Jay Jay?" she warbled at the baby. "Does Junior want some stush christening outfit...?"

We put them in the basket anyway while I looked for practical things to make my job as a mother as effortless as possible. A baby rocker, breast pump, feeding bottles and electric steriliser, breast pads to stop the infernal milk stains on my clothes. Bibs, disposable nappies and dummies/soothers to shut him up. A couple of maternity bras.

Junior soon started to whinge, so we headed for home. There was absolutely no way I was going to breastfeed in public.

On the way I picked up a copy of Essence. The magazine is just made for me, written by professional women for professional women. Women who have the same tastes in clothes, hairstyles, careers. But what do I find? Page 50 was a true life story about a woman reporter who got pregnant on holiday. The father-to-be wanted her, but thought neither of them was ready for *a kid. She didn't feel ready either but against all odds decided to keep her baby and was telling the world that it was the best decision she ever made. How could having an unexpected baby be the best decision a dedicated career woman could make? I didn't understand. Why didn't I feel like her?*

Later that day I started to take the plaits out of my hair. I'd had them in for four months and my hair had grown thick and long. My hairdresser appointment was for the next day, until then I wouldn't start to feel like myself again. I missed the hairdresser's. Missed the people, the gossip. The proprietors of Hair Shack in Camberwell were more like old friends and I always received a warm welcome, good advice and a delicious cup of coffee. Maybe then I'll start to feel more like the old Jennifer Edwards.

After two weeks of working from home and adjusting to the life of a housewife/mother Jennifer was becoming restless for the outside world again. The first week had seen people coming and going, visitors asking stupid questions about the labour and the weight of the baby. She hadn't realized how tired she was until Junior stopped sleeping through the day as well as the night. Cooked meals had become a thing of the past and Jennifer survived on takeaways unless Donna was around.

Hiring a nanny became a priority. There was no way she could work from home, and she needed to get back to work as soon as possible. She needed someone who was not overly expensive and didn't mind doing housekeeping as well. Qualified nannies only need apply.

Jennifer interviewed the candidates over the next two days, with Donna at her side for a second opinion.

"So you've been child minding for five years now," Jennifer referred to the paper in her hand.

The woman opposite her was fortyish with hair just beginning to grey and tied back in a bun. A very matronly figure. Her skin was already wrinkling even though her face was like dumpling dough. Her huge arms were crossed under her hefty chest and she sat on the edge of the sofa, feet spread in front of her. "Yes. An' me bring up eight pickney ah me own." She pulled the red cardigan she wore over her bosom.

"Eight! Goodness," Jennifer swallowed.

"Dem faada was a no good layabout, but 'im did bring in de money somehow, yuh know."

"Right. How did you find time to study?"

"Study?"

"Your qualifications."

"Me have me firs' aid."

Jennifer waited for her to continue.

"Yuh don't need no certificate to chilemine yuh know. I run my home wid a heavy han' an' a tongue of fire. Let one pickney step outta line an' he will know nuh fe do it again or else, nuh fe let me fine out about it."

Jennifer smiled nervously. A look passed between the sisters.

"You young people dem nowadays cyaan stay home an' bring yuh pickney dem up properly. I tell you," she pointed an accusing finger at Jennifer, "if me was nevah home fe me pickney, dem woulda end up skylarkin' 'pon street. Dat's another t'ing...when I was young a man's family was 'im priority, yuh understan'?"

Jennifer saw she was getting nowhere with this one.

"Bwoy pickney need a man aroun' de place," the woman continued. "Anyhow my son was to get a gal in trouble he wouldn't dare lef' her, 'cause he would have me to answer to."

"Right," Jennifer forced a smile. "Tea?"

"You 'ave coffee? Me only drink coffee."

"Okay, I'll be right back."

Donna followed her sister into the kitchen. "There's no way I'm going to allow you to let that old battle-axe look after Junior."

Jennifer sighed. "I know you're right, but I've seen five already and I'm getting worried that we won't find a suitable person by the end of the week. I really need to get back to work next week."

"We've still got time. Besides, if you can't find someone qualified, Shanika will do it, she ain't got not'n better doing and she's at home all bloody day with Naomi anyway."

Jennifer had no intention of allowing any such thing, Shanika wasn't exactly her idea of a responsible person. The idea wasn't even worth considering. "I can't burden your friend with another baby and besides she's not qualified. If anything happened we wouldn't be able to complain to the authorities."

Donna just gave her a look and mumbled, "She brought up her own child, didn't see no harm coming to her."

"I know she's your friend, but Junior's my baby and it's my duty to make sure he's looked after properly."

Donna lifted Junior in the air. "Did I say anything?"

The kettle boiled. Jennifer made the coffees and carried them through to the living room.

"Yuh nuh 'ave no biscuit...?"

Jennifer could hear Deborah's laughter through the walls.

The next candidate arrived an hour later. She was tall, slim and reminded Jennifer of a primary school teacher she'd once had.

"Tell me more about your experience please, Mrs Gregson."

"Well, I went to school around here and studied child development, child psychology, human biology, and sociology," her voice was soft and somewhat soothing. Almost like a hypnotist. "I then went on to work at a nursery as that was where I felt my talent lay."

Jennifer nodded. All of this was already on her CV.

"I was at a nursery in Camden for three years before going on to be a childminder in my own home and then a nanny in other people's homes," she giggled.

It was such a strange reaction that a chill ran down Jennifer's spine. There was something not right about this one. If she could bore you to death just telling you about her career, heaven only knows what she could do given the chance to tell her life story.

One more candidate to go.

"I absolutely adore children. Could just eat them up if they were edible. Couldn't have any of my own you see," she leant forward to whisper to Jennifer, "Men, dirty creatures the lot of them. Couldn't bear to be touched by them."

"Ha-ah," Jennifer laughed nervously. Junior had begun to cry upstairs.

"Aah is that the little tike now? Perhaps I should meet him."

"Not right now, Mrs Gregson," Jennifer stood up and held out her hand. "I've got your number, I'll be in touch."

Donna was coming down the stairs with Junior as Jennifer shut the door behind the man hater.

"Okay, give me Shanika's number."

SEVEN
Live well smaddy nuh know hard time

I remember someone saying to me that because I had money my job as a mother would be so much easier, because at least I could afford to pay for full-time childcare. True, I can still afford expensive holidays, I can give my child all the material things he needs, but there's more to bringing children up alone.

Junior is now three months old and has colic so bad that no amount of hugging, feeding or lullabies will calm him down. I usually get home around seven every night. By this time Donna has relieved Shanika and is taking care of him. I used to love spending a bit of time when I got home checking my work schedule, reading or preparing briefs, then taking a glass of wine up to the bathroom with me and immersing myself in scented hot water and bubbles for an hour at least. Then I'd slip into a silk negligee and watch television or listen to the radio until I was ready to sleep.

This is how things go now: I get up at six thirty, exhausted after only about a couple of hours sleep. With every bone in my body aching, because of all the awkward positions I've had to sleep in to accommodate him, I ease baby off my chest, put him in his cot and tiptoe cautiously out of the room.

Even before the invigorating effect of a morning shower has worn off Junior is awake and hungry. If Donna's up by this time she deals with it, if not I have to throw a towel over my shoulder and bottle feed him. Unfortunately he's still not yet old enough to have a bottle propped up to feed from himself while I carry on.

I'm generally at chambers by eight so as soon as Shanika turns up, sometimes in her nightclothes, I'm out of the door.

I work harder on my cases than I did before to prove to everyone that having a baby has not affected my abilities. I'm still as sharp as I always was.

When I get home Donna's usually waiting on me to take over so that she can go out with her new boyfriend, who I haven't had a chance to meet yet, or raving with her friends. I envy them as they dress up, laugh and go out to enjoy their freedom, leaving me behind with a screaming child. I've complained to the nurses and midwives at the clinic that it can't be normal for him to carry on screaming all the time like this. They assure me that it is, he'll grow out of it. Lots of gripewater and cuddles. I spend the evening walking about with him strapped to my chest because every time I put him down he screams until I feel like screaming.

I lie in bed at nights with Junior on his back beside me. I can't help thinking of his father. I remembered the nights we'd spent together in each others arms. I want so much for someone to hold me while I cry. To put their arms around me, a warm male body caressing mine. Whispering with a warm breath that he'd be there for me. That he loved me and, no matter what, was going to take care of me and our child. I wanted someone to share what I was going through and I wanted that person to be his father.

I've been forced into having a christening. I don't understand this tradition. The child was officially named when he was registered. Why go through this naming before God when I don't even go to church? If there's one thing I hate it's a hypocrite and that's exactly what I'm being forced to be. Seems like a waste of time and money to me. When I convey this to Donna or my friends they're all blasting me:

"Your child won't go to heaven if he's not christened."

"Mum would have a fit if she found out you weren't going to christen him."

"How's your son going to feel when he grows up and there are no christening photos in the album."

"You can't bury him on consecrated ground if he dies."

"Everyone needs a religion. You're Christian aren't you?"

Am I? The last time I was in church was for Elaine's wedding and even then I wasn't too happy about singing hymns that meant I was a sinner no matter what I did.

They were the ones who wanted a christening, they could organize it. Donna dug out our christening gown. The one we'd both worn at our own christenings. I said I'd do the food for the reception. That was before the discrimination case came up and I was again deep in paper work. Two days before the christening I called Karen for help with the cooking. The phone was answered by a man.

"Hello, is Karen there please?" I could hear the sound of kids playing in the background and unmistakable pop music.

"I'm afraid not. I'm holding the fort for a couple of hours," his deep voice said. "Kyle's birthday party. Who should I say called?"

"It's Jennifer." I was beginning to think that Karen was holding out on me. Had Charles come back?

"Jennifer, it's Philip."

Philip? The same Philip who had come to collect her after the reunion? It must be over a year now. With one lover. From what I had heard of her affairs, this was a record for Karen. "Hi Philip. Look, it's urgent that I speak with her."

"A problem?"

"You could say that."

"What's up?' He sounded genuinely interested.

"Well you probably know all about the christening this weekend."

"Yeah, I'll be there with Karen."

So Karen was even showing him off in public now! Boy she had been keeping this a secret. "The problem is I haven't been able to prepare any food yet. I've got relatives coming in from all over the country and nothing for them to eat."

Philip laughed. "Sounds like one of Karen's dilemmas."

I didn't think it was so funny but I laughed anyway. "So can you get her to call me as soon as she gets back?"

"I can do even better than that," he said, "I can do the cooking."

"Sorry?" I thought I heard wrong. This was Karen's himbo talking.

"I used to be a chef, owned my own Caribbean restaurant before we went bust. I could cook you up some curry goat and rice, ackee and saltfish, roti..."

"You're not pulling my leg are you Philip?"

"No! I'm serious. I'll go out and buy everything and come round. You can pay for the stuff, but it's a favour, okay? Any friend of Karen's is a friend of mine."

No wonder he was lasting so long in Karen's home. Which woman would want to lose a man who cooked and looked after her children during a birthday party?

"Thanks Philip but really, I couldn't..."

"I insist. I'll come over tomorrow."

What could I say? I backed down and let him do it. It was either that or go out and get tons of Marks and Spencers ready meals, crisps and peanuts. Besides I was alone with Junior and he had started to make noise. I was about to call out for Donna to get him, but remembered that she was out with her mates.

We recently started Junior on solids to supplement his formula milk. I wasn't with him enough to keep my own breast milk going, but it was almost impossible to get him to take a bottle from me. Donna seemed to have no trouble. It was as though he knew by instinct who should be giving him the breast milk and who gave him the bottle. By the time I got to his cot Junior had stopped crying but when he saw me he immediately started again.

"Oh, so now you're playing games."

Oh where was Donna? I picked him up and held him at arms length. I had learnt by experience to protect my clothes before picking up a baby. I reached for the towel at the end of his cot and draped it over my shoulder. Once placed comfortably against my body he settled down, opened his eyes and looked right at me.

"I wonder what you're thinking, boy." I hadn't looked at him properly in a while. He had simply become that screaming tiny human I had to put up with. His hair had grown thick and was soft and silky. He had filled out and the wrinkles he'd had at birth were now just creases in his pudgy joints. He seemed to be watching my face as I opened his palms, stretching his fingers out. He had the same shape fingernails as Paul. How strange that I should remember the shape of his nails. I saw Paul in Junior's eyes, mouth and even his eyebrows. All he had of mine was my forehead and nose.

"It must be about time you were fed," I told him. Junior looked at me not understanding. He gurgled and stuck a fist into his mouth. The sooner he was fed, changed and put back in his cot to sleep, the sooner I could get on with my work.

True to his word Philip turned up the next day with two huge carrier bags full of provisions. When I answered the door I almost didn't recognize him as the dishevelled, but cute man I had seen over a year ago. Philip now wore Malcolm X style glasses. His hair was shorter and he'd grown a moustache and goatee. Wow!

He handed me the bill, donned an apron, washed his hands and set to work. While I chopped onions he browned the meat. While I added seasoning, he stirred sauces. This was true cooperation, Karen was a lucky woman. For the first time since I had split with Paul I began to feel the loss of a relationship. I had thought about the physical, but had not missed having a man around. I had been so consumed with the pregnancy, the baby and keeping my career afloat that I was often too tired to think about a male/female relationship.

Would I have time for one? What would my priorities be then? Would another man be interested in me once he found out about the baby? If I did find a man willing to take me on, how would he feel about living with my sister as well? Would a man be intimidated by my career? While I had a man in my kitchen I decided to use him to my advantage.

"Philip?"

He turned to me while chopping fish. "Yes Jennifer."

He was cute, I could see why Karen had been with him for so long. Nice butt too. "Would you think I was a good catch...I mean, if you were looking?"

"I like women like you," he said. "You're intelligent, beautiful, a lady with her own independence and means and you're good company. I admire women like you. I don't know how you find time to fit in the demands of a career, friendships, family, and other commitments."

I was grinning with pleasure and tried to hide it behind my cup of coffee. "Thanks. But women like me also come with a lot of baggage, like a child for instance. What is it that frightens men off about going out with a woman who already has kids?"

"Firstly, men are afraid the children will start looking at them as fathers and the mothers will expect commitment. My parents always steered me away from getting involved with single mothers — not that I listened to them." *He paused to fill the kettle with water.* "Men are like free spirits and sometimes they like to make their own decisions, move from place to place without anything to hold them back. As we grow older, we want to settle down and have children and don't mind if they happen to be someone else's."

"Like you?"

"Ye-es. Although I wasn't thinking that when I met Karen... When we met she told me she just wanted one thing: someone to share her bed occasionally. Someone to take her out and give her a good time. Even warned me not to mix with her children or her personal life."

"How did you take that?"

"I wanted her. At first it was just sex. Then I started to spend more time, weekends and the odd couple of days. I'd fix things around the house, take the children off her hands..."

"You made yourself indispensable."

"Not on purpose. It's just the way I am and the way I feel about her. I wanted to do things to help her."

"How do you feel about Karen?" *I pushed.*

He smiled shyly.

"Go on I won't say a word," *I crossed my heart.*

Philip scratched the back of his head then scraped the diced fish from the chopping board into the frying pan. It sizzled and the aroma of peppers and onions filled the kitchen.

I got up to switch the extractor fan on. "Do you love her?"

There was hurt in his eyes. "I do," *he shrugged,* "but I can't tell her that."

"Why not?"

"She won't let me."

That sounded about right. Karen fighting not to get hooked and messed up by a man again. I kind of knew how she felt, but here was a man willing to do anything for her and yet he had to keep his mouth shut about his emotions. What I wouldn't give for a man to feel that way about me. I touched his arm and he turned to me and gave me that smile that I had first noticed at the front door. Aah, the scent and closeness of a man. If he wasn't my friend's man I could have fallen in love with his honesty and kindness, not to mention his good looks, fit body and cooking skills. Whatever Karen was up to, she'd better wake up soon or he'd be gone before she realized what she had.

The day of the christening. A warm May sun beat down on the small entourage. Karen climbed out of the Ford Escort and opened the back door for Beverly and her son. On the other side of the car Karen's children Natasha and Kyle hopped out and ran towards Jennifer's house. Karen straightened her clothes under her coat. Behind them a Fiesta pulled up. Elaine stepped out, locked up her car and approached them. Karen slammed her car door shut. "Do you think she's getting any yet?"

Philip removed a cake from the boot and followed a few paces behind.

"Who?" Beverly was trying to iron out the creases in her skirt with the palm of one hand while keeping Jerome upright with the other.

Karen rolled her eyes. "Jennifer, of course."

"Wouldn't bet on it. The woman's never at home, she's either at work or sleeping." Having seen the other two children take off Jerome, now twenty one months old, was struggling to be allowed the same freedom. Beverly let him down but kept hold of his hand.

"She should need some relief right about now, you know her baby is three months old. The man disappeared when she was around four months pregnant. I make that at least eight months without any nookie."

Elaine cracked up. "Karen you're disgusting. There is more to life y'know. Maybe she's happy with a celibate life."

The women all looked at each other — Beverly who had been without a man for two years, Elaine, who was a married woman and Karen, whose lover still gave her goose pimples when he sucked her toes. "Naah," they chorused.

The smooth soul with a touch of hip hop was pouring out onto the street from Jennifer's flat. A group of youths, Donna's friends, hung around outside sipping cans of Dragon stout and, the new lick, Hooch and Two Dogs (alcohol which tasted like lemonade so you wouldn't feel too guilty). The women pushed through the group. A couple of the youths were about to make a move on Elaine when they spotted Philip bringing up the rear and decided otherwise.

The guests of honour made their way towards the tiny dining area crowded with relatives and old friends, many of them cooing at the baby.

In the midst of it all they could hear Jennifer's voice. "He puts on a pound a day, I swear. I don't need to go to the gym, all I have to do is carry him around for a few hours a day, enough to burn a few hundred calories."

"Yaow, anybody home!" Karen called out. The rude stares she got didn't faze her at all.

Jennifer appeared from the centre of the gathering and came towards them, arms empty and open. "Where have you been?" Dressed in a long white twenties style dress with a fringe, she looked magnificent.

"Well we had to go home, have a nap, do our hair..."

"Again," Elaine finished.

"Your fault ya know, dragging us outta bed nine o'clock inna de morning fe go ah church."

"Your godson's christening! It was an exception."

"Well so is my Sunday morning lie in."

Jennifer embraced Karen. "You didn't bring your mother?"

"I told her you only wanted her for one t'ing and she said she ain't coming," Karen said good naturedly.

"So no Johnny cake?!" Jennifer put on a distraught face. Back in the day Jennifer had had a thing for Karen's mum's Johnny cakes, not to talk of her fried dumplings.

Karen poked her friend in the stomach. "Looks like you could do with losing a bit of weight anyway girl."

"You serious?" Jennifer examined herself.

Beverly laughed along with Karen. "She's ribbing you. You look great."

Jennifer laughed with them and turned to Philip who was still carrying the cake he'd spent last night baking and this morning icing. Philip handed Jennifer his hard work. "Hi Philip, thanks for everything. It's beautiful. We've got enough food to last until next weekend."

"My pleasure," he said modestly.

"So where is our godson?" asked Beverly still holding Jerome who was no longer trying to escape his mother's reach. This was unfamiliar territory and maybe he was better off with Mummy.

"He's somewhere in here," Jennifer said, handing the cake to a passing relative. "Where's Allan, you didn't leave him at home on his own?"

Elaine explained her husband's absence. "No, he had to work last night. Being a nurse he sometimes has to cover other's shifts. He'll be by once he's got some sleep."

Jennifer nodded. "Let me take your coats upstairs. Help yourself to drinks."

By this time Junior was becoming extremely confused with all the new faces coming at him from every angle. Donna, meanwhile, was busy socializing with her friends. A number of relatives had asked her if she had any plans to settle down and have pickney as well. She'd grown tired of explaining that that was the furthest thing from her mind.

"So now you 'ave de baby you t'ink you can fine a man?" Aunt Iris asked Jennifer. She was studying Jennifer closely so she could report back to her brother, Jennifer's father. This was exactly why Jennifer hadn't wanted to invite her family. Married for God knows how many years, she didn't understand how the youngsters of today could bring up children without a father. As far as she was concerned, if the baby father was not available it was the mother's duty to find a replacement and get married as soon as possible.

"You want to fix me up with your son, Auntie?"

Aunt Iris threw her hand up to Jesus. "Lawd me God. Yuh t'ink I want my son slaving for somebody else's pickney. Fine de culprit an' bring 'im before God, mek 'im face 'im mistake."

"Yes Auntie."

"Yuh ah feed 'im yuhself?"

"I expressed my milk so he could have it in his bottle at first, now he's on formula and solids."

"Yuh a tell me yuh useta squeeze out fe yuh milk an put in a bokkle?"

"Yes Auntie. I didn't have time to breastfeed."

"Chile, yuh miss out 'pon the pleasure an' happiness you an yuh baby coulda get from breast feeding. Yuh nuh watch a baby breastfeeding an see how 'im lickle fingers and toes jus' a curl up wid pleasure?" she curled her hands into fists and let them go again.

Karen rescued Jennifer in the nick of time and dragged her away from Auntie Iris who was already turning to find someone else to share her views.

"Karen," Jennifer kissed her full on her cheek with gratitude, "I love you."

Karen wiped the kiss off quickly. "Don't mek no one see you do dat again, yeah?"

Jennifer laughed.

"Elaine's fawning over her husband enough to make you sick. Come mek we sort this deejay out."

Beverly came up to them. "Can't you get that deejay to play something else? Do we look like gangsta bitches?"

Jennifer had been too busy talking to people she hadn't seen for years to notice that about twenty of Donna's friends, each with a drink in their hands, had taken over the living room and were distressing her Wilton carpet with a 'jump up' they called dancing.

"Excuse me!" Jennifer shouted above the music. No one paid her any attention. She moved closer to the deejay's set. "EXCUSE ME!"

The deejay, his baseball cap turned backwards, looked up at her feeble attempt to attract the crowd's attention. He smiled at her before turning back to his records, his head bopping in time to the hard core rap.

Jennifer was in no mood to pop style however, and grabbed him by his collar.

"Hey man! Mine my garms," the deejay said, straightening his silk shirt and dusting down his trousers unnecessarily.

"I don't give a damn. I've told you once before, change that music NOW. Put on something decent, this is a christening."

"Awright, awright. Bwoy yuh touchy, eeh?"

As Jennifer walked back to her friends, Barry White replaced Biggie Smalls.

Over in a corner of the living room, Elaine and Allan weren't seeing eye to eye. "Always the same t'ing," he said, raising his voice. "I can't even walk inna de house good before yuh start hassle me 'bout pickney."

Carrying Jerome on one hip, Elaine tried to reason with him. "I just want us to have the tests..."

"What did I tell yuh? I don't need nuh test. There's nothing wrong with me." Just then Philip appeared, providing Allan with an opportunity to escape. "Yaow Phil man, I been trying to reach you."

Elaine sighed and turned around to face a dozen or so people staring at her, including her friends.

She shrugged and joined them as Allan sloped off for a chat with Philip. The two men were the only two in their age group and even if they hadn't known each other too well to start with they would probably have become acquainted just for the company.

"Everything all right, El?" Beverly asked, taking Jerome from her arms and letting him back down onto the floor.

"With me, yes. But the black man's ego could do with some therapy," she glanced over at Allan who was now laughing as though nothing had happened.

Donna, dressed in a long satin skirt and chiffon blouse, now had Junior on her lap on the sofa which was pushed back against the wall. She was holding him under his armpits and trying to teach him how to dance. His strong little legs were pushing against her thighs and he was actually taking steps.

"Let me have him," Beverly begged. But Jerome wasn't having that. As soon as Beverly took the baby from Donna's arms he started to bawl.

"Best see to your jealous husband," Elaine took him from her arms and Beverly bent to pick up Jerome. It was as if they were playing musical babies.

Junior fell asleep on Elaine's shoulder. It had been a long day of being dressed, undressed, handed from one stranger to another and quick feeds. Jennifer and Donna would pay for all the disruption in his day later that night.

As it got darker and the guests got more drunk the music slowed down, and people began coupling for a dance. Elaine had disappeared, Beverly and Karen were talking old times, while their children played outside in the communal back garden. Jerome seemed to have more energy than the rest of them. Jennifer excused herself to go to the bathroom and climbed the stairs on legs that had been in heels all day. Once upstairs she slipped her shoes off, threw them into her bedroom and slipped on her comfortable slippers.

As she going back downstairs she thought she heard someone choking in the bathroom. She knocked on the door. "Anybody in there?"

"Jen?" The word came out as a broken cry.

"Elaine, is that you?"

The latch was drawn back and the door opened. Elaine stood inside, her face tear streaked. "Come in will ya."

Jennifer did so reluctantly. Big women crying always meant big trouble. "What's wrong? Have you and Allan had another fight?"

Elaine broke down as though the world had come to an end. Jennifer pulled her over to the bath tub and they sat side by side on the edge. Jennifer put an arm around her friend's shuddering shoulders. "What is it?"

"My period," Elaine sobbed.

Jennifer slapped a hand to her forehead. "You mean you've missed it, you're pregnant?" she said ecstatically.

Elaine let out a wail and doubled over hugging her knees. Jennifer was confused. Hadn't Elaine been trying for a baby? Then it dawned on her. Of course, if you were pregnant the last thing you wanted to see was your period. "You haven't missed your period, you're not pregnant?"

"We've tried so hard, Jen," Elaine sniffed. "I've done everything the doctor told me to."

"I know."

"You don't, none of you understand how I feel. You all got pregnant with absolutely no effort at all. I want to and..." she broke off again sobbing. "Allan won't go for the tests. It's possible he's got a low sperm count."

"Is that what the argument downstairs was about?"

Elaine nodded. "If only he would come with me and get checked out, then we could be sure."

"You've still got Allan, don't force the point. Maybe the problem is that you're trying too hard."

"I was so sure," she said. "So sure this time. I was a week late." Jennifer reached for the spare toilet roll, ripped a handful off and handed it to her friend. Elaine stood and faced herself in the mirror. "Look at the state of me. Could I use some of your make-up, Jen?"

"Sure, come on," arms around each other they left the bathroom for the bedroom.

By about eleven o'clock people started to leave. Jennifer made her promises to keep in touch and kissed so many wrinkled cheeks she made a mental note to get a stronger strength moisturizer as she got older. The remainder of Donna's crew had gone up to her bedroom, and the sounds of muffled jungle music drifted down the stairs.

Junior was asleep in Jennifer's room with the intercom switched on in the living room and kitchen. Exhausted Natasha and Kyle were stretched out on the sofa end to end. Jerome was laid out on his mother's lap in the armchair adjacent. Philip, Allan and Trevor, a husband of one of Jennifer's family friends were in the kitchen playing a three handed game of dominoes. Philip had even insisted on clearing up while the women took a break.

"So did Paul get an invite?" Elaine asked sarcastically.

"Ha-ha?" Jennifer laughed. She still received two hundred pounds a month from him, occasionally with an accompanying letter but most times just the cheque. The money was all in an account for Junior, but Jennifer never answered his letters and he never called.

Pat, a long-time friend of the family was now handing out christening cake from an oval shaped plate. She was self-employed, the owner of her own successful textiles business. Not one to miss a business opportunity she had brought a copy of her brochure with her in the hope of getting some orders.

Beverly accepted a slice of cake, and shifted in her seat a little. "I invited Devon's parents to our christening."

"And what happened. They turn up?" Elaine asked admiring a set of ruffled blinds from Pat's brochure, that would look great in her baby's room if and when she had one.

"Yes they did. Then they had the cheek to ask me if the baby was his."

"You lie!" Karen's cigarette nearly fell from her lips. The other women had turned their attention towards Beverly who immediately felt uncomfortable.

"They walked in handed me an envelope with ten pounds in it for the baby and then his Dad said, 'He doesn't look much like Devon does he, you sure is his baby?'"

"Bwoy, I'da tear up the money and dash it back in his face," Karen said.

Pat was furious. "What right do these people have to come into her house and ask a question like that? Why the hell would she invite them if the kid had nothing to do with them?"

"They were always really good to me when Devon and I were together, I couldn't leave them out of their grandson's life altogether."

"You heard from them since?" Elaine asked.

"Christmas card every year that's all."

"God that makes me so sick..." Pat sat cross-legged on the floor, listening.

"Do any of you still like your children's father?" Elaine asked.

Karen stood and reached for the bottle of Brandy on the coffee table. She poured a large measure and swaggered back to her seat on the floor, "Him! I don't even waste my time thinking about him."

"I hate Paul. How else can you feel about someone who puts

another woman and his career before his child. As far as he was concerned the child was my responsibility and my mistake."

"Trevor's a good father..." Pat's eyes caught each women's in turn. "We didn't plan to have children until we were well-off and set up but when Iesha came along we were happy, Trevor takes just as much care of her as I do."

Beverly remained quiet.

"Bev?" Elaine prompted.

"Hmn?" she pretended she hadn't heard the question.

"How do you feel about Devon?"

Dropping Jerome's hand she picked up her glass from the floor, but instead of drinking from it she twirled it between her fingers. "I try not to feel anything, but I was in love with him. Sometimes I feel that if he came back and said he was sorry and wanted to raise his son, I'd take him back."

"He left you pregnant, Beverly!" Elaine gasped.

"We were having problems before then," she sipped from the glass feeling the warmth of the alcohol burning its way to her stomach. "Sometimes I feel that I didn't try hard enough to help him with his problems. We never talked enough."

"Charles couldn't stop tell me dat me talk too much," Karen huffed. "He was seeing the children regular after we broke up. Bringing lickle money every now and then." She giggled unexpectedly. "You know what I used to do whenever he came round...I'd mek sure I wasn't cooking and any food in de cupboards or fridge I'd tek it all out, hide it in the hall cupboard. Then when he arrived an' asked if I needed anyt'ing I'd jus' show him the empty cupboard dem an' ask him if he see any food in de house. The man would hand over some money quick-time. Same t'ing wid the pickney clothes, show him all the ones wid holes in dem. If they see you doing well yuh don't get not'n'."

The other women nodded and laughed with her. Elaine slapped her thigh. "He stopped doing that when he caught Philip there though, innit."

"Damn right. He come in, saw Philip lying on the settee and walked out again. Change 'im mobile number an' didn't even leave an address to reach him at."

"Naaah, that's bad. What, did he expect you to live your life like a nun, while he spread his wild oats?" Pat asked.

"I don't care what he thought. It's his kids suffering for his own selfishness. You wait 'til dem grow big an' he can't explain where he was when they was growing up."

"No conscience," Jennifer said. "That's what makes women so different. Men have no conscience."

"At least when they're young they don't have no conscience," Pat leaned into the circle. "When old age ketch dem then they start to t'ink 'bout family and want to mek amends. By then the kids are big, grown up people wid they're own families, and couldn't care less about his lonely, sick arse."

"You go girl," Karen said. They all laughed.

"Mummy," Kyle woken by the laughter, raised his head from the sofa, a line of dribble sliding down his cheek.

"Lay down boy," Karen said almost harshly, "I'm only over here."

The boy looked too much like his worthless father for her liking. Her mother had always said a child conceived from love will always look like the father, a child conceived outside of love will take after the mother's side. Kyle seemed to have proved his grandmother right. He rested his head back on the arm of the sofa and was gone again.

"Allan told me that when we have our children he's going to set up a trust fund for them," Elaine said. "So that if anything happens to him or our relationship they'll still have that money put by."

Karen looked at her incredulous. "What's he expecting to happen? And just how much does he think he's gonna be able to put away when you've got children to feed?"

"We're both working. We can afford children."

"Anyway, by the time you have your kid you'll have a nice lickle nest egg there," Karen snapped.

Jennifer met Elaine's eyes and saw the hurt in them. Sometimes she could just slap Karen. Even if she had guessed Elaine's problem correctly, it wasn't fair to tease her.

"I never realized how much a small baby needed until I had to shop for Junior," Jennifer said, changing the subject.

Beverly lifted Jerome off her lap and heaved her large body off the sofa. Elaine watched her. For some time now she'd been thinking that her friend could do with some afrobics classes and a calorie controlled diet. Even going out more or getting a job would do, anything that would stop her sitting around alone eating tubs of ice cream and chocolate. She had once spent an afternoon at Beverly's house in which time her friend had put away two portions of chips, four pork sausages, eggs and beans and still had room for dessert. Elaine could show her the right things to eat and how to tone up painlessly. And, perhaps, she wouldn't have to be on her own once she was looking trim. The men would flock to her.

"Out of a group of five women, three of us have children here and on our own. Why? Because our men are weak," Karen spat, lighting up another cigarette, she blew a stream of smoke into the air.

"I don't know about weak," Beverly said, "but they have no staying power that's for sure."

"Please! Charles was all right about having kids until they wanted his time and his money, then he couldn't hack it. What choice have I got?"

Jennifer sunk deeper into the armchair and sipped her drink, enjoying the company of women her own age and the chance to get a lot of her pent-up frustration off her chest. "Our choice was in the beginning when we first got pregnant whether to have the child or not?"

"But should that be our only choice?" Elaine asked.

"What do you mean?" Beverly looked at her friend.

"Men tend to say, yeah have the baby, because they're not carrying it. If they had to get pregnant would they still say, yeah we'll have the child?"

"So what you're saying is that a man doesn't see it as a living person until the child's actually born, so it's not a problem."

"Exactly, Jen. Do a role reversal, tell him when the baby's born that he'll have to stay at home with it, feed it, change its nappies, wash it, get up at least three times in the middle of the night. Tell him that every move he makes the baby will be the first thing he'll have to think about. Let him know exactly how much stress it will entail and then see if he still wants to have a baby."

"So wha'? We mus' siddung wid dem an' tek dem through child rearing step by step? Get outta here! Anyway, it still wouldn't work because so long as you're there to take care of the kid he can do what he damn well likes."

"That's another thing, Karen. Why are you treating Philip like a sex object when he's trying his hardest to make you see that he wants to take care of you." Jennifer couldn't help herself. Karen didn't appreciate the good thing she had going — one of the most loving men around.

Karen defended herself. "I came to a decision in my life that I'm not gonna sit around waiting for Mr. Right or anybody else for that matter. When I grow old an' look back on my life I don't wanna see me sitting on my arse waiting for him to float through the door. I did that with Charles, I ain't doing it again. One day I'll have a Jag in my garage, minks in my wardrobe, and a jackass to pay for it all. Philip's only acting the way he does because he knows his place. Once I let him think he's got me, I'll never get it as good as I'm getting it now."

"You don't know that?" Elaine reasoned.

"I'm telling you, girl. Charles was exactly the same, promising me this and that. When we first started going out I was sixteen. He would always turn up with something for me, a rose, a teddy, a packet of jelly babies..."

The women giggled.

"We were only kids, wid no money. Useta lay in each others' arms and dream of having our own kids, our own house and earning enough so I wouldn't have to work."

Beverly nodded in recognition.

Karen continued. "Two years after we had Natasha we bought the house, Charles got a promotion an' we were living large, man. We had money, jobs, and friends all over. Then the mortgage rates went up. He started to take out loans and things got harder." Karen sipped from her glass of brandy. "You know, we thought having another baby would ease the tension. I can't believe I was so stupid, or so in love."

"But what actually split you up?" Jennifer asked.

"A lot ah t'ings, but I feel his dick was number one. He had the damned cheek to call the woman while I was in the same room and chat her up. It wasn't even like he went for another woman, it was dat woman's lifestyle he wanted. Y'know, she was single, no kids, no stretch marks, an accountant, her family were all lawyers, doctors, police officers. She had freedom and money," Karen spouted bitterly.

"What's wrong with these men?" Elaine marvelled. "They get it good and yet they've still got to get it better." She wondered how she would feel if Allan ever did that to her. She trusted him so much it would kill her. Elaine wanted to console Karen and reassure her that Philip was not like that. In the short time Elaine had spent with him she felt sure he was sincere. But Karen wasn't having it.

There was no point in arguing about men, Beverly reasoned. It was hard enough bringing a child up on your own without spending all your spare time thinking, 'if only I had a man'. They were all strong women who could raise confident, stable children into successful adults. *That* was the point.

Each woman thought about it for a moment, considering her own priority in life.

Beverly wanted to be married, have a house, and garden. She had exams in a few weeks and she was using every spare moment to study and revise. This was important to her.

Elaine wanted children, but it seemed there was obviously a problem there that she wasn't ready to tell her friends about.

Karen wanted her independence, to show the world that she was tough, so tough that not even love could break her.

Jennifer just wanted her career, the only thing she'd ever really wanted. The thought of being pitched into a meaningless life made her nervous. Who would she be? The need for money, status and a useful role in society had kept her going all these years. She had struggled for success, worked hard for it and at last she had reached the pinnacle of her chosen field. There was no way she would give it all up to be a mother.

EIGHT
Every fish eena sea nuh shark

Things have worked out quite nicely for myself and my little family. I'm back into the swing of the legal world. Donna is putting her head down and is going to university to study graphics and interior design. I'm so proud of her. Junior's still being looked after by Shanika and so far so good. At first I was worried about what she would expose him to, but I've grown to trust her.

Remember Tony Carnegie, the cute detective I gave a hard time on a case last year? Well, he's blown back in my life like a blast from the past. I was coming out of court today, a million things on my mind when I walked straight into him.

"So you ignore old friends now," he says.

I had to look up to see who it was. I recognised the face right away. "Tony." I was glad to see him. We hardly know each other but I felt close to him, like he was a link to my old life. Dressed in a suit that looked brand new and a little stiff on him, he still reminded me of Denzel Washington. Dark, tall, edible. "How nice to see you again."

He looked surprised. "Well Miss Edwards, this is a change from the cold efficient reception I received the last time we met."

I remembered our last meeting well. I'd really given him a hard time. I flashed him a warm smile. "I don't know what you mean?"

His expression was unreadable. "I suppose you've got yet another meeting to rush to, or a court case, or piles of paper work back in your chambers."

"No, actually..." I was about to tell him that I was going home to relieve my sister of my son when something stopped me. I couldn't tell this man that I had a baby. I was afraid that the first thing he'd ask me was when had I got married, just like all the others had done. I felt at that moment that if I told him about my son I'd miss out on the chance of getting to know him better. One thing I've learnt from my friends about single men, is that, to them, a single mother is for one thing only. Sex.

"...I was just about to go for a drink, why don't you join me."

He turned around and looked behind him and then turned back to me, studying my face quizzically as if he wasn't sure I'd spoken to him. "No one else around I suppose you must be talking to me."

I laughed.

"And I suppose you want to pay for your own drinks," he beamed and then winked.

"Hey I'm a liberated woman, remember? You can pay for the pleasure of my company," I flirted mildly.

"Should we go now?"

I thought about Donna sitting at home with my six month old son, waiting for me to come back. "I have to make a phone call, why don't you meet me at the wine bar around the corner?"

"Montenegro's?"

"Yes. I'll be five minutes behind you."

"Don't stand me up now."

"Would I?"

He was backing away from me. "Be there or be square."

I laughed as he backed into a wall.

"I meant to do that."

I laughed harder.

"I did!"

I used the phone in the outdoor clerk's office. Donna answered almost immediately. "Sis, you on your way?"

I lied. "I've been held up, D."

"What?! You promised you'd be back to take him."

"I know but I can't help it. Look, take him round to Shanika's, I'll pay her."

"Jen, I'm going out with Shanika."

"Well where is she leaving Naomi?"

"At her mum's."

"Can't you..."

"Are you sure you can't get back?"

I chewed my lip, considering. My options were to either go back to a teething baby or have a drink with a witty, good looking young man. It was no contest. "I'll drop her mum a few pounds. Please D," I pleaded.

There was a deep sigh down the line before Donna said, "All right," and hung up. I renewed my make up and headed back down the road. The guilt

154

wore off as I walked up to the wine bar and when Tony stood to greet me with a kiss on the cheek it disappeared completely.

I spent the whole afternoon entertained. Tony was not only funny but he was intelligent and caring. He told me of his family. Being the only boy with four sisters he felt he had an empathy with women that he got from watching his little sisters grow into adulthood. His mother and father had struggled to stay together for the good of their family and had instilled in him a deep respect for women and family.

He told of how he had been at the birth of one of his nieces and reminisced about the anticipation, and longing for it to be a boy only to find out that yet another girl had been born into his family.

He said if he had the chance to raise a son he would teach him how to treat a woman. How a woman is supposed to be loved and treasured for what she does for mankind. There was a sincere sadness in his eyes when he talked about the way boys thought that being hard and dominant was the way to go. He really seemed to know what he was talking about.

"So did your sister take your advice?"

"Eventually."

"She got rid of Fitzroy then?"

"Yes."

"And she didn't end up being another single mother statistic?"

"No, thank goodness."

Three hours later we were still talking and then I remembered I had a life outside of this liaison. I thanked Tony for his company, stood up and swayed on my feet.

"Never fear, Tony Carnegie is here," *he grabbed my elbow.* "My car is right outside. I'll give you a lift home."

"No...! That won't be necessary." *I couldn't let him come home with me. I still hadn't told him about my son and I didn't want to spoil the past three hours with the revelation.*

"Au contraire. Besides, what kind of man do you take me for? I wouldn't get a woman drunk and take advantage of her... Not unless she was well aware of what she was getting," *he said, raising an eyebrow mysteriously. I giggled.*

"All right then, we're agreed. I take you home." *I had no choice. I nodded and was led out to his car.*

The drive home was uneventful. I couldn't concentrate on anything other than how I was going to get out of inviting him in.

In front of my house I jumped out of the car quickly and headed for the door, then I realized I'd left my handbag on the dash and my briefcase on the back seat. Tony was sitting there watching me through the car window with a grin on his face and my purse in his hand. I walked back to the car and he reached into the back seat, retrieved my briefcase and got out of the car.

"If I didn't know better I'd think you were running away from me."

"Ha!" I laughed, swallowing nervously. "Course not." I took my belongings from him. "Give me a call sometime I might have some more work for you."

"Ah so yuh treat me?" He put on a yardie accent.

God, this man was so irresistible. I fished my business card out of the handbag. "Call me." This time I let my tone of voice do the talking.

"You better mean that 'cause I will."

As I turned to walk up to the house, I felt his eyes on me. Even after I'd opened the door he was still standing at the gate, a smile on his face.

"I didn't get a kiss," he pouted like a little schoolboy.

I curled my finger at him, beckoning. He shuffled up to the door and I kissed him on his cheek. Just then we both heard the sound of Junior crying. I nearly bit my tongue. Why wasn't Junior at Shanika's mum's house? I didn't want to have to make any explanations but before I could pull the door to, he looked past me into the house. Donna was coming down the stairs.

"Hi!" he waved.

"Hello." Donna replied coming towards us. "I heard a noise," she continued, "I was just making sure..."

I turned around and gave her my sweetest smile. "Everything's alright, Sis."

Donna looked at me nervously, then at Tony, then back at me. She got the message finally and made her way back upstairs.

"You have a baby living with you?"

Oh, why did I have to lie? I had completely forgotten that I'd previously told him Donna hadn't got pregnant when I replied, "My sister's."

He looked taken aback. "But you said, Fitzroy..."

"Yes, well it happened anyway. Another boy."

"Right," he nodded. "Must be tough having them live with you."

"They're family, what can I do?"

He nodded. "I'll see you around then."

"Bye Tony."

I closed the door behind me and floated up the stairs and into the living room of my flat where I fell onto the sofa, wondering why it had been so easy to lie. It had come out automatically as if Junior really was Donna's son and not her nephew. He just seemed more hers than mine.

"So was he the business that held you up?"

I glanced up to see Donna standing in the living room doorway, Junior held to one shoulder. Dressed in shorts and a huge jumper she looked like a child herself.

"It was work, D. He's a detective I'm working with."

She came into the room, sniffing as she walked past me, and sat on the armchair opposite which was big enough for her to bring her legs up, cross them and place Junior in the cradle they made. "You stink of cigarette smoke and you don't even smoke."

I stood up wearily, "What is this? Am I suddenly on trial for going to a business meeting in a bar?"

Donna gave me a cutting look. "Shanika's mum is gonna call you for her money. She could only look after Junior for a few hours so I had to get back early." She began unbuttoning Junior's babygrow as he watched me through upside down eyes. I sometimes wondered who was the big sister when she carried on like this. All I had done was take a little time out for myself. Now I was feeling as if I had no right to feel good about spending time with a man.

To get rid of the guilt that was seeping its way into my psyche, I offered Donna some money to go back out and enjoy herself.

A frown creased her pretty face. "Was he worth it?"

"Was who worth what?"

She lowered her lashes. "Forget it. Just remember, Junior's your baby and not mine." She unfolded herself from the sofa, handed me my baby and walked out. I heard her bedroom door slam shut upstairs. What had I done wrong?

How you feeling?
Hot hot hot.
How you feeling?
Hot hot hot.

"Come on girls, you're not trying hard enough. Work it." Elaine Goulden, dressed in a two-piece leotard and leggings with matching carnival coloured headband, walked between the twenty or so hot, perspiring women who were doing the shimmy in the gymnasium hall of the leisure centre. Women who had decided this was the way they wanted to lose weight or get fit. She passed Jennifer in her cut-off top and jersey shorts and slapped her backside. "Go on, girl." The girl was good. If only most of the women that came were that fit, but then she'd probably be out of a job.

"Come on Elaine, man. I thought we were friends," Karen puffed, sweat dripping off her chin.

"That's why I'm doing this, honey. Gotta be cruel to be kind."

Beverly stopped mid star jump and bent double clutching her

sides. Her chest straining in the leotard she had squeezed herself into.

Elaine rushed to her side. "You all right, Bev?"

Beverly could only signal that she had to sit down, she didn't have a breath left in her body.

"All right girls, take ten minutes out," Elaine announced to the rest of the Afrobics class. There was a huge sigh of relief around the room as the women all stopped their exercises and walked off into groups. Elaine stopped the cassette player and joined her friends on the gym benches.

"Bev, I should kiss you. Thought I was about to have a heart attack."

"Karen you were doing great, especially that whine yuh waist, girl," Elaine slapped her on her back.

"Now she waan bruk me back!"

Jennifer was dabbing her neck and chest with a towel. "I don't know why I didn't come before. This is much more fun than jogging every day."

"You always used to say you never had time."

"Now she 'ave baby she 'ave time," Karen flung Jennifer a disbelieving look. "You better start talk 'ooman, tell us what we doing wrong."

Jennifer wrapped her towel around her neck. "I make time for myself that's all. Plus I've got a minder and a younger sister. It's not like Junior's a small baby anymore. He's nearly a year old now you know."

"Bwoy, where does time go?" Elaine whistled.

"I know, I took Jerome to his first day at nursery last Friday to kinda get to know everyone," Beverly laughed at the memory. "Boy didn't want to come home and then all weekend it was, 'When we going back mummy', or 'Can't you take me now?'"

"My two was exactly the same when they started. Now I have to drag them outta bed. Especially Natasha now she's in secondary."

"What's happening wid you an' that detective?" Karen asked, raising a bottle to her head and taking a swig of mineral water.

"Nothing's happening. We're just friends. I like it that way."

"You're not sleeping with him yet?"

"Maybe he can't get it up," Karen laughed.

Elaine winced.

"He's a nice guy, we get along really well and to tell the truth I would hate to spoil that with sex," Jennifer replied.

Elaine nodded, glad they had got off the subject of children. It had become like a thorn in her side. She and Allan still hadn't managed to conceive and even though they'd both been checked out and knew the problem was his, he wouldn't accept it. "Come on girls, back to your steps, we're gonna step it up!"

"Aah man," Karen dragged herself up from the bench and made her way out to the middle of the floor. Jennifer jogged back, while Beverly hauled herself up with as much enthusiasm as a man going to the gallows.

After aerobics and steam baths the women went their separate ways. Jennifer picked up a leaflet entitled, *Beauty From The Inside Out* and read it on the way back to the car. The author, Toni Lee, was a black American who was in England running a series of interesting seminars for black women at the leisure centre. Before the baby, Jennifer had taken a keen interest in black women's support groups. But since having Junior the single item on her agenda seemed to be work. Now that Junior was a bit older it was time to start doing things that she enjoyed again. Maybe even go on a skiing holiday this year.

Later that night as Jennifer prepared her bath, she chided herself for allowing Donna to go out tonight. Tony had asked her to go bowling. *Bowling!* The first time anyone had suggested going bowling since her school days. She enjoyed his company and would have liked to have gone. Over the past few months they had begun calling each other regularly, to talk or invite each other out for drinks, dinner, a show. He had become one of her best friends.

Still only a good friend, Tony was the break she needed from baby things, family problems, the hassles of work. He was the sunlight entering her prison. She wondered about their relationship as she lathered her body. She had never thought it possible, but now she noticed that she was developing muscles where she had never had them before. Did Tony like his women hard, or soft and pliable? A smile spread across her face at the thought of him answering the question. He would probably say something like, "Give me one of each, I'll squeeze them and then tell you."

She only thought about the future when she really had to, because it didn't look good. Each day for the rest of her life would be like a slap in the face. Each year would be saying to her, your son is a year older and still doesn't have a father. She had to admit that the older he got the more she worried about the lack of a father figure. The boy had plenty of 'aunties', but no male role models. Tony sprang to mind again.

She stepped out of the bath and briskly dried herself with a large towel. There was one problem with her getting together with Tony Carnegie. She had a son she had lied to him about. Lied! She'd told an untruth in the spur of the moment five months ago, and now it had caught up with her.

"Mamma!" The call came from her bedroom down the hall.

Jennifer's heart sank. She slipped into her satin nightie, the one with thin shoulder straps. A nightie made for seduction on a night like tonight. Instead she had to see to Junior.

"Smile baby," Donna kneeled down with the camera and caught a toothy grin from Junior. Around them children ran back and forth from the living room to the kitchen. It was a shame it was freezing outside. January was grey and although it hadn't snowed it was cold enough to. Jennifer wished his birthday was in the summer then she could have sent them all outside.

Donna had spent the entire morning turning the flat into a toddler's paradise. Balloons hung around the front door with a huge clown face attached to the actual door.

Junior had a squashed chocolate roll in his fingers. "He's going to ruin that suit," Jennifer fretted.

"It's his birthday, leave him. Besides Mummy can always afford to buy him a new one," Karen laughed. Junior was dressed in a white shirt, with pressed pleats in the front and one in the back, with a navy bow tie. He wore baby suit trousers, and with his fade haircut he looked for all the world like a half pint sized man. His first birthday and it seemed as though everyone was having more fun than he was.

Karen's daughter Natalie lifted him up and carried him out to the hallway where they had set up a small slide. Junior struggled to be put down and eventually became too much for the eleven year old.

"He's growing up so fast isn't he?" Beverly watched him try to crawl up the short ladder.

"He's growing up and I'm growing old," Jennifer frowned.

"You're gonna be twenty nine this year. Girl, if you'd started when I did you'd feel like forty by now."

To Jennifer that was no comfort. Junior hadn't taken away her youth, as having Natalie had taken away Karen's, but he had taken away her freedom. Her choice. She often thought like this and hated herself for it because she knew it wasn't Junior's fault. If she had used her own common sense and taken her own advice Junior wouldn't be here now and she wouldn't have children running around trampling cake and soft drinks into her carpet and parquet floor.

He was something, though, wasn't he? An accomplishment that had gone well so far without affecting her career either.

"*I feel good!*"
I had earlier bathed in jasmine aromatherapy oil and was getting ready for enlightenment, that fulfilling feeling that I was expecting from tonight's lecture. American lecturers were always the most enthusiastic, the most passionate about their subject.

I wanted to look like a sista, a sista that had found her roots, who knows where she's coming from and where she's going. I picked out an ankle length trouser suit with a long knee length blouson, in Kente cloth. There was even a scarf to match, which I wrapped my hair in. My make-up was very light, almost natural. These women don't go in for the Westernized look.

My drive to the leisure centre was accompanied by the gospel sound of The Sounds of Blackness singing "Black Butterfly". I felt free. My first leisure trip out without my friends, Tony, Junior, Donna or work colleagues. There'd be women there like myself. Women who wanted to be told that they had a right to be selfish. After decades of liberated slavery, they could now go to work, buy themselves expensive gifts etcetera, without feeling guilty.

For the lecture the leisure centre had reserved the same hall I had taken my Afrobics class in. It was set out with chairs side by side in a large circle. In the centre stood a microphone stand. Women were milling around. Some had already chosen their seats, others were helping themselves to food and drink from the buffet, a few gathered around the stall tables selling books and self-help tapes written by Toni Lee, but glancing around it appeared that the speaker had yet to arrive. I walked over to the book stalls and browsed through the titles. 'Treat Yourself To The Relaxation Experience,' 'Confidence, Composure and Competence for the Black Woman,' 'Self Empowerment,' 'Stress Skills for Turbulent Times,' '30 days to Self-Discovery,' 'The Black Man: A Translation For Women'. I was tempted by that last title but decided that I'd had enough of them for the time being. On another table I discovered products for black parents, 'The Working Woman's Guide to Raising Your Child and Still Finding Time for Yourself,' 'Building Self-Esteem in Your Child'. There was a tape and workbook set that claimed it would instill cooperation and respect in your child through songs and play and I bought them both. So that I wouldn't have to spend the whole evening alone I made my way to the makeshift bar and buffet.

"*Is Toni Lee here yet?*" *I asked a young black woman, dressed in jeans and a white t-shirt.*

She looked up at me. "I haven't seen her but the whisper is that she likes to make an entrance."

I smiled, now curious to meet our mentor. I helped myself to a pineapple juice.

"Have you been to one of her talks before?"

"No."

"Neither have I," the woman bit into a sausage roll before putting it back on her plate. "I can't wait."

I held out my hand to her. "Jennifer Edwards."

"Reverend Fay Turner," she shook my hand and then chuckled. I thought it must have been the look on my face and was ready to apologize.

"I know what you're thinking," she said, "my name sounds like an old movie star. I think that's what my parents intended."

I laughed with her. Reverend Fay Turner fitted in perfectly with what was to come for the rest of the evening.

We got into an easy conversation about what we did for a living and our reasons for coming tonight. It had been a hard day and I told Fay that this was my way of pampering my mind. She agreed and told me she would love to have me come by her church one day and give a mentoring speech for her girl guides and brownie groups. I handed her my card.

Suddenly, over the loud speakers came the sound of drums. The rhythm deep and resonating. Before the drums there had been no music, just the sound of people talking. We saw it as our cue to find a seat but, before we could make a move, in stormed a huge woman, clapping her hands loudly. The room full of women turned to see the extravagantly dressed woman wearing the type of African costume that you only saw on the television — the turban shaped headdress, long, flowing multi-coloured cloak. Heavy wooden jewellery adorned her ears, throat and wrists. She was followed by another woman who was smaller, dressed in a business suit and carrying an armful of office files. Fay and I quickly found a seat together.

"I have arrived. I am woman and I have arrived," the accent was clearly American. It was loud and authoritative and she wasn't even using the microphone.

Fay and I looked at each other. Was this her?

"For those of you who have never met Toni Lee, let me ask you, which one of us is she?" She turned to her companion. "This neatly dressed office type with perfect make-up, or me big, proud of being African, loud and domineering?" her eyes were scanning the circle. "You want it to be me..."

The other woman hadn't said a word. She placed her armful of files on the table behind her and stood in the background watching the leader. "The truth is it's neither of us." Everyone began to mumble among themselves. The big woman began to unbutton her cloak and as she undressed, handed it to the woman behind her. Underneath it was a padded body suit which her assistant unfastened from the back. She took her jewellery off and packed them away. *"We all wear an outer image,"* she took the turban from her head and shoulder length relaxed hair fell free. Underneath the suit she was dressed in jogging bottoms and a long baggy jumper. *"This is me. This is how I am comfortable."* There was a vast outlet of breath from everyone around me and I'm sure mine was among them. She looked nothing like the woman we had all seen come in. Toni Lee now stood before us, dressed like any of us on a day out shopping. She was stunning nonetheless.

Toni introduced herself and then her assistant, Ashanta. She had begun by showing us just how an appearance can get a reaction, that she wouldn't have got by walking in as herself. *"Would you have felt disappointed?"* she asked rhetorically. She already knew what we'd have thought.

She didn't disappoint us however. She talked of liberation and our struggle against racism, sexism and the manipulative controls of society upon the black woman. What she also did was tell us that although we wanted to rush ahead of our black men into the twenty first century, we had to first ask ourselves why? What the satisfaction would be to ourselves. Were we still just being controlled, wanting to prove to others that we could do just as well, if not better, than the men? Or were we doing it for ourselves?

We had discussions on literature, white feminist writers and how their writing compares to our own. How their experiences became so much different when tainted with colour. Toni told us how her seminars grew out of impatience. Impatience with the all too few women's magazines and women's liberation groups that were the half-hearted attempts by black women to copy white women's groups. And impatience with men trying to give us equality. Equality derived from their needs, their fantasies, their second hand knowledge, their agreement with the experts, Toni explained.

By the time she passed us over to Ashanta we were all spellbound. If she had been a man I would have fallen in love with her. Ashanta was to teach us how to tap that beauty within.

"Let's turn beauty inside out!" she started.

"For black women, a personal commitment to take time out for you..." she gestured to the whole room, *"...may mean reshuffling priorities. We have the unique roles of being a homemaker, lover, wife, mother, confidante if you're lucky, student, artist and career women and sometimes all of the above at once, our schedules are already packed. How can we maximize our energies to nurture ourselves when there are so many pressures and so little time?"* Unlike Toni's voice her tone was that of a mother speaking to her

teenage daughter.

"The answer to is to flex that self esteem! Since we've so much to do it's your only choice. Girls, what do you do?" she threw her hands up indicating that we follow her lead.

"Flex that self-esteem!" we chorused.

"Louder, I don't think Toni heard that. Come again."

"FLEX THAT SELF-ESTEEM!!"

"Because the woman that feels good about herself inside is the woman who makes certain she always looks her best outside. Whether you need to jump some emotional hurdle, schedule time for exercise, lose forty pounds, or pull yourself out of depression, self-esteem will pull you through every time."

Ashanta covered everything from weight loss to nutrition, psychology to exercise, make-up and hair to being a mother. The latter being the part I was most interested in.

Up on the screen from the overhead projector was a guide that we all laughed at. Ashanta questioned us as she read out each one, "Isn't that true?"

A mum has to learn to...
* Do five things at once — and do them all properly.
* Shower very quickly.
* Enjoy tidying up.
* Only iron what's absolutely necessary.
* Like cold coffee.
* Plan the day's activities meticulously.
* Change every plan at the last minute.
* Shut doors on mess now and then and get out!
* Talk in shorthand when little ears are wagging.
* Guess the end of her friends' sentences.
* Fall asleep within seconds as soon as the baby does.
* Be selfish occasionally.

The last one she had underlined. "Don't be afraid to be selfish, just don't forget that sometimes you also have to make sacrifices."

By the time she had finished I was ready to go out into the world and practice self-expression, openness, to show people that I am freer in the mind than I thought I was. I even wanted to get up there and share my story with those women, show them that I knew exactly what they were talking about.

I was still full of Toni's parting words when I pushed open the front door and entered my quiet flat. "I leave you love, I leave you the challenge of developing confidence in one another, I leave you a thirst for education, I leave you responsibility for our young, I leave you desire to live harmo-

niously with your fellow black man, I leave you, power, faith and dignity."

The Savoy was full when they walked into the lobby that evening at just after seven thirty.

Tony was nervous and kept fiddling with his collar. He'd never been to these places socially. Once, on a case, he had to spend two nights in the Hilton, at the expense of his client. He remembered how uncomfortable he'd felt, despite the fact that everything around him was designed for the guests' comfort.

"Will you relax?" Jennifer slapped his hand playfully.

"I'm not used to this kind of place. Do you realize we'll probably be the only black faces in there. All ah dem looking at us and wondering who we are."

"If it bothers you so much we'll go somewhere else."

"Dressed like this?"

Jennifer smiled at him. He looked good in his black suit and had even been practicing his posh-speak on the way there in the car. The Savoy had been an old haunt for special occasions and Jennifer felt a thrill coming back again as she entered for the first time in two years.

"Evening, Miss," the familiar top hatted doorman saluted her with a smile. They turned left in the lobby, walked past the grill room and up the thickly-carpeted steps into the American bar. She took a seat at a table. Tony sat down beside her, awkward and out of place.

"Should we have a drink first?"

Tony shrugged looking around at the glamour. "It's your date."

"It might help to relax you."

"If it does I'm game. Let's go for it."

A nod to the barman brought him to their side. "What can I get you Miss?"

"I'll have a vodka martini," she looked to Tony and he cleared his throat before answering.

"Whisky and soda please." The waiter walked away back to the bar.

Tony gazed at the woman by his side as she looked around the room. She was strong, intelligent and sensual. The type of woman he had only ever dreamed of dating. He often disgusted himself with the occasional one night stands over the years. A quick lay, no real conversation, no meeting of the minds. Girls who thought that wearing a weave and tight, short skirts was the way to a man's heart. Together their IQs wouldn't match Jennifer's.

Yet there was something stopping him from making the move on her. Every time he thought of them together...alone...in bed...making love, he wanted to call her, turn up on her doorstep, take her in his arms. It was an ache that only one woman could cure. But was someone else in her life? Was that why she kept him at bay? Just good friends. Jennifer was more than just a passing diversion, a companion. Of that he was sure. The lifestyle she led, this place, he would never fit in. But he could learn to couldn't he?

Jennifer gave a cursory look around the room, and she too began to feel nervous. There was a time when she had fitted in here amid the talk of politics and law; expensive second homes on remote islands; universities, celebrities. Her eyes met Tony's. She smiled and touched his hand affectionately. "We'll just have our drinks and leave, okay?"

"Look if you really want to stay..."

"No, I want to have a good time. I guess I must have changed. This place doesn't impress me anymore."

She could see Tony visibly relax. They chatted briefly over their drinks, finishing them quickly so they could leave that much sooner.

They were walking back towards the exit when Jennifer suddenly stopped. She pulled Tony to a halt. "What's wrong?"

"...I've just seen someone I know."

Standing near the cloakroom was Paul Harvey. A middle aged white woman standing just behind him. Deliberately Jennifer took Tony's arm and walked towards them. Tony was surprised by the sudden intimacy but followed her lead nonetheless.

"Good evening Paul."

Both Paul and his date turned to face them. Paul made a croaking sound in his throat before coughing to clear it. "Goo...Good evening," he stuttered. His eyes flitting between Tony and Jennifer were filled with a kind of silent pleading that made Jennifer want to laugh.

She extended her hand and he shook it woodenly. She then turned to the woman beside him who was sizing her up and down.

"Ah...darling," Paul said turning to her but keeping his eyes on Jennifer, "this is Miss...I'm sorry I don't remember your first name..."

Jennifer glared at him. "Edwards, *Jennifer* Edwards."

"Yes, Miss, ah, Edwards. She...uhm...joined the Worshipful Company of Black Barristers...last year wasn't it?"

"Nearly two years ago," Jennifer shook the woman's cold hand. "And you are?"

"Paul's wife, Hilary. It's good to see so many young black women joining the profession, isn't it?"

Jennifer felt her stomach tighten and her eyes became bleared with a sudden rush to her head. It was her! The woman who had greased his path to success and he'd even gone as far as to marry her!

Jennifer wasn't sure what the look on her face conveyed as all she could feel was a nerve jumping in her temples. She ignored Hilary Harvey and again clung to Tony's arm. "My...my date Tony Carnegie," she said introducing him.

"Nice to meet you," the Harveys said as one, shaking his hand in turn.

"Darling, we really must be off, we have a dinner engagement," Hilary said, tugging at Paul's sleeve. "Maybe you'll come to one of our dinners, Jennifer?"

"If I'm invited, I don't see why not." Her eyes never left Paul's.

"Good. Are we ready?"

Paul nodded. "Nice seeing you again, Jennifer. Good luck."

Jennifer's heart was beating so fast that she thought she would have a heart attack. Before she could say another word the Harveys were gone.

"An old friend?" Tony asked and then when she didn't answer, "Are you okay?"

Jennifer's jaw was hard and her eyes held such a look of scorn that Tony let it drop, for now.

"I'm fine let's just get out of here."

NINE
Me feel relief not a teef can teef me education

"What's this Junior?"

The nearly three year old studied the picture in the 'open the flap' book thoughtfully. Then a cheeky, dimpled grin spread across his face. "Chicken."

Donna kissed him loudly on his cheek. "See he can read."

Jennifer looked at her cynically. "He memorized it. Don't you know children remember pictures easier than words?" she slipped a file into her briefcase. Dressed in a beige, classic silk suit with a complimentary shirt and pearl beads, she looked her usual stylish, confident self.

"No he didn't," Donna stood up and took the book over to Jennifer. "You bought this book for him two days ago. He's known his alphabet since he was two."

Junior mounted his tricycle and weaved in between his mother and aunt. "Dee-daa, dee-daa."

Accidentally he brushed Jennifer's leg with his handlebar. With a tut of annoyance she immediately checked her stockings for snags. "All right, so he's developing fast. I don't have time now, but I'll read with him as soon as this case is over."

" 'As soon as this case is over'," Donna mimicked. "Ever since he was born it's been as soon as this case or that case is over, 'I'll spend more time with him', 'I'll take him out', 'I'll take him to nursery', 'I'll pick him up'."

Jennifer stopped what she was doing and watched her sister's ranting. "He's doing all right, isn't he?"

"He may be doing all right but it's no thanks to his parents."

Jennifer took that remark like a slap in the face. "Thanks Sis," she said drily.

"God," Donna threw herself onto the sofa. "Why am I always the one getting stressed out, when you can come and go as you please? I'm single, I'm not a mother and yet I feel like one. I have a life too you know. Every time the chance of a job comes up I've got to check with you first that's it's all right for me to go for an interview, or leave for a few days. Why is your life so much more important than mine?"

"I'm sorry you feel that way about my career. The career that is paying for you to live in luxury while you study. The career that pays for your food, clothes and raving..."

"I'm not talking about your career, Jen, I'm talking about your son. For most of the time since he was born Shanika, Naomi and I have been the only company he's had in this flat."

"Is it my fault that I'm out before he wakes up and he's asleep when I get home at nights?"

Donna met her eyes. "You want the truth?"

"Not having my permission has never stopped you before."

"You could make time if you really wanted to. You're not the only barrister in London. You don't have to work all the hours God sends. I see you making time to shop with your friends, to go keep fit, or out with the detective. How can you go out with a man who doesn't even want to meet your son anyway? I just don't think you care about your Junior enough."

If only she knew that Tony had no idea Junior was her son. She had managed to keep Tony at a distance, never letting him get closer than a kiss between friends. After all that's all he could ever be now. She never let him come back to her house for fear the truth would come out and she was too afraid to go back to his because the temptation to let the relationship get sexual would become a reality. "Donna, how can you say that," Jennifer was indignant.

Donna placed her hands on her hips. "Action speaks louder than words."

It sounded like a challenge. "All right. I'll talk to Julian when I get to work, I should have some leave due. I shall spend some time with my son."

"Damn right, 'cause as soon as you get the time off I'm moving out for a while. I need a break too, and so does Shanika. We might even go on holiday."

For a few moments Jennifer panicked. She was doing this deliberately to wind her up. Then she thought, what could be so hard about spending two weeks with an infant. He was her son. Many women before her had managed it and if Donna thought she couldn't then she'd show her.

The thought of being totally alone with her son dominated her day. She had never actually spent time with him as a mother. Junior was three years old and all she could remember about his baby years were the worst months. The painful breast feeding, the colic, the struggle to stop him spitting out the solid food during weaning, the teething when she had spent whole nights pacing up and down with him. Sleepless nights because he wanted to play instead of sleep. Baby food or milk spilt on her homework or worse still, on important briefs for that day. Cancelled appointments due to the lack of a babysitter. The potty training that had meant having a potty in every room of the house and asking him every five minutes if he wanted to go. The times she'd been walking around the flat bare footed and stepped in something wet or soft and squishy.

Had that really been a skip of her heartbeat when he'd read the word 'Chicken' or had that just been her imagination? After three years of motherhood she had to admit that she was practically a stranger to the little boy running around her home. The cute dimpled face that sometimes bugged her to play with him. The strong determined mouth like his father's that asked "Why?" over and over until you answered satisfactorily. But Jennifer knew he needed a man in his life for balance. But she could only give him herself.

Jennifer's son. The son she hadn't even bothered to give a real name.

Two weeks later I was on my way home to begin a fortnight alone with Junior. Donna had decided to go off on a holiday to Tenerife with Shanika. They would be leaving tonight after dinner. You know, I'm not even bothered about what the two of them are going to get up to. My worry is that I won't have anyone to call on.

By the time I reached my front door I was hyperventilating. I barely made it to the sofa before Junior had come running in, nearly knocking me flying.

"Mummy look," he said holding up a cardboard model he'd made and painted. It looked like...well, it looked like nothing ever invented.

"That's nice, Junior." I had heard that giving praise was very important to a child of his tender age."What is it?"

He opened his eyes wide at me and said with a huff, "An airplane."

I nodded and smiled, that was encouraging wasn't it? Yes, I'd learned that on a customer care course once.

"It's for you," he said handing it to me.

I shook my head. "It's too good for me, Junior. And besides I don't play with aeroplanes so why don't you keep it and then I can come and see it whenever I want."

He liked that, he was beaming. Donna was upstairs I could hear her stereo and for once it wasn't shaking the house. "Let's go and see Auntie Donna, okay?" I suggested.

Before my sentence was finished he was dashing for the stairs. Did this child never walk. It was a miracle he hadn't broken some part of him by now. I followed him up and we made it to Donna's door almost at the same time. Donna was folding a pile of clothes she had taken from her wardrobe into a suitcase. She had had her hair plaited into extensions again so that she wouldn't have to be bothered with styling it on the holiday.

"Hi Donna."

"Sis," she whirled around and her braids flew over her shoulder, "I'm nearly ready."

I went in and sat on the bed. "So I see." Junior climbed up on the bed and sat cross legged, his cardboard model still in his hands.

"Auntie Donna gonna buy me present," Junior informed me.

"Is she now?"

He nodded enthusiastically. I felt my heartbeat speed up again nervously. In a few hours I would be left completely alone with this bundle of energy. I hadn't brought much work home for the two weeks, just one brief which I wouldn't have to read until I was ready to go back.

"What d'you think of this?" Donna held up a tiny bikini against her T-shirt. Well I never! The top part would just about cover her nipples. Not only did my baby sister have better hair than me she was also better endowed, if you know what I mean.

"You're not going to wear that out on its own are you?" I gasped.

"Course," she threw it into the suitcase. "Cost me twenty five, I'm not hiding it."

Junior bounced up and down on the bed, "I like it."

"You would, you're a man," I told him.

"Not man," he pouted. "Am a boy."

Donna and I laughed. He had a point, but boys turned into men and one day he might remember this conversation and know exactly what I meant.

"So, you going to be all right?" Donna asked me.

"What do you think I am...Sixteen?" I wrapped a plastic bag around my travel iron that I was letting her borrow. "Yes dear, I'll be just fine."

"Well, you know," she stopped folding to study me, "you haven't really *had to do this alone before. But I've left a list downstairs of what he eats, what he likes to do, where he likes to go, his favourite books..."*

"Donna, I am his mother," I reminded her yet again, "I do know him, I live here too."

She touched my arm affectionately. "I know Sis, but..." her words drifted off and I suddenly felt incompetent. What was it that she thought I couldn't do? Communicate with him? Play with him, be his mother? I could do it. The hard thing would be the loneliness. Day in, day out of baby talk.

An hour later Shanika turned up and soon after that they were gone. Luckily by this time it was Junior's bedtime. I put him to bed and then went myself. Tomorrow would be the first day of being a real single parent.

Saturday morning.

Jennifer settled herself in for a lie in. She didn't have to work, she didn't have to shop and she couldn't go for a jog now that Donna had left her alone with Junior.

She had only just drifted off when the door slammed back into the wall and a tiny body flung itself onto the bed on top of her. Jennifer groaned.

"Mummy, mummy," Junior chanted and then not getting an answer decided to use her as a trampoline. Jennifer turned over and opened her eyes. She wished she could tell him to go and bother Auntie Donna. The child was just a blurry, coloured shadow. His Batman pyjamas made her dizzy.

"Junior, stop," she said hoarsely. The bouncing ceased, for a second, and then as she closed her eyes and relaxed he started again.

"Mummy, mummy, Donna not in bed."

"Hmn I know, she's gone," Jennifer whispered.

"Gone where?" He stopped bouncing and crawled up beside his mother.

"Holiday."

"Where's 'oliday?"

Jennifer sighed and sat up, flipping Junior over onto his back with the motion of the duvet. "It's far far away, Junior," she swung her legs off the bed and slipped her feet into her slippers.

Junior kneeled on the bed, "Can we go wiv her?"

"No Junior, she's gone in an aeroplane." Drawing her arms through the sleeves of her dressing gown, Jennifer yawned and headed for the door.

"Why?"

It was going to be one of those never ending conversations that Junior so much loved. If she indulged, it could carry on all day.

"Why don't we go and have some breakfast?"

"Yeah!" He jumped off the bed and followed his mother to the bathroom.

Jennifer helped him brush his teeth first and then while she brushed hers he stood on the toilet seat watching. "I can sing mummy," he boasted.

"Can you?" Jennifer asked through a mouthful of toothpaste.

He nodded. "My teacher learn me song 'bout brushing teet'."

"Teeth, Junior."

"Yeah, I said teet."

"Teeth," she pushed her tongue between her teeth and pronounced it slowly.

Junior watched and followed. "Teetha."

"Not teetha, just teeth," she did it again.

"Teeth," he replied.

"Good, give Junior a gold star."

He smiled proudly puffing up his chest. "You want to hear my song?"

"Okay, sing it to me as we go downstairs."

He climbed down off the toilet seat and followed his mother down the stairs singing:

"Dis is the way we brush our teeth, brush our teeth, brush our teeth.
Dis is the way we brush our teeth on a cold and frosky mornin'."

He applauded himself at the end and Jennifer clapped too. "I did that one at school too," she told him as he sat down at the dining table for his breakfast.

He looked at her quizzically. "You don't go school."

"No, but I used to. A long time ago."

"An den you got too big?"

"Yes," she smiled. This communicating with children was easy. Why, it was even easier than talking to an adult. She poured milk on his cornflakes and brought it over to the table for him.

Junior cocked his head to one side, then sat back on the pine chair and crossed his arms.

"Junior? What's wrong with it?"

"I din't want dat. You din't ask me what I want."

Jennifer screwed up her mouth and was about to tell him off and then thought, no, that's perfectly fine, he was right. Adults have a choice, why shouldn't children? If that was the way things worked for him then she would adapt. "Okay Junior, what would you like?" She opened the top cupboard where they kept the cereals. There were two rows of the individual serving boxes of Kellogg's and she brought one set out and laid them in a row in front of him.

"Uhm," Junior scratched his head looking for all the world like a professor trying to solve a difficult equation.

This was going to take longer than she thought. Jennifer pulled out a chair opposite and watched as her three year old son picked out one box, set it aside and then had a rethink and swapped it for another one. "Junior, if you don't hurry up and choose one we're not going to be able to go out later."

"A'right, dis one," he picked out a box of Coco Pops and handed it over. "An' I only drink warm milk," he informed her.

Cheeky! No, Jennifer. She was beginning to see why Donna had thought it necessary to leave her the list. Junior was a very fussy child. Things had to be done just so. How had that happened? There was no way she wanted a spoiled child. He had to know the difference between not having something, and getting something without earning or deserving it. He had to learn respect for other people and their time. *Looks as though whatever he asks for he gets.* And if he didn't get it right away he would keep on until he did. Did that remind her of someone? *Paul Harvey.* Yes, Junior was taking after his father even without having him around. But cycles could be broken, she had seen it happen often enough with families that had passed through her career.

Jennifer decided that they would spend today at play indoors. Tomorrow if the spring weather stayed the way it was today, they would go out and then, starting Monday, they would begin to explore his education. Donna had pointed out that he was bright so it was about time she found out for herself.

Water was dripping from his glistening, taut body as he positioned himself on the diving board for a second dive. He easily executed a complicated dive before his well-developed body hit the water.

Junior was jumping up and down excitedly by the side of the pool, as Tony swam the width under water before emerging on their side of the pool.

"Tony, Tony..." Junior was heading for the side of the pool. Jennifer rushed to grab him.

"It's okay, I've got him!" Tony called out.

"I can swim."

"Can you?" Tony lowered the little boy into the pool beside him.

"He can't," Jennifer smiled.

"I can," he was indignant. "Auntie show me, she did."

Jennifer eased herself over the edge of the pool into the cold water of the swimming pool. What a break this had been. She had spent the whole morning trying to occupy the energetic toddler when Tony had called.

"I'm babysitting," she had told him.

"Need help?"

"From you?"

"No Santa's elves, of course me. I'm chief babysitter in my family you know."

Jennifer had considered it and then thought better of it. She couldn't afford the risk of bumping into someone who knew that Junior was her son. Besides Junior had learnt to call her mummy now and that was the big giveaway, he was now a baby who could talk. It wouldn't take Tony long to find out the real relationship between babysitter and baby. Children this young didn't know how to lie.

Then Tony told her that taking Junior swimming would tire the little boy out, that was all she needed to hear. She went and got Junior ready and told him to call her Jennifer for the day. He was curious as usual and asked, "Why?"

"It's a game Junior. Just for today," she lied, trying to make the idea sound exciting. It seemed to have worked perfectly.

Now Junior was proving he could indeed swim. Jennifer watched them swim away from the side together. Tony staying above water and close to Junior's side in case he should need help. At the other end they hugged each other and Jennifer felt a pang of jealousy. When had her son ever hugged her like that? Only on the odd sleepless night when he crept into her bed. She never encouraged it. That wasn't the only reason for the pang of jealousy though. Jennifer also wanted to hug Tony like that and because of Junior she was holding back on her romantic life.

"Mu..." Junior caught himself, a twinkle came into his eyes, and then he continued, "Jennifer, see I did swim."

"Yes you did, didn't you?" She smiled, pleased that he'd remembered to call her Jennifer. He certainly was a bright boy.

She bobbed in the water watching them whisper conspiratorially. They were swimming back towards her, man and boy. *Father and son.* The thought had crept into her mind suddenly and she pushed it out just as quickly.

"Jen, you telling me you didn't know your nephew could swim?" Junior giggled.

"I've never been with them when they go swimming. He's Donna's son after all and I am a very busy woman."

"Sure, sure," Tony winked at Junior and they giggled again, completely throwing Jennifer for a second. "GET HER!"

Jennifer was soon splashed to a soaking, shivering screaming mess. She swam away and they came after her. In the end she gave in to the game and began to splash them back. The three of them played pool kiss chase, until they were exhausted.

Back at the flat Jennifer again stopped Tony at the door. "We had a great afternoon Tony, thanks."

"It's me that should be thanking you two. Bwoy, I haven't played kiss chase since primary school." He winked at Junior who was yawning. "Pity there weren't more girls, hey champ?"

"Yeah," Junior rubbed his eyes.

"I'd better get him up to bed, I'll call you soon."

"You off for the rest of the week?"

"Yes, while Donna's away."

"Good, we can do something else in a couple of days."

"I don't think so Tony."

"And why not? Junior will enjoy it."

"I just don't think it's a good idea letting him get attached to a man. He's never had a father you see, kids this age make attachments..."

Tony looked offended. He shoved his hands into his jacket pockets and turned to go. "I'll see you around then," he said and was already walking away when she said goodbye. Jennifer closed her eyes. *Tony didn't deserve that.* She was sorry she had to do it, but she knew she wouldn't be doing him any favours by encouraging him. Hurriedly she closed the door, put Tony out of her mind and lifted her sleepy son to take him upstairs to bed.

"Never mind baby, you've got us," she kissed his head surprising not only Junior but herself.

Monday morning, the first thing I did was turn the kitchen into a class-

room. We used the dining table as a desk, the notice board as a blackboard and me as the teacher. Junior was excited at the fact he was going to get to play school. I had dressed him up as though he was going to school. And I dressed like I remembered school teachers dressing.

In front of him he had a pad of plain paper and a felt tip pen. I decided we would start by giving him some first words. To my surprise Junior already knew some six letter words. He was telling me that he could 'draw' the words, Cat, Dog, Rabbit, Pig and Donkey. I said, okay so you know the farm animals what about street words? I gave examples: Taxi, Road, Shops, Crossing.

Would you believe out of those the only things he got wrong were Road which he spelled Rod, and Crossing.

I remembered the self-esteem tape I had bought for him and brought that down from the bookshelf. Together we listened to the moralistic story told by a black woman and a black man then sang along to the song:

"Now can you move right to the beat?
I can do that, I can do that.
Can you touch your head, your shoulder and your feet?
I can do that, I can do that.

Can you shake hands with a neighbour or a friend?
I can do that, I can do that.
Can you spread peanut butter and jam?
I can do that, I can do that."

We stood in the middle of the living room floor doing all the actions, laughing at the funny bits and dancing around the coffee table. God, I hadn't had so much fun since primary school. I promised Junior he'd have to practice what he was saying he could do. The song went on like that. Giving the child accomplishments, like tidying your room, dress yourself, right down to pedalling your bike.

By the time we settled down in the afternoon I had learnt so much more about my son and his potential. I'd been missing out on this and all because of my work schedule and my refusal to let him disrupt that.

It's his father I really feel sorry for. There is so much he is missing and unlike me he will never have the chance to catch up. He might have photos to look at and I could sit and tell him just how bright our son is but there is no way he could relive these moments in Junior's life: seeing his small milestones happening before your eyes and knowing that this little talented person had come from you.

No, Paul Harvey will never have what I have — the love and respect of his son, even despite the lack of time I have spent with him during his short life. I'm now determined that years from now my son isn't going to be able to turn around to me and say, "Where were you when I needed you Mum?"

"Mummy?" Junior looked up and his face was illuminated by the television. I was busy typing up a record of my day on the laptop and as I looked up I noticed Junior was running a toy car along the surface of my glass-topped table. No matter how many times I tell him not to, he only listens long enough to forget.

"Yes Junior," I looked up from the computer.

"Well, you know daddies, right..."

He sounded just like Donna. At some stage I would have to start correcting his grammar. "Fathers you mean."

He looked up at me with puzzled eyes. "Is dat the same?"

"Yes Junior."

"Well, why come I don't have one?"

"A father?"

He nodded.

I should have seen this coming. I'd had months, years even to prepare an answer and yet I was speechless. "Why mummy?"

"Not everyone has one Junior. Some mummies don't need daddies to bring their children up."

"Oh," he said and carried on scratching my table top with the toy car. I assumed he was satisfied with my answer so I started typing again.

"Mummy?"

I sighed, "Yes Junior."

"But don't kids need daddies?"

"Not always," I paused. What do you tell a child who was not yet four years old about the real world? The realities of relationships. The ups and downs. Money problems, careers, sex!

"Did you used to have a daddy?"

"Yes I did."

"Where is he den?" I remembered the photo album we kept in the storage cupboard in the kitchen. Donna and I occasionally spent evenings going through them. Photos of us growing up. Pictures of mummy and daddy, friends, neighbours. I went and fetched them. Junior followed me, and we came back to sit on the rug in the living room. I opened one that contained pictures from five years ago and it showed photos of the four of us one Christmas.

"This is your grandma and grandad, my mum and dad. We were having our Christmas dinner in this picture."

He looked up into my face. "Where are dey?"

"In Jamaica. I've sent them pictures of you and told them all about you."

He turned the page and studied the next set of photos closely. "Does auntie have a mummy and daddy?"

We were getting awfully close to the truth now and I knew he wouldn't be satisfied until he got answers. "Yes."

He came right back with, "So why don't I?"

I sat back against the settee and pulled him to me. Junior was watching my face closely. I knew I couldn't lie. "It started before you were born, your father was a man who wanted to be rich, and if he'd kept you it would have stopped him from getting rich and so he left us."

"He wanted money more dan me?"

"He wanted his..." I stopped, suddenly realizing that I really didn't know what he wanted. I was not prepared to make his excuses for him. I was also not going to make anything up about Paul Harvey. Junior would only know the truth about his father. I wasn't the one stopping him from seeing his child, it had always been his decision.

"Mummy, did you want money as well?"

"Why?"

" 'Cause I didn't have you for a looooong time," he dragged out the word.

"I know and I'm sorry." I felt guilty. "I was so angry at your father that I became angry at you too...because you were a part of him. Do you understand?"

It was obvious he didn't. He was turning the pages of the photo album. Images of my happy childhood family were planting themselves into his head. I felt tears in my own eyes at how much I had missed out on his life because of my own selfishness.

My son had had to grow up without his father and without the attention of his mother, and for what? Money! Status! What is all that without the love of your family? Your own flesh and blood. I hugged him to me and he put one small chubby arm around my neck and we sat like that for the longest time.

Jennifer had been trying to shut off her alarm clock for several seconds before she realized it was the telephone that was jarring her nerves.

"You were asleep?" The familiar deep voice brought her slowly round to consciousness. Her heartbeat increased and her temperature shot up ten degrees.

"Tony...no, no not really," she stammered.

"Mmm. What does that mean? Could it be that you're in bed but not alone?"

She chuckled, this was just what she liked about Tony. The ability to make her smile in any situation. She was exhausted, after spending half the night with a fretful toddler. Junior had had a stomach ache and wouldn't sleep in his own bed, but even in hers she had to keep getting up to rush him to the toilet. Jennifer touched her head, her soft curlers were askew under her fingers. Her silk headscarf lay on the pillow.

"Of course I'm alone. Where are you?"

"In bed."

"In your own bed?"

"Of course I'm in my own bed," he mimicked her coquettish tone making her laugh again.

Jennifer imagined him laying on top of his duvet with nothing on but his boxer shorts. Before her imagination could go any further she rolled over to look at the clock. It was only eight o'clock, but usually she was up by now. Junior moaned and curled his little body up into a ball. "What are you doing up at this time of the morning?"

"I was woken by a dream of you in your swim suit and couldn't get back to sleep." She was his closest female friend and yet he often found himself thinking about her in ways he knew he probably shouldn't. She had trim legs, a nice bust, the most remarkable eyes. Maybe he wouldn't mind taking her to bed, but would she mind being taken? And what would happen after that? More than once he had found his eyes wandering down to the V of her blouse and had to remind himself that *your little head could often get your big head in a lot of trouble.* It worked every time.

Jennifer was smiling, it was the first time Tony had made a sexual reference to her and she liked it. "Yeah?" If only he could see her now, with her bleary eyes and curlers he wouldn't be thinking what he was thinking.

"Mmm hmm."

"I suppose I should be flattered that I was your first thought of the day."

Now he laughed. "What are you doing for the rest of the day?"

"Sleeping most probably. Junior was up all night with a stomach ache." There was silence on the other end.

"I had a good time the other day, with you and Junior," Tony chuckled. "Boy makes you want to have kids of your own doesn't he?"

"Yes he does," Jennifer replied meaning every word.

"So when can I take you two out again?"

"Tony..." she said hesitantly.

"Don't start with that 'not getting attached' business," he interrupted. "I don't mind being his uncle." There was a second's silence. "Don't you trust me?"

"Tony, it's not a matter of trust."

"You're a very protective auntie, I like that. But you don't want to rob your nephew of male companionship."

Jennifer thought about it. "I'll need to discuss it with his mother. I'll call you later, okay?"

"Mmm. Promise?"

She imagined his face, the way he pouted his lips and fluttered his eyelashes when he was teasing her. "Promise."

They finished the conversation with a jokey phone kiss and Jennifer leaned back on the pillow glowing from the conversation but still feeling exhausted. Junior woke up a few minutes later and Jennifer rolled out of bed, stood stock still in the shower, dragged on a long jumper and an old pair of leggings and moved mechanically through her new morning routine.

Junior seemed to notice her lethargy and decided to take full advantage of it. He dragged every single toy he owned out of their boxes and placed them in all the places she'd told him not to. Midmorning, they did another self-esteem lesson. They were now onto feel good about yourself songs such as *I Love You No Matter What*, and *Positive Power*. Each day they would sing one song together. It didn't always have to be at the same time of day either — morning, lunchtime, bedtime. Junior had even remembered one as they walked through the streets of Lewisham the day before and had began singing happily to himself:

"I love you when you're happy, I love you when you're mad,
I love you when we disagree or when we're holding hands."

He'd squeezed Jennifer's hand then and she'd looked down into his sweet chubby face and had to bend down to give him a hug.

After their song she realized what a mess their home was and sent him outside with his bike while she tidied up indoors. She had taken to watching the afternoon soaps and chat shows with a cup of tea and a doughnut whilst Junior took his afternoon nap and she set about the task of cleaning so that the flat would be in order when she came to sit down.

When the doorbell rang Jennifer was reluctant to answer it. *Who could it possibly be?* She hadn't even bothered to take out her curlers. Had Tony decided to overrule her decision not to see him and come over anyway?

She got up and looked down the stairs to the front door. What was she doing, she didn't have x-ray eyes? Tentatively, she walked down in her slippers and half opened the front door, peering through the gap, and immediately wished she had followed her first instinct not to answer it.

Paul Harvey stood there with a bunch of flowers in his arms. He was dressed in his business suit. "Jennifer?"

She didn't say a word, one hand went to her head. *The curlers!* The way she was dressed! *Oh my god!* Jennifer had always thought that if she saw Paul Harvey again she would be showing him how having his child hadn't changed her. She was still working full-time and living the life she had planned to live. But right now she looked a mess and felt like a cleaner out of *Coronation Street*.

"Aren't you going to let me in," there was a wry smirk on his face.

"I'm not dressed. What do you want anyway?"

"Jennifer..."

She shivered involuntarily, remembering how she'd loved the way her name rolled off his tongue. "Don't start with any explanations and you can keep your flowers, we don't need you."

"My son might feel differently."

"Your *what?!*" She pulled the door fully open, facing him in all her charwoman glory. "*My* son wouldn't want anything to do with you no matter what you were offering as a bribe."

Paul looked around disconcertedly, he coughed. "Can we talk about this inside?"

Jennifer crossed her hands over her chest. "I have nothing to say to you, Mr. Harvey."

"Jennifer, I have found a way to disperse our grievances," he told her, leaning closer to the door. "If you let me in perhaps we can discuss them."

Jennifer scrutinized him hard before letting him into her home. Junior was still out in the back garden playing, she hoped he would stay out there until she got rid of this intruder. "Well?" she asked, as he stood opposite her in the living room.

He looked around at the toy box in one corner, the pile of children's books on the coffee table and her mug and plate sticky with the jam from her doughnut. He cleared his throat.

"You said you had a way to stop me hating you?"

"Not quite the way I put it, but yes. May I?" He gestured towards the sofa. Jennifer nodded but remained standing herself. Paul still held the bunch of roses and orchids.

"How is...our son?"

"My son is doing just fine, healthy, intelligent and prosperous, like his mother."

"I see. And you received the money I've been sending?"

"Yes, although I haven't touched a penny of it, you're quite welcome to have it back," she spat back at him.

Paul Harvey shot her a look, but it quickly disappeared as she stared him down with a look of her own. He clasped his hands around the stem of flowers. "I'm married now."

"I know," she sniped, "How is *Mrs*. Harvey?"

"As a matter of fact that was what I came to talk to you about."

"Your wife?"

"In a way. My wife and I want to start a family. She is a little older than myself and we've encountered some...complications."

Jennifer breathed out exasperatedly. *Get to the point*.

She saw Paul swallow hard and then run a hand around the inside collar of his shirt. "Our son..." he coughed, "needs a father. You have no idea how overjoyed I was to find out I had a son." His eye met hers and she stared him down again.

"Just in case you'd forgotten, Paul, you gave up all rights to your son the moment you took up with that bitch for your career."

Paul placed the flowers on the coffee table, freeing his hands. "Let's not get heated, Jennifer," he held up his hand. "What I have to say may be to your advantage. I realized that when you fell pregnant with our baby..."

There he goes with that 'Our' baby again. Since when did he have anything to do with this child other than providing the sperm? She didn't seem to recall him going through pregnancy, labour, or sleepless nights in order to call himself a parent.

"...That you didn't want to go through with it on your own. I also realize what a terrible time it must have been for you to find yourself in that position. He must be a real handful now, about three isn't he?"

Jennifer was too angry to speak without screaming.

"Anyway, my proposition is this," he cleared his throat again, "I want to have custody of our son."

Jennifer's mouth fell open, "Whaat...?!!"

"Please, hear me out first. Just think of the benefits to yourself. You wouldn't have to do this on your own anymore. I could let you have full visitation rights as agreed with my wife. I could even run to giving you maintenance when he comes to stay with you."

Blood was pumping in her ears, her heart was beating way too fast. She felt so hot she was afraid she would pass out, then she heard the back door open and close. The sound of the little boy's footsteps raced up the stairs and stopped in the doorway to the flat. Jennifer turned and went to her son's side.

Paul stood up a smile on his face. "This must be the little man in question."

Junior looked up at his mother questioningly, wrapping a hand around his mother's leg.

"And what's your name, son?"

Jennifer grimaced at his use of the word 'son', she wasn't finished with him yet.

Junior grinned because he knew the answer to that question, "June-ya Edwards," he said proudly.

"Junior, so your real name's Paul," he said, crouching down in front of Junior.

Junior looked confused. "No, my name's June-ya."

Paul looked up at Jennifer. "You named him *Junior*?"

"That's what he said, didn't he?"

"I can't believe you would do that," he shook his head and muttered. "Never mind, that's easily remedied." Paul turned on his smile again and touched the boy's shoulder. "Well Junior, it's nice to finally meet you."

"Who're you?" Junior asked.

Jennifer tensed and was ready to stop him when Paul said, "I'm your daddy."

Jennifer felt Junior's arm grip her leg tighter. "No. You're not my daddy. I don't 'ave a daddy." Paul looked up at Jennifer accusingly.

"Junior, it's okay," she bent down to him trying to soothe him, his little cheeks had turned red.

Junior continued to shout at Paul, "You're not my daddy. Leave my mummy alone, we hate you, leave me alone!" He struggled out of his mother's arms and headed for the spiral staircase, climbing it as fast as his little legs could carry him.

Jennifer waited until he had gone before turning her wrath on Paul. "What the hell did you do that for?"

"He has a right to be told."

"Jus' like you think you've got a right to come in here and tell me that you think you and your bitch can raise my son better than I can."

"I never said that."

"You damn well did," Jennifer felt her street self erupting, her hands flew in his face. "You can take your blasted self-righteous self back out that front door just like you did when you left me pregnant to marry for money."

"You've turned my son against me..."

"What was there to turn against? He doesn't know you, and even if he did he wouldn't like you Paul." She looked him up and down, eyes burning with hatred, dragging him down to something she would wipe off her shoe.

Paul approached her, "I know how you must feel..."

Jennifer was enraged, "You *know!!* Know what? I'd be very interested to know exactly what it is you think you know," her head bobbed from side to side.

Paul's expression changed from fake compassion to a sneer. "I can see I'm wasting my time here. Don't think you've heard the last of this. I'll see you in court."

Jennifer ran up behind him as he reached for the door handle and as she did so she raised one leg and caught him square in the centre of his back. His head slammed into the front door with a thud. He let out a cry and when he turned back to her his nose was bleeding.

"You shall be hearing from me," he said through his hand, his voice muffled. "Maybe I'll add assault to my list of charges."

"In that case maybe I should make a good job of it," her hand went automatically to the vase on the table by the front door. Paul noticed this and he was out the door before the vase even left the table.

Jennifer shut her eyes and fought back tears of anger. Then she laughed. She laughed so hard that her sides hurt. Junior came down the stairs, watching his mother leaning against the front door laughing.

"What's funny mummy?"

"Nothing baby, nothing." Junior looked at her, his baby face puzzled and then he started to laugh too. "We showed him didn't we?" Jennifer said through tears.

Junior wiped her cheek with a chubby hand, "Yeah."

Just what makes a man think he has the right to walk back into a woman's life after three years and tell her how to run it? What is it with them? Yes, I had the hots for Paul. I wanted him body, mind and wallet, but that was nearly four years ago!

This is a new generation of women he's dealing with. Unlike our grandmothers and even our mothers before us, we don't need to wait around for a man to marry us, get us pregnant and turn us into his personal housekeeper and sex slave. Oh no! This generation is taking care of its own business. We're not standing for any of their macho crap either, because sometimes a woman's got to be a bitch to survive.

Paul Harvey obviously hasn't woken up to that fact, nor will he until he stops looking for an easy way to the top and wakes up to reality. If he thinks marrying a white politician's daughter will make him fit in and guarantee him status, he's wrong. They're still looking at a black man, no matter who he's married to or how he speaks.

Take my son away from me! Ah, if he thinks I'd stand by and let him be taken away by a complete stranger, he's got another think coming. I would seriously consider murder before I let that happen. When I told Karen and Elaine the other night they thought I should get a hit man and just scare him a little. Between Karen and myself I'm sure we could come up with enough hard cases that would be only too glad to do it for a few pounds. But seriously, if he does come after my son he's got a fight on his hands.

Anyway, that's enough about Paul. Over the past few weeks I've gotten to know two males a lot better, my son and Tony Carnegie.

Junior is just so bright, and loving. He's reading well, attentive, inquisitive and on the odd occasion he has a helpful streak. Don't get me wrong, he's as boisterous as most three year old boys but when I need a hug or a kiss he seems to sense it and comes to my aid. He's back at nursery now. I went back to work two days ago and Donna got back from holiday too. At the moment I'm trying to reschedule my work pattern and case loads so that I can spend time with Junior in the evenings, before he goes to bed. I miss him like crazy. I've got a photo of him and Tony together on my desk, it was taken the last time we were in the park together.

Tony, now he surprised me. Just last night he told me a well kept secret. He shared this with me on our first...romantic night together. After years of being just good friends and colleagues, Tony asked me out on a 'real date' as he put it. He told me to wear something sexy so that he could stop seeing me as Miss Edwards. He wanted to see the real Jennifer.

"So where exactly would the lady like to go?" he'd asked me.

"I don't know," I said, "surprise me...I just want to have a good time...take me where I can have a good time..."

So I asked Donna to babysit and spent ages trying to find 'the real me' as Tony put it. I parted my longer length hair down the middle and swept the front behind my ears, letting the back hang to my neck and then the ends were flipped up for that sixties look. I wore a short lilac sleeveless dress with a matching bolero jacket and fashionable platform silver shoes. Tony pretended not to recognize me when I stepped out of the taxi in front of the wine bar, then he twirled around and whistled. "Miss Edwards, where have you been all my life?" before putting an arm around my back. It felt exciting.

We started off in King's wine bar in Dulwich, but didn't stay longer than it took us to finish two drinks. The atmosphere wasn't right. We then went back to his flat. I hadn't realized how much private detecting pays. Tony's flat was simple but tastefully furnished courtesy of Ikea. He put a video on and we settled down on the sofa, side by side, to watch 'The Last Boy Scout' over microwave popcorn and diet coke.

Tony was laughing so hard at one point that he spilt coke down the front of his T-shirt and without a care in the world whipped it over his head and threw it in the direction of the bathroom. He leaned back on the sofa dressed just in his black jeans and socks. How lucky men are. They could take off their tops in public, walk the streets in nothing but a skimpy pair of shorts, a woman doing that would either get arrested or whisked off to the local loony bin. Now if I had just taken my top off and sat there as normal, he would have thought I was getting fresh.

I hadn't really noticed his body before. Even when we had gone swimming I was too worried that Junior would forget to call me by my name, to take in his fine physique. Now as I took in his lean, toned frame, broad muscle capped shoulders, I wanted to touch him. He smelt of cocoa butter and aftershave, a lickable smell. What I was feeling surprised me because, right at that moment, I wanted him to be mine. Every time his bare flesh brushed mine, I broke out in goose pimples.

This had never happened with Tony before. When we'd first met he was just an annoying PI with a cheeky smile. Then he'd become an arrogant self assured MAN, then a witty companion and friend. But now...Now what?

There was an electronic keyboard in the corner of his front room covered by a dust sheet. I asked him if he could play.

"I played a bit at school," he shrugged.

"Play for me."

"Now why didn't you just ask me to sing?"

"Because I've heard you sing," I said wryly. Tony had this habit of singing along to songs on the car radio as he drove. He sang terribly.

He whipped the dust sheet off of the keyboard and switched it on. "Well, you'll be happy to know that during my performance you will be so taken aback by the fact that I can't play that you won't even notice my singing."

I laughed. Tony cleared his throat, cracked his knuckles and then played a couple of bars before starting a bluesy tune. I knew it, it was the intro to Gershwin's 'Summertime'. He was obviously being modest, because he could actually play the thing.

"Summertime, and the living is easy," he sang with a deep exaggerated Southern accent, "...fish are jumping and the cotton is high. Oh your daddy's rich and your ma is good looking, so hush little baby don't you cry." He chuckled to himself as he played on.

A sweet shiver went down my spine. My heartbeat quickened. I was amazed. There were hidden depths to this man that I hadn't realized.

"You can play."

"I surprise myself sometimes," he said arrogantly. I knew he was joking. "Come sing with me," he said and opened the book on top of the keyboard. I went over and squeezed onto the seat next to him.

I sang the next verse on my own and when I'd finished we both started laughing while he played on through the chorus.

Afterwards Tony put some music on and we got talking. We talked about movies we'd seen, places we'd visited and ambitions. He always had amusing stories to tell about his work. Finally the conversation had come around to families, ex relationships and children.

"I have something I need to tell you."

For a moment it took me back to when Paul had said almost the same thing. I wondered why I couldn't stop comparing them. "You know you can tell me anything, T."

He was playing with the gold bracelet he wore and then he stopped and looked me straight in my eyes with a look of sincerity that took me aback. "I'm not like other guys," he said in a high-pitched Michael Jackson voice.

I giggled and curled one leg up under me. "I know that you fool, you're a mad man."

He laughed too but kind of shyly, he really did have something to say. "You know how I feel about you don't you?"

"How's that?" I asked.

"Come on, you don't need me to spell it out."

"I think I do. Indulge me."

He laughed in that cute way he had, "I L. O. V. E. Y.O.U."

"Come again!"

"You wanted me to spell it out."

I placed one hand on his bare chest and pushed him, he fell back on the sofa, his legs came up and fell across my lap. A strategic move on his part. I was laughing with happiness by this point. He crossed one arm across his chest and reached for my hand with the other. I took it happily.

"That wasn't all I had to tell you," he said.
"Stop playing around. Spit it out man."
"There is someone else," he was dead serious.

Now I knew this had been too good to be true. I could feel my throat constricting and my eyes glazed over, but he was smiling and squeezing my hand tighter. "I didn't mean another woman silly," he sat up and kissed my forehead. My confusion must have shown on my face. Why was he doing this to me? A joke is one thing, but why did he have to be so good at winding me up.

"I have a son," he confessed. "Wesley is eight and I get to see him only when I make an appointment with his mother or when she needs him out of the way, so that she can go out."

I searched his eyes waiting for the, 'Gotcha', but it didn't come. "You're serious?"

"Never been more so...except for when I said I loved you."

That brought another smile to my face, but also a sense of guilt to my heart. "So why didn't you tell me before?" I wanted to know.

"I didn't want you to think of me that way. You were always going on about baby fathers and how the lot of us couldn't care less about our kids. I do, but I knew you wouldn't believe me."

I felt sad. He was right I wouldn't have. Although now that he had opened up to me I so much wanted to tell him the truth about Junior. I touched his face with one hand, his smooth youthful face, so trusting and open. I kissed his lips lightly. "I love you too. I'm glad you told me about Wesley."

He grinned at me. "So do you have any secrets you wanna tell me about?"

"No," I said hastily, "Do you have any pictures of Wesley?"

He was up and had the pictures in his hand within a minute. He showed me pictures of Wesley from the beginning. His girlfriend had been pretty, was pretty still I presumed. When I commented on it he said that was all she had going for her.

Wesley looked more like her than Tony. He had a round face, but was tall, and lean like his father. "Gonna be a basketball player," Tony said proudly. Watching him talk about his son made me want to share all I'd discovered about my own, but I couldn't yet, not now.

"...One more chance, baby
Give me one more chance..."

Later we lay on the sofa together, my head on his chest, the CD left to repeat over and over. Just talking as easily as we always did, about everything and nothing, finishing each other's sentences. I could feel his breath tickling my forehead with each word. Our first kiss was unlike I'd imagined it would be. His lips brushed my forehead, settling on each eyelid so softly as I turned my face up to him. It was as though every nerve in my body were transmitting signals to each other. An R. Kelly track was playing in the background and our bodies were already moving to the beat of 'Downlow'.

"...You want me but he needs you.
Yet you're telling me that everything is cool,
Trying to convince me baby to do as you say,
Just go along and see things your way..."

He kissed my nose, then looked at me, "I want you," he said. "Is that all right?"

"...Keep it on the downlow,
Whispering, nobody has to know, nobody..."

A shiver ran down my back to my toes and then burned its way back up the front of my body, setting my vagina alight and then sending burning little fires alight in all my erogenous zones. My lips found his, our lips touched for a whole minute before I opened up to him and our tongues met. I felt his mouth on my neck, sucking my flesh tantalizingly, I sighed with the new senses awakening. One of his hands went to the zip at the back of my dress. The little jolt of electricity began again and the tingling along the surface of my skin. We swopped places so that he was on top. I grabbed the back of his neck and held him to me while I lay back, his arms made struts on each side of my body, his body like a tent. I was kissing his chest, sucking his tight little nipples and he moaned as his body came down on top of mine. I could feel his erection strong against my groin. "You're beautiful," I told him, "Your body is so beautiful."

There wasn't the hurried passion I'd had with Paul. We were taking our time. Taking our time to remove our clothes bit by sensuous bit. Tony hadn't closed his eyes the entire time, which at first I found unnerving and then erotic. He was taking in every inch of me.

Tony pulled one nipple into his mouth, and then the other, his mouthing so soft that I couldn't tell his mouth from my own skin, with little flicks of his tongue he had me digging my fingers into his hard back. His fingers found the moistness between my legs, he stroked lightly and I felt myself melting. I twisted to pull down the zipper on his flies to release him from his *jeans and he grabbed my hand.*

Pulling me up from the sofa he led me into the bedroom. He didn't pull back the bed sheets, we undressed in the middle of the floor, still exploring, tasting each other's bodies. That night I discovered that the soles of the feet are one of our most erogenous zones, but Tony must have known this already. Before he pushed me back gently onto the bed, he took a packet of condoms from his dresser drawer and kneeled in front of me. He rolled it on so sensually making sure I was watching him that instead of being a passion killer it became a sexy part of the foreplay. At that moment I longed to be penetrated whilst the rest of me wanted desperately to hold onto that feeling, to memorize the warmth of being held, the ecstasy of being in a state of desire.

At last, he took me into his arms and laid me down. He brushed kisses onto my cheeks and neck and then across my breasts. As he entered me I remember saying all those things that lovers say that sound so corny afterwards. Already I was coming, but he waited for me to come again and again.

Afterwards, laying dreamily in his arms, I knew this was what love was all about. So when he turned around and said, "Jen will you marry me?" I almost said 'yes' straight away before reality crowded my senses again and I stopped myself.

"Can I think about that one?"

He kissed my forehead. "Sure, as long as the answer's yes."

I loved the shape of his jaw and chin and the way his lips always seemed to curl upwards. I realized I'd wanted to kiss those lips since the very first day I'd met him. So I kissed them now to my heart's content. Soon his arms were around me and we were off again.

The week passed quickly. Tony had called her every night. Sometimes just to talk and other times to ask if she had made a decision yet. She hadn't, and by Sunday night she had a permanent headache. Self-induced pain, she thought glumly. Thoughts of Tony came and went in her mind. Her moods would swing from joy and warmth to confusion and guilt. One moment she was willing him to call and the next, wishing he would disappear off the face of the earth.

She had told Elaine about her problem of owning up to disowning her son and Elaine had said, "Don't make fire where there's no smoke — tell him."

When she told Beverly, she said, "How could you do that? How would Junior feel if he found out you were ashamed of him? And what about Tony? He's proposed...Who would want to marry someone who lied about something like that?"

Okay, it had been foolish to lie. She hadn't thought he would ever have to know the truth. How could she have predicted the future?

After Beverly's reproach Jennifer decided not to mention her dilemma to Karen. She dreaded what she would say to her.

"So when are you going to invite him round?" Donna was asking.

"What?" Jennifer looked up from her computer.

Donna got up from the floor where she had been eating sausage and chips in front of the telly. Junior was sprawled out asleep on the sofa. "Tony. When are you going to invite him round to meet his new family?"

Jennifer frowned and turned back to the computer, her hair fell over one eye and she threw it back irritably. "It might not be his new family, I haven't made a decision yet. I've been thinking, maybe it's too soon to be introducing a stranger into Junior's life."

Now it was Donna's turn to frown. "What are you talking about? Junior knows Tony and he likes him, you told me that yourself."

Jennifer breathed deeply and evenly. "It might turn out to be a complete disaster. You know how quickly Junior bonds with people. What if it doesn't work out with Tony and we break up, what will that do to Junior? I don't want to risk it."

"Have you told Tony this?" Donna placed her plate on her sister's desk and leant against the wall to her sister's right.

Jennifer was suddenly angry. "I will okay! Why is everyone hassling me nowadays?"

Donna's eyes widened, "Jen, what's the matter?"

Jennifer jumped up, pushed her chair back and made for the door, "Just leave it." Her life, it seemed, was in everybody's hands but her own.

Donna was shocked and wanted to go after her, but knew that when her sister was angry it was best to leave her to deal with it alone. She hadn't expected that kind of reaction from mentioning the man Jennifer was supposed to be madly in love with. It could be that Jennifer was just being careful because of what had happened with Paul. Whatever it was, she would find out eventually. Donna went over to the sofa and picked Junior up, hugging his cuddly, warm body against her chest. She lay back on the sofa with her nephew snuggled against her and turned back to watch the Eddie Murphy movie on the television.

Jennifer glanced at the clock. It was almost eleven o'clock on a Thursday night. She'd been in the office since ten o'clock that morning. There had been paperwork to finish. She dropped her pen on the blotter and stretched. Rubbing her eyes she poured water from the jug on her desk. There was a big discrimination case tomorrow afternoon and she hadn't been able to concentrate all week.

Tony had wanted her to go shopping with him on Saturday...for an engagement ring! He was still trying to convince her to say 'yes'. And Donna was excited at getting another chance at being a bridesmaid. *Marriage!* Her second proposal. Jennifer wished she had kept it to herself but she had been too excited when he'd asked her. She'd felt like an excited fool. The perfect opportunity for her to tell Tony about Junior and she had chickened out. All of this week she had managed to avoid seeing Tony, claiming that she had too much work on. To Tony it must have seemed as if she had second thoughts because of his son, but the truth was she was still trying to find a way to tell him about Junior.

After a moment or two of contemplative silence, she wandered down the echoing corridor to the ladies.

"Evening Miss Edwards," Ken Power, one of their regular security guards, was rounding a corner as she pushed the door.

"Evening Ken," she smiled tiredly.

"Working late again? Young girl like you should be home snuggling up with your boyfriend not sweating over dusty books."

"I know Ken, maybe one day I'll find the time."

Life was a bitch. If this was a movie she could have the bit where she had lied to Tony edited out, but this was real life. Anyway, if Tony had told her about his son from the start she wouldn't have had to lie in the first place. Jennifer freshened up and made her way back to her office dragging her feet on the polished wooden floor. The office door was still open and as she walked back in her semi-sleepy state she didn't even notice the man in her seat until her chair spun around. Tony smiled broadly at her.

She was too startled to smile. "How did you get in here?"

"Your kind security guard let me in on my fake ID."

"God, you just can't get the staff nowadays," she said sarcastically, hands on her hips.

"Ready?"

Jennifer was somewhat bemused. "For what?"

"I thought you'd be hungry. We could get something to eat..."

She cut him short. "I'm tired, T," she walked over to the coat stand. "I just want to go home, maybe it's my time of the month."

"Why don't you come back to my place? If it's your monthlies we don't have to..."

"I just want to get home." *Tell him, put him out of his misery.*

He clasped his hands on the table and nodded, his smile fading, but still flickering on his lips. "Maybe Saturday night?"

She nodded, reaching for her coat, Tony jumped up and helped her put it on. He put one hand on her shoulder turning her towards him. He bent forward and kissed her, aware that she was keeping her arms by her sides. He frowned. "Talk to me Jen, what's wrong?"

"I told you," she turned her back to him again, "I'm just really tired. I've had all this work," she indicated her desk full of books and folders.

He followed her and standing behind her he pulled her close. "Jen, this is me you're talking to. I *know* you."

"You don't know anything about me," she pulled away walking to the other side of the desk out of his reach. "Tony...I can't see you again."

His arms dropped to his sides.

She glanced up and looked for a brief second into his sad brown eyes. "There's someone else," she lied.

"You expect me to believe that?" he placed his knuckles on the desk leaning towards her. "Last weekend we made love, I proposed to you. We've known each other for over two years..."

"I just can't have you in my life anymore."

He swiftly covered the space between them and stood directly in front of her. Jennifer's heart was pounding and she wanted to cry, but her lie wouldn't ring true. If she was really finishing with him for someone else why would she be crying over it? He was so close now she could smell his mouthwash. "Jen," he reached out and placed a finger under her chin, turning her face up towards him. There were tears in her eyes. "Jen...I *know*."

She sniffed. "What do you know?"

"I know about Junior. This is what this is all about, isn't it?"

Jennifer wasn't giving anything away. "What do you know?" she repeated.

"I know he's your son and not your sister's. I know who his father is and who he's married to. I know that you're paranoid about being labelled. I told you a long time ago, I *know* women. I'm a detective, it's my job to know these things."

She stared at him incredulous. He'd known all along and he'd let her carry on this charade! Had he been laughing at her? Was this supposed to make her feel better? Well it didn't. And what was all this detective stuff all of a sudden?

"You've been spying on me?" her voice was angry and husky.

Tony jumped back. "Don't you think I'm the one that's supposed to be angry here?"

"Don't give me that," she glared at him. "You've been digging up my past without my permission. God, Tony! How low do you go?"

He sighed, and his shoulders sagged. "I was curious, and then when I found out I figured it would only be a matter of time before you told me. I thought telling you about my son would get you talking to me, trusting me."

Jennifer lowered her eyes. "Touché," she said and walked into his arms. "How long have you known?"

"A year."

Her tears started afresh. What a fool. How could she have carried on that way for so long? What must he think of her?

Proving how close they were, he answered as if reading her mind. "I don't think any less of you. Remember I told you I loved you, I knew then and it doesn't make any difference." He kissed her nose and then her lips.

Her lips trembled. "I'm so sorry, Tony," she choked. "As time went on I wanted to tell you..." she looked up at him "...but I just didn't know how." She rested her head on his chest and he caressed her face until her sobbing ceased.

"Come on, enough already. Big 'ooman ah bawl like lickle pickney."

She laughed.

"That's better. I understand," he said softly. "So, your place or mine?"

"That's another thing, about us getting married..."

He had one eyebrow raised. "Yes?"

"How would you feel about us living together first?"

"I'm down with that."

"It's just that I feel Junior should have an adjusting period."

He let a breath out through his lips. "Bwoy, this is a big move...Are you sure?"

She looked up into his eyes. "The question is, are you?"

He nodded. "Never been more sure."

She hugged him before going to her desk for her briefcase and handbag. She wiped salty tears from her eyes. "Home, Jeeves."

He put on an American drag queen accent, he let one hand go limp and placed the other on his hip. "Girl, when we get home, we is gonna do some talking."

"Yes sir, or should I say, sista," she laughed.

He smacked her bottom lightly as she passed him. She leant on his shoulder as they left the building, arms crossed behind each other. "So, what are we having for dinner?"

"How about microwave lasagne."

"Mmm, my favourite."

TEN
Lovin' heart mek backbone strong

Donna took a month to make up her mind about Tony moving in. We had told her together, sitting side by side holding hands like teenagers facing my parents. Donna had looked from one of us to the other and then said, "I'll have to think about it." It wasn't as if I was asking her permission, I just wanted to know what she thought of the idea. But as this would mean a disruption in our household, I felt it only right to hear her views.

Junior had taken to him from their first meeting and was impatient for Tony to move in with us. Donna said that seeing as she would be moving out to live on campus in September that I could do as I pleased.

Tony wanted me to meet his parents.

"It's best that you meet them now before we start cohabiting, so you don't chuck me out 'pon de streets afterwards." He was always joking around, I was never sure whether he was winding me up or not. He had given me a pretty good idea of his parents and their views on family so I basically knew what to expect. And I felt it was only right that I was introduced to his parents with Junior in tow. Tony said that was fine by him but he'd warn them in advance so that they could put away all their breakables.

We went in Tony's car. It was pouring with rain, the traffic was moving lethargically through the streets of south east London. As we turned off Peckham's Rye Lane I suddenly got nervous. I turned around and looked at Junior who had fallen asleep in his booster seat in the back of the car.

Suppose they were fond of Tony's ex-girlfriend and had wanted them to stay together. Wouldn't they see me as an intruder? Would we end up with all those old arguments like, why did he run from one relationship and leave his son to raise someone else's? I hadn't voiced these fears to Tony because they hadn't raised themselves until now. Tony must have felt my anxiety too *because he placed one hand on my knee and gave it a squeeze, I covered his hand with mine and our eyes met.*

Tony was carrying a still sleepy Junior. I stood silently by his side and waited for that blue painted front door of his parent's home to open and reveal his background to me. It was still raining and memories of those old horror movies where the travellers turn up at a spooky house in the country came back to me. The door opened.

"Hello Dad," Tony smiled at the man standing in front of us in a short sleeved shirt. He was as tall as Tony and thin, his eyes lit up at the sight of his son.

"Come in boy, we expected you later. Yuh madda's still cooking," he smiled warmly at me. "Come in, come in." He invited us into the narrow hallway and I followed awkwardly. The door closed behind me and my heart leapt. This was it, no escape.

"This is Jennifer," Tony turned to me. "And this is her son Junior."

"Hello Jennifer," he took my hand and I looked at him properly for the first time. He was in his mid-fifties with very young lively eyes. His hair was still jet black and there was no bald batch. Which meant that Tony would hopefully be just as lucky.

"Hello, Mr. Carnegie."

"Derek," he said. "Come t'ru, come t'ru," Tony was already heading up the staircase into the flat above. The smells of Jamaican cooked chicken were wafting towards us as we ascended. Junior's head rose and he looked around him and then at me. His inquisitive eyes were everywhere at once. Inside the flat stood the woman who had brought the man I loved into the world.

"Derek, open some wine, my son is home," the woman's voice was loud and confident. I almost stood to attention. She was a large imposing woman, streaks of grey hair were just beginning around her temple. Her mouth had the same cupid's bow as Tony's and her brows and eyes would probably look like his if she smiled. Instead, there was discontent etched in those eyes as she looked at her son. He turned, handing Junior to me before moving across to her. He folded his arms around her affectionately and they embraced.

"Hello Mum." I met her eyes over Tony's shoulder. Had I just imagined that she was imposing because of the tension I'd felt? In Tony's arms, she was smaller in height than she'd first seemed. However, in every other detail, Tony really was his mother's son.

"Anthony, yuh not eating? Just like yuh faada, bwoy I can feel yuh ribs."

He laughed. "That's hard muscle, mum. By the way, this is Jennifer and Junior."

"Nice to meet you Jennifer," her eyes passed over Junior and he clung tight to my neck. "Is he shy?"

"Not usually," I said feeling like a teenager all over again. She walked towards me, three steps and it was like it happened in slow motion and took the longest time.

"Would Junior like an ice lolly?"

Junior's face immediately lit up and he pushed to be let down. I put him down and he followed Tony's mum into the kitchen.

"Come upstairs, nuh," Derek called. Following Tony's lead I took the two steps up to their split-level living room. It was an overcrowded little room, filled with furniture that they probably couldn't bear to part with. Beautiful ruffled blinds hung from all three windows along one wall. I sat down on the dark leather couch, in the centre so as not to disrupt the plump yellow cushions in each corner.

"Move over," Tony said lowering himself next to me. "It's hard to believe, but two can sit on it."

Derek chuckled and handed us both a glass of wine. My throat was dry and I wanted to knock it back all at once but instead I sipped it ladylike. There was a glass coffee table in front of me, on top of which was a vase of nylon flowers. There were photos of the family all around us. Black and white ones of their daughters and son growing up as well as newer portraits of the grandchildren — Tony's nephew and three nieces. Everything was dust free. Junior came back in with an ice lolly and I immediately started searching for tissues.

"Relax Jen. Mum's had kids in here before, you know."

I breathed deeply trying to relax. When his mother came in and took a seat opposite me, Tony got up and went to sit on the arm of her chair, taking one of her hands in his. I didn't know where to look. I felt lost, so I pulled Junior closer and said, "You've got a lovely home."

Her smile widened at the compliment. "You known Anthony long?" she asked me.

I looked over at Tony and he was smiling. He probably found this very funny. "About three years Mrs. Carnegie," I replied. "We worked together before we became...friends."

"Please call me Rose," she smiled. I know she was trying to put me at ease but I was still waiting for that punch line.

"Jennifer's a barrister," Tony said.

Derek raised an eyebrow and slapped his thigh, "Big time lawyer!"

"My son always did have an eye for quality," Rose said. I took another sip of my wine to avoid her eyes. "So, you're divorced?"

"No, uhm, Junior's father just didn't want to know."

They both nodded. "How is Wesley?" Rose asked her son, but was looking at me.

I watched Tony's face. "He's fine mum, why don't you phone him sometime and ask him yourself?"

"I shouldn't have to, you should be bringing him down to visit me," she slapped his hand lightly. "Have you met my grandson?" she turned to me. I knew it was coming, my test.

"No, but Tony's told me all about him, I look forward to meeting him soon." Tony was looking at me with pride. I wanted him beside me not over there holding his mother's hand.

I had almost forgotten Junior while we were talking and when I looked around he was playing with a porcelain horse on the floor. His lolly-sticky hands leaving marks all over it. "Junior, can't you leave things alone."

"It's all right," Rose reassured me, "I can clean it." She rose from her chair almost regally and made her way to the door. "I'd better serve up dinner. Why don't you come with me, Jennifer." This was not a request but an order. I placed my glass on a coaster and glanced over at Junior who was admiring himself in their mirrored drinks cabinet. Tony saw my worried look "I'll watch him," he said.

"So, did he buy you a ring?" she asked as soon as we were out of earshot of the men.

"Yes," I held out my hand and showed her the emerald and diamond ring we had chosen together.

"Anthony knows how to treat women right. Some take advantage of it," she said giving me a look out of the corner of her eyes.

I faced her and mustered up the courage to put her mind at rest. "Rose...I can see that you and your son are very close. I love him too, how could I not?"

She smiled at me in a kind of, 'I know what you mean', way.

"Tony and I fell in love after being friends for years, I wouldn't want to hurt him and if you're thinking that I might be trying to replace Junior's father, then you're wrong. Junior has only had me and my sister all his life, there was never a father to replace. You can see for yourself how much they love each other."

"Jennifer...I like you," she wiped her hands on a tea towel and faced me. "You're honest and I can see you're not after Tony for his money, you have a career all of your own," she crossed the kitchen her arms open to me. "Welcome to my family. Just take care of my boy for me."

"Don't worry I will." It was all I could wish for, but I knew she would be watching me still.

Rose got me to chop the salad while she finished off the cooking and we talked. She told me about Tony's childhood. How he was a spoilt child, being the only boy. She laughed as she reminisced about the girls dressing him up *in their clothes and putting make-up on him. He was never short of girlfriends as he grew up because his sisters' friends often fell in love with his cute smile and his jokey ways. Tony had always been loving. One of his sisters, Deniece, still regularly came to him for advice on her love life.*

The mother of Tony's son was exactly the type of woman Rose had been scared of him meeting. She took advantage of his caring attitude, and knew she could get whatever she wanted from him without giving. Especially once she had his son. Rose had actually breathed a sigh of relief when Tony had told her he was leaving that woman, but he insisted he was still going to see his son as much as possible.

I had yet to meet his sisters and hoped I could give it some time. More women in this family of protective females would be too much straight after this one.

We left their home at around nine o'clock that evening.

"Don't leave it so long to come back and see us again Anthony," his mum kissed his cheek and there were tears in her eyes.

"I'll phone Mum."

Both his parents kissed Junior and told me to feel free to come up and see them anytime and bring my son with me. I still felt more comfortable with Derek than Rose, but I felt that I would get to like her eventually and she would grow to trust me.

"You met his what!"

"His mum and dad."

"And?" Karen was eager to get the news out of her. Ever since Jennifer had told her about the engagement and the decision to live together, the couple had become big news.

Jennifer switched the phone to her other hand and crossed her legs. "Don't sound so surprised Karen, we are getting married."

"Me know. Yuh know how long I been seeing Philip and I've only met his brudda...once."

"Well that's your choice. Once you've met the folks it's like you're his wife, and I know how you feel about that."

"So how'd it go?"

"Dad's a real nice guy. I got the feeling he would have married me himself if he had the choice. Mum pretended to be a hard nut to crack but I managed it."

"Brave, brave 'ooman. By the way, Phil's moving in properly next week."

Now it was Jennifer's turn to be shocked. "Was that my fault?"

"Naw, I just thought it'd save on the bills, you know. He's here most time anyway," Karen deftly changed the subject. "You know Beverly's lost weight?"

Jennifer smiled to herself. Why did Karen find admitting getting close to a man embarrassing? "No, I haven't seen her for months. How much?"

"Ten pounds, you should see her. You can see it in her face."

Jennifer didn't want to admit that since she had been seeing Tony she had started to neglect her friends again. Maybe when Tony moved in they should have a housewarming. She'd get to meet his friends and family and he could meet hers.

"I spoke to Elaine the other day she didn't say a word."

"Yuh lucky if you get anything out of Elaine these days. She nuh start dem test to get pregnant."

"I know, she said that much. Artificial insemination," Jennifer said, suddenly feeling sad.

"You see how God wicked? Gal can get pregnant in seconds by accident, but when it come to people who really want pickney, dem haffe suffer."

"Mmm."

"Look, Jen, I gotta go, catch you later."

"Take care Karen." She hung up and was about to call Elaine but thought better of it. She called Beverly and congratulated her on her weight loss instead.

Jennifer was pleased with herself for taking the time to catch up with her friends. Just a simple phone call could make such a difference to the way people felt. She didn't want them saying behind her back how she never kept in touch now that she had a man. By the time she had replaced the receiver she realized her own life still had a couple of loose ends that needed tying up.

Tony, of course, knew of Paul's existence, but she hadn't mentioned the visit he had paid on herself and Junior, the threat that he had issued and the summons that had arrived by courier yesterday. Paul was going ahead with his case for custody. She had promised there were never going to be anymore secrets and she wanted to explain to him, tell him that Paul Harvey was a part of her life that she would rather forget. Over the months she had been seeing Tony she had all but forgotten the threat and at the time had thought it was nothing more than a vindictive jab at her. Just when everything had started to go so smoothly Paul shows his balding head and upsets the apple cart, throwing Jennifer's emotions into turmoil. The only weapon he had against her would be to win the right to her son.

The date was set for three months away. By then she and Tony would be cohabiting. Jennifer had tried enough of these cases to know that the most custody Paul would get would be weekend split custody, but even that could disrupt the new life she had planned for her family.

It was time that she spoke to Paul Harvey, person to person.

Jennifer raised her arms sensually and stretched. Getting up she crossed to the mini bar. She wore a cream loose fitting linen and wool mix top over navy slacks belted with a black velvet belt. She poured herself a brandy. Before she made that call she needed a drink.

Tony moved in in July. Between us we decided what furniture we'd sell. To be honest it was mostly his. I was comfortable with my home and so was Junior and I didn't want too many changes all at once. The first night Junior didn't leave us alone at all. He followed Tony from the living room to the kitchen, from the bedroom to the bathroom and decided he was going to help him unpack. Having a three year old help you pack or unpack anything takes almost three times as long as doing it on your own. He would take something from a box and ask, "What's this, Tony? What does this do? Can I play with it? Can I have it?"

Several times I told him to go play in his bedroom or the back garden but he kept sneaking back in. Tony seemed to enjoy Junior's attentions and spent time answering his questions and even having a break to play with him. Watching them together made me feel so content. He finally had a man around the house and he seemed determined to make the most of it. They were like kindred spirits, and that night we had to take him to bed with us too, until he fell asleep. Then Tony carried him back to his own bed.

"Hi lover," he slipped back into the bed beside me.

"Finally alone," I whispered back. He folded his arms around me and we kissed. "Do you mind if we don't make love tonight?" I asked.

"Course not babe, so long as I can feel you next to me."

I snuggled closer if that was possible, and breathed in his scent. He was my man. Handsome, talented, gentle, sensitive, humorous and he made me so happy. We loved each other and one day he wouldn't be just my man, he would be my husband and Junior's father. I could hear his heartbeat and feel his breath on my forehead. I was falling deeper in love with him by the second. As I fell asleep I was thinking...my man.

Sunday morning he got up early. While I was showering I could hear him downstairs with Junior. Donna was still in bed. We wouldn't see her on a Sunday before midday. I arrived downstairs in my summer jogging gear. Junior was on Tony's lap tucking into a cooked breakfast. Bacon, eggs, beans and toast.

"Morning mummy."

"Morning baby, and how are my handsome men this morning?" I went over to the fridge to get myself a glass of fruit juice. Tony's eyes were following me around the kitchen.

"We saved you some," he said.

I looked at the food and said, "You eat it."

Tony looked wounded so I went over and kissed him. "I'm sorry," I said in my baby voice, "I just never eat before my run and then never fry ups."

"Well neither do I," he eased Junior off his lap and stood up in front of me, grabbing my bare waist with his gentle hands, "but muesli and orange juice just doesn't look like hard work." He shrugged and I kissed him again just for being so cute.

"I didn't get a kiss," Junior pouted. So I picked him up, held him against me and planted a big wet kiss on his cheek making him giggle.

"Can I run with you?" Tony asked, flicking a stray hair off my forehead.

"Could you keep up?"

"Try me," he was already heading for the bedroom to change into his track suit. Junior was sent to go and bother Donna while we headed out. He wasn't happy about having his new companion taken away from him.

Three miles later Tony and I were back and panting against the front door frame. Okay, so he could run. He had good lung capacity and strong legs. I'd taken him on some of the toughest slopes I knew and he'd kept up.

"What d'you say to moving to the Caribbean when we're married," said Tony a little later, catching his breath from a kiss in the middle of the kitchen.

I looked at him. "Move...to the Caribbean?"

"Why not? What do we have holding us here?"

I pulled away returning to the dining table. "My career for one, Donna, your work, Junior's schooling..."

"Stop," he pulled up a chair opposite me. "Your career, you can practice something else. Donna is a big twenty year old woman she can take care of herself. Junior would have a much better education in the West Indies than here, even if we had to pay for it. I can get work out there doing exactly the same thing..." his eyes glazed over. "Or we could open our own agency together, a law and detective agency."

"Get outta here!" I waved him away turning back to the paper.

He gave me that wounded dog look. "Will you at least think about it...for me."

"Mmm," I said, through a mouthful of muesli.

"Great," he jumped up from the chair. "Junior, we're going to Barbados...Oh, we're going to Barbados," he sang. I glared at him as Junior came running and giggling into the kitchen and he whirled him around his head.

He was like a big kid! There was no way I was leaving, not after having had to struggle through so many obstacles to get where I am now. That was another of men's differences. They never liked to put down roots. A woman wants to find somewhere were she can settle and build, a man prefers to pack his clothes and his walkman and move on at the drop of a hat. Pick up some trade or other along the way to make a living. After all, they didn't have to work as hard as a woman to build a career, make a home for their family. Family ties meant nothing to them. What about his own son, Wesley? If we just picked up and left, he would never see him.

I had hoped that Tony would soon drop the idea but instead, he took every opportunity to remind me of how beautiful Barbados was. If there was a travel programme on we'd have to watch it. He brought home brochures that I would find under my pillow, in the fridge and wrapped up in the towels in the bathroom. Honeymoon shots taken on beaches or lush green mountains would find themselves into my briefcase.

He even went as far as to enlist the help of my son. Junior would come up to me and look up at me with his big eyes and say, "Mummy, I want to wear uniform like kids in 'Bados. Can we swim everyday if we went there?"

I still stuck to my guns.

In the three months since Tony moved in Jennifer seemed to be living in perfect bliss. She had a man who was deeply in love with her and her son, living under the same roof. She loved Tony and saw how much he cared for her, their love seemed to grow and grow. Moving in with him was the natural progression, to give both of them the chance to find out if this was what they wanted or if he could handle bringing up someone else's child. She couldn't possibly marry him without finding out if he could cope with an inquisitive, time consuming infant and an over busy mother.

Tony, true to his word, had done everything he promised and more. The panic about the invasion of her privacy, space and independence didn't disappear overnight though. There hadn't been a man in her life in a long time and nothing as intense as this. When he had first moved in there had been the dilemma of where to put his stuff. So she had had a clear out. Clothes and shoes that would never again see the light of day were given to charity, her dressing table was cleared enough so that they had a his and hers side, as were the shelves in the bathroom.

Then there were things to learn about him, such as what he liked eating — they would have to shop together. Did he do his share of the housework, washing, ironing? Did he have habits that would drive her mad? Rules had to be laid down as to who would discipline Junior. What Tony could do without referring to Jennifer, who would Junior ask permission from. Who was Tony to Junior anyway? All these questions and more raised their heads and between them they dealt with it.

Jennifer found herself rushing to get home in the evenings now, which she hadn't done ever. She liked the fact that he was there to share the load, he was there to give her reassurance, a hug, a compliment, a massage after a hard day, an ear to listen to her troubles. She could feel comfort in his scent. In the middle of the night she could reach over and touch him or snuggle up on the sofa, when the house was still and quiet, for heart to heart talks, or put on a smoochy record and rock together in the middle of the front room.

What a difference having a man around the house had made to Jennifer and Junior's lives. There had been a three foot painting of a Black family — parents and three children ranging from teens to baby — having a picnic, painted by a young artist, which Jennifer had fallen in love with but had never got around to hanging. Tony knew all about it, she had shown him where she would hang it and one evening she had come home and it was there, on the wall, facing you just as you came out of the living room. The embodiment of a happy family.

Junior had someone else to read to him, a male voice to add new perspective. He had a man who not only played football with him, but knew all the rules of football too. He promised to take Junior to judo classes where he would not only learn the art of self-defence but would learn the discipline of the power of the mind and physical fitness. But there was more to being a father than playing football with Junior, and Tony understood this. They had what Tony called their 'man on man day' which was Sundays. Women excluded, it was a day where Jennifer either had to leave the house or they would go out for the whole day, just Tony, Junior and sometimes his son Wesley. At home they would talk about growing up, doing things around the home, 'taking care of the women' (Tony joked trying not to make it seem heavy). This was basically a talk about how females developed and were brought up, what makes them different. For

Junior some of it went right over his head, but Wesley, who would be going to secondary school in two years listened intently and asked questions. For them there would be no men's work or women's work, just hard work. Outdoors they would go camping for a day, learn how to build barbecues in the woods, basic first aid, cycling and bike repair. They would talk about and play sport, climb and build, and most importantly, bond.

Jennifer found herself having to fight down jealousy when Junior would want to take a bath with Tony instead of her, when he wanted to play a game with him, when he would sit by the window just waiting for Tony's car to pull up and then dash to the front door to jump into his arms. It was only natural the boy would take to Tony, he is the most selfless person Jennifer knew. One day, Junior would be a man like Tony, a man who had character, ambition, determination, sensitivity and the intelligence to learn how to use the gifts he was born with as well as the ones she had instilled in him.

Of course she still had the worry that Paul Harvey would come back and undo all that she had managed to achieve with her son, but after talking it over with Tony she knew she had no worries. Tony was like her right arm, although she told herself over and over that she shouldn't become too dependent on him. She couldn't let love mess her up, she had to stay focused and in control.

Tony had taken to doing his case notes on my laptop computer. I came home one night and he was sitting at my desk reading something from the screen.

"Hi honey," I said, dropping my briefcase and planting a kiss on his cheek.

"Mmm, oh hi," he turned back to the screen almost immediately. Curious, I walked back to the desk and looked over his shoulder.

"Tony, you're reading my diary!"

"Babe, why didn't you tell me you kept a journal?"

"Why didn't you ask permission to read it?" I swatted his head with the palm of my hand.

"Jen, this is really good, especially the parts about me," he grinned and I'm sure I blushed.

I stormed out and heard him pushing back his chair to follow me. I hung my coat up in the hallway and went to the kitchen. I swung open the cupboard where we kept the glasses and took one out.

"I thought we didn't have secrets from each other anymore?"

"It's not a secret, you can read it," I slammed the cupboard door. "Why couldn't you have asked first?"

"All right, you're upset," he came towards me and laid his arms on my shoulders. "I was looking for a disk to save my work on and came across the box of disks labelled 'journal'."

I looked up at his pitiful face. He was dressed in one of my big jumpers and his green track suit bottoms, and stood bare footed on the cold kitchen floor. "So you opened up the box that obviously did not contain blank discs and put one into the computer, and when you saw it did indeed have something on it, you proceeded to read it..."

"Caught red-handed, Guv," he put on a cockney accent and raised his hands in the air submissively.

I lowered my eyes laughing. "Silly. It's okay, I don't mind you reading it. You know it all anyway."

"You sure?"

"I said so didn't I?"

He kissed my nose and then my lips. "You ever thought of publishing it?"

"Now you are being silly. Who'd read the perils of being a single career mother?" I chuckled, but Tony was serious.

"Well if the perils of being a baby father can get two bestsellers, why shouldn't yours?"

"It's not fiction though, Tony. That's my life on those discs, it would be open to public ridicule."

"Well then we pass it off as fiction, change the names, places, dates, give you a pseudonym. Baby, I know someone in publishing, why don't you let me show it to him."

"No," I was already backing out of the kitchen. "It's not even worth considering wasting someone's time for."

"How do you know unless you try?" He was giving me that look again.

"Okay do it, then I'll get a chance to tell you I told you so."

Tony spent most of that night with the lap top on his knees in bed. In the morning he woke up bleary eyed and told me he just couldn't put it down. I was bemused, I hadn't even read the thing back to myself. Twice a week I'd recorded my thoughts and feelings on my life without ever expecting anyone else to read it and now my fiancé wanted to have it published. I let him go ahead. Maybe it would take his mind off Barbados.

Tony came into the room and stood behind Jennifer's chair in the middle of their bedroom with his hands deep in his pockets. "Junior finally fell asleep after the fifth story," he grinned.

Jennifer applied her lipstick with a lip brush and sat back to view her made up face. "Thanks T." Junior had been hyper all evening. At one stage Jennifer had suggested giving him a drop of brandy to knock him out. Tony had managed to tire him by first singing his self-esteem songs with him and then reading to him. Tony watched Jennifer getting ready for her date. "Do you have to do this?"

Jennifer met his eyes in the mirror as she fastened her gold droplet earrings. "Babe, you know I do."

He sighed. "Then let me come with you."

He cared so much. Standing there with his hang dog expression, his eyes were pleading, so full of love. Jennifer pushed her chair away from the dressing table, she stood up and her long black dress fell to her calves. She had to meet with Paul, once and for all, before this got as far as the courts making the decision. She wanted to lay down her feelings, spread her cards on the table so to speak. Tony could never bring Junior up the way he so much wanted to, as his real father, while Paul had rights to see him whenever he pleased.

When she had called Paul's office he seemed so surprised he was speechless. Then he went on the defensive, threatening to call his lawyers. Jennifer had remained calm and simply told him she wanted to see him to talk about their son. Paul was then flabbergasted, she could almost see him grinning into the phone. She told him where they should meet and when, and that it would be his one and only chance.

Tony felt awkward, like an outsider. He had no say in this situation. Choosing to move in with Jennifer and her son in the first place was a big decision. Whenever a man moved into a ready made family he had to prepare himself for the absent father turning up one day. Tony had thought about it and even talked about it with Jennifer but he had never felt any threat before until now.

Jennifer felt this was her business. Something she should have cleared up months ago. Tony shouldn't have to become involved. He loved her and Junior unconditionally and there was no way she was going to jeopardise that. Junior was her responsibility and any decisions concerning his life would have to be made by her.

"I know you want to be there for support, but honey I know Paul. He'll see you coming along as a weakness and attack it. Plus neither of us would be able to say what really needs to be said with you there."

"You forgot to say 'no offence'," Tony smirked.

"I'm sorry..."

Tony's eyes fell on her dress. "I guess I'm jus' jealous. I mean look at you... You're beautiful."

Jennifer smiled.

"Look, I know how you felt about him, you wrote it all in that diary. He was supposed to be your husband, you had his baby. How could he not want you back?" He reached for her and she stepped into his arms.

"Tony, I love you. The way I felt for Paul Harvey is history. Did you ever once hear me mention love in connection with him? I have nothing but contempt for him, but he wants to try to take my son away from me. I want to make sure not one of us has to suffer. I want to make sure that any rights he gets will be with my consent and not one forced onto us by the courts."

"I know that..."

"But?"

"But look what he can offer you and Junior. He's got money, power and fame... Who am I compared to that?"

Jennifer could feel his uncertainty. Maybe it had been a mistake to let him read her journals. She had almost forgotten how she had lusted for that power and status that Paul Harvey had. She had acted like a child promised a trip to Disneyland. A dream come true. The real cost had been of no consequence, only the result. Thank God she had changed.

"Paul Harvey is not the man I'm in love with. He is not the man I want by my side raising my son. He is selfish and vindictive and the only reason he wants custody of my son is because he and his wife can't have children. He doesn't want me and he doesn't want Junior. What he also doesn't want is for people to think *he* has the problem."

There was a silence between them. They held each other and their eyes locked. Communication was the key here. There was a childlike quality in his eyes that said, 'I want to believe you, it's him I don't trust'. "Don't let him sweet talk you into anything, y'know."

"I won't," she smiled.

"An tell him if he so much as raises his voice to you, or lifts a finger in your direction he's got me and Junior to answer to." Tony's hand caressed her neck and hair.

That was more like the old Tony. God, it was good feeling this secure about a man. She was a lucky woman and if there was one thing the Toni Lee seminar had instilled in her, it was never to bemoan what you didn't have, but to appreciate the hell out of what you did have.

Before she left to meet Paul Harvey, Tony had hugged her so hard that, for a moment, she nearly changed her mind and stayed at home.

Paul still had his flat in Lauderdale Tower. The Barbican apartment was his private domain. His escape from the pressures of politics and his wife's socialite friends. Jennifer's heart was beating triple time as she rang the intercom buzzer and Paul's clipped voice came out at her. His old fashioned charm and patronizing manner came flooding back to her, and she wondered how she could ever have contemplated marrying him. He stood in his doorway waiting for her as she stepped from the lift. They stood for a moment sizing each other up, sensing the mood, the attitude, the tone their conversations would take. Paul's thinning hair was now balding. He was dressed the most casual she had seen him, in a t-shirt which he wore over jeans.

"Good evening," he let her in with a flourish of his hand. It had been nearly four years since she had been there and it hadn't changed. She suspected there was no need for him to make changes in an apartment where he no longer lived.

Silently, she stepped over the threshold and felt his eyes burning into her back. She turned to face him.

"Can I take your jacket?"

Jennifer had wanted to impress him with her fit body. Wanting him to see that physically she hadn't changed a bit despite having a baby. After seeing the way he dressed, she felt overdressed. "No thank you."

He shrugged his shoulders and led the way into the sunken living room. "Can I get you a drink?"

"Water will do, thanks." Her palms were sweating. She pretended to study a painting on the wall until he left to go to the adjoining kitchen and then she sat down on the edge of the seat of one of the armchairs. Paul came back, carrying her water and a glass of wine for himself.

She took the glass and held it firmly in her hands, the ice cold glass cooling her palms. Paul sat opposite. "How are you?"

"I'm very well, thank you." It was the third time she'd said anything and the third time she had said 'thank you'. Her nerves were at breaking point but Paul looked as cool as a cucumber. But then he was a politician now, who knew what was going on behind the mask.

"You look fabulous." His compliment was met with an icy glare and he cleared his throat before continuing, "I'm glad you called... you know a lot could have been avoided if you'd talked to me months ago."

Jennifer took a sip of the water and felt her throat open up again. "Are you saying if I had let you walk out with my son, I'd have been a lot happier?"

"I'm not saying that... Look I don't want us to start out on the wrong foot. We are two civil people.."

"One of us is," she interrupted bluntly.

"Jennifer, please let me finish. I've thought about what I said, and I know I'm not the best when it comes to affairs of the heart. The way I came across may have been very callous and I apologise."

Jennifer silently watched him.

"I apologise for the way I treated you four years ago, leaving you with my child to raise alone. I thought money would take care of you both. Then when I saw you with that man..."

Jennifer's eyes glared at him, her jaw set hard.

"I felt a longing," he quickly held up a hand, "no, not in that way... I felt a longing for what I could have had. A son. I felt a longing for you too, but I knew I had lost you, but there was still a chance for me to be a father to my son."

Jennifer shook her head and imagined she could hear violins playing somewhere overhead. This was so sickening. Had Paul digested some soppy romance, or one of William Cosby's books on good parenting?

He continued. "I hadn't realized the extent to which you had come to hate me..."

Jennifer felt she ought to stop him before she puked. She held up her hand, halting him in mid sentence. "Paul, let's not pretend this is some kind of reconciliation. I'm here because you are taking me to court to get rights to see my son."

Paul's mouth clamped shut.

"All right, you are his biological father, but you are not his daddy. A daddy is someone who is around for his child through the good times and the bad, offering support and love, encouragement, a positive role model for the child to follow. A daddy is not an envelope containing two hundred pounds every month. Do you think you fit the bill in any way?"

He said immediately, "Given the chance..."

"Given the chance!" Jennifer interrupted once again. Oh, he was so full of it this one. He had probably sat up all night planning his little speech. "What did you get when I told you I was pregnant? Wasn't that your chance? When you had a choice between having a wife and a family of your own, you chose a white woman for status. I'm not going to bring your wife into this, I'm just using her to make you see what you've lost."

Paul swallowed the rest of his wine. "I am content with my life, except for not having my offspring beside me."

"Oh, so now you just need that one little accessory to add to your collection and your life will be complete?" she asked sarcastically.

"I do not see my son as an accessory. I want him to know who I am, I want to make up for what I've missed out on in his life."

"And what about him? Have you thought about what you are doing to him?"

"What? Giving him the father he hasn't had for three years, I hardly see that as a disaster."

"He has a father. I'm going to be married to him one day and he has already expressed a wish to adopt Junior legally."

Paul let out a hiss and got up. He stomped noisily to the kitchen and she heard the fridge door open and close. Sitting down again with a bottle of wine in his hand, she watched as he poured for himself and then offered it to her. Jennifer took the bottle.

"You can't do that." His voice was now low, not as confident as before.

Jennifer knew what he was talking about. He expected the world to stop for him. He could go on and live his life as he pleased but everyone else's life had to be held in suspended animation until he walked back in. "We can and we will."

"Where do I fit in to your plan? As a visiting uncle? A long lost relative?"

"If you hadn't turned up and ruined that plan, yes."

Paul shot her a look, then looked down at the glass in his hand. He breathed deeply and then relaxed in the chair, crossing his legs. He looked hard at her. "I'm not some street thug who is going to cause either of you harm. I don't want to take him from you, I just want to be part of his life. Why are you so against me?"

Jennifer poured herself wine and coolly sipped before answering. She slipped her jacket off her arm, now warm and the wine was making her relax. Where should she begin? Did he want to hear about how he had ruined the life she had planned for herself and her son? Did he want to hear about her humiliation, her pain, her loneliness?

Did he want to hear about how Junior had been registered without the signature of his father on his birth certificate, how they had to spend hard times making explanations and excuses for him? Did he want to hear about Junior asking why he didn't have a father? She didn't think so.

"You have no idea," she shook her head sadly. "You left me pregnant, a week away from my wedding day. I didn't hear from you again until after Junior was born, when you couldn't even pick up the phone. For three years Junior had no father. I didn't trust another man in all that time until I fell in love again. Then you suddenly decide now that he is walking, talking, potty trained, feeding and dressing himself that you want in. He has a life of his own. He is settled, content, he loves Tony as I do..."

"What's to stop him getting to love me?"

"He'll ask questions you won't be able to answer. Remember it was you who walked out. I've never lied to him. No one stopped you from turning up as he grew from baby to child. We never moved or changed our phone number and yet you couldn't call. How are you going to explain that, Mr. Harvey?"

All he could do was hang his head. What excuse could he offer? He was ashamed and had every right to be. Jennifer would have gloated if she didn't feel so wretched about the whole thing. This was the moment she had waited for, making Paul humble, wanting to hear him beg.

"I'm so sorry," when he looked up again his eyes were filled with water. "Haven't we all been punished enough?"

"It's up to you."

He searched her eyes. "You mean the court case."

"You want to punish me and Junior just a little more. You want to put me in court to tell the world why I can't have you disrupting this happy little boy's life."

"You think I haven't thought about him in all those years, don't you?" His voice was breaking on every other word.

"Prove me wrong."

He leaned forwards so that she could see his whole face a lot clearer. "Look, I didn't get a secretary to send those cheques you received every month. I sent them all myself. Not a week went by when he wasn't in my thoughts. I knew when his birthday was coming up, I followed his development stages in a book I hid from my wife. I wondered whether he thought about me. I thought about you after we... broke up," he shrugged. "I wondered if you kept the baby or not. I found out while having drinks with a colleague that you had gone into labour in court, turns out it was big news."

Jennifer remembered it all too vividly.

"I wanted to come and see you both, but how was I to know when the right time was? How was I to know what kind of welcome I would receive?"

"Turns out you weren't welcome at all."

"I know that now and I understand why, but can't you see my point of view?"

"Believe me, I want to see your point of view but I want you to realize mine and Junior's. How can you be so selfish?"

"And you're not? By stopping him seeing me now, aren't you being selfish? If I have to live with the questions he's going to ask, then why don't you ask yourself if you can take the questions he'll ask you ten years from now, when he might want to see me."

Now it was Jennifer's turn to feel guilt. Yes, Junior might well want to find his father someday. Would she just cross that bridge when she came to it or sort it now? "It might never happen. I'm sure he'll see enough of you in the papers anyhow."

Paul laughed. He laughed real belly laughter. Jennifer wondered if he was becoming hysterical, or drunk. "Oh Jennifer, I remember why I fell in love with you. You have a knack of finding a solution to every problem. You must be an extremely successful mother."

"I am now," she swallowed. "It wasn't always that way as I'm sure you'll realize."

Paul raised an eyebrow, "Am I to take it that you're giving me the chance to prove I can be a good father?"

Jennifer shifted in her seat. Was that what she meant? "I'll need to discuss it with my family first. There have been a few changes at home recently and I wouldn't appreciate any more."

Paul was grinning incredulously.

"Does your wife know about your son?"

"Of course," he coughed clearing his throat, "although only recently."

Jennifer nodded and poured more wine for both of them, "I didn't tell Tony at first either."

Paul watched her curiously.

"Well... I'm sure you can guess why. The stigma of being a single parent. It just wasn't me. I wasn't sure how men would take me." As the words left her mouth she wondered why she was telling him this, of all people. Then again, they had always been able to talk, she had once felt comfortable talking to him about most things.

"I'm sorry..."

"Stop apologising, Paul. Saying sorry now means absolutely nothing to me. What would mean more to me would be you making things up to us by being a man now."

"That's what I'm trying to do..."

"And I'm trying to punish you. But I wouldn't go as far as taking you to court to fight this. I've seen too many families pulled apart by courts."

"Again you're right, and I'm wrong. I want to make it up to you. Just tell me what to do."

Power! Now she had him eating out of her hands. Guilt ridden, he was begging to ease things. Did he have sleepless nights, pangs of guilt everytime a child crossed his path, nightmares that he may never have another child, dreams that his one and only would grow up to hate him?

Jennifer stood up and felt the alcohol suddenly rush to her head. On her empty stomach she had only had to have three glasses of wine and she was feeling drunk. Paul saw her wobble on her feet and jumped up, lending her his arm to steady herself. Jennifer jerked away from it as though he was offering her a red-hot poker. "I'm fine."

"Look, sit down I'll make some coffee."

Jennifer obeyed, not that she had a choice she felt suddenly ill. "Paul, did you ever love me?"

"In the only way I think I'm capable of loving someone. You were dear to me, I cared for you as... I don't know, as I did my mother."

"Hmph."

Like his mother indeed. What, did she look like the housewife, matronly type? No wait, that could be a compliment. Every man loves his mother more than life itself, before the woman he marries. She smiled drunkenly.

Paul brought the coffees in and sat closer to her on a pouffe. "Tell me about Junior," he requested.

"What do you want to know?"

"Remember, I know nothing. Tell me all."

So she did. She told of his reading achievements, his inquisitive mind. Laughed at reminisces of the funny things he said, and did. Told of his maturity, and dexterity. Most of all she talked about the way she felt about him and he about her. How through the emotionless beginning they had grown together and now he was the centre of her world. Her most precious possession. She loved him so much that sometimes she felt it must be impossible for anyone to love that much. She explained how Tony had come into their lives and Junior had taken to him right away. Now there were three of them. She loved Tony, and he loved the both of them. They were a family and would stick together to fight anything that threatened to ruin that.

It was nearly two o'clock in the morning when Paul dropped her home. Tony was at the door before the car had even parked up. Jennifer raised a hand to him as she stepped from the car, to tell him she was fine.

"Jennifer," Paul called.

Jennifer leant back inside the car and looked at him questioningly. "Yes?"

He dropped his eyelids for a second, like an embarrassed schoolboy. "Forget the court case... so long as I can see him occasionally... so long as he knows me... I want him to be happy too."

She reached back into the car with her right hand. "Thank you."

He took her hand and kissed it. "He's a lucky man, and I"m a fool."

She watched the car drive off before walking up the pathway and into Tony's arms.

He was worried, and no wonder, she had left at seven o'clock yesterday evening. "What happened to you?"

"Everything's okay. We talked."

Tony, still dressed the same as when she left, closed the door behind her. "Until two o'clock in the morning... and where's your car?"

"Tony! You don't trust me?"

"Once bitten..."

She stopped in the hallway and turned to him with a smile on her face. "I had a bit to drink and couldn't drive back that's all. Baby, why have tough steak when I can have succulent chicken. Paul Harvey is not going to be a bother. I made him see that he could only cause disruption by interfering now, he understands that now. This is our time, he had his chance."

"I can't believe he would give in that easy."

"Not exactly," she climbed the wrought iron staircase. "I had to promise him some visiting privileges. I don't want Junior growing up knowing I kept his father from seeing him. So if Paul doesn't see his son it won't be down to me."

Tony followed her up the stairs, his hands on her waist. "I love you, Miss Edwards."

"And I love you," suddenly she turned towards him. "Tony, will you marry me?"

He grinned. "Didn't I ask you that question?"

"Well?" she asked excitedly. Her tired eyes had a mischievously bright light in them.

"Yes. Wherever and whenever you want me to," Tony replied. "You're my lady."

"Make love to me," she breathed before her arms flew around his neck and she kissed him passionately. He held her and kissed back. They walked backwards up the stairs.

"My lady's wish is my command."

Just last week I received a phone call from a very excited X press publisher. They loved my journals and wanted to publish it as fiction. Would I be interested in doing the rewrite? Would I be interested?!? I was too flabbergasted to speak, but after we talked editing and contracts, I accepted and put the phone down. For just a few seconds I sat there letting it sink in and then danced around the living room before calling Tony on his mobile, because I couldn't wait until he got home. People, strangers would be reading about my life. They would like it enough to pay money to read something I had written through some very emotional times.

There was no feeling in the world like it. In fact when I started to tell my friends that I was going to be a published novelist they were more impressed than when I told them I was a barrister.

An author! I stared at the contract with my name on it. I have this new sense of worth. Like before I only meant something to my family and now I have two careers and a fiancé and a beautiful son.

Paul wrote me a very touching letter. He says that he will not intrude in our lives anymore, all he asks is that I keep him up to date with photographs, letters and a current address so that he can keep track of his son. I agreed, I feel it is the least I could do for a peaceful life.

I'm going to be married, but then you knew that already. But I've actually set a date now, June 24th, it's my mum's birthday. Both my parents will be flying over from Jamaica for the wedding.

This idea of Barbados isn't all that bad, you know. I've been thinking about it and the more I think about it the more I think, why not?

Junior is still young enough to start again. I don't have to be a barrister. With the book contract signed and sealed and a commission to write a sequel, I could write full time. What a beautiful place to write my next novel. I'll feel like Terry McMillan. Plus I'd be so much closer to mum and dad.

Donna visits from university in the summer. She is being very coy about her sex life, although I get the distinct feeling that she isn't about to become a nun.

I'll miss her if we go, and I'll miss all those friends that I have grown to love, but I can't limit myself. Being a barrister was an ambition that I fulfilled but I don't need anymore. It is in no way as spiritually or emotionally fulfilling or gratifying as my creative ability.

"Mummy can I have some new trainers," Junior held up his old ones with holes already in the toes.

"Yes Junior. Ask daddy to buy them."

Junior had been calling Tony 'daddy' for about a month now. It had been his choice after hearing Wesley calling the man that he thought had belonged to him, daddy. Junior had asked if he could as well. Tony had accepted it as fate.

Junior ran out of the room again. "Daddy..." *How many times had I told him about running in the house?*

The publisher's agreement was still open on the last page and I turned it over again reading my name on the front cover. Jennifer Edwards, author of 'Baby Mother — When a Man Leaves a Woman.' X Press publishing had accepted the book two weeks after reading it. The wedding was six months away and I now had a book to rewrite as well as organize the wedding and work full time. They say things happen in threes what next?

"Babes," Tony was standing in the doorway in his boxer shorts, "I've just thought. With your new career we don't have to stay here for anything."

I sighed happily. Number three.

"Oh, we're going to Barbados," Tony picked me up and spun me around the room, before we fell on the sofa giggling and kissing like newlyweds.

"I'm jealous," there were tears in Karen's eyes. She stared at Jennifer's traditional white silk and lace gown, the veil thrown back to reveal hair that had taken Donna an hour and a half to tong, getting each individual curl to sit perfectly.

"You!" Elaine and a new slimline Beverly said together. Donna caught the joke and they all burst out laughing. Jennifer beside her groom, turned around and they all saw the radiance and excitement surround her like a glow.

"Please ladies, we are trying to take a picture here," the photographer, a short effeminate man with a tape measure around his neck, bustled over to them and pushed and pulled at the ladies' peach satin dresses until he had them in an orderly line outside the church.

"Smile."

The flash went off and Jennifer looked to her left at her new in-laws, then to her right at her own mother and father who had flown in just a week ago to be at their eldest daughter's wedding. Her mother had been eager to talk to the two sisters, lecturing them, especially Donna, on the evils of the nineties man. "Don't follow your sister," she had said, marring Jennifer's excitement over the wedding. But as soon as she'd met Tony, they'd got on immediately and when she saw her grandson for the first time she had burst into tears. Now she looked happier than the bride and groom. Jennifer smiled at her before looking back at Tony. He kissed her gently on the lips as camera flashes went off all around them.

After a long and tiring reception, it was time for the newlyweds to leave for their honeymoon in Barbados, their new home.

"She's going to throw the bouquet..."

Jennifer stood at the front of the hall watching her friends come forward. As soon as she saw that everyone was in position she turned her back to the throng of excited women, raised the bouquet and threw it back over her head. She turned in time to see Beverly and Donna almost catch it before it bounced off their fingertips to land in Karen's crossed arms.

She was more surprised than the rest of them. Philip was by her side in a second lifting her in the air. Beverly, Elaine and Donna came to Jennifer's side and as a group they surrounded Karen.

"So what did you say?" Beverly asked.

Karen looked at them all and then turned to look at Philip. "Yes!"

There was a scream from all the women as they jumped up and down excitedly, then they realized that Philip might want to get in there as well and parted. Jennifer clasped her hands in front of her and looked around at her friends, she marvelled at how beautiful they all looked. She was so happy that when Tony circled her into his arms, she jumped for joy nearly knocking him down.

"Think we better be going."

Jennifer and Tony Carnegie took hold of their son's hand and left the church hall, followed by a cheering crowd and a shower of confetti. A limousine waited outside. Before Jennifer climbed in, her hand was grabbed by someone from behind. Jennifer turned around and faced a tearful Elaine. She searched her eyes.

Elaine was nodding. "I'm pregnant."

"Aahh," Jennifer was crying with her, their tears of joy mingling on made up cheeks. "Why didn't you tell me before?"

"This is your day," she smiled tearfully.

Jennifer hugged her once more. "Congratulations, honey, you deserve it." She let go of her and climbed into the car beside her husband and her baby. She waved to all her friends. Then she saw Donna squeezing through the guests to get to the car, her beaded headdress already askew.

Jennifer wound down the window. "Did I forget something?"

"Yes," Donna said. "Would you be disappointed if I decided to get pregnant and not get married?"

Jennifer turned around to look at her family in the car beside her. "It's your choice baby sister. Just promise you'll love the child and not get married or pregnant for the wrong reasons."

Donna smiled. "See, who needs to be single to survive?"

Exciting new novels from The X Press
COMING soon

RUDE GAL by Sheri Campbell
As her man's snoring echoed in the night, Angela Seymour wondered if there was more to life than the boredom of a long-term relationship with a man who took her for granted. Weeks later a chance meeting with a stranger starts her on the most exciting and sensual adventure of her life.

THE HARDER THEY COME by Michael Thelwell
The film starred Jimmy Cliff and wasan international hit. The book is even better! The unabridged, no-holds barred account of Jamaica's original 'Johnny-Too-Bad', Rhygin aka Ivan O. Martin.

I SPREAD MY WINGS AND I FLY by Nubia Kai
In America's Deep South, Caleb refuses to remain a slave and despite the shackles and the whippings, his one aim is to remain free by any means necessary. Only the love of a woman is able to keep him on his master's plantation. But eventually even that is not enough.

IN SEARCH OF SATISFACTION by J. California Cooper
Cooper, one of America's hottest writers, weaves this powerful human drama of two families linked by the same man. Josephus's daughter Ruth is born to a hard working mother and seems destined to a life of poverty, while Yinyang is Josephus's daughter by his alcoholic but rich mistress. In seeking the legacy left by their father, both end up pulling themselves and their families onto an emotional roller coaster.

FLEX by Marcia Williams
'Woman ah run t'ings!' But not when a man's involved! Three best friends show some sisterly solidarity when faced with the joys and pains of modern relationships. *Baby Mother* author Andrea Taylor writes under her real name for this seriously steamy sex romp. You have been warned!

For a colour catalogue of all X Press novels, write your name and address on the back of an envelope and send to:
Mailing List, The X Press, 55 Broadway Market,
London E8 4PH

NEW! Black Classics

Only from The X Press – an exciting collection of the world's greatest black novels.

THE BLACKER THE BERRY by Wallace Thurman/Emma Lou was born black. Too black for her own comfort and that of her social-climbing wannabe family. Rejected by her own race, she drifts from one loveless relationship to another.

TRADITION by Charles W Chesnutt/When a black man is wrongly accused of murdering a white woman, the black population, proud and determined, strike back.

IOLA by Frances E.W. Harper/Iola is duped into slavery after the death of her father but snatches her freedom back and starts the long search for the mother whom she was separated from on the slave trader's block.

THE CONJURE MAN DIES by Rudolph Fisher An African king is found dead in Harlem then turns up later, very much alive! *The world's FIRST black detective thriller!*

THE AUTOBIOGRAPHY OF AN EX-COLORED MAN by James Weldon Johnson/The Ex-Colored Man thinks he's white until his teacher calls him 'nigger'. As he grows into adulthood, he discovers a pride in his blackness. *A true classic!*

THE HOUSE BEHIND THE CEDARS by Charles W. Chesnutt/Can love transcend racial barriers, or will the rich George Tryon reject his fianceé the moment he discovers her black roots?

THE WALLS OF JERICHO by Rudolph Fisher/When a black lawyer buys a house in a white neighbourhood, he has to hire the toughest removal firm in Harlem to help him move in. *Hilarious!*

A LOVE SUPREME by Pauline Hopkins/Sappho is beautiful, chaste and has a dark secret. Only a man with the greatest love for her will be prepared to overlook it. Will she find that man?

THE PRESIDENT'S DAUGHTER by William Wells Brown/The black daughter of the United States president is sold at slave market while her indifferent father sits in the White House.

THE SOUL OF A WOMAN/ Stories by the world's greatest black women authors: *Zora Neale Hurston, Jessie Fauset, Nella Larsen*

ONE BLOOD by Pauline Hopkins/ A black doctor embarks on an expedition to Africa with the sole intention of plundering as much of the continent's loot as possible, but soon discovers his roots and culture.

JOY & PAIN by Rudolph Fisher/ Jazz age Harlem stories by a master of black humour writing.

AVAILABLE FROM WH SMITH AND ALL GOOD BOOKSHOPS
call The X Press hotline: 0171 729 1199 for your nearest stockist

Books with ATTITUDE

THE RAGGA & THE ROYAL by Monica Grant Streetwise Leroy Massop and The Princess of Wales get it together in this light-hearted romp. £5.99

JAMAICA INC. by Tony Sewell Jamaican Prime Minister, David Cooper, is shot down as he addresses the crowd at a reggae 'peace' concert. Who pulled the trigger and why? £5.99

LICK SHOT by Peter Kalu When neo-nazis plan to attack Manchester's black community they didn't reckon on one thing...A black cop who doesn't give a fuck about the rules! £5.99

SINGLE BLACK FEMALE by Yvette Richards Three career women end up sharing a house together and discover they all share the same problem-MEN! £5.99

MOSS SIDE MASSIVE by Karline Smith When the brother of a local gangster is shot dead on a busy Manchester street, the city is turned into a war zone as the drugs gangs battle it out. £5.99

OPP by Naomi King How deep does friendship go when you fancy your best friend's man? Find out in this hot bestseller! £5.99

COP KILLER by Donald Gorgon When his mother is shot dead by the police, cab driver Lloyd Baker becomes a one man cop-killing machine. Controversial but compulsive reading. £4.99

BABY FATHER/ BABY FATHER 2 by Patrick Augustus Four men come to terms with parenthood but it's a rough journey they travel before discovering the joys in this smash hit and its sequel. £5.99

WICKED IN BED by Sheri Campbell Michael Hughes believes in 'loving and leaving 'em' when it comes to women. But if you play with fire you're gonna get burnt! £5.99

FETISH by Victor Headley The acclaimed author of 'Yardie', 'Excess', and 'Yush!' serves another gripping thriller where appearances can be very deceiving! £5.99

PROFESSOR X by Peter Kalu When a black American radical visits the UK to expose a major corruption scandal, only a black cop can save him from the assasin's bullet. £5.99

UPTOWN HEADS by R.K. Byers Hanging with the homeboys in uptown New York where all that the brothers want is a little respect! A superb, vibrant humourous modern novel about the black American male. £5.99

GAMES MEN PLAY by Michael Maynard What do the men get up to when their women aren't around? A novel about black men behaving outrageously! £5.99

DANCEHALL by Anton Marks Reggae deejay Simba Ranking meets an uptown woman. He thinks everything is level vibes, until her husband finds out. £5.99

WHEN A MAN LOVES A WOMAN by Patrick Augustus *Baby Father* author is back with his hot new novel. The greatest romance story ever...probably. £5.99

OBEAH by Colin Moone Mysterious murders and family feuds in rural Jamaica, where truth is stranger than fiction. *Winner of Xpress Yourself '95 writing competition!* £5.99

AVAILABLE FROM WH SMITH AND ALL GOOD BOOKSHOPS

Keep updated with the hot new novels from The X Press. Publishers With Attitude. Join our mailing list. Simply send your name and address to:
Mailing List, The X Press, 55 Broadway Market, London E8 4PH

INTRODUCING AN EXCITING NEW RANGE OF CHILDREN'S BOOKS: The DRUMMOND HILL CREW

Welcome to the *Drummond Hill Crew* children's books. This addition to the X Press list is the start of a new range of books aimed at a younger readership. Set in Drummond Hill comprehensive school, the books, aimed at 9-12 year-olds, show a group of school friends in a variety of exciting adventures. These books are certain to become hot property so order your kid's copies today!

X PRESS CHILDREN'S COLLECTION — NOW Available!

AGE AIN'T NOTHING BUT A NUMBER
by YiNkA AdEbAyO

When some of the pupils from Drummond Hill School go on a summer holiday to the mysterious Headstone manor, they find themselves right in the middle of an adventure! Are the strange noises in the night really that of a ghost?

BOYZ TO MEN
by YiNkA AdEbAyO

Darren and Tyrone have been best mates since way back when. But when Darren starts lying and hanging out with the Smoker's Corner Crew, their friendship is seriously put to the test.

LIVIN' LARGE
by YiNkA AdEbAyO

When a show-off arrives at school, the Drummond Hill Crew all decide that he's acting too big for his boots. It can only be a matter of time beforethere's TROUBLE!

AVAILABLE FROM WH SMITH AND ALL GOOD BOOKSHOPS

X PRESS *yourself '97*

WIN £1,000 AND GET YOUR NOVEL PUBLISHED

You have a novel inside your head. We want to publish it. Send for details of the UK's biggest black book prize to: Xpress Yourself '97, 55 Broadway Market, London E8 4PH

CLOSING DATE: December 31st 1996

SKANK

Call the X Press Hotline:
0171 729 1199 for your copy

Pure Ragga!

The slackest magazine....

Out Every two months. £1.25

THE VICTOR HEADLEY COLLECTION

3 Tuff Novels From The Number One Black Author In The UK:

YARDIE

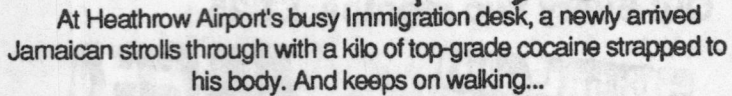

At Heathrow Airport's busy Immigration desk, a newly arrived Jamaican strolls through with a kilo of top-grade cocaine strapped to his body. And keeps on walking...
By the time the syndicate get to hear about the missing consignment, D. is in business — for himself — as the Front Line's newest don. But D.'s treachery will never be forgotten — or forgiven. The message filters down from the Yardie crime lords to their soldiers on the streets: Find D. Find the merchandise. And make him pay for his sins...

EXCE$$ – THE SEQUEL TO YARDIE

Things got really hot after D.'s arrest. The police virtually closed down Hackney for business. The posses have had to take stock and regroup. But the shaky truce that followed their turf war, is getting shakier as Sticks, a 9mm 'matic in his waist, dips deeper and deeper into his own supply of crack...

YUSH! – THE FINAL SCORE

The final curtain comes down on the superb Yardie trilogy. An all guns blasting end, worthy of Britain's most popular black writer. If you enjoyed reading it remember to big up the book to your bredrin.

The Ragga & The Royal

"Monarchy will never seem the same again. A hilarious mick take of the British class system"
THE VOICE

"Surely one of the funniest and most outrageous comedy novels for years. Even the Queen would have to smile."
PAPERBACKS REVIEWED

WHEN The Princess decides to include inner city problems as part of her charitable work, little does she know where it'll end!

As 'community representative' at a large urban development project, Leroy Massop is about to start working very closely with The Princess on her charitable mission.

They are worlds apart but The Princess is taken by his streetwise charm. Soon a cool working relationship starts to develop into something a lot hotter!

It's an illicit liaison that could destroy the monarchy and her husband, The Prince, is determined that it MUST be stopped. In the meantime Leroy is desperately trying to keep not only his long-term woman sweet, but his 'runnings' as well!

THE HOT NOVEL BY **Monica Grant**

From the publisher who brought...

Single Black Female

By Yvette Richards

When thirtysomething **CAROL'S** marriage ends dramatically, she gives up on men and is convinced she'll never find happiness again.

American advertising executive **DEE** moves to London looking for new horizons and maybe 'Mr Right.'

DONNA leaves an empty relationship in Bristol and heads to the Capital in the hope of making it big as a model.

They all end up sharing a house and soon discover that black women wherever they're from, have the same problem...**MEN**!

Together they experience the ups and downs of single life in the 90's. They finally discover that something special can happen with a man when you least expect it.

"Excellent...no woman's bookcase should be without this hugely entertaining and uplifting novel."
THE VOICE

"A compulsive read... written with humour, Single Black Female hits us men with some real home truths."
PATRICK AUGUSTUS

"Yvette Richards 'tells it how it is' and entertains with a story that echoes the experiences of women from all walks of life."
PRIDE MAGAZINE

Moss Side
MASSIVE

By Karline Smith

"The side of Manchester few people ever get to see...wicked stuff."
VICTOR HEADLEY

"Karline Smith is an author that's certainly going places...She brings an amazing insight and human dimension to crime writing."
THE VOICE

AS baby-faced drug dealers on mountain bikes ply their trade, gun shots shatter the mid-day bustle in Moss Side, Manchester. A young gang leader lies dead on a busy road. No witnesses come forward to help the police.

THE victim's hot-headed brother, now in control of their posse's empire, swears revenge on the boss of a rival gang and his entire family. The score MUST be settled at any cost!

MEANWHILE a mother who once dreamt of 'streets paved with gold', struggles to raise her children alone in Moss Side, unaware of her eldest son's role in the killing and the gangland contract that threatens to destroy everything she lives and works for.

40,000 people will read this page

You can advertise your product or service to them for as little as **£125** per half page

Telephone Steve Pope on **0171 729 1199** for details

South London's No: 1 letting agency

Whether you're looking for a flat to rent or have a property to let, we are THE AGENCY to phone!

CREARY'S
PROPERTY LETTING & MANAGEMENT SERVICE

421 coldharbour lane * london SW9 8LJ
Tel: 0171 733 3997

GORDON & KEENES
Estate Agents
93 Acre Lane, London SW2.
Tel: 0171 274 7000

FOR SALE

We offer a quality of service very few can match

Jamaica

★★★★★

Five star accommodation...at guest house prices!

Guest House De Dolphin
Dolphin Bay, Portland, JA

Located near to some of the most beautiful beaches in Jamaica, Guest House De Dolphin offers a quality of accommodation that no one else can match at the price. For just £15 per night (based on a couple sharing), you will enjoy the plush surroundings of this brand new three bedroom villa. Fully fitted self-catering kitchens, marble floors, antique style wooden beds and luxury en-suite bathrooms are just some of the features that will make your stay a truly special event.

FOR FULL COLOUR BROCHURE TEL:
PAULINE DA COSTA ON 0171 955 9550